T0304945

Hope
Street

**Mike Gayle: emotions you'll never forget,
stories you'll want to share**

MIKE GAYLE

Hope Street

HODDER &
STOUGHTON

First published in Great Britain in 2025 by Hodder & Stoughton Limited
An Hachette UK company

2

Copyright © Mike Gayle 2025

The right of Mike Gayle to be identified as the Author of the Work has been
asserted by him in accordance with the Copyright, Designs and Patents Act 1988.

A CIP catalogue record for this title is available from the British Library

Hardback ISBN 978 1 399 72449 4
Trade Paperback ISBN 978 1 399 72450 0
ebook ISBN 978 1 399 72451 7

Typeset in Plantin Light by Manipal Technologies Limited

Printed and bound in Great Britain by Clays Ltd, Elcograf S.p.A.

Hodder & Stoughton policy is to use papers that are natural, renewable
and recyclable products and made from wood grown in sustainable forests.
The logging and manufacturing processes are expected to conform
to the environmental regulations of the country of origin.

Hodder & Stoughton Limited
Carmelite House
50 Victoria Embankment
London EC4Y 0DZ

The authorised representative in the EEA is Hachette Ireland, 8 Castlecourt
Centre, Castleknock Road, Castleknock, Dublin 15, D15 YF6A, Ireland

www.hodder.co.uk

For all my fantastic readers. I couldn't do this without you.

Prologue

Bernie: 2020 – The morning of the day she goes missing

Bernie McLaughlin made her way up the narrow flight of stairs, the treads squeaking and groaning with each step as she carried her son's morning mug of tea. She was so exhausted she felt more like eighty-four than sixty-four. She had one of her terrible headaches again and hadn't slept very well. She'd recently cut down her hours at the minimarket and the launderette, but retirement was still a whole nine months away and, on days like this, she felt it couldn't come around quickly enough.

Reaching Connor's room she gently knocked on his door to the rhythm of 'How Much Is That Doggie in the Window?' It was their silly tradition, a joke from way, way back when he was small and she'd wake him up for school. Somehow it had lasted until now, even though – at nearly twenty-seven – her son was a grown man, and his musical tastes had long since moved on.

'Morning, sleepyhead. I've got a really good feeling that today is going to be a wonderful day.'

Despite the warmth of her greeting, Connor was rolled up in his duvet like a caterpillar in a chrysalis and barely moved as she cleared a space amongst the clutter on his bedside table – an iPad, his mobile, headphones, glasses and two empty cans of Vimto – and set down the mug of tea.

Perching on the edge of his bed, she switched on the bedside lamp, gently rubbing his arm, and as she did so took in the posters on the walls, all of them of Metallica, his favourite band. She didn't understand the appeal personally – it was all just noise and shouting to her – but for some reason Connor loved them.

'Morning, Mum,' he said eventually opening his eyes and yawning.

'And good morning to you too, sunshine. You were so fast asleep there I thought I was going to have to throw a bucket of water over you to wake you up!'

Laughing, Connor squeezed her hand gently. 'I know you wouldn't do that. You love me.'

'Well, you've certainly got me there!' She kissed him on the cheek, revelling in the warmth of his skin. 'So, what's made you so tired this morning? Were you up late playing your video games again?'

He nodded sheepishly. 'I did try to get to bed early but I was at a really good bit and I didn't want to stop.'

'So, what time did you come up? Midnight? One in the morning? Two?'

'Er . . . I think, it might've been around two-thirty.'

'And if you're telling me, your mother, it was two-thirty, I'm guessing it'll have been more like three!' she said, her southern Irish brogue becoming all the more pronounced as it always did when she was annoyed, even though she'd lived in Derby far longer than she'd ever lived in Ballyea. 'Oh, Connor, what are we going to do with you, eh? We've talked about this a hundred times at least! You need to get your sleep, especially when you've got work in the morning.'

'I'm not in until twelve. I swapped shifts with Alan. He's got a dentist appointment because his back tooth is giving him problems.'

Bernie smiled. 'Well, that was kind of you, Connor. You're a good friend to Alan, but it's really beside the point. Even if I'd have let you sleep until just before it's time for you go to work, it still wouldn't be enough. You know what you're like; you need a solid eight hours at a regular time or you're all over the place.' She reached out a hand, and stroked his hair fondly. 'And you need a good haircut as well! It's curling under at the back it's so long.' She sighed heavily. 'Anyway, drink your tea, then come down and have some breakfast with me.'

Back down in the kitchen, Bernie flicked on the radio and began preparing breakfast: muesli and toast for her, strawberry-flavoured Pop Tarts and scrambled eggs for Connor. She'd long since grown used to her son's eccentric breakfast choices; he'd had them ever since he was a toddler. They always went in phases and she knew better than to try and fight them. And yes, Pop Tarts and scrambled eggs might seem unusual to some but she didn't care. Connor liked them and they made him happy and at the end of the day that was all that really mattered.

Bernie was spooning Connor's eggs onto his favourite plate, a bright yellow one he refused to let her get rid of despite it being so cracked and chipped it seemed more suitable for putting a plant pot on than a meal, when her son came into the kitchen. He was wearing what he had slept in, his favourite Metallica T-shirt, and boxer shorts.

'Pop Tarts!' Grinning from ear to ear he scratched absent-mindedly at his armpit. 'Mum, you're the best!'

Though he'd said this, or some version of it, to her every morning since he could string a sentence together, Bernie never, ever tired of hearing it.

Much as she would've loved for them to sit down to breakfast at the table in the back room, she instead followed Connor into the front. Rather than sitting on the sofa he lowered himself into what to her eyes looked like an oversized black and red car seat, but which her son insisted on referring to as a 'gaming chair'. Bernie hated the thing. She thought it was ugly and looked out of place amongst all of her nice furniture. Worse still, Connor loved it so much he insisted on sitting in it even when the TV was off and he wasn't playing games. But it made him happy, and so this was yet another sacrifice Bernie was more than willing to make.

They chatted as they ate, Connor telling her how excited he was about his upcoming birthday and how he hoped he was getting some new video games, going on to describe, in great detail, a new one he had his eye on. She'd never really seen the attraction of video games, reasoning that life was challenging enough as it was without adding zombies and warfare into the mix, but then again what did she know? She was a woman nearing retirement and he was a young man with his whole life stretching out before him; it would be more strange if they liked all the same things.

In return Connor asked his mother about her plans for her day off. As a rule she didn't like lying to her son, and rarely did if she could help it, but today she had reason not to be entirely truthful.

'I'm just running a few errands this morning and then I might go and see Becky – you know the girl who used to work at the launderette with me. Remember I told you she had a baby? Well, I'm going to go and see how she's getting along. I'm not sure what time I'll be back, but chances are it'll be late as she can talk the hind legs off a donkey! What shift did you say you're working today?'

He took a bite off the corner of the Pop Tart in his hand. 'Twelve 'til eight.'

'So, you'll be home around half eight, nine then I suppose?'

'Depends,' said Connor gravely, 'these days the drivers on the one-two-five don't even seem to bother about the timetable in the evening. They just come when they come.'

Bernie smiled, and was about to take a bite of her toast when a familiar figure flashed past the window, the letterbox opened and a pile of post plopped onto the mat.

Connor looked at his watch. 'Seventeen minutes early? I wonder what's going on there, then?'

'Probably wants to get home and work on that garden of his,' said Bernie, who only knew about the new lawn the postman had recently laid because Connor had told her about it after talking to him at length when he'd delivered one of her son's new games.

'I think you're right,' said Connor. 'I think he told me he's starting on his borders this week.'

Later, as her son played on his PlayStation, Bernie collected the plates, took them to the kitchen and washed them up before heading upstairs to get ready.

Today is not going to be like any other Monday, she thought as she stood in front of her wardrobe picking out her outfit for the day. *Today is going to be different.*

She then dressed and did her hair and make-up before returning to her bedroom where she pulled out the top drawer of her chest of drawers, the one where she kept all her shirts and blouses, and reached right to the back, searching until she found what she was looking for. After taking out the envelope she removed the money inside and carefully counted it. Once, twice, and a third time for good measure. Resealing the envelope, she was about to take it downstairs when she heard people talking outside.

Always more than a little curious to know what was going on in the street, she went to the window. It was Bev talking to the Kennedys, yet another family who had taken the council's blood money and agreed to move out of Hope Street. As if sensing she was being observed, Bev suddenly looked up towards the house, causing Bernie to quickly pull back from the window. Though she and Bev were best friends, they were currently not on speaking terms after Bernie took offence when Bev revealed a couple of weeks ago that she too was seriously thinking about

5

accepting the council's offer. 'I mean, we're never going to beat them,' she'd said. 'They're the council, and they've got more lawyers and what-have-you than you can shake a stick at. Plus, with my arthritis the way it is, I'm telling you, if they offered me a ground-floor flat I think I'd bite their hand off.'

Bernie had tried her best to talk her friend round but in the end they'd argued, and words had been said. Though she was sure she'd forgive Bev at some point in the future, for the time being she was finding it hard to get over what felt, to her, like the ultimate betrayal. This was her home and she would fight tooth and nail for it, and until now she'd thought Bev had felt the same.

Heading downstairs Bernie slipped the envelope into her hand-bag before putting on her shoes and coat. It was a relatively cool March morning and rain-free at home in Derby but when she'd looked at the weather on her phone earlier that morning, much to her displeasure it was forecast to rain where she was going. Still, she thought, she had her coat and her umbrella so she was sure she'd be okay.

'Right then, I'll be getting off,' she said to Connor as she returned to the living room. Her son didn't respond, and it was then she real-ised he was wearing his headphones. She wasn't keen on the things and was forever worrying about what all that noise would do to his hearing, but the alternative was having to live with the constant soundtrack of guns, bombs, and zombies crying out as they got sliced in two. Anyway, he'd promised he wouldn't listen to it too loud, al-though as she stood staring at him she did have to wonder if his opinion on what was loud and her own were even remotely similar.

He must have been completely absorbed in the game because when she tapped him on the shoulder and exclaimed, 'Connor, can you even hear me in those things?!' he'd nearly jumped out of his skin.

'What?' he asked, bewildered as he removed his headphones.

'Didn't we agree that you wouldn't have the volume on too loud when you've got those things on?

'But . . . but . . . it's not quite the same if it's too quiet. But you're right – it's bad for my hearing so I promise I'll turn it down now.'

Bernie smiled. 'Good, now come and give your mum a kiss.'

Without any resentment Connor got out of his gaming chair and gave her a kiss and a huge hug.

'Ohhh,' said Bernie, her voice full of delight. 'Have I ever told you, you give the best hugs in the world?'

'Every day,' said Connor.

'And do you know why I do that, son?'

'So that I'll keep on giving you the best hugs in the world?'

'Exactly,' said Bernie smiling. 'Your hugs are the stuff that keeps your old mum going. Now, like I said, chances are I'll be back before you get home but if for any reason I'm not don't forget there's mini pizzas and oven chips in the freezer, but you must have some peas with it, okay? It's good to eat your greens.'

'Okay, Mum,' said Connor sitting back down in his gaming chair and slipping on his headphones. 'I'll see you later.'

1

Lila

'I'm sorry, would you mind repeating that? I don't think I heard you properly.'

The birdlike face of the elderly woman in the high-backed chair sitting opposite is full of disdain, as if she thinks I'm being deliberately dense.

'I said, "Nothing,"' she replies. 'N-o-t-h-i-n-g. Nothing!'

Shocked and more than a little amused I glance down at the open notebook in my lap in order to compose myself. She's confused. She has to be.

'No, Winnie,' I say raising my voice in case her hearing aids aren't working. 'I don't think you heard me right. What I actually asked is, "What's the best thing about being one hundred and eight?"'

Grimacing, the woman raises a finger and jabs it in my direction. 'Of course I heard you! You asked me what's the best thing about being a hundred and eight and that's my answer: nothing! There's not a damn thing that's good about it! Everyone I've ever loved is dead; I can't get out of this chair without asking one of these idiots to help me up!' She waves a spindly liver-spotted hand in the direction of one of the young care assistants distributing cups of tea to the residents gathered in the communal lounge. 'And to top it all, I haven't had a decent bowel movement in at least fifteen years! Being one hundred and eight isn't a prize, it's a pain in the backside, literally! Now go and print that in your stupid rag, and leave me alone!'

9

Stepping out of the boiling hot care home into the weak May sunshine a short while later, I return to my car. After flinging my bag into the passenger-side footwell, I get in, close my eyes and rest my forehead against the steering wheel wondering what on earth I'm doing with my life.

When I'd gone into local journalism three years ago my friends had all thought me insane. 'It's a dying industry,' they'd said. 'Ten years from now there won't be a local newspaper left in the country.' And those very same friends I'd made on my postgraduate journalism course had of course headed to London, full of dreams of working for one of the nationals or getting into PR with all the prestige and glamour such jobs would afford. But thanks in no small part to my late granddad – a diehard local newspaper journalist himself – I'd grown up believing that being a journalist on a local paper was a noble undertaking. I'd always loved hearing his stories of life at *The Exeter Examiner*, the paper he'd worked on for his entire career, and he'd always encouraged me to believe in the vital importance of local news. He had great faith in its ability to hold those in power accountable, give voice to local communities, and turn a spotlight on issues deemed insignificant by the nationals but vital to the people living with and affected by them.

However, in my naivety what I hadn't really anticipated, what I hadn't truly foreseen was that for every story unearthing a crooked local MP fiddling their expenses, there were a hundred more about charitable donations from local businesses (complete with obligatory oversized cheque), secondary school controversies ('Local Girl Excluded Over Skirt Length') and of course, fluffy, feel-good stories of which my 'Oldest Woman in Derby Shares Secret to Long Life' article was supposed to have been a shining example.

I'd get the story written of course. There wasn't a miserable centenarian in the world I couldn't get a decent heart-warming piece out of even if it took longer than usual and required the application of some judicious editing. Even so, after three long years of this, I'm tired, really tired. And broke too, really broke. Which is one of the many, many reasons why I finally gave in a couple of weeks ago and applied for a job on *The Correspondent* down in London. Although apart from my boyfriend Gabe I haven't told anyone yet in case it doesn't come off, I'm trying to stay hopeful. And so right now I've got no choice but to sit tight, cross my fingers and hope beyond hope that soon I'll be swapping the delights of curmudgeonly old ladies for hard-hitting interviews in Westminster.

The other reason for wanting to get down to London is to be with Gabe who lives and works down there. We've been together five years, been doing the long-distance thing for most of it and, to put it mildly, it hasn't been easy. It's difficult spending so much time apart, and when we are together there's so much pressure to make the most of every minute that we almost ruin things by trying too hard. If this job comes off it will be a huge relief to finally be under the same roof, like a proper grown-up couple.

Trying to hold on to this positive thought, I check my watch. It'll practically be the end of the working day by the time I get back to the office, and I soothe myself with the thought that in less than an hour I'll be at home, parked in front of the TV, sipping on a cold glass of wine and tucking into the yellow-stickered Marks and Spencer ready meal I picked up at lunchtime.

My car is ancient, held together with gaffer tape and positive thinking, and so when I turn the key in the ignition I instinctively hold my breath, willing the engine to turn over. Thankfully it starts, but there's a new high-pitched whistling sound coming from somewhere that doesn't bode well. I turn up the radio to drown it out and then head back to the office.

Along with *The Echo*, the BFK Media building, is home to a stable of titles including *The Derbyshire Post*, YourDerby.com and *The Derby Advertiser*. Once upon a time walking into this building had seemed almost impossibly exciting and, armed with my newly issued security pass, I'd march into work imagining myself to be Woodward or Bernstein reincarnated for the modern age. Now, however, I feel nothing other than a kind of world-weary exhaustion, and once again I think about how wonderful it will be to move on from this place.

After taking the lift, I get out at the fourth floor, home to *The Echo*. Once upon a time we took up two whole floors of the building but thanks to numerous cuts over the years we've been whittled down considerably. As I begin my trek across the newsroom, I wave to Gary and Paul on the sports desk, nod briefly in the direction of the permanently grumpy Angela Sawyer and her unwilling protégé, Sahil, on the crime desk before stopping by the arts and culture desk to chat to Patrick, who as usual is surrounded by several huge piles of books and unopened post. Skirting round the politics desk staffed by *Echo* veteran Sharon Chapman, a no-nonsense Yorkshire woman who terrifies everyone she meets, I finally reach my destination, the junior reporters' desk, which I share with my best friend Niamh and my sort of friend Lewis who is actually more like an annoying younger brother than anything else.

'How did you get on with Derby's oldest granny?' asks Niamh as I slump down in my chair. 'Did you learn the secret to long life and happiness? Should I be taking a daily draught of port and going to bed at nine?'

'She was a monster,' I reply. 'An absolute nightmare of a woman. Honestly, if she'd been more mobile I'd have been lucky to make it out of there alive.'

'The old ones are the worst,' chips in Lewis, from behind his computer. 'I once tried to interview a group of nannas for a piece about the bingo hall at Rushforth closing. I swear on my life, while I wasn't looking one of them pinched my backside and then tried to make out she was brushing some fluff off my trousers.'

'Did you get her number though?' quips Niamh. 'You did, didn't you?'

'Unlike you, Niamh, I'm not that desperate for a date,' snaps Lewis. 'But I've got the number for the local bowls club if you're at a loose end at the weekend. I'm sure one of those old boys would take pity on you if you smiled a bit more.'

Niamh picks up her stapler ready to launch it at him but then I sigh heavily. She stops and raises an eyebrow at me.

'Got the regional news blues again?'

'I'm not sure how much more of this place I can take,' I reply. 'The same old stories, the drudgery, it's getting me down.'

'We've all been there,' says Lewis. 'Only last week when I was covering the magistrates' court, listening to the hundredth person of the day explaining why they'd been driving without a licence or insurance, I seriously thought about packing it all in and going travelling.'

Niamh grins. 'Where to? Anywhere exciting?'

'I was thinking Colombia, Ecuador, Peru, Bolivia, Chile, maybe ending up in southern Argentina, but then I made the mistake of checking my bank balance and realised that even if I saved really hard for a year I'd be lucky to make it to Scunthorpe let alone South America.'

'Aww, poor baby,' says Niamh. 'That new café up the road has got a Brazilian blend on special this week. Why don't you treat yourself to one and drink it with your eyes closed instead?'

I idly check my email on my phone, hoping beyond hope to find a life-changing message waiting in my inbox. But there's nothing save for half a dozen marketing emails and one from my landlord saying he'll get someone out to fix the shower by the end of the week, which bitter experience tells me will be more like a month.

Disheartened I set down my phone, then immediately pick it up again to check the time. There are just fifteen minutes to go before I can head home without seeming like a slacker. I offer to do a tea run, in the hope of filling up a few minutes, but before anyone has a chance to tell me what they want, a voice I immediately recognise calls out across the newsroom: 'Is Metcalfe back yet?'

I stand up from behind my computer and wave at my editor, Peter Fordham, framed in the doorway to his office. He's small, bearded and neat, and looks a bit like I'd imagine a badger might do if they were forced to wear a suit to work.

'I'm here, Boss, what do you need?'

'A quick word,' he replies, and then turns and disappears back into his office.

'Oh, golden girl's in trouble,' says Lewis with a smirk. 'What have you done now?'

'Nothing,' I say casually, even though it could be any one of a number of minor infractions from taking one too many packs of Post-it notes from the stationery cupboard to my car leaking engine oil all over the car park. 'He probably wants to pick my brains about the best way to sack you without making you cry.'

Ignoring Lewis's retort, which is something both childish and obscene, I briefly exchange a look of panic with Niamh, before taking a deep breath and heading to Peter's office.

I've always quite liked Peter. Though he's at least a generation younger than my granddad, he's so old-school he reminds me of him quite a bit. His hard work and commitment have seen him rise through the ranks to become *The Echo*'s twenty-fourth editor in its one-hundred-and-sixty-two-year history. And he's not exactly had an easy time of it. His tenure has coincided with some of the toughest times in local newspaper history, and while *The Echo* is doing better than most he's still had to manage huge budget cuts and oversee massive redundancies, and even though I'm looking to jump ship, selfishly I'm rather hoping he's not about to cut me too.

'How did you get on with that old dear's story?' he asks gesturing for me to take a seat.

'All good. I'm probably going to write it up in the morning if that's okay?'

'Well, there's no rush on that. Although, I suppose, given her age there perhaps ought to be!' He finds his own joke so funny that it's several moments before he can speak. 'Anyway, the reason I wanted to see you is because I've got a job for you. You go home past Cossington Park don't you?'

I think for a moment. Even after three years in Derby some areas of the city are still a bit of a mystery to me.

'I think so. Why?'

'I've just had a whiff of a possible story over that way and I thought you could check it out on your way home.'

My heart sinks. There go my plans for a wine and TV night. I try to imagine what the story might be: 'Ghost Haunts Local School'? 'Asda Worker Slapped with Sausage'? 'Fugitive Terrier Causes Mayhem at Fete'? None of these are made up. Sadly.

'What's down at Cossington Park?'

Peter glances at a Post-it note stuck to his desk. 'You know they've been emptying out the houses round there for the past couple of years to make way for that new development?'

It rings a vague bell. I think the paper had run a couple of articles about it and I knew local opinion was divided.

'Well,' he continues, 'a little bird's just told me that the council are having kittens because there's a bloke there refusing to move, and he's holding everything up and costing them a fortune.'

Confused, I look at my boss. 'Can't they just kick him out?'

'If it was that straightforward, I think they would've done it by now. Chances are it's some sort of legal thing, but I don't know the details. Which is where you come in.'

He plucks the Post-it note from his desk and hands it to me. Scrawled across it in Peter's barely legible handwriting is an address: '121 Hope Street, Cossington Park.'

I look up from the Post-it to Peter.

'No name? No number?'

'Just what's there.'

'So, I'm guessing you want me to do the usual: find out what his game is and see if there's a story there?'

'Got it in one, Metcalfe. I doubt it'll come to much but we're a local paper, and it's a local story, so you know . . . just do what you can.'

2

Connor

Ignore them.

'Spaz!'

Ignore them.

'Retard!'

Ignore them.

People are always calling me nasty names. Well not always. And not all people. But sometimes. And some people.

The names they call me are always the same, and never anything I haven't heard before. I get spaz and retard a lot. Sometimes I get 'weirdo' too, and if they're old enough I might get 'Rain Man' as well. Sometimes I get them joined up together like this: 'oi-spaz-retard-weirdo' or like this: 'oi-retard-weirdo-spazman' but really, it's all the same.

Usually it's people who don't know me, or just know *of* me who call me names. People like the kids who used to live on Hope Street, or who went to St Mary's, my old primary school, or Charlecote, my old secondary school, before I stopped going. But right now, as I sit on the top deck of the number forty-three making my way home after work, the name-callers are a group of teenagers I have never seen before. They are all wearing school uniforms but not from a school I recognise.

'What a retard!' calls one of them from the back of the bus. 'Can you hear him? He's singing on the bus like he's on *Britain's Got Talent!*'

They are right. I am singing. But because I'm wearing my head-phones I didn't actually realise I was doing it out loud.

I don't normally sing loudly.

I know singing on buses is not something people usually do.

I know that even when I do it quietly it sometimes makes people feel uncomfortable.

But the boys are making me nervous and when I get nervous I try to calm myself down by singing.

My favourite songs to sing along to are by Metallica.

And my favourite Metallica song is 'Enter Sandman'.

Out of the corner of my eye I see something. But I daren't look.

I take a deep breath and count: one, two, three. Then I do look and immediately feel scared. One of the boys has moved from the back of the bus to the seat across from me. He's looking at me and all his friends are laughing.

I try my best to ignore him. I stare straight ahead so that all I can see are the windows of the bus and the road. I know that the boy is doing something horrible though. I just know it.

As the bus pulls in at the next stop, I count to three in my head, or at least I think it's in my head – it's hard to tell sometimes – and when I get to three, I quickly stand up and try to get off the bus. But as soon as I do the boy grabs my bag. I can't let him take it. It has my house keys in it, and my phone, and anyway, why should I let people take my things? Why should someone else have the things I've worked so hard for?

I don't think about it. I just do it.

I push the boy and he goes flying back into his seat and straight away all his friends get up and run towards me, shouting. But I'm too quick for them. Before they can get to me I rush down the stairs and squeeze off the bus just before the doors close.

I turn and look at the bus as it pulls away. The boys all bang on the windows with their fists and their faces are twisted in a horrible way, but they can't get me.

I am safe. For now.

I look around, trying to work out where I am and see that I'm on Newhall Way, a busy dual carriageway. This stop is six stops before the one I should have got off at. I suddenly feel very tired and think about waiting for the next bus, but it isn't due for another twenty minutes. Even then, there's no guarantee it will turn up on time. These days buses almost never stick to their timetables, which is a shame because I know them all off by heart.

There is nothing for it, I'm going to have to walk the rest of the way home.

As the traffic roars past me I put my headphones back on. They slipped off when I escaped off the bus, but at least they're not broken.

I press play on my phone, and as the music starts I begin my journey home. I walk past the petrol station, then the Crown pub, where I sometimes go with my friend Marcus. I walk past where the old Comet building used to be. They knocked it down two years ago to make space for a car park, but they haven't started building it yet so it's just a big space with loads of rubbish and weeds.

I turn off into Linton Road. There is a row of shops here, selling everything from hair extensions to Polish food. I walk past St Mary's, my old junior school. I smile when I think about my days there when I used to play superheroes on the climbing frame. I loved that climbing frame, loved scrambling to the top and looking down at all the other children below, playing their own noisy games that gave me a headache.

I walk past the door of The Fresh Fryer, my favourite fish and chip shop, and catch a whiff of the hot vinegary air and suddenly realise how hungry I am. I don't buy any, even though I am really tempted, because Marcus and I have fish and chips when he comes round to see me and Mum always used to say, 'Chips once a week is more than enough!' So, I hold my nose to stop the lovely smells getting in and keep walking. I go past the shoe repair shop, and the travel agents before turning off the main road until I get to the railway bridge.

Sometimes, because it is fun, I make noises when I go underneath because it is all echoey but today I don't.

Soon, I'm on the other side and round the corner turning into the road where I live: Hope Street.

When people first started to move out I couldn't get over how different all the houses looked with metal grilles attached to their front doors and windows. But these days I barely notice. Sometimes there's a new bit of graffiti across one of the grilles; other times there's a new collection of those little metal canisters naughty people have scattered across the pavement.

Before it was just me left, people from other roads would sometimes park their cars in Hope Street, but as more families moved out and the road got emptier the cars started to get broken into or vandalised overnight. These days the only people who park in the street are people who don't know any better, or Marcus, when he is coming to see me.

Reaching number one-two-one, I take my keys out of my bag and unlock the front door. There's no hallway; I just step straight into the living room, drop my bag on the floor by the sofa and go to the kitchen.

The house is quiet and still, having been shut up all day, but as I fill the kettle and put it on to boil and turn on the radio it starts to feel a little bit more cheery. As I make my tea, I help myself to two slices of cheese from the packet to take the edge off my hunger. I always have the same thing on the days when I eat tea at home instead of at work: an individual frozen cheese and ham pizza, a slice of buttered bread and a mug of tea. Sometimes, if I'm in the right mood and have done my weekly shop, I might have a packet of crisps too (ready-salted, or salt and vinegar at a push but never beef, bacon or prawn cocktail). Today, though, isn't one of those days.

I turn on the oven to preheat it, just like Mum taught me, take the pizza out of the freezer, put it on the baking tray and when the oven's hot enough I put the tray in the oven and, as I'm setting the timer on my phone for eight minutes exactly, there's a sharp knock at the front door.

These days it's very rare for anyone to knock on my front door. Marcus has his own key, and it's too late in the day for it to be the postman.

I start to feel uneasy.

What if the boys from the bus have followed me home?

I creep upstairs, careful to avoid every creaking step, and tiptoe into Mum's room. Kneeling on her bed I gently pull a tiny corner of the net curtain to one side and look down into the street below.

The good news is that there is no sign of the boys from the bus.

The bad news is that there is a yellow car, which I do not recognise, parked across the road. It looks very old and battered.

I make up my mind not to answer the door.

Since everyone else moved out of Hope Street, Marcus is always telling me not to answer the door to anyone I don't know.

The first time he said this I asked if this included the postman, because although I recognise him, I don't actually know him. To this Marcus said that the postman was okay, but no one else.

Then I'd asked if this included the man who came to read the gas and electricity meter, and Marcus had said, 'No, but you have to check their ID first.' As soon as he said this, I searched online to see what genuine meter readers' ID looked like. Since then, I've checked three meter readers' ID badges and have a record of them on my phone.

As I'm carefully watching out of the window, the person knocking on the front door takes a step backwards, looks up and sees me. It is a young, pretty lady and as I drop the net curtain and duck down she waves at me.

From downstairs I hear the creaky letterbox open and a woman's voice shouts: 'Hello? I know you're there! I saw you at the window! My name's Lila Metcalfe. I'm a journalist from the *Derby Echo*. Have you got a few minutes to talk?'

I freeze. Mum used to have *The Echo* delivered when I was younger. I used to like reading the tiny adverts in the back, especially the ones that said puppies for sale because I always wanted a dog. Even though I haven't looked at *The Echo* in years there's always someone reading a copy in the break room at work.

Why has someone from *The Echo* come to see me? I'm just Connor, Connor who lives in Hope Street and works at the DIY-Depot at the retail park.

Maybe this is exactly the thing Marcus has been trying to warn me about. People pretending to be people they aren't. People who are up to no good.

I tiptoe downstairs, through the back room and edge into the living room.

'Are . . . are you really from *The Echo*?' I shout.

I hear the letterbox open and then the pretty young lady says: 'Yes, I am. Am I speaking to the owner of the house?'

'I'm . . . I'm not the owner; it's rented from the council.'

'But you live here?'

'Yes.'

'Great, what's your name?'

I think for a moment. I'm not sure I should tell her my name. It is very strange to talk to people through my letterbox.

'I'm sorry,' I call towards the door. 'But I don't talk to people I don't know.'

'And that's a good policy to have,' says the lady. 'But I promise you, you've got nothing to worry about from me.'

I think again and then ask a question. 'Do you have any ID? If you have ID that I can check I might be able to talk to you.'

There's a moment of quiet and then the voice through the letterbox says, 'I've only got my work ID.'

I feel a little shiver of excitement.

I've never seen a journalist's ID badge before. Will it be anything like the meter readers' or do they make special ones for journalists?

I move closer to the door. 'If you really are from *The Echo*, post your badge through the letterbox so I can check it.'

There's another short pause and then the voice through the letter box says, 'I'm sorry, I can't do that. What if you don't give it me back? I won't be able to get into the office.'

'But I will give it you back. I'm not a thief.'

'I'm not saying you are. But I have to be careful.'

I consider the problem. 'Is your ID on a lanyard?'

'Yes, yes, it is.'

'Well, why don't you push the ID bit through the letterbox but keep hold of the strap? That way I can't take it from you but I can have a proper look.'

There's another pause, this time longer and then the letterbox opens wider and I see the woman's fingers pushing the ID badge through.

I look at it carefully.

On the one side it says: 'NUJ Press Member, Lila Metcalfe,' along with her union number and an expiry date, which I'm pleased to see has not yet been reached. In the bottom left-hand corner is a black and white photograph of the young woman with shortish hair. She is not smiling. I take a photo of it on my phone, and then flip the badge over. Here is a different ID. This one says, '*Derby Echo* Reporter,' and underneath is a photo of the same young woman, smiling this time, and then a long black magnetic strip like the one on my own ID badge for work.

I take a picture of this side too, and feel pleased to have added not just one but two brand-new IDs to my collection. Then, putting my phone back in my pocket, I push the badge back through the letterbox. I'm not sure what Marcus would say about this. But I do have a record of her ID now. I don't think there's any harm in just seeing what she wants and so I take a deep breath and open the door.

3

Lila

Even if the man standing in front of me hadn't just made me conduct a whole conversation with him through a letterbox, I would've known he was a bit odd just by looking at him. It's hard to pinpoint exactly what the oddness is, but it's there nonetheless. Perhaps some of it's down to his glasses, the lenses so thick they look like the bottom of milk bottles, making his eyes large and cartoon-like. Or maybe it's the DIY-Depot uniform he's wearing, his polo shirt just a touch too tight, the trousers a little too short. Or maybe it's the fact that sprouting from the base of his jaw is a small tuft of hair he's clearly missed whilst shaving. Then again, maybe it's all of these things, and something else too, that indefinable yet unmistakable air of oddness some people seem to emanate, and which others can spot from a hundred paces.

In short, he looks like the sort of person you'd avoid sitting next to on the bus, or hesitate standing behind in a queue. He's odd through and through but not in a frightening or threatening way, I'm sure. No, he's just plain-old odd, and that I can cope with.

I hold out my hand. 'I'm Lila Metcalfe. So pleased to meet you. What's your name?'

'Connor . . . Connor McLaughlin, but you can call me Connor,' he says tentatively accepting my greeting.

His hand feels warm and strangely puffy, and I'm relieved when he lets go. I decide to get straight to the point. 'I'm so sorry to drop by unannounced, but I recently heard about your situation.'

He frowns. 'My . . . my . . . situation?'

'Your refusal to leave your home here in Hope Street to make way for the new development.'

He raises an eyebrow, and shakes his head vehemently. 'No, I don't want to move.'

'Of course, of course,' I say not wanting to upset him. 'Obviously nobody wants to be forced to leave their home. It isn't right and it sounds like just the thing the readers of *The Echo* would love to know more about. Would it be okay if I came in and asked you a few questions about it?'

He frowns again, and for a moment I wonder if he's not going to let me in, and if I'm going to have to conduct the entire interview on the doorstep. It wouldn't be the first time but it never exactly results in the interviewee opening up in any meaningful way, and there's always the potential for the door to be slammed shut in my face. As it is, however, his phone alarm begins to sound, and his expression changes.

'My pizza's ready and I don't want it to burn.' With that he turns and goes back inside leaving the front door open.

For a moment I wonder if he's going to come back, then I look at my watch lamenting how if I hadn't gone back to work, then right now I'd be tucking into my bargain king prawn linguine and bingeing on episodes of *Love is Blind*. Instead, I'm standing here on a street that looks like a scene straight out of a post-apocalyptic zombie film while the smell of cooking pizza fills the air.

Hope Street is just so spooky and desolate. Rows of typical terraces, which in any other area would've been teeming with life and character, rendered bleak and forbidding by the absence of their inhabitants and the metal grilles over the windows where there should've been curtains. I regard Connor's house once again, the only unboarded one in the street. Two distinct but related questions form in my mind: what kind of person would willingly choose to continue living in the eerie and empty graffiti-covered houses of Cossington Park, and why on earth would they do so? I take a deep breath and finding myself wanting answers to these questions I step into the house and close the door behind me.

The front room is small but neat, and decorated in calming, muted shades of pink and green, suggesting a feminine presence somewhere in the picture. Directly in front of me is a small cream leatherette two-seater sofa, with a matching armchair against the adjacent wall. Rather incongruously in the middle of the room there's one of those gaming chairs that sits directly on the floor, positioned in front of a large TV. The chair is black and red and has 'X-Force' written on the side in shiny silver letters. It's an odd mix, a slightly dated gran's living room, with a sprinkling of teen-age boy, and I wonder if Connor lives with an older relative, and if so, where she is.

Keeping an ear open I cross the room to the gas fire and examine one of the photos on the mantelpiece above. It's a colour photo, of a young bespectacled boy, of perhaps ten or eleven, who I assume is Connor. He's standing proudly next to a slim middle-aged woman, with shoulder-length jet-black hair and smiling eyes. She looks like she could either be a young grandmother or an older mother, though it's clear from their features the two are definitely related.

I reach out to take a closer look at the photo but then I hear someone approaching. Taking a step back, I turn around to see Connor returning to the room. He's carrying a tray on which sits a depressingly pallid-looking meal consisting of an individual pizza and a slice of bread and butter, along with two mugs of tea.

Setting the tray down on the sofa, he picks up one of the mugs and offers it to me.

'You're a guest,' he explains sounding as though he's parroting the words of someone older, 'and you should always offer your guest a cup of tea . . . but I didn't know how many sugars you take so I put in one and a half like I have.'

I try my best not to wince as I take the mug from him. I can't recall ever having had tea with sugar in, even when I was a child. Still, there's a first time for everything and having got this far the last thing I want is to cause any offence. With a bit of luck, I can find out what I need to know and be out of here before my drink is even cold.

Mug in hand I take a seat in the armchair, but rather than sitting down on the sofa opposite Connor picks up the tray again and then with great difficulty sits in the gaming chair and proceeds to eat his meal.

I'm not sure what to do as I'm now looking at the side of his head and he's making no effort to look at me. I consider moving the armchair into a position better suited to an interview but reason that as we've only just met, I can't exactly start rearranging his furniture. No, I'll just have to get on with things and hope for the best.

'So,' I begin, as Connor chews loudly on the pizza in his hand, 'I don't want to take up too much of your time, Mr McLaughlin, but—'

'I said you can call me Connor,' he interrupts, his mouth half full of pizza. 'Can I call you Lila?'

'Yes, of course.'

'Good. Because that's your name, isn't it?'

'Yes,' I say, somewhat thrown. Is he joking or being serious? It's impossible to tell. 'Anyway, as I was saying, I don't want to take up too much of your time, especially while you're eating, so I'll just make a start, shall I? So . . . Connor . . . why exactly is it that you're refusing to move?'

He doesn't reply; he doesn't even register that he's heard the question. Instead, he just chews, and chews, and chews, until eventually he swallows loudly and then picks up his slice of bread.

As a journalist I've faced many difficult interviewees – some angry, some frightened, some grief-stricken, others outraged – but someone distracted by their evening meal is a new one on me. Perhaps I've gone in too hard, too quickly, especially for someone who has obviously got some sort of learning difficulty. What's needed now is a bit of time spent laying the groundwork. It will take longer, which is slightly irritating, but should yield results in the end.

'So, you like video games?' I begin, hoping this will warm him up.

He puts down his slice of bread and for the first time turns to look at me. 'Yes, and I really like Metallica too.'

I've never quite seen the point of video games myself, though Gabe is partial to playing them with his friends now and again. And as for Metallica, the only person I've ever known to be a fan was Florian, the pretentious French exchange student my family hosted when I was sixteen, and I'd found them about as appealing as I'd found Florian and his passion for playing the lute. I search my mind trying to recall something, anything that might keep the conversation alive but the best I can come up with is: 'Great, it's good to be interested in things.'

This is clearly the wrong thing to say because he returns his attention to his meal, and the slice of bread he'd been eating. For something to do I pick up my tea, take a sip, and immediately regret it. It's so sweet that it sets my teeth on edge but not wanting to appear rude, I swallow it down.

'So, have you always lived around here?'

There's a moment of silence, and then still without looking at me he says, 'Yes.'

I want to kick myself. What am I doing asking closed questions like some sort of rookie? He doesn't need yes or no questions. He needs them open-ended to get him talking. I try again.

'And where did you go to school?'

For a moment he stops chewing. 'St Mary's. I didn't really like it.'

Two whole sentences. It's all I can do to stop myself from punching the air. 'Oh, that's a shame. Why not?'

This time he turns to face me though he refuses to meet my gaze. 'I got bullied a lot. And then I got bullied at secondary school. And so, I stopped going.'

He says this so matter-of-factly, so without asking for pity or even showing any to himself, that it almost breaks my heart.

'I'm so sorry to hear that, Connor. School can be really tough, can't it?' I pause, hoping he might respond but he doesn't, and so I follow up with another question.

'So, what did you do instead of school?'

'I stayed at home mostly, watching TV and listening to Metallica and then when I turned sixteen, I got a job at DIY-Depot at Derwent Retail Park.'

'Well, that's good – and what do you do there?'

'I work with Alan, mainly. He's old, but he's my friend. Me and Alan sometimes work in the garden centre bit, which is the best because Alan likes plants and he tells me all the names, and I get to use the hose, which is fun. Sometimes though we just restock the shelves, work in the warehouse, or collect the trolleys, but the garden centre is definitely my favourite.'

This is more like it. He's really opening up to me now.

'And how was work today?'

'Not too bad,' he says. 'I helped unpack the deliveries. It's hard work but it can be fun too. We've got these special ladders – warehouse ladders they're called – they've got wheels on them and you can move them around the aisles when you need to put stock on high shelves. I went on them today, and Alan and some of the others pulled me around the store while I was up there. It was really good fun.'

I smile encouragingly. Despite my earlier impression Connor really is quite sweet, but he clearly needs a lot of help. For the first time it crosses my mind that perhaps I shouldn't be interviewing him without some sort of guardian present, but before I can think what if anything I'm going to do about it out of nowhere he says, 'Because of Mum.'

I'm confused. 'I'm sorry?'

'Because of Mum.' His voice is a little louder this time.

I don't know what he's talking about. Is this something to do with his job? Does his mum work at DIY-Depot too?

'I'm not following. What do you mean because of Mum?'

He sighs clearly frustrated at my lack of understanding. 'You asked me before why I won't leave Hope Street.'

'Yes . . .'

'Well . . . it's because of Mum.'

I take a moment to make sense of this. 'Are you saying it's your mum who doesn't want you to move?'

He shakes his head. 'No, I'm saying I can't move because of Mum.'

'Because she's ill or something?'

He shakes his head again. 'Because she's gone.'

Now I'm completely lost.

'Gone, how? Do you mean she's passed away?'

For the first time he looks directly at me and our eyes meet.

'I mean she went out one day three years ago and well . . . she never came back.'

4

Connor

Lila, the journalist lady, is giving me a funny look but because I don't know her, I'm not sure what it means.

'Let me get this straight. Are you saying that your mum went missing?'

I nod.

'Three years ago?'

I nod again.

'And she's never been found?'

'No, not yet.'

'And the police know about this?'

'Yes, they investigated for a while but they didn't find her.'

'And the reason you don't want to move is . . . ?'

'Because I know she'll come home one day soon and when she does, I want to be here.'

Lila takes a notepad out of her bag, opens it and starts scribbling something down. It looks like she's writing quite a bit but then she stops and looks at me.

'I know this must be difficult for you, Connor, but could you tell me a bit more about your mum and how she went missing?'

I open my mouth to speak but no words come out. Even though I like talking about Mum I don't really like talking about when she went missing because it makes me too sad. I think about her; I think about her a lot. How she looked, how she smelt, and the lovely things she used to say to me. I think about her every morning when I first wake up, and I always, always think about her last thing at night too. But I try not to think about when she went missing, otherwise I get too sad. But now Lila wants me to talk about it and I'm not sure how I feel.

If I start thinking too hard about the time Mum went missing right now, I'm not sure if I'll be able to stop. I'll think about it and think about it, and think about it until it is all I can think about. And if I'm thinking about this all the time then I won't be able to think about anything else. And I'll just make myself sadder and sadder and sadder until I can't sleep or eat or go to work.

'Connor?'

I look at Lila. 'I don't really want to talk about it.'

'Oh, I'm sorry.' She tilts her head to one side. 'I imagine it must be really difficult for you. But I really do think that *Echo* readers will get something from hearing about your story.'

I'm still not sure. I don't really care about *Echo* readers. I just care about me and Mum.

'Why would *Echo* readers want to know about Mum?'

'Well, she's from the area, isn't she?'

I nod.

'Then I can almost guarantee her friends and family will want to read all about her.'

I screw my nose up and pull a face. 'We do have friends but we haven't got any family. It's just me and Mum.'

'Then don't you think all your friends and all your mum's friends would really love hearing about her again?'

I think for another moment, imagining Mum's friends reading about her. It's the sort of thing Mum would like.

'We had breakfast together,' I tell Lila. 'Mum had a bowl of muesli and a slice of brown toast, and I had two strawberry Pop Tarts and scrambled eggs.'

33

For some reason this makes Lila smile. 'And did you and your mum always have breakfast together?'

'Not always but that day I was doing a late shift.'

'And your mum? Did she work too?'

'Yes, she worked at the launderette on Lucas Street and at the minimart on Linton Road.'

'So back to that day,' says Lila. 'You had breakfast together and then what happened?'

'We talked about my birthday for a bit.'

Looking down at her notepad she wrote something down. 'And when's your birthday?'

'The 6th of April.'

'And you would've been how old on your birthday?'

'Twenty-seven. But I'm thirty now. I went out for burgers with my friend Marcus and his mum Bev.'

'That's nice,' she said and again, she scribbled something down.

'Okay, so, back to the day your mum went missing. You chatted about your birthday and then what?'

'Mum said she was going to get ready to go out and while she was upstairs I sat in here playing video games. Then after a bit she came in wearing her coat, told me that she was going to run a few errands and see one of her friends who had a new baby. She said she might be home late and that there was pizza in the freezer for tea if she wasn't back. Then I gave her a kiss and a hug and she left.'

'And did you see her again after that?'

I bite my lip, and shake my head.

'Oh, I see,' says Lila. 'That was the last time you saw her?'

I nod, but don't say anything. I didn't even look when she went out the front door. I just carried on with the game I was playing.

'I didn't know it would be the last time. I thought it was going to be like any other day. I just . . . I just . . . didn't know.'

For a moment Lila doesn't say anything and neither do I. We just sit there in silence. Then after a bit she says, 'Are you okay to carry on?'

I say yes, and so she says, 'So, tell me about what happened when you came home from work.'

'It was about nine o'clock and I remember the house was dark. But Mum had said she was going to be late so I didn't worry too much. But then when it got even later and she still wasn't back I thought that maybe I'd got it wrong and that she had come back but gone to bed.'

'Why did you think that?'

'Mum sometimes used to get quite bad headaches and so she'd take some tablets and lie in bed with the lights off. So I thought that might be what had happened.'

'So, when did you realise she wasn't there?'

I look down at my hands. I don't want to tell Lila this bit.

'Connor?'

I squeeze my eyes shut.

'Connor?'

I squeeze them shut even tighter.

'Connor, are you okay?'

I open my eyes, and a small tear rolls down my cheek. I have always felt bad about this. Always. I should've checked. 'I didn't realise she wasn't there until the next morning.' I look at the empty space on the sofa, and wish Mum was here so I could tell her how sorry I am that I didn't check on her earlier. 'Instead of checking on Mum . . . well . . . I played video games until midnight, and then I went to bed and didn't get up until after ten.'

'And that's when you found out that she was missing?'

I shift in my seat. 'Even though it was a little bit late there was no sign of Mum and everything was just as I'd left it the night before. Mum always used to get up early so she would have at least tidied away my plates but they were exactly where I'd left them. I checked to see if she'd left a note to say that she'd gone out but there wasn't one, and so I knocked on her bedroom door, and when there was no answer, I went in. The bed was made but she wasn't there.'

'So, what did you do then? Call the police?'

'I went across the road to get Mum's friend Bev. And she didn't know where Mum was either. She hadn't seen her since the day before. She came over here and checked the house with me, and then we tried calling her again, and when that didn't work, Bev called the police.'

'And what happened next?'

It's really hard to think about that time. And I get all jumbled up when I try. I remember some bits but not others. Mostly I just remember feeling scared. Very scared.

'Two police officers came to the house and they spoke to me and Bev, asking us lots of questions just like you're doing right now. Then when they were done, they said that we shouldn't worry and that Mum would probably turn up in a few days. But Mum didn't turn up. Bev called the police again and again until finally they sent different police officers round and this time they took some of Mum's things with them like her toothbrush and her hairbrush, and they told us that she was now a missing person.'

'Oh, Connor,' says Lila. 'That must have been so hard for you.'

'It was. Very. All I wanted was Mum to come back but I was glad that the police were looking for her.'

'And did they find any clues? Any trace of her?'

'Well they checked with her friend Becky, the one with the baby, but she told them Mum had been to visit the week before, not the day she went missing. Then after a bit they said they'd found

CCTV of her in town, which is strange because she hadn't said anything at all to me about going into town.'

'Could you have misheard?'

'Mum would've told me if she was going into town. She didn't really like it. She always said it was too busy. But if she was going to go there then she would've asked me if I wanted anything from the nice cake shop by the bus stop. She always got me something from there whenever she went into town.'

Lila scribbles lots in her notepad. I don't say anything while she's writing. Instead, I just listen to the sound of her pen scratching on the paper.

After a while she stops writing and looks at me again. 'So, the police had CCTV of your mum but still couldn't find her?'

'They said that some of the cameras in town weren't working like they should. They said they lost her. They said that they would carry on looking for her and would let us know if they found out any more.'

'And how long did they carry on looking for her?'

'Things were quite busy at first and there were always people ringing or coming to the house, but then there was the pandemic and lockdown, and everything just went quiet.'

'Of course, lockdown. For something that affected us all so much it's amazing how easy it is to forget about it sometimes. Anyway, when was the last time you heard from the police?'

I think about her question. 'I can't really remember. A year ago. Maybe a year and a half. I'm not sure exactly but it was quite a long time. I remember they didn't say anything very much when they called. When I told Marcus about it he got angry and said they were just "box ticking".'

'And who's Marcus, again?'

'He's Bev's son, and my friend. He comes round to visit me once a week and we have fish and chips together.'

Lila puts her pen down and gives me a funny look. 'So, one day out of the blue your mum left the house and never came back, and three years later no one knows what happened to her?'

'It's like she just disappeared,' I say.

'And what do you think happened to your mum?'

I think hard about the question. I have thought and thought about where Mum went and where she could be, but the truth is I have no idea. 'I don't know. I really don't know. She's out there though. I know it. She's out there and she is trying to get back to me.'

'And what makes you say that?'

I get up from my gaming chair and sit on the sofa. Not on Mum's side but next to it. I look down at the empty cushion, and try to imagine Mum sitting there but it's too hard. I just can't do it. I lift my head and look at Lila.

'I just know. Mum will be back because she has to come back. Mum will come back because I know she would never leave me forever.'

Lila gives me a sad smile, and is quiet for ages before she asks me another question.

'So, that's why even though all your neighbours have moved out you're refusing to leave your home?'

I'm happy she understands because not many people do. 'I have to stay here; I have to. I can't leave Hope Street because if I do, how will Mum find me when she comes back home?'

5

Lila

The moment Peter's in his office, I silently start counting to sixty in my head in order to give him time to take his coat off, settle in his chair and perhaps even turn on his computer. I don't want him to feel ambushed but after a night and an early morning thinking about nothing other than Connor McLaughlin and the amazing story I'm going to write about him, I just can't wait to get started. My impatience, however, is such that I don't even get to twenty before I've launched myself in the direction of Peter's office.

'Have you got a minute, Boss? It's really important.'

'My door is always open except when it isn't,' says Peter jovially. 'What can I do you for?'

'It's about that guy over in Hope Street you sent me to yesterday. I think it's a much bigger story than it looks.'

Peter raises an eyebrow. 'How do you mean "bigger"? You mean it's not just some mardy bloke giving the council what for just because he can?'

I reach for my notepad. 'Do you remember a couple of years ago, not long after I started, we did a big splash on a woman who went missing over Cossington Park way?'

Peter's forehead furrows in deep thought. 'It rings a bell. An older woman, wasn't she? The CCTV picked her up in town, but then half the bloody cameras weren't working and so they lost her. Is that the one you're thinking of?'

'That's the one. Bernadette McLaughlin. And guess who her son is . . .'

Peter raises an eyebrow. 'The guy from Hope Street?'

'Got it in one.' I tell him all about my interview and the moment I'd understood the connection between the two stories. As I bring Peter up to speed I find myself reliving everything I'd thought and felt sitting in that tiny front room listening carefully as Connor told me his story in his own unique way. Every now and again, as if too big to contain, his sorrow would break through, in a crack in his voice, or a pause that was just a moment too long, betraying the depth of feeling coursing through him.

In my time as a journalist I've encountered all manner of people in their moments of deepest crisis: mothers who have lost children, families who have seen all they own destroyed in terrible house fires, old people reduced to poverty after being cheated out of their life savings. And my heart had gone out to all of them – how could it not? But I've learned the hard way that I can't get too involved in any of these people's stories. That isn't my job. My job is to shine a light on their situation – nothing more, nothing less – and so in a way I suppose I've grown a little more hard-hearted over the years, partly to protect myself, partly to make sure I remain impartial and do a good job.

But something about both Connor and his story has managed to worm its way under my skin. He'd filled my thoughts all the way back home from Hope Street last night, and had even haunted my dreams in the few hours I'd managed to sleep. Whatever the reason, I know in my heart that I have to write his story; I have to shine a light where before there has only been darkness. On the surface it's a run-of-the-mill story: crazy guy refusing to play ball; but after meeting Connor and learning more, I realise that it's much more complex and poignant than that.

'Poor bugger,' exclaims Peter, once I've told him everything. 'If I remember correctly he wasn't quite . . . how shall I put it . . . the full ticket?'

'I think he's got some sort of learning difficulty, if that's what you're getting at, although I have no idea what kind and wouldn't presume to make a diagnosis.'

He runs a hand across his chin thoughtfully. 'So, what's this got to do with him not wanting to move?'

'Well, the thing is he's somehow convinced himself that even though she's been gone nearly three years now, one day his mum will come home. And he's worried that if he moves and she comes back she won't know where to find him. It's proper heartbreaking, the sort of story *Echo* readers will really love. A missing woman, a poor local lad who has clearly fallen between the cracks of a broken system, and who is now at the mercy of a heartless council in thrall to desperately greedy developers. It's got it all.'

He sits back in his chair and regards me carefully. Have I done enough to convince him how good the story is or am I about to be dismissed from his office for wasting his time?

'You see?' he says, his tone betraying just a hint of triumph. 'This is what local newspapers do best. Could you imagine one of the nationals being interested in a story like this? Not in a million years. But for us, this is our bread and butter. It's going to be a cracking piece, absolute front-page material. What are you thinking? A front-page splash, and an in-depth follow-up the day after?'

I can't help but grin. That was exactly what I had in mind.

He sits back in his chair thinking. 'How long do you think it'll take you?'

'There's a fair bit of background,' I admit. 'And obviously I'd like to chase up things with the police and see how their investigation stands . . .'

'So do you think she's still alive then?'

'She might be. It's impossible to say with the information I've got at the moment, so I'll have to do a lot more digging.'

Peter sucks air in loudly through his teeth. 'Sounds like a lot of work.'

'It is. I reckon I'll easily need two, maybe three weeks to do a proper job on it.'

Peter chuckles as if I've just cracked a joke. 'Nice try, Metcalfe. You've got seven days.'

After leaving Peter's office I head back to my desk grinning like an idiot and give Niamh a double thumbs up, prompting her to let out a little cheer, which immediately grabs Lewis's attention. As I sit down at my desk he cranes his neck around the side of his screen and gives us both a questioning look.

'Okay, then, interest piqued. What was that in aid of?'

'Wouldn't you like to know?'

'Oh, come on,' he whines. 'Just tell me.'

Feeling benevolent I give in. 'Oh, alright then, if you're begging. That guy over in Hope Street Peter sent me to see yesterday . . . well . . . it looks like it's going to be a much bigger story after all.'

I fill Lewis in and can't help but notice the mild look of irritation on his face. I can tell he's jealous and would love to get his hands on a story like this, especially as it's been a while since he's had a front page.

'I suppose I should say congrats,' he says, begrudgingly. 'It'll definitely make a good piece. Where are you going to start?'

'I was going to ask that too,' says Niamh. 'Obviously you're going to want to connect the two stories, but what's your angle?'

'I was thinking maybe central government's countless cuts to local services, police overstretched, real people with real problems falling between the cracks in a broken system and then finish off with a massive dig at the council for getting into bed with greedy developers who don't care about communities.'

Lewis laughs. 'So, a bit of everything then? Throw it all at the wall and see what sticks?'

'Well, it's worked before, I don't see any reason why it shouldn't now. And if it ends up causing a bit of a stink all the better; it's always good to rattle a few cages when you get the opportunity.'

I grab my second coffee of the morning and then make a start by putting in a few calls in the hope of getting some quotes. I call the council's press office and give them a list of questions I'd like responses to by the end of the day. I ask about the plans for Hope Street, how they came about in the first place, details about the developers and any declared conflicts of interest. Next, I put in a call to the press office at Derbyshire Constabulary and ask them for their most recent update in relation to the disappearance of Bernadette McLaughlin – and a comment to go along with it.

It feels good to have a story to really sink my teeth into, to really believe in what I'm doing, rather than simply churning out everyday stories, that no one – often not even the people I'm writing about – are really invested in. If only every day was like this, I'd be concentrating all my energies on trying to persuade Gabe to move up here rather than messing about applying for jobs down in London. Not that he would of course. These days it feels like it's all I can do to get him to come up for the weekend, so the thought of anything more than that is almost laughable.

Picking up my phone I'm about to put in a call to the office of Sheila Conway, the MP for the Cossington Park area, to see if she knows anything about Connor's situation and what if anything she's going to do about it, when it starts to ring.

'Hey, you,' says Gabe as I picture him sitting at his desk at work, looking smart and well turned out as always. 'Sorry I missed your calls last night. I thought it was only going to be a quick drink after work but it turned into a late one. How are you?'

'Really good actually,' I say too excited to be mad at Gabe for not being available last night when I desperately wanted to talk to him about my encounter with Connor. 'An amazing story's just dropped into my lap – it's the reason I called last night – and I can't wait to get started on it.'

'Oh, that's good. Makes a change, eh?'

'Certainly does. Anyway, I'd better go. I'm swamped right now but I'll talk to you later tonight and tell you everything, oh, and chat about plans for the weekend. Suffice to say it'll involve great food, cocktails and possibly dancing.'

'Actually, about that . . . I know you're going to hate me but I can't come up this weekend.'

My heart sinks. 'Why not?'

'Andreas managed to get tickets for the England match on Saturday, and I couldn't say no, could I? I'm sorry, Lils, really I am, but looking on the bright side if you come down here instead we'll still have Friday and Saturday night together, plus most of Sunday too.'

I feel myself getting riled and before I can stop myself I snap, 'Oh, thanks very much for squeezing me into your busy schedule!'

'Don't be like that,' he pleads. 'It's not like I asked for the ticket.'

'Well, you could turn it down.'

He sighs. 'Why are you being like this?'

'Being like what? A girlfriend who actually wants to spend time with her boyfriend? Of course, it's not like I didn't see you last weekend, oh no wait, I didn't because you were "slammed" at work. And the weekend before I had to come down to London even though it wasn't my turn because you had something on, and the weekend before that I didn't see you because you were away with the boys. And now yet again I'm going to have to cancel all the plans I've made for us up here and suffer the nightmare of weekend train travel all over again! You're not being fair, and you know it.'

Gabe snorts. 'And you're not being reasonable, so I guess we're both in the wrong here.'

'I'm not having that! You're twisting things.' I lower my voice as I see Lewis looking at me over his computer. 'Look, maybe we should give this weekend a miss.'

'Maybe, you're right,' Gabe says flatly. 'Maybe it would do us both good to have a bit of space.'

'Okay by me,' I snarl, feeling myself once again letting the pressures of being so far apart get in the way of my better judgement. 'Have a great weekend, enjoy your match and I'll see you when I see you.'

Gabe and I started going out together in my final year at Bristol. I'd been studying English, while Gabe had just returned to his degree in business and finance after a year out working at a management consultancy firm in London. That was the only time in the course of our five-year relationship where we've actually lived in the same city. After graduation I headed up to Sheffield to do my postgraduate degree in journalism, while Gabe was offered a job in London, with the very company where he'd spent his year out. Though it was difficult, we'd made it work, each of us taking our turn to travel to see the other at weekends, and talking constantly on the phone during the week.

It was only for a year, we'd told each other; in no time at all we'd be together down in the capital. But then towards the end of my course I'd had a call from *The Echo* offering me a place on their graduate trainee programme. I'd loved my time on placement there. It had been a real in-at-the-deep-end, hands-on experience, the kind I was sure I wouldn't have had if I'd served my time on a national. Besides which, when Dad had heard the news, he'd been really touched. 'Following in your granddad's footsteps, eh?' he'd said. 'He always used to say a local paper's the best grounding for a career in journalism you'll ever get.' And so, even though Gabe had made his disappointment plain, I'd accepted the job.

Quite why it had taken me until now to feel even remotely up to the challenge of applying for jobs in London, is anyone's guess. Maybe I'd grown a little too comfortable at *The Echo*, maybe I was scared of discovering I wasn't good enough to make it on a national. Perhaps even, subconsciously, there was an element of fear jumping back into a full-time relationship after having spent four years living apart. Maybe it was all these things and more besides, but the bottom line is the way things are at the minute is unsustainable, causing us both a huge amount of pointless stress.

Usually, when we've had one of our long-distance arguments I'm the one to call and make peace, but this time Gabe's so in the wrong, so out of order that I'm determined to wait it out. And so rather than give in, I bury myself in work for the next couple of hours to take my mind off things. But then, just as I'm about to head out to get a late lunch with Niamh my phone rings.

When I see it's Gabe, I immediately melt. He's come to his senses. He wants to apologise. He cares about what we've got enough to put his pride to one side and try to make things right. And so that's what I want to do too.

'Just give me a sec,' I say to Niamh and taking the call I race across the newsroom to the hallway outside the loos, which is, in an open-plan office like this, one of the very few places a person can talk privately.

'Sorry about that. I was just going somewhere a bit quieter. Listen, before you say anything, I'm sorry. I shouldn't have jumped down your throat like that. I really hate it when we row.'

I expect Gabe to immediately echo my words, to tell me that he's sorry too, and that us arguing is all down to the stress and strain of being so far apart. But instead of an apology of equal warmth and sincerity, all I get is silence.

'Gabe? Gabe? Are you there?'

Finally, he speaks. 'I'm really sorry, Lils, I am, but I just don't think I can do this anymore. It's not just this argument, it's a lot of things and it's been a long time coming. The thing is I've tried and I've tried, but I really don't think we can make this work. The truth is, I think we might be over.'

6

Connor

I'm standing at the bus stop waiting for the one-two-five to take me into work for my late shift, when my phone rings. I check the screen and see that it is Marcus calling. Normally, I would answer because Marcus is my friend, but today I'm not sure what to do because I don't know if I should tell him about last night when Lila the journalist lady came to see me. I'm worried that he'll be upset with me for letting a stranger into the house, even though I did check her ID first.

'Hello, Marcus, how are you?'

'I'm good thanks, Connor, mate. You okay?'

I think for a moment. I am definitely more than okay. Even though it had made me a bit sad talking to Lila about Mum, it had also been nice. There aren't many people I can talk to about Mum these days. I think people don't bring her up because they think it makes me sad, but I do miss talking about her, and Lila had really listened to me and had seemed interested in everything I had to say. I also really liked having my photo taken by the photographer that Lila sent for. His name was Paul, and he had a beard and a really expensive-looking camera. When he was done he let me look at all the photographs he had taken of me. Some were really funny, and he said he would send me copies of the funniest ones if I gave him my email address. I can't tell Marcus any of this though, not about Lila, or the interview, or even the photos. It has to be a secret.

'Yes, I'm fine. I'm just on my way to work.'

'Late shift, is it?'

'Yes, a two-ten.'

'Okay, well I won't keep you. I was just calling to say that I called that plumber mate of mine, Jax, about the leaking tap in the bathroom that the council haven't sorted. And he'll be giving you a call this week to arrange a time to come round. Don't worry about the bill – I'll sort it.'

Marcus is really thoughtful to have done this, and I feel even worse not telling him the truth about the journalist.

'Thank you, Marcus, that is very kind of you.'

'No problem, mate. Any issues, just give me a bell and otherwise I'll see you next week as usual.'

As I end the call I look up to see that the one-two-five is coming down the road. When it pulls up, I say hello to the driver, and he says hello back and then I'm about to head upstairs when I remember the boys from yesterday and decide to sit downstairs instead where it's safer. The only free seat is next to a lady about my age, but when I try to sit down she gives me a funny look and puts her bag on the seat and so I stand instead.

Holding on to the rail with one hand, I slip on my headphones, turn on my music and think about Marcus. I've known him for as long as I can remember. His family used to live in the house opposite and Marcus's mum, Bev, and my mum were best friends. After Mum went missing, it was Bev who looked out for me, popping over with food and washing my clothes for me, and always making sure I was looking after myself and keeping the place tidy.

Bev carried on checking in on me even after she accepted an offer from the council to leave Hope Street. They gave her a ground-floor flat on the other side of town and it took two buses to get to me but she did it every single week. But then a year ago her arthritis got so bad that she couldn't check in on me anymore and that's when she'd asked Marcus to take over.

Mike Gayle

Once a week, after a day working at his garage, Marcus drives to the chip shop on Linton Road, picks up two portions of fish and chips, a can of Vimto for me and a Coke for him, then we eat it in the living room in front of the TV. It's one of my favourite times of the week. Like I said, I don't like lying to him but I don't think he would care that I had very carefully checked Lila's ID before opening the door, or even that I had taken photos of it for my records. He would just be annoyed that I'd let a stranger into the house and would be even more cross if he found out that the one stranger was actually two.

I eventually get a seat when the bus reaches The Old Crown, and so I'm a bit more comfortable for the rest of the journey, so comfortable that I fall asleep and almost miss my stop. Luckily, an old lady getting off the bus accidentally bangs me with her shopping bag, and when I open my eyes I realise that we're at the retail park. I make sure to thank the driver before I get off the bus, and then I start making my way across the really big car park to DIY-Depot where I work.

I've worked at DIY-Depot for fourteen years now, since I turned sixteen. I love working here. It is one of my favourite places to be. Because I've been here so long I know everyone and everyone knows me. Best of all, it's not like school where nearly everyone was horrible to me; in fact, it's the opposite, because nearly everyone is nice. People bring in cakes for us all to share when it's their birthday and when it was Wimbledon last year someone brought in a load of strawberries and cream for everyone to enjoy when watching the matches on the TV in the break room, and at Christmas we always go out for a works party and sometimes, but not always, we have a Secret Santa too.

It was Mum who got me the job at DIY-Depot. She heard from one of our old neighbours that they were looking for people to collect the trolleys from the car park and so she called them up

50

and got me an interview. It was the old manager, Jenny, who gave me the job, and I really liked it because I could make collecting the trolleys into a game, first getting them from around the car park pretending I was Pac-Man and they were power cookies, and then slotting the trolleys together to make a massive train and pushing them back to the front of the store.

I don't do trolleys much anymore though. When we got a new manager he said that I could do some training and learn to work in different parts of the store and so that's what I do now.

Arriving at the staff entrance at the side of the store I open my jacket, untangle my lanyard and swipe my employee card to open the door.

You would think that after all these years this would get boring but it doesn't.

Even after all this time I still feel special that I can go through a door that normal people aren't allowed through.

This door is just for people who work at DIY-Depot and no one else.

I walk up the corridor and let myself into the locker room to hang up my coat and put away my bag and the first person I see is my friend Alan.

My friend Alan is old.

He has short white hair, tired-looking eyes, a neatly trimmed grey beard and long, straggly grey eyebrows, which have a life of their own.

He reminds me a bit of an old terrier type of dog, like the one Mrs Harris our old next door but one neighbour used to have.

Sometimes when Alan speaks, I don't actually listen to the words he says; instead I watch his eyebrows dancing crazily about and imagine how funny it would be if one day they flew right off his face.

Alan and I became friends on his first day at DIY-Depot five years ago. He's seventy-two, and used to be a bus driver. Then he retired but then his wife died when he was sixty-seven and he got lonely staying at home without her and so he got a job at DIY-Depot. He always jokes that the reason we're friends is that most people are too annoying but that I am only partly annoying so that makes me okay. I don't really think he thinks I'm annoying. I actually think he really likes me, just like I really like him too.

'I didn't know you were in today,' I say, surprised.

'I wasn't supposed to be, but the gaffer asked if I'd make an exception, because there's some health and safety training thing going on this afternoon in the warehouse. Apparently, Ranjit's leading it so they needed someone to cover.'

I laugh remembering the advice Alan had given me when I told him I had some early shifts coming up. 'You shouldn't let them take advantage of you like that, Alan!'

'Too right,' he says, getting the joke. 'Still, at least you and me can hang out for a bit today. I feel like I haven't seen you to talk to for a while. Everything okay?'

I think about telling him about how Lila from *The Echo* came to my house yesterday. I think it is a story he would like. But before I can say anything Ryan, the assistant manager, comes in.

I don't like Ryan very much. I like Andrew, the store manager, much better. Andrew is always quite smiley and waves whenever he passes me on the shop floor. Ryan is not smiley. He is bossy, and not just because he is assistant manager. I think he is bossy because, like Alan says, he likes the sound of his own voice.

'Come on, you pair!' he shouts. 'A delivery's just come in and it's not about to unload itself! Chop chop!'

'Chop, Chop!' says Alan, once Ryan has gone. 'I'll give him a bloody chop, chop! Where does he get off talking to the pair of us like we're his own personal slaves? If he did his fair share instead of swanning around with his clipboard bossing us about like a tinpot dictator we wouldn't need to chop, chop!'

We go down to the loading bay. There isn't just one lorry to unload but two, and we both know this will take ages.

'I'm too old for this malarkey!' says Alan. 'And I can tell you for nothing, this is the last time I do anyone around here a favour!'

It takes us three long hours to unload and unpack the lorry, and afterwards Alan and me are both very sweaty and tired. Even though our break isn't for another hour yet, Alan says that we have to stop.

'If me and you don't have a drink now we'll pass out and if them upstairs don't like it they can lump it!'

Even though I know that DIY-Depot doesn't have an 'upstairs' I don't want to correct Alan when he's in this sort of mood. Instead, I follow him to the break room where he makes a mug of tea, while I get my Vimto from my jacket in the locker room.

During our break we talk about lots of different things. Alan always has lots of interesting stories to tell, and I enjoy listening to them. He tells me one about the time he was looking after his next door neighbour's cat and it brought a live mouse into the house, which is so funny and makes me laugh so hard that a little bit of Vimto comes out of my nose.

Because Alan's story is really good I want to tell him a really good story of my own, and then I remember that I was going to tell him all about Lila from *The Echo* and how I'm going to be in the paper soon. Even though I think Alan will like the story, I'm a little bit worried that he will be like Marcus and get cross because I let a stranger into the house, especially one who is a journalist. Alan doesn't really like *The Echo*. Sometimes he calls it 'a rag' and says that it's 'only fit for wrapping chips in' – even though chips don't come wrapped in newspaper; they come in boxes.

Instead, I tell Alan a story about how when I was small my mum and I used to feed Bev's cat whenever the family were away. 'It was called Cuddles,' I tell him, 'but it wasn't very cuddly at all. If you ever tried to give it a stroke it would wag its tail and hiss at you, and it was so mean that it actually once bit the postman and Mum said that they ought to get a sign for the door that said, 'Beware of the Cat.'

Alan laughs, and starts to tell me a story about a mean cat he once knew when the break room door opens and Briony from the office comes in, followed by a group of people I've never seen before.

'That'll be the new recruits,' whispers Alan. 'Someone said there'd be some new blood coming in soon. Poor beggars, they have no idea what they're letting themselves in for.'

Alan nudges me hoping I'll laugh, but I don't. I can't. In the group of new recruits there is a face I remember straight away even though I haven't seen it for years. It is a face that sends a shiver down my spine. Her hair is long and blonde now instead of being short and mousy brown like it used to be, but there's no mistaking who it is.

It is Adele Sharpe.

The girl who made my time at secondary school a nightmare.

Bernie: September 1992

'Pregnant? Are you absolutely sure, doctor? I mean, I'm thirty-seven!'

Dr Agyeman reached for the calendar on her desk, and looked as if she was trying her best to conceal a smile. 'Eight weeks according to my calculations. I take it this is somewhat unexpected news?'

Bernie sat back in her chair and shook her head in disbelief. 'But I'm on the pill.'

Dr Agyeman nodded sagely. 'I'm afraid to say that no method of contraception is a hundred per cent effective.'

'But pregnant? I mean, I haven't even got the means to properly look after myself let alone a baby.'

'Well, as I said, it's very early days so there's no need to rush into any decision right now. The important thing is to take the time to digest this news properly. I'll book you in for a follow-up appointment for the beginning of next week and we'll take things from there. How does that sound?'

Bernie had no idea how it sounded as she hadn't been listening at all. All she could hear was the sound of the blood rushing through her ears, and she wondered if the baby could hear yet and, if so, whether it could tell just how terrified she was.

'I'm sorry,' said Bernie, and she got the doctor to not only repeat what she'd said but also write it down on a piece of paper. 'Honestly, nothing's going in right now; my head's all over the place. At least if it's down in black and white I'll be able to take it in properly once I've calmed down a bit.'

Thanking the doctor, Bernie left the consulting room, feeling as if everything outside the four walls she had just left seemed different, off-kilter somehow. Had the corridor back to the reception always been this wide? Had the chairs in the waiting room always been that violent shade of orange? Had her shoes always made this terrible squeaking noise against the vinyl flooring under her feet?

Outside she took several deep gulps of fresh air and leaning against the wall next to the entrance instinctively reached into her handbag, pulled out her cigarettes, lit one and had almost got it to her lips before she remembered something vague about it being bad to smoke when you were pregnant. Had it been something she'd watched on the telly? Or maybe something she'd read while flicking through one of the magazines at work? Wherever it had been, however hazy the memory, it was enough to make her stub out the cigarette on the wall beside her, throw it on the ground, and then crush it with a twist of her heel. For the time being at least, she was going to have to find another way to calm her nerves.

'You're pregnant?' exclaimed Bev, the following morning, as the two friends stood restocking the bread aisle of the Hudson's SuperSave where they both worked. 'I didn't even know you were seeing anyone!'

'Shhh!' hissed Bernie. 'Not so loud!'

Bev gave her a funny look and narrowed her eyes. 'You're not saying . . . ?' Bev's eyes widened and she lowered her voice so much that Bernie could barely hear her question. *'Is it someone from here?'*

Bernie nodded and her heart sank. The secret she'd been carrying around for months was about to come out and she wasn't proud of it; she wasn't proud of it at all.

'Let's not talk about it here,' she said trying her best not to cry. 'My shift's over in half an hour. I'll wait outside for you and we can talk when you're on your break.'

As they carried on with their work, Bernie fell silent, lost in thought about the mess she was in and how much she regretted the events that had brought her to this.

She'd always known that Kevin, the deputy manager, was married. His wife sometimes came into the store, young kids in tow, to pick up her shopping. Bernie had even served her a couple of times and as she'd put her items through the till she'd thought she'd seemed nice, so quite why she'd let herself succumb to Kevin's advances was anyone's guess.

She'd never been great at relationships, in part she'd always assumed because her own parents hadn't been what you might call a great example. A dad who drank himself to death and a mum who was full of rage and self-pity had made her long for stability and yet ironically attract a whole series of men who wanted the opposite.

Kevin had been flirting with her for ages, complimenting her on her hair, make-up, or figure, and always finding excuses to get her on her own. Then had come the works Christmas party, and he'd offered to give her a lift home and foolishly she'd accepted. And what began as a one-off, somehow developed into a regular occurrence, one that was always at his convenience. He'd call when his wife was out of town with the kids seeing family, he'd call when he was on his way home after a night out with friends and was a bit the worse for wear, and he'd call whenever he was down about work, about being passed over for promotion or whenever he was stressed because the store had missed its sales target and he was getting it in the neck.

After several months of this Bernie began to tire of all the guilt she felt. She reminded herself that she was better than this and so she broke things off. She'd ignored him at work, refused to take his calls at home, but rather than putting him off this had only served to make him pursue her more ardently. He'd call her his Irish beauty, find every excuse to take her aside at work, wait outside her bedsit for her to come home, and though she knew better, she'd give in, and as much as she would tell herself she deserved better, the fact of the matter was deep down she didn't really believe it enough to make any kind of difference.

The last time she had seen Kevin outside of work had been about a month ago. He'd called late at night, pleading and cajoling to be allowed to come round. When she'd finally agreed he brought a Chinese takeaway with him, along with a bottle of wine that she knew full well was from the bargain bin at work. They'd eaten the food while half watching a late-night film, and after clearing away the containers into her tiny kitchenette, together they'd opened up the sofa bed and made it up before climbing under the cold duvet to make love as the smell of sweet and sour pork and peanut oil lingered heavily in the air. She hadn't known she was already four weeks pregnant then; she hadn't even got the slightest inkling that the catastrophe that awaited her had already happened.

'Kevin?' Bev's voice was heavy with disbelief.

'I know,' sighed Bernie. 'Believe me I know.'

'But he's not even that good-looking.'

Bernie cringed. 'Don't. I hate myself enough as it is, alright? Just help me work out what to do.'

'Are you going to have it?'

'I haven't even got that far.'

'And are you going to tell him?'

'That there is the other six-million-dollar question.'

Bev hugged her friend. 'You'll be okay, you know. Whatever happens you'll be okay. You're strong; you'll get through this. I know you will.'

At work the following day, Bernie found herself staring at Kevin whenever he loomed into view. He'd make a terrible father. He already was one, but still maybe he deserved to know. The question was when and how to bring it up. In the end, things sorted themselves out, because later that evening, as she sat at home eating beans on toast in front of the TV, she heard someone ring the front-door buzzer several times in a row followed a few moments later by a knock at her door.

'Hello, love,' said Kevin, brandishing another cheap bottle of wine in her direction, 'aren't you going to invite me in?'

She stared at him for a moment not speaking, as if seeing him for the first time. How had she ever allowed this man into her life? How had she ever allowed him to touch her when right now his proximity alone was enough to make her feel nauseous? Leaving the door ajar she headed to the kitchenette, grabbed two wine glasses and a corkscrew and returned to the room to find that Kevin had already made himself comfortable on the sofa.

'So how you've been?' he asked as he opened the wine and poured out two glasses. 'Have you missed me much? I think you have. Seemed like you couldn't take your eyes off me at work today.'

She took a sip of her wine, and almost spat it straight back out. Though she'd had this very same wine before, and it had been half decent, for some reason it now tasted like vinegar in her mouth.

'I'm pregnant,' she heard herself saying.

He put down the glass in his hand. 'You what?'

'I'm pregnant. Eight weeks apparently.'

Kevin's face was the picture of disbelief. His eyes were wide, his mouth hung open, and for a moment Bernie was struck by how closely he resembled the whole salmon on the fish counter at work.

'But you said you were on the pill.'

'I was, but apparently that's no guarantee of anything.'

His face contorted in anger. 'You stupid bitch!' he snapped, and he picked up his glass and flung it at the wall with such force that it made her jump as it smashed into a million pieces and sent a scarlet splatter across the room.

'You need to go,' said Bernie standing up.

'You don't tell me what to do, you whore,' he growled, getting to his feet too. 'I mean, is it even mine?'

Bernie didn't miss a beat. 'Unfortunately, yes.'

'I don't believe you. And nor will anyone else.'

'I don't care what you believe,' said Bernie not quite sure where this strength was coming from. 'I don't care about you at all. I just want you out of my place right now, or I'm going to call the police, do you hear me? I'm going to call them, and make such a fuss that you'll regret crossing me.'

He held up his hands in surrender. 'Okay, okay, no need to be like that, is there? Just tell me you're going to deal with it and I promise I'll go. Just tell me you're going to make all of this go away and I'll be out of here.'

'I'll do no such thing!' snarled Bernie, much to her own surprise. 'Whether you like it or not, I'm having this baby.'

All the blood seemed to drain out of Kevin's face. 'You don't mean that.'

'I do.'

'You can't. I'm married – this will ruin everything.'

'And this is only just occurring to you? I don't remember you worrying about that too much before now or did I miss something?'

He bit his lip, and Bernie could see in his eyes that he was torn between wanting to fly into another rage and getting as far away from her as he possibly could.

'I'll get you a promotion.'

In the heat of the moment it took her several seconds to understand what it was he was proposing.

'You're offering me a promotion?'

'To a supervisor. More money, more responsibility – you could get out of this place and get yourself somewhere better to live.'

'And in return . . . ?' She wanted to make him say it, to spell out exactly what it was he was asking her to do.

His gaze shifted to the floor by Bernie's feet. 'You know . . .'

Bernie felt a wellspring of anger rising up within her. 'Let's say I don't know. Come on, Kevin, be a man; say it, say exactly what it is that you want me to do.'

Kevin wasn't exactly a small man but at this he seemed to shrink before her eyes and then finally, in words that registered just above a whisper he said, 'Get rid of it.'

'That's the second time you've called this baby it,' she said and turning towards the coffee table, she picked up the heavy glass ashtray and raised it above her head. 'Leave, leave now, or I swear on this baby's life I will cave your stupid head in!'

Other than to Bev, Bernie never said a word about who the father of her baby was, and if anyone at work suspected or made the connection between the swelling of her belly and Kevin's hasty transfer to a store down in Gravesend, then they kept it to themselves. And so it was she became a single mother to baby Connor, and gladly never gave his father a second thought.

7

Lila

'So, that's it? Five years over just like that? What an absolute tosser! And he did it over the phone?'

'Like the man he is.'

'Well, if you ask me, you're better off without him.'

I think for a moment and switch the phone to my other ear. It's all very well for my sister, Robyn, to make such proclamations from the safety of her happy marriage but I'm not so sure.

'Am I?'

'Are you what?'

'Better off, really.'

'Yes, you are,' says Robyn firmly. 'If he's not prepared to make the effort after all your time together then yes, kick him to the kerb I say, and get back out there. See how he likes it when he sees you on Insta with a buff new beau.'

I'd smile at the picture my sister has painted were it not for the fact that it feels like my heart is breaking. After Gabe had dropped his bombshell I'd been shocked of course but I hadn't for a minute believed he was really serious. I'd convinced myself that he was just angry, saying things he'd come to regret because after all he and I were solid as a rock and in it for the long haul. But over the course of that phone call and multiple subsequent conversations I'd come to understand that he'd actually meant every word, which was as painful to accept as it was humiliating to acknowledge.

'Thanks, sis. That's just the sort of thing I need to hear even if it isn't likely to happen anytime soon.'

'I know it must feel like that now,' says Robyn, her tone softening. 'It's still raw. It's only been a few days. But it will get better. I promise.'

As I end the call, my stomach rumbles, but I can't muster up the energy required to put a meal together. Instead, I pour out a bowl of cereal, drown it in milk, and then as an afterthought as I return the carton to the fridge, I grab a bottle of beer, open it, then carefully take everything back to bed.

Setting it all down on my bedside table, I climb under the covers, having already exchanged my work clothes for my fluffy onesie the moment I came home. Reaching for my laptop, I queue up an episode of something suitably mindless to distract myself but despite my best efforts I just can't concentrate, and so finally, inevitably, I switch it off and allow myself to be consumed by thoughts of Gabe, and how much I already miss him.

I think about trying to call him again, imagine myself begging his forgiveness, pleading for him to give us another chance. But something, I'm not sure what exactly, stops me. Perhaps it's my sense of pride, the stubborn streak running through all Metcalfes, or maybe even feelings of anger at the thought Gabe had given up on us after so long together. An awful thought strikes me. What if this isn't about the long-distance thing at all? What if he's simply been looking for an excuse to call it a day? I tell myself I've cried my last tear over that man, and with that thought, I'm about to turn out the lights and cry myself to sleep when my phone rings.

'Hello,' says a female voice I don't recognise. 'Am I speaking to Lila Metcalfe?'

'Yes,' I say, wondering what on earth this is about. 'Yes, it is.'

'Oh, good,' she says. 'My name's Brooke Cheung, I work in the HR department of The Correspondent News Group. I'm so sorry to be calling outside of normal office hours but it's just come to my attention that due to an IT glitch a number of candidates have failed to receive the email inviting them for interview the day after tomorrow. So, I'm personally contacting everyone to double-check. Can you confirm you received yours?'

'My . . . my . . . what . . . invitation to interview at *The Correspondent*?' I can barely believe I'm actually saying these words. 'No, I'd definitely remember an email like that. Are you saying they want to interview me?'

The woman laughs. 'You might want to sound a bit more confident when you come, but yes, they do want to interview you. Thankfully, despite the error all the other candidates are able to make the date we had planned, and we're really hoping you can too.'

At work the following morning I pull Niamh aside first thing and tell her everything.

'Talk about timing!' she says. 'So, are you going to go for it?'

'Well, I've said I will, but part of me wonders what's the point now that me and Gabe are over.'

'And the rest of you?'

I can't help but smile. 'I'm curious to see if I could do it.'

'I know it's easy for me to say, but forget Gabe. This is about you, not him. And as for the question of your abilities, of course you can do it. They wouldn't have called you in otherwise. If you want my opinion, I think the question you really need to ask yourself is do you want it? And how much?'

I think for a moment. Having wrestled with this question all night, I'm still not sure. 'Of course I've complained about this place, but isn't that just what we do? Moan about life in local journalism and assume the grass would be greener on a national?'

'Well, yeah, but what if it actually is greener? What if this is the move that takes your career to another level? I mean, obviously you've got to get the job first, but just think how amazing things will be if you do. Besides . . .' she grins '. . . I'll need friends in high places if I'm ever going to get out of here.'

I spend the rest of the day alternating between continuing to work on Connor's story and laying down the groundwork for calling in sick tomorrow. At various times throughout the day whenever Peter is in earshot, I cough, or fake-sneeze, so much so that he even asks me if I'm okay. Much as I hate the subterfuge, I know after having sat through countless HR presentations to the staff about the necessity of giving at least four weeks' notice for any time off, it's the only way I'm going to make this happen without revealing that I'm going for an interview.

The following morning I board the 9.15 to London and as I take my seat it doesn't escape my notice that the last time I made this journey was in order to spend the weekend with Gabe. Pushing the thought from my mind, I take out today's edition of *The Correspondent* and determine to read it from cover to cover, and even make notes on it.

Later, as the train pulls into St Pancras, I gather my things and make my way over to *The Correspondent*'s offices in Battersea. By rights, I should be a bundle of nerves as this is the first job interview I've had in three years but for some reason I feel strangely calm. Perhaps it's because now that Gabe and I have split up, it doesn't feel like all of my future happiness is riding on this one thing. Then again, it could be down to working on Connor and Bernie's story, meaning that I'm feeling better about being at *The Echo* than I have in a long time.

Whatever the reason when I finally arrive at *The Correspondent*, I don't even pause for thought at the entrance, I just step right into the revolving doors, and once I'm through the other side into the bustling lobby, stride confidently towards reception and give them my name.

As I take a seat in the waiting area I look around at all the people coming and going and can't help but wonder what it would be like to be one of them. There's an energy and excitement here in this building where so many globally important news stories have been broken and so many prize-winning journalists have made their names, an energy that *The Echo* even at its best can't compete with. What might it feel like to work here? To be at the beating heart of a news operation like this?

Before I can take this thought any further I look up at the sound of footsteps on the marble floor and see James Neate walking towards me. I recognise him from his by-line photo, and, of course, the countless times I've seen him on *Newsnight* and it feels a little bit like meeting a rock star.

'Lila Metcalfe?'

I stand up and shake his hand. 'Yes, so pleased to meet you.'

'You too,' he replies. 'Have you come far?'

'Not too far. Just Derby.'

'That's right, you work on *The Echo* don't you? I did a stint there as part of my journalism course many, many moons ago. Such a great paper. Really solid.'

'Yes, yes, it is.'

'Right then, just follow me up to the boardroom and we'll get started.'

The interview panel is made up of James, two senior editors and the head of HR, and they ask me questions covering everything from current world events to my opinion on the paper's recent major redesign, and without faltering once I answer everything they ask and even put forward some ideas of my own. In fact, I end up enjoying the experience so much that I'm almost disappointed when they tell me we've run out of time and start thanking me for coming to see them.

It is, without doubt, the best interview I've ever done and as I get into a packed lift with a bunch of cool-looking people talking animatedly about a spate of recent political protests taking place in Beijing, I feel a little thrill of excitement at the prospect that these people could be my work colleagues.

As I head to the Tube I open up Google Maps, and look up Gabe's work address over in the City. The plan I'd hatched last night, if I could give it such a grand name, had been to message him after my interview and ask if he'd meet me for lunch. Once he'd agreed I'd tell him about *The Correspondent* job and hopefully he'd see how serious I am about changing things for the better. Then maybe, just maybe he'd agree to give us a second chance. That had been the plan. But as I tuck my phone away it dawns on me that my excitement at being at *The Correspondent* has reignited my enthusiasm for my job, and actually the thing I really want to do is get back to writing pieces that make a difference, helping people like Connor and his mum, by doing what I do best, and Gabe, well . . . he'll just have to wait.

8
Connor

I am standing in the decorating aisle at work looking at Adele between the gaps in the paint tins. I feel like a spy.

A spy keeping watch on an evil villain from a distance.

Adele is in the garden furniture display helping Georgia, one of the other customer service assistants, put together a parasol.

She is not doing a very good job and keeps getting things wrong but for some reason Georgia seems to like her because they are laughing together like they are sharing a joke.

I used to quite like Georgia but now I am not so sure.

I have never liked Adele.

She is my enemy.

When I saw Adele in the break room yesterday, I knew it was her straight away even though the last time I saw her was more than ten years ago.

I know Adele from when I went to school. And she was one of the reasons I stopped going.

I was two whole school years above her, but that didn't make any difference at all. She and her friends Chloe Larimar, Tonya Piper and Sophie Atkins used to bully me every day and make my life a misery.

They would kick and punch me whenever they could, and if I ever looked like I might fight back they would threaten to get their boyfriends or their brothers to beat me up.

Sometimes when I was eating dinner on my own in the canteen they would spit in my food. One time Adele took one of the jugs of drinking water from one of the tables and poured it all over my head. She and her friends would start all sorts of rumours about me too, saying the most horrible things. They even called the police on me one time, saying I had attacked one of them, but all I'd done was push Chloe away because she pulled my jumper so hard it nearly ripped when I was on my way home from school one day.

After the police came round to my house and told me off, I told Mum that I wasn't going back to school again.

She told me to give it a few days and things might seem better but I knew they wouldn't. I can be quite stubborn when I want to, and even though Mum went up to school and had lots of meetings with the head teacher I did not change my mind.

I never went back to school, not even when the council sent Mum a letter and threatened to take her to court.

For a while I had a teacher, Mrs Barnett, who came to my house twice a week and gave me work to do. She was really nice and I quite enjoyed her lessons too, but then one day she stopped coming. It was something to do with budget cuts, Mum said, and so that was the end of that. For a bit Mum tried to teach me herself but that didn't work out very well because she wasn't very patient. So, in the end on the days when she was working at the launderette I helped her out, and on the other days I stayed home and played video games. Not long after Mum told me about the job at DIY-Depot and I thought I'd never have to see Adele again. But I was wrong.

'What are you doing, lad?'

It takes me a moment to realise that someone is talking to me. I turn around and see Alan.

'Nothing.'

'Doesn't look like nothing to me.' He leans forward and looks through the shelves to see what I've been looking at.

'Adele Sharpe,' he says sounding unhappy. 'I didn't recognise her at first, but then I heard someone calling her name and put two and two together.'

I look at Alan, surprised. 'You know her?'

'Sadly yes, I had two sets of the Sharpe family living on my road at one point, the two sisters, their various partners, and a gaggle of kids you couldn't keep track of, and Adele was one of them. Feral they were, roaming the street until all hours, causing all manner of mischief. You want to stay clear of that one, if you want my advice, bad to the bone the Sharpes, the lot of them.'

Before I can tell Alan that I will never, not ever, be talking to Adele, Pawel, who is staffing the customer service desk, calls Alan over the Tannoy to do a price check.

'I can't get five minutes' peace in this place!' says Alan. 'Sorry about this. I'll have to catch up with you later, lad.'

As he walks off, I turn back to the shelves to carry on with my spying on Adele, but she isn't there and neither is Georgia, and the display still isn't up properly. I tell myself maybe they have gone to get Musa from the warehouse because I know he is really good at putting together garden furniture. I look around to see if I can see Adele, or Georgia or Musa, but I can't, and so I decide to stay where I am and wait for them to come back.

A voice from behind makes me jump.

'Excuse me?'

I turn around expecting it to be a customer.

But it's not. It is Adele Sharpe.

'Hi,' she says, smiling. 'It's Connor, isn't it? Connor McLaughlin? You probably don't remember me but I'm Adele, Adele Sharpe. We used to go to school together.'

I want to say of course I remember you.

I want to say you're the reason I left school early.

I want to say that even though it's been years since I've seen you I still have nightmares about you sometimes.

But instead, I say nothing.

'You are Connor, aren't you?' she asks taking a step towards me.

My mouth has suddenly gone really dry but my hands are so wet with sweat that I have to wipe them on my apron. I want to run but my legs feel like they are made of jelly.

She wants to know if I am Connor.

I think about telling her that I am not but then remember that I am wearing my name badge and it's this that she is staring at.

I have no choice. I have to answer her question.

I nod again, but still don't speak.

'Listen,' she says taking another step towards me, 'I don't know whether you remember this but I was really horrible to you at school. I was really mean, and I just want to say I'm sorry. I was hanging around with the wrong crowd, and things weren't brilliant at home – not that it's any excuse – but I shouldn't have taken it out on you. I was like, a total bitch, and I'm sorry. I've done a lot of growing up over the last few years and all I can say is I'm not the same person I was back then. I've changed. So, what do you say? Can we start again?'

She holds out her hand for me to shake but I don't move. Instead, I just stare at her. This doesn't make any sense. Adele Sharpe is apologising to me. She was so cruel, so mean, for so long. Can it really be true that she has changed? I know it was a very long time ago and both of us are grown-ups now. She looks different to how I remember her looking when we were at school together. Back then she had brown hair, and now it is long and blonde. Back then she had no tattoos but now I can see that she has them on her hands, and her neck too. She does look different on the outside but can people really change who they are on the inside?

I get worried that if I don't shake her hand she will be offended and might do something bad to me. I reach out to shake it, staring at her long pointy red nails but then over her shoulder I see Briony from the office coming towards us down the aisle. She's not alone. With her are Pam from kitchen designs, Maryam from home furnishings and Alan, along with loads of other members of staff, and they are all looking at me.

'Connor McLaughlin!' calls out Briony, her curly brown hair bouncing in the air as she marches towards me, holding a newspaper in her hands. 'You're a dark horse, aren't you? On the front cover of *The Echo* and you never said a word!'

She turns the newspaper in her hands around so that I can see the front page. Under the headline: 'NOT LEAVING! Son of Missing Local Woman Holds Up Multi-million-pound Development' is one of the pictures Paul the photographer from *The Echo* took of me standing in front of my house, arms folded, and looking sad.

The whole thing takes me by surprise. I knew I was going to be in the paper but I thought that Lila might give me a call first to warn me. I don't know what to say and then I remember that I am supposed to be shaking hands with Adele, but when I look for her, she has gone. Before I have time to think I am surrounded by people congratulating me on being in the paper and wanting to know more about the story.

'So how did it all come about?' asks Pam. 'Did you call them?'

'No,' I say, 'they came to me. I was at home and there was a knock at the door and a nice lady said that she'd come to interview me.'

'And how did she hear about you?' asks Maryam.

'I don't know,' I say. 'Maybe from the council.'

'Poor lad,' says Pam, putting an arm around me. 'I'm ashamed to say that I'd all but forgotten about your poor mum going missing. It must be so terrible for you.'

'It's not very nice,' I admit. 'I miss her very much.'

'And now the council are threatening to bulldoze your house!' says Jason from the warehouse. 'It's disgraceful!'

'But he can't stay there forever,' Briony pipes up. 'He's the only one living in that street now. It must be dead spooky at night.' She shudders. 'For what it's worth, Connor, I think you should move.'

'Well, I don't,' says Alan firmly. 'I think Connor should stick it out if that's what he wants to do. Bloody council throwing their weight around like they own the place! They can't even get the bins sorted so what they're doing getting involved in a multi-million-pound development is anyone's guess! Why don't they just mind their own business and let him be?'

'My mum's going to come home,' I say trying my best not to have angry thoughts about Briony and her comment. 'I know lots of people think she won't, but I know she will. And when she does, I want to be there waiting for her.'

'That's a lovely sentiment,' says Briony. 'It is, really. But what are you going to do if she doesn't come back? Just stay in that empty street for the rest of your life? That's no way for a young man like you to live, is it?'

As I decide to ignore Briony my phone vibrates in my back pocket. Phones aren't really allowed on the shop floor, but it's a rule everyone, even Ryan, ignores. Even Andrew, the store manager, turns a blind eye as long as it doesn't stop us doing our work.

While everyone else carries on arguing about what they think I should do, I take out my phone to see Marcus's name there. My stomach flips. This can only mean one thing: like everyone else he's seen me in the paper and now I'm in really big trouble.

'What are you doing on the front page of *The Echo*?'

I swallow hard. 'I'm sorry, Marcus, I should've told you. I didn't know it was coming out today.'

'Well, that's okay, then,' says Marcus in a way that I know means something different. 'It's not like I've had my mum on the phone for half an hour giving me an earful about how I'm not looking out for you properly.'

I feel really bad. Marcus's mum is usually really kind but when she gets angry she can be very scary indeed.

'I'm sorry, Marcus,' I say again. 'I'll call Bev and tell her it was all my fault not yours.'

'Fat lot of good that'll do,' he says and he sounds angry. 'You know what she's like.' He stops and sighs, and when he speaks again he sounds a bit calmer. 'It's not really you I'm mad at, it's the journalist who interviewed you. How did she even find you?'

'I don't know. She just came round.'

'And you answered the door even though I've told you a million times not to?'

'She had ID. She passed it through the letterbox so I could look at it and I checked it over really carefully before I let her in. I've still got a picture of it on my phone.'

Marcus laughs. 'I bet you have. Why don't you zip it over to me so that I know who I'm talking about when I call the editor of *The Echo* and complain? I'm not having it, you being taken advantage of like this. It's not on.'

'But she wasn't trying to take advantage of me. She was really nice and interested in what I had to say.'

'Of course she was,' says Marcus. 'I bet she was all sweetness and light to get you to talk. That's how these people operate. They get one whiff of a story and then go in for the kill.' He sighs. 'I can't believe they made you talk about your poor mum.'

'It was quite nice, talking about Mum. People don't really ask me about her anymore. So, I didn't mind, really.'

'Well, I do,' says Marcus. 'And I'm going to tell them exactly how much I mind and why, when I speak to them. Don't you worry, after I've finished no one from *The Echo* will be bothering you ever again.'

9

Lila

'Well, love, I'd better let you go. I don't like to chat too long to you on the phone when you're driving.'

I look down at my rubbish phone lying on the passenger seat next to me. Mum's voice is coming through its hopeless speakers.

'I'm fine Mum, really, I am. I've got both eyes on the road, and the traffic's at a standstill as it is anyway.'

'Well, you need all your wits about you with the number of idiot drivers out there, so I'll leave you now. Have a great day, and congratulations again on that story of yours. I know your granddad would've been over the moon with it.'

'Thanks, Mum,' I say swallowing down the lump in my throat. 'That really means a lot.'

When I eventually pull into the car park at work, my thoughts shift to the day ahead and I'm grateful for the distraction. My front-page piece on Connor and Bernie made huge waves yesterday. Virtually all the local radio stations picked up on the story. BBC East Midlands ran a piece that included a live grilling of a disgruntled-looking leader of the council and even before I left the office yesterday there had been a record number of readers' comments left online, all clamouring for the police to renew their efforts to find Bernie. The article has certainly struck a chord with the people of Derby, and I'm already thinking of a few tweaks I can add to my follow-up piece before we go to press later today. Hopefully, this and some additional quotes that came in late last night, should keep the story on the front page and alive in the local consciousness for the rest of the week at least.

'Morning, mate,' says Niamh hurrying over to me the moment I enter the newsroom, 'sorry to be the bearer of bad news but Peter said you need to go and see him as soon as you get in. I think he's had a bit of blowback about that Hope Street splash of yours.'

'Blowback from who?'

'Beats me. He just said to go and see him.'

Suddenly I feel panicked. When I'd written the article Peter had been the first to read it, and he'd loved every word, but I know from experience that an editor's opinion of a piece can change overnight depending on how much aggravation they get as a result of it. Maybe he'd had it in the neck from his bosses, or maybe he'd had an earful from someone at the council. I rake over everything in my head trying to work out what I might have done wrong. I mean, what if I've made a glaring mistake of some kind, or overlooked something crucially important that even an intern would've picked up?

Since starting work at *The Echo* I've been threatened with legal action at least a dozen times by everyone from local gangsters who like to pretend they are bona fide businessmen through to city councillors, caught in compromising positions, both personal and financial. So far, however, they've never amounted to anything because I've always been careful. But perhaps breaking up with Gabe has thrown me more than I'd like to admit and so there's every chance I could have really messed up this time.

Heading to my desk I slip off my coat and hang it on the back of my chair, trying my best to ignore Lewis who is drawing a finger across his throat as though I'm heading off to the executioner's block, then walk over to Peter's office. Straightening my skirt, I take a deep breath, exhale and then finally pluck up the courage to knock on his door.

'You wanted to see me, Boss?'

Peter looks up from his computer. 'Oh, yeah.' He begins rummaging around through the chaos of papers strewn across his desk. 'It's about that Hope Street story.'

I meet Peter's gaze bracing myself for whatever's coming next.

'You know that lad, Connor, did you ask him if he wanted anyone there while you interviewed him?'

My stomach tightens. So, this is the issue. Something to do with safeguarding?

'No, should I have done? He seemed perfectly capable of making his own decisions to me. Has he said something?'

'Not him,' says Peter, 'some family friend of his phoned as I was leaving last night. I'll tell you he gave me a right earful. I don't think he's going to get legal or anything, but before this blows up into something it's not, could you maybe just nip round to where he works and hear him out? I'm sure he just wants to vent a bit and then hopefully that'll be that.'

My heart sinks. I've had to make apologies for things I'm not even remotely sorry about on behalf of the paper before, and it's my least favourite thing to do. It's never nice being shouted at, but being shouted at for essentially doing your job is as upsetting as it is galling.

'Oh, come on, Peter, I've got loads on today. Can't I just call him?'

Peter pulls a face. 'To be honest he was so irate that I don't think a call will cut it.' He rummages around on his desk again, then lifting a finger in the air as if he's just remembered something, picks up a block of Post-it notes, peels one off and hands it to me. 'But I'll tell you what, as you're so busy, don't go now, just leave a bit earlier tonight and whizz in on your way home from work. It shouldn't take long.'

The rest of my day is manic. In addition to making the changes to the follow-up article on Connor and his mum, I cover a breaking news story about a huge factory fire on the outskirts of the city, interview the new local crime commissioner, and write up several other pieces due in for the end of the day. It's only when I go to turn off my computer and spot the Post-it stuck to the bottom of the screen that I remember I still have to fight through rush hour traffic to make my apology to Connor's family friend. Snatching up the Post-it, I shove it deep into my pocket, say my goodbyes to Niamh and Lewis and gritting my teeth head out of the newsroom.

As I pull up outside MC Auto Services on the Chester Green Industrial Estate, I'm relieved to see that the lights are still on as the traffic over here had been even more of a nightmare than usual, and the last thing I need is to have come this far only to find the place closed for the night. Checking the Post-it again, I commit the name on it to memory, and then forcing my lips into something that hopefully resembles a smile, get out of my car and make my way into the reception.

As there are a couple of people in the queue ahead of me I take the opportunity to look around, wondering if there are any clues to be found that might give me an indication what the owner's like and how much of a drubbing I'm in for. The reception area is sparsely furnished, and looks like it hasn't been decorated in years. I find myself painting a picture in my mind of a curmudgeonly old man in greasy overalls, that day's *Daily Star* rolled up in one hand and a spanner gripped tightly in the other.

When my turn comes, I flash the oddly stern-faced young re-ceptionist with short purple hair my warmest and most sincere smile, but it seems to do nothing to soften her.

'I'm here to see Mr Campbell.'

'And you are?'

'Lila Metcalfe from *The Derby Echo*. I think he's expecting me.'

The woman disappears through a door to the side of her, which I suspect leads to the workshop because the moment she opens it there's a cacophony of male voices, machinery noises and a radio blaring out a Blink 182 tune. A short while later she returns and resumes her position behind the desk.

'Take a seat. Mr Campbell will be with you shortly.'

Obviously, I just want to get this over and done with, so I can get home and start my evening, and the fact that Mr Campbell is making me wait, which is clearly a deliberate power play on his part, is intensely annoying. But what choice do I have? I take a seat in one of the grubby chairs as instructed, and look at the pile of magazines – a mixture of old *AutoTraders*, car mags and ancient, dog-eared women's glossies – stacked on the coffee table next to me. Refusing to look like his delay is bothering me I pick up the magazine at the top of the pile, which turns out to be a well-thumbed copy of *Top Gear*, but no sooner have I opened it than I hear the workshop hubbub again and I look up to see a man not much older than me come through the door into the reception area. He's tall and unnervingly good-looking, with soulful dark brown eyes and cheekbones you could cut glass with. He's wearing overalls emblazoned with the company logo and for a moment I think there must have been some sort of mix-up, and that this is one of Mr Campbell's employees assuming I'm just another customer, but then I clock the expression of pure fury on his face and realise my mistake.

'Mr Campbell?' I stand up and hold out my hand. 'Lila Metcalfe from *The Echo* – lovely to meet you.'

His top lip morphs into a snarl. 'Don't give me that. I was told you'd be coming to see me first thing this morning! What time do you call this?'

I try my best to look remorseful. 'I can only apologise, Mr Campbell. Things have been manic at the office and this was my first opportunity to come by, and now I'm here I'd like to apologise for—'

He jabs a finger in my direction. 'Where do you get off barging into a vulnerable young man's home and pumping him for information for one of your stupid stories? I thought you journalists were supposed to have ethics! I suppose that all goes out the window once you think you've got hold of a juicy story. Poor Connor had no idea he was going to have his whole life splashed across the front of your rag, and he was really upset about you bringing up all that business with his mum again. Haven't you got any sense? How did you think that was going make him feel?'

I'm completely thrown. The Connor this man is describing bears almost no resemblance to the one I'd interviewed. What is he on about saying that Connor is upset over talking about his mum? He'd been the one to bring it up in the first place. I couldn't possibly have read the situation this wrongly, surely?

'Mr Campbell,' I begin determined to keep my cool. 'I can assure you that—'

My phone rings from inside my bag, which makes him look even more infuriated. Under normal circumstances I wouldn't have dreamed of answering it while I was in the middle of an apology but I'd been waiting all day for a call from a local MP about a story I've been working on and I really can't afford to miss it.

'I'm so sorry about this, Mr Campbell, really I am, but I have to take this.' As I head back outside I take the call. Much to my surprise it's not the MP, but someone else entirely. We talk briefly and then I ask the caller to stay on the line while I head back inside the building where the outraged Mr Campbell is waiting for me, arms folded, looking like he's about to give me both barrels.

'I'm so sorry about that,' I say with a beatific smile. 'The perils of being a journalist I'm afraid. So, before we were interrupted you were telling me how upset Connor was about my piece in *The Echo.*'

'Upset doesn't even begin to cover it,' he growls. 'He was beside himself. And it's all your fault.'

I sniff carefully. I'm enjoying this moment perhaps more than I ought. 'So, he was "beside himself", was he?'

'That's what I've just said, isn't it?'

'Oh, then perhaps you'd like to tell him that.' I turn my phone towards him. 'Because not only has he told me how delighted he is with yesterday's piece and today's too, but he's also just asked me for a favour.'

Now it's his turn to look completely confused. 'Connor's asked you for a favour? What kind?'

I try my best not to sound as smug as I feel. 'Well, I suppose I might have misheard him but I'm pretty sure he said he wants me to help him find his mum.

10

Connor

'Evening, Connor,' says Lee, the landlord of the Crown, 'haven't seen you in while. You meeting Marcus?'

'Hi, Lee, yes, I am meeting Marcus, and Lila, a journalist from *The Echo*.'

Lee raises an eyebrow. 'Of course, you were in the paper the other day weren't you?'

'Yes, but that was about me not wanting to move out from my house. Today we're meeting because she's going to help me find Mum, or at least I hope she will. She hasn't said yes yet.'

'Well, good luck to you, lad,' says Lee. 'I know it can't have been easy for you being without your mum all this time.' He wipes down the top of the bar with a cloth and then looks at me. 'So, what are you having then?'

I think for a moment. I am in the mood for a Vimto but I don't think they sell it here and anyway I know Marcus will have a beer so maybe I should have something similar. 'I'll have a lager shandy please, Lee,' I say and then suddenly feeling a bit hungry I add, 'Oh . . . and a packet of ready-salted crisps too.'

I had the idea to call Lila after Marcus said that speaking to *The Echo* would rake everything back up about Mum again. Marcus had said it like it was a bad thing, but I thought that maybe raking up everything about Mum was exactly what needed to be done. The police had told me ages ago that Mum's case was officially still open, but I can't remember the last time they called me. So maybe Lila, being a newspaper reporter, will be able to do what the police can't, especially if she is like the journalists that were sometimes in the TV shows Mum used to like, doing everything it takes to uncover the truth no matter what.

Once I'd decided to call Lila, I had to get the courage to do it. I'd tried to make myself call yesterday, and loads of times again today but I only got brave enough forty minutes ago. I was shocked when she said she would meet me, and even more surprised when she'd told me where she was and who she was talking to. The next thing I knew she put Marcus on the phone and he asked me if I'd asked her for a favour and I said yes. And then he sighed like he was really, really tired and said, 'Be at the Crown in half an hour, and the three of us can talk it all through.'

I have only taken a couple of sips of my drink when I see Marcus come into the pub with Lila. It seems strange seeing them together like this, especially after how angry Marcus was about her interviewing me, but I'm glad they're both here because it might mean that they both think my plan is a good idea.

'Hello, Connor,' says Lila. 'Good to see you again. Can I get you another drink?'

I shake my head. 'I'm fine thank you.'

Then with a different tone of voice, Lila turns to Marcus and says, 'And what can I get you?'

'Oh,' he says sounding a bit embarrassed. 'No, I'll get these.'

'No,' says Lila firmly. 'I insist. Compliments of *The Derby Echo*.'

As Lila goes to the bar to get their drinks, Marcus sits down, his face really serious. 'Thanks for the heads-up, mate. You could've told me you were going to call this woman. You've made me look like a right idiot.'

'How?'

'I told you I was going to complain to her boss about her taking advantage of you, and then you go and call her up!'

'But she didn't take advantage of me,' I say. 'I told you that. She was really nice.'

'Well, it's done now,' says Marcus grumpily. 'Although how you think she's going to be able to find your mum when the police can't, is anyone's guess.'

I feel annoyed with Marcus. He is treating me like a child, like I don't know what I'm doing. I'm about to tell him that when Lila comes back from the bar.

'Well, this is nice,' she says putting the drinks down on the table. 'So, you two used to live in the same road then? I used to have a really good friend who lived on my road when I was small . . . What was her name now? It'll come to me if I give it a minute . . . That's it, Jasmine Cook.' She shakes her head and grins. 'I haven't thought about Jas Cook in years. I wonder what she's up to now?'

I'm not one hundred per cent sure, but I get the feeling Lila is doing what Mum used to call, 'making polite conversation'. I try my best to think of something to say but my mind is blank. And so, after a few moments of no one talking at all I say the thing that is weighing on my mind.

'Lila,' I begin, after brushing my lips to make sure there are no stray crisp crumbs there, 'will you help me find my mum?'

Lila puts down her drink. 'Look, Connor, I'm really sorry if my article has brought up a lot of upsetting feelings for you, but I don't think I'm the person to help you with this.'

My heart feels heavy. This is not what I wanted to hear at all. 'But why not? You know how to find things out and people will talk to you because you're a journalist. I just know you will find Mum if you say yes.'

Lila looks at Marcus and then back at me. 'You're right, I do know how to find things out and maybe people will talk to me because of my job, but that still doesn't mean I'm the right person to try and find your mum. This is something for the police really; I'd be way out of my depth on this one.'

'But the police aren't doing anything, are they? You said in your article yesterday that they hadn't got any new leads and had sort of given up. They're not doing their job, they're not looking for Mum, so if they won't then I think you should. You'd be really good at it.'

Lila looks at Marcus and he looks up from his drink. 'Mate, she's trying to be nice, but the horrible truth is no one knows what happened to your mum and . . . well . . . maybe we never will. Like I've told you before I just think the best thing you can do is find a new home, live a good and happy life, and know that's what your mum would've wanted more than anything.'

Suddenly the noise in the pub becomes too much for my ears and the lights so bright that my eyes hurt. 'No, no, no, no!' I shout. 'Mum would never leave me and not come home! She wouldn't! She is coming home! We just need to find her!'

When I open my eyes, everyone in the pub is looking at us. I look down and see my drink has tipped over and is dripping on my jeans and the crisps I'd been eating are all over the floor.

'What's going on?' yells Lee from behind the bar and Marcus stands up. 'It's all sorted, mate. We'll be out of your hair in a minute.'

Lila gets up from the table and comes back from the bar with a cloth and starts wiping up the spilled drink while Marcus picks up the crisps from the floor and when it's all done Marcus takes a twenty-pound note out of his wallet and hands it to Lee. 'Apologies again, mate,' he says and then we leave the pub and go and stand outside.

For a minute I think I've ruined everything, that Lila is going to leave and never talk to me again but then, very gently, she puts her hand on my arm. 'I'm sorry we upset you like that, Connor.

You're right, there's always hope, there's always a chance your mum might come home.' She stops, looks at Marcus and then back at me. 'Look, I can't make any promises. To be honest I don't know if I'm even up to the task. I've never done anything like this before, and that's before I've asked my boss's permission to get involved. Oh, and I certainly can't do anything unless Marcus is on board, either. But if you really want my help, if you think this is the only way you'll find your mum, then I'll try my best to make that happen.'

I look at Marcus. 'Please tell her it's okay! Please tell her she can help us find Mum.'

He puts his hands in his pockets and stares at me. 'Look, Connor, you know I've got your back but I just don't want you to get your hopes up. Are you one hundred per cent sure this is what you really want?'

'More than anything.'

'I mean, I know you want your mum back . . . but are you sure about this being the way you want to try to do it?'

'What other way is there?'

He turns to Lila. 'Look, I'm sorry about before . . . it's just . . . well you know.'

Lila nods. 'I get it, some of my profession have definitely let the side down in the past. But I promise, I'm not here to exploit anyone; you can trust me.'

Marcus is silent for a minute and then he looks at me. 'I'm really going to get it in the neck from my mum when she hears about this . . . but okay, if it's what you want then I'm okay with it too.'

Me and Marcus then both look at Lila.

'Right then,' she says. 'I suppose we'd better get started. If you don't mind I think we all ought to go back to yours, Connor, so I can ask you a few more questions before I take this to my boss.'

Back at the house, I make Lila and Marcus a cup of tea and then Lila asks me to tell her the whole story of Mum going missing again. This time she asks lots of different questions, things about what Mum was wearing, what time she left the house and even what the weather was like. I try my best to answer her and Marcus sometimes adds something to what I say too, and Lila writes it all down in the notepad that I remember from last time. After this she turns to a fresh page, writes something down at the top of it and then looks at me.

'That's great, Connor, thank you. What I think would be useful now is for me to try and get a sense of who your mum really was . . . I mean is. You know, as a person.'

I think for a moment. It's such a big question that I don't know where to start. 'She's nice,' I say.

Lila smiles. 'I bet she is. What kind of things does she like doing?'

A picture pops up in my mind of an ordinary night in with Mum. She'd sit on the sofa knitting and watching *Coronation Street*, while I relaxed in my gaming chair with my headphones on listening to Metallica. She never made me do the things she liked to do, but she did like us to be in the same room.

'Knitting,' I say, 'and watching soaps, and helping people.'

'And you said she had two jobs, I think. Is that right?'

'Yes, she worked at the minimart and at Clarkes, the old launderette on Linton Road.'

Marcus smiles. 'I'd completely forgotten about that place. The hours I used to spend in there with Mum before we got a washing machine.'

'It closed a few years ago,' I tell him. 'Mr Clarke, the man who owned it, died.'

'And did she keep in touch with anyone who used to work there?'

'A few people.'

Lila tears out a couple of pages from her notebook. 'Well, could you write down any names you can remember and their contact details if you've got them, plus the names of anyone else she was friends with, including, if that's okay your mum, Marcus.'

Marcus nods. 'Of course, if you think it'll help. I know Mum would be more than happy to do anything to help Connor and Bernie.'

'Great,' says Lila, and she looks down at her notepad again. 'Connor?'

I look up from the list I am writing on the paper she's given me and see that her face has changed.

'I know this might be difficult for you, but would you mind if I took a look through your mum's bedroom?'

I think for a minute then nod. 'I don't mind. You can go in there.'

I take her upstairs and along the hallway to Mum's bedroom at the front of the house. Nearest the door is her chest of drawers. On top of that is a mirror, a photograph of me when I was a baby and a small, pink silk-covered jewellery box. On the opposite side of the room is Mum's big pine wardrobe, then in the far corner there is an old armchair with some of Mum's clothes on it neatly folded. In the middle of the room is Mum's double bed with the light green striped bed set that matches the wallpaper.

'What a lovely room,' says Lila. 'And you've kept it so beautifully for her.'

'I clean it every week,' I tell her, 'just like Mum did. I want it to be nice for her when she comes back.'

Lila gives Marcus a look but doesn't say anything for a moment or two. Finally, she says, 'Why don't you leave me to have a look around and I'll come back down when I'm done, okay?'

It is half an hour before Lila comes back downstairs. She is holding a box file and two photo albums. 'Would it be okay if I borrowed these for a little while? I'll look after them, I promise.'

'Okay,' I say. 'I trust you.'

Smiling Lila picks up her jacket and puts it on. 'Right, I'd better be off. I've got an early start in the morning, but I'll be in touch as soon as I've spoken to my editor.'

'I'd best be getting off too,' says Marcus standing up. 'But I'll talk to you soon, Connor, alright?'

As I wave to them both from the doorstep, I have a funny feeling in my stomach, a bit nervous, a bit excited. I've done it. Someone is finally looking for Mum again, and I look up at the night sky, hoping that wherever she is, she is doing the same and knows I've never given up on her and never will.

11

Lila

Lewis doesn't even bother to hide the disbelief in his voice.

'He wants you to find his mum? What does he think this paper is? *The New York Times?* We've barely got the budget to keep the loos stocked with paper towels, let alone fund some in-depth investigative piece.'

As the office drinks machine dribbles hot water onto the instant cappuccino powder in Lewis's cup, Niamh scowls and punches him on the arm.

'Alright, Negatron, no need to spread all your joy quite so widely. Lila knows what she's doing, don't you, Lils?'

Do I? I smile weakly. 'The important thing is that I haven't even said yes yet. All I've agreed to do is put it to Peter and who knows if he'll even bite.'

Lewis stirs sugar into his drink. 'And if he says yes, what then? Where exactly do you think you're going to find the time to look for this missing woman? You can bet your rent money he isn't going to free you up from your day job to do it – we're stretched enough as it is.'

'What's wrong with you?' Niamh jabs Lewis with one of the wooden coffee stirrers. 'Remind me not to call you next time I'm on the ledge of a building in two minds whether to jump off or not.' Sighing heavily, she shakes her head and turns back to me. 'Just ignore him, Lila. I personally think it would be great, and if Peter says yes and you need any help, I'm here for you.'

As I sit down and switch on my computer, ready to begin my morning's work, I can't help wondering if maybe Lewis has a point, especially as it's something I'd thought myself. Connor's proposal had completely taken me by surprise, and initially I'd only agreed to meet with him and hear him out because I felt so sorry for him. But the more he talked, the more convinced I became that this was something I wanted to do, and the depth of feeling that led to his outburst only served to convince me more. The police seem to have all but given up on trying to find Bernie, and so too it appears have friends and neighbours, and yet Connor hasn't. So, in a way I feel like I'm his last chance – his only hope – and if I don't help him, who will?

Those, at least, are the reasons to take this on, but there are plenty not to. For starters as Lewis said, I'm already backed up with more work than I know what to do with, and even though my weekends are freer now that Gabe and I have split, who knows how I'm possibly going to find the time to pursue all the potential leads around Connor's mum's disappearance? And then of course there's the job at *The Correspondent* to think about. While there's every chance I might not even get it, if I did I'd almost certainly have to drop the investigation, which would be worse than if I'd said no from the outset. And then there's the small matter of getting Peter's approval, because while he'd been in favour of the front page and the follow-up piece I'd written about Connor and his mum, there's no guarantee he'll go for another one, especially when there's no telling when, or even if, I'll be able to bring the story to a satisfactory conclusion.

And yet, despite all of the reasons not to do it, something in me feels that this is worth pursuing, something in me knows that there's more to this story than first appears, and something in me believes that if anyone's going to get to the bottom of things then the best person for the job is me. And if nothing else it'll stop me from having time on my hands to do any more thinking about Gabe.

Before I can change my mind I stride straight across to Peter's office and after knocking on his door tell him everything about my meeting with Connor and Marcus last night.

'So, let me get this right,' he says once I've finished talking, 'I send you over to calm down an irate bloke who sounds like he's about to sue us and you talk him into agreeing to another story? Crikey, you're a smooth operator!'

'You've got the wrong end of the stick, Peter. I didn't say anything; it all came from Connor, the lad whose mum's gone missing.'

'Oh right, and what about the fella who complained? What did he have to say about it all?'

'He was there for the whole thing and he says that as long as Connor is happy and I keep them both in the loop then he's fine with it.'

'And so all that's stopping you now, I guess, is me?'

I give Peter my most plaintive look. This is the moment that could make it or break it.

'You do know we haven't got the resources to free you up from your regular workload?' he says.

'I know, but I'll find a way to fit it in, I promise. You won't even know I'm doing it.'

Still thinking, Peter runs a hand over his beard. 'You know it's going to be a lot of work, don't you?'

I nod in agreement. 'I know, but I'm up for it.'

'And, you have considered that even if you do find out what happened to this woman it might not be the happy ending this Connor lad is hoping for?'

This is something that had crossed my mind more than once while going over it all in the middle of the night, and yet I still can't help thinking it's the right thing to do.

'I know, Boss. But more than anything he wants to know the truth, and I think I can help him with that.'

Peter's expression is so inscrutable I have no idea which way he might go. Then just like that, he grins and shakes his head, as if he's just heard the punchline to a corny joke.

'You're going to do this, even if I say no, aren't you?'

I flash him a guilty smile. That exact thought had literally just crossed my mind.

'I've got to help him. I have to, and I just know there's something in this for *The Echo* too.'

'In that case, Metcalfe, you have my blessing,' says Peter. 'Just don't make me regret it.'

As I head back to the newsroom I give Niamh and Lewis a delighted thumbs up and then go straight to the corridor outside the loos to call Marcus.

'Good news,' I tell him. 'My boss has said yes, which means – unless anything's changed your end – I can go ahead and get started.'

'Wow,' says Marcus, 'that's great. I know Connor will be over the moon. I felt really bad upsetting him like that last night. I had no right to say what I did. If it was my mum, and she'd gone missing like that, I don't think I'd ever give up looking for her either.'

'Like I said, I can't make any promises, but I will do my best to get some answers for him.'

'So do you want me to let him know the good news?'

'If you don't mind – the sooner I can get started, the better.'

Only all too aware of the need to keep up with my regular workload, I try my best to finish the piece I'm due to file before mid-morning but my head is fizzing with so many ideas about Bernie's case that I find it almost impossible to concentrate. In a bid to quiet my mind, and make a start on my investigation, I go and talk to Angela on the crime desk and ask her what, if anything, she can remember about Bernie's disappearance.

'It's all very noble,' says Angela, once I've explained what I'm up to, 'but you do know you're on a hiding to nothing with this, don't you? Have you any idea how many people go missing in just a single year in Derbyshire?' She doesn't even wait for me to respond. 'Over five thousand. And do you know how many of those five thousand people are ever found? Not many, I can tell you, and besides which a lot of them don't want to be found.'

'But her son's convinced that she would never leave him – surely that's got to count for something.'

Angela is grave. 'Well, if it does then statistically speaking the only thing it'll count towards won't be the rosy outcome you're hoping for.'

'But surely if something awful had happened to her then Connor would've heard something by now?'

'Not necessarily, bodies can be found years, sometimes decades after the person's gone missing, and sometimes they never are. I can tell you now, it's not going to be an easy case to solve.'

'But not completely impossible?'

Angela's expression softens slightly. 'No, not necessarily impossible.'

'Okay, so, let's say she is still alive and for whatever reason hasn't come home. Where and how do you think I should start?'

'Establish a timeline for her disappearance; find out as much as you can about her; talk to as many of her friends, family and neighbours as possible to find out what her state of mind was like at the time. Oh, and talk to the police and see whether they're willing to share anything with you, which given the roasting you gave them in your article the other day I'm guessing will be zero.'

I sigh, recalling how, thanks to me, the chief constable had to spend two days doing press interviews with TV and local radio defending the force's investigation into Bernie's disappearance. If anyone was going to be in Derbyshire Constabulary's bad books, it was me.

'Leave it with me,' says Angela as if reading my mind. 'There are a couple of contacts I've got in the force who owe me one and I'm more than happy to call in a favour.'

That evening, after a full day at work, rather than going out to the pub with Lewis and Niamh I head home and start trawling through all the information I have on Bernie, some from my initial investigation and some gathered during my lunch break today, and start to pull together a timeline for Bernie's disappearance just as Angela had suggested. Once that's done, I draw up a list of names of people I need to interview and then finally, as I'm microwaving my evening meal I start to go through the box of things I brought back from Connor's last night. I'm not even five minutes into this task, when I'm hit by a wave of tiredness so overwhelming that I have no choice but to call it a day.

Taking my sad ready meal for one to bed, I stick on an episode of something mindless to watch on my laptop when it suddenly dawns on me that the last time I'd watched this series had been with Gabe when he'd last come to stay. Much as I'm determined not to cry, I'm not quite as resolute about allowing myself to wallow and for the first time since we split I permit myself the indulgence of looking at Gabe's Instagram.

As I pick up my phone, and search for his profile, my hope is I'll find evidence that his life is as empty without me as mine is without him. Perhaps an artfully taken picture of a solitary rainy day walk captioned with something cryptic that I'll know is about how much he misses me. Or a snippet of Harry Nilsson singing 'Without You' over a snap of the sun setting that encapsulates just how much his heart is breaking. What I find, however, are just some boring pictures of Gabe and his friends in the box at that stupid football match that started this whole mess off and a few others of various courses taken during a meal at a posh restaurant.

Just as I'm about to put my phone down it occurs to me that perhaps these post break-up pictures have been carefully curated for my benefit, to make me think that he's actually doing okay when he isn't. If I really want to see how he's coping, perhaps I need to try something else, and so scrolling through his friends list, I find his best friend Barnaby, and take a look at his account.

Barnaby's account bears no small resemblance to Gabe's. Snaps of friends, nights out and of course that football match, but there's one notable exception: the photos in the restaurant are different. Rather than just featuring shots of the gorgeous food and décor, there are pictures of the people Barnaby was dining with: his girlfriend, Citra, and of course Gabe, but there's one other: a glamourous-looking woman, with long dark hair. In the first photo she's sitting next to Gabe, and they're both smiling into the camera. In another she's feeding him a forkful of food from her plate and Gabe is laughing as he angles his mouth to catch it, and then finally there's a shot of the two of them, posing cheek to cheek, with their arms around one another as they wave to the camera.

I sit back in disbelief, my hands shaking as I try to make sense of it all because this woman is no stranger; this is a face I know very well, or at least did once upon a time. If I'm not mistaken, the woman fawning all over my ex-boyfriend is none other than Orla McKenzie, Gabe's ex-girlfriend, the girl he had been seeing before we got together back in our university days.

12

Connor

'Okay, then, Ryan, I'm going home now it's the end of my shift.'

'Alright for some!' says Ryan. 'Don't forget to clock out and check the app to see what shifts you're on next because there's been some changes.'

I want to tell Ryan that I'd already been at work for three hours when he started but I don't bother because he won't care anyway. Instead, I just nod, then get my stuff from the break room and leave to catch my bus home.

Today has felt like a really long day. It started at six o'clock this morning with me helping unload two deliveries, then after my break I spent three hours on the click and collect desk with Alan, and after that I had to restock some of the paints in the decorating section and had a very long and confusing conversation with a posh lady about two colours in the Farrow and Ball range that both looked black to me.

I take out my phone as I walk across the retail park towards my bus stop to see if I have missed any calls or messages from Lila. I was so happy when Marcus called yesterday to tell me that her boss had said it was okay for her to help me. I think I even jumped up and down because I was so excited. Lila is so clever and I just know that she will find Mum and bring her home and then we can get back to the way things used to be.

There are no missed calls or voicemail messages and I think about calling Lila myself to ask if she has any news yet, but then I remember Marcus told me not to bother her in case she gets fed up and changes her mind about helping. 'I know it's hard,' he'd said, 'but you've just got to let her get on with things. If she has anything to say she'll call you – until then you'll just have to stay strong.'

Feeling a bit sad that it's taking so long, I put my phone back in my pocket, and then slip on my headphones before carrying on to the bus stop. I only get through the first two tracks on *Load*, my least favourite Metallica album, when I reach the bus shelter, and sit down on one of the tiny ledges that is barely big enough for my bum. I check my watch to see how much longer I'll have to wait. It looks like I've just missed the 14.07 and so I'll have to wait for the next one that should be here at 14.22.

Just then I see something move out of the corner of my eye, and when I turn I see a teenage boy standing at one end of the bus shelter looking at me. He is dressed in a school uniform of grey jacket and black trousers but has got a scarf covering the lower half of his face. Suddenly I feel scared and I think about going back to work and getting a later bus, but before I can move I hear something behind me and I turn to see another boy with his face covered by a scarf at the other end of the shelter.

'Oi, retard!' shouts the boy nearest to me. 'Did you think we'd forgotten about you? You pushed our mate on the bus the other day and now you're going to pay.'

I scramble to my feet. 'I'm sorry. I don't want any trouble. I only pushed him because I—'

Before I can even finish what I'm saying I feel a sharp blow on the back of my head and crash into the side of the shelter, my headphones flying up into the air. Another punch slams into me, knocking me off balance and onto the ground. I try to get up but one of the boys kicks me in my side, making me gasp for air, and then I feel another kick, in my back this time, which is so painful that I let out a loud cry. As I lie curled up in a ball on the cold hard ground, with the boys kicking and punching me, I beg and beg for them to stop but they just carry on until suddenly I hear someone shouting and swearing at the boys, and just like that they run off.

The pain is so bad that for a moment I just lie there on the ground with my eyes squeezed tight shut but then I feel someone bending over me. I open my eyes a bit but because of the blood running down my face, I can't see who it is. I try to give my eyes a wipe with my hand but it doesn't help, and then I feel someone dabbing at my face with a tissue, drying up the blood, and this time when I look I can see who it is. I can't believe it. It is Adele Sharpe.

'Connor, are you alright?' She looks really worried and helps me to stand up. 'Little scumbags, setting about you like that! I tell you what, if they hadn't run off I would've battered them.'

I wobble and nearly fall over, and she settles me back on to the ledge I'd been sitting on. I feel like crying, and then reach up and touch my face to find that I already am.

'My glasses. Where are my glasses?'

Adele reaches down to the ground and picks up what is left of them. One of the arms has snapped off, and a lens has popped out of the frame.

'I'm so sorry, Connor,' she says offering me the pieces. 'I don't think these can be fixed. I don't suppose there's any chance you've got a spare pair?'

'I have, but they're an old prescription.'

'Well, I suppose that's better than nothing.'

I look down at the twisted mess in my hands. Why do people have to be so cruel? Why can't they just leave me alone?

'I tell you what,' says Adele, 'why don't we head back into work and get some stuff from the first-aid box to clean you up?'

I don't want people at work to see me like this. It will be embarrassing. 'I don't want to go back to work. I just want to go home.'

'Okay.' Adele hands me a clean tissue from her pocket and makes me press it against my bleeding forehead. 'I mean to be honest you really ought to be going to the hospital to get checked over.'

I shake my head and regret it. The pain is really bad. 'I don't want to go to hospital. I just want to go home.'

'Okay, if that's what you really want to do. But I'm going to go with you, make sure you get home okay, and get you sorted out.'

I'm not at all sure how I feel about this. Even now being so close to Adele makes me feel scared, but I'm so shaken by what has happened, and feel so helpless without my glasses, that I know I can't say no.

'So, what happened?' asks Adele as we wait for my bus. 'Did they just beat you up like that for nothing or did they try to rob you?'

'They were bothering me on the bus the other day and one of them tried to grab my bag and I pushed him and ran off. They didn't like it and so they must have been waiting for me to get me back.'

'Little scumbags,' she says angrily. 'You didn't deserve any of that. Honestly, I didn't know what was going on for a minute there. I'd just finished my shift and was thinking about grabbing some stuff from Aldi before I got the bus home when I heard all that noise, and I couldn't believe it when I came over to see what was happening and saw you on the ground with that lot laying into you. Honestly, I saw red.'

'Thank you for helping me.' I look down at the blood-covered tissue in my hand and feel a bit strange. 'I don't know what would've happened if you hadn't come.'

Adele shivers. 'I don't like to think about it.' She hands me another clean tissue from her bag. 'I'm so sorry this has happened to you, Connor. I know I'm not exactly one to talk after the way I treated you at school, but I hope I wasn't that bad.'

I think about saying, yes, Adele, you were that bad just in a different way, but I don't because right now it doesn't feel like the right thing to say. When I don't say anything, Adele looks embarrassed and says, 'I really am sorry about how I was back then. You didn't deserve it, Connor; you really didn't deserve it at all.'

'Thanks,' I say, because I don't know what else to say and just then the number one-two-five turns up. I check my watch, and see that it is 14.15, which means that this is either the 14.07 and it's eight minutes late or the 14.22 and it's seven minutes early.

When we get on the bus, the driver isn't one that I know and he gives me a funny look probably because of all the blood on my face and the fact that the collar of my DIY-Depot polo shirt is half hanging off. Adele says that we should sit upstairs to stop people staring at me and even though I don't like sitting upstairs on the bus anymore I follow her and then the bus pulls away.

I don't really feel much like talking on the journey home but it doesn't matter because Adele does all the talking. She talks about how angry she is with the boys who beat me up, and about work and how much she is enjoying it, and she even tells me about when she went out at the weekend, and about the best bars and nightclubs in Derby. When we get off on Linton Road, she talks all the way (this time about how her gran's brother and his family used to live out this way) but the moment we reach Hope Street she stops.

'Is this really your road?' she asks looking at all the boarded-up doors and windows of the houses.

'Yes, but I'm the only one living here now.'

'Oh, yeah, of course – that's why you were in the paper, wasn't it?'

I nod again but don't say anything because I'm too busy thinking about how weird it is to be walking towards my house with Adele Sharpe. I can't quite believe it. She and her friends bullied me every single day for so long that in the end I stopped going to school and now she is acting like she is my friend. I suddenly feel scared again and don't want her to come inside my house.

'Thank you for walking me home,' I say when we get to my front door, 'but you don't have to come in. I'll be alright now.'

'Are you sure? I thought you lived here alone. You'll need some help seeing to those cuts and bruises.'

'Thank you, but no,' I say firmly. 'I'll be okay.'

For a moment Adele looks like she might not take no for an answer, but then she sighs. 'Well, I'm sure you know what you're doing. Just take care, Connor, won't you? I'll worry about you being all alone here.'

'I will. Don't worry, I'll be fine.'

I wait until Adele is right at the end of the road before taking out my keys and opening up my front door. There is a pile of post on the mat, and when I pick it up I see that on the very top there is a letter in a brown envelope with what looks like writing on it. Because I haven't got my glasses on I have to hold it right up to my face to see what the words say. Stamped across the top it says, 'Derby City Council' and along the bottom are the words 'IMPORTANT – DO NOT IGNORE.'

I know this will be another letter trying to get me to move. Another letter full of flats I don't want to see. I'm so fed up, I just can't be bothered to read it. I'm so fed up that I just don't care. I take the letter and shove it in the drawer in the back room along with all of the other council letters I haven't opened and then go upstairs to find my spare glasses, wash my face and change into clothes that haven't got blood on them.

Later that evening Marcus calls round as usual and when he sees the state of my face, he is furious.

'They just attacked you for no reason?'

'I've had trouble with them before,' I explain, and tell him about the other day on the bus. 'I think the boys got me because of that.'

'And do you think you'd know them if you saw them again?'

I shake my head even though I'm almost positive that I would. If I say yes, I know that Marcus will want me to get in his car with him and drive around until we find them. But I don't want any more trouble. All I want to do is forget it ever happened.

'Marcus, please don't worry,' I tell him. 'I'm fine. I just need to get some new glasses – that's all.' I reach up and rub the side of my head. 'These old ones are giving me a bit of a headache.'

'It's not just about the glasses though, is it?' says Marcus. 'People have got no right to treat you like that. No right at all.'

I look at the carrier bag with our fish and chip supper in it that Marcus put down on the armchair when he came in. The smells coming from it are so delicious they're making my mouth water.

'Can we just eat now? I'm really hungry.'

Laughing, Marcus shakes his head as if I've just said something funny and then gets out our food. We eat in front of the TV, with Marcus on the sofa, and me in my gaming chair.

While the adverts are on, I press mute on the remote, turn to Marcus and ask him a question that has very much been on my mind.

'Do you think people can change?'

Marcus sits up and gives me a funny look. 'What are you on about?'

'People,' I say. 'Can they change? Like if they were really horrible once can they ever change and become nice?'

Marcus frowns. 'What like those toerags who beat you up? People like them never change. They'll move on from beating up people at bus stops, to shoving their way into the homes of old ladies, and then they'll end up doing time, because . . . well because it was always going to end that way.'

'So,' I say, not thinking about the boys, but Adele, 'you think if you're bad that's it, you're that way forever?'

He thinks for a minute. 'I suppose there are some exceptions, but only some. For the most part, Connor, people are depressingly predictable. If they start off as losers, they'll end that way too. The fact of the matter is change takes effort, and most people are too lazy.'

In bed that night I think about something Mum always used to say. That I shouldn't judge people by what they say but by what they do. I think by this she meant that people can say anything, so it's their actions that are more important than anything that comes out of their mouths. When Adele tried to apologise for how she'd been at school that was just words, but today when she helped me that was different; that was an action. I think maybe Marcus is wrong, maybe people can change and Adele is proof of that.

I think perhaps she might be a nice person now after all.

Bernie: 1995

Bernie looked at the man in confusion. 'I don't understand. Why are we going up the stairs?'

The housing officer, a large middle-aged man with a beer belly and a sorrowful expression, smiled patiently. 'Because it's on the first floor.'

Bernie reached into her jacket pocket and pulled out the photocopied list of properties she'd picked up from the housing association. 'It says here it's on the ground floor,' she said pointing out the property she had circled in blue biro.

The man nodded and shrugged. 'Don't know what to tell you, love, the only maisonette available at the moment is on the first floor. Do you still want to see it?'

Bernie hesitated. The reason she'd chosen to look at this flat was precisely because it was on the ground floor and had a garden for Connor, even if that garden only consisted of a minuscule patch of scrubby grass and a couple of cracked paving slabs. As much as she didn't want to appear ungrateful, she'd spotted that all of the first-floor maisonettes had balconies jutting out from the living room, which wouldn't have been a problem if it had just been her, but a nightmare with an overactive toddler like Connor. All it would take for disaster to strike would be a warm day, an open patio door and a momentary lapse in concentration.

Bernie sighed. 'Actually, I don't think I'll bother. It's not for us.'

The housing officer shrugged again. 'Fine by me, but just to be clear this will count as one of your three offers, and it says here you've already turned one down.'

Bernie was outraged. 'Because it was on the twelfth floor of a block of flats! The day we went to see it the lift was broken and I asked someone and they said it'd been like that for months! How am I supposed to be carrying a baby, and a buggy, and shopping and who knows what else up and down twelve flights of stairs, day in day out? And as for this place there's no way I'm letting you count it as one of my offers when it's you fools who made the mistake saying it's on the ground floor when it's up there with its death-trap balcony!'

'According to what I've got down here this is your second offer and I've got to treat it as such unless I hear otherwise.'

Was he deliberately not understanding her? Was she not speaking English? 'But I wouldn't have even booked in to see it if I knew it wasn't on the ground floor!'

'Look, I don't make the rules,' said the housing officer despondently. 'Now do you want to see the place or not? It's no skin off my nose what you do, love. If you've got any complaints take it up with the office, not that it'll do you any good, mind. They're a right clueless bunch.'

Bernie felt her heart sink. If they were going to treat it as one of her offers even though it wasn't her fault then she might as well see it. Kneeling down she undid the straps of Connor's buggy, and scooped him up with one arm, while folding down the buggy with her free hand. She looked pointedly at the housing officer hoping at the very least he might offer to help, but instead he just turned and started walking up the stairs and so – with no little effort – she carefully balanced Connor on one hip, picked up the pram and followed after him.

That evening as she lay on her bed with Connor babbling away next to her looking around the tiny room in which they lived, she really did feel like she wanted to cry. The only thing holding her back was the knowledge that if she gave in to her deepening despair even for a moment, there was a very real danger she might never recover.

Though the bedsit was awful, she was in no doubt that accepting the maisonette would've been the wrong choice for both her and Connor. And not just because of the balcony, but a quick walk around the neighbourhood with its piles of rubbish on every street corner, roaming gangs of bored kids seeming as if they were looking for trouble and even an abandoned car on the pavement – windows smashed, doors open and seats ripped out – all spoke of a level of neglect she didn't want her son growing up around, suspecting as she did that things would be hard enough for him as it was.

Bernie wasn't quite sure when she first became aware that her son wasn't quite like other babies. He'd never exactly been a good feeder, and when it came to sleep he'd been even worse, but this she put down to nothing more sinister than random bad luck. Some mothers got quiet contented babies and others didn't and that was just the way things were. But as time moved on, as Bernie took Connor to playgroups, met other mums and observed the children Connor's age up close, she began to wonder if he was a little different. Other babies seemed so much more alert and interested in what was going on around them while Connor seemed to inhabit a little world of his own.

When these babies started to crawl and her son remained happily in one spot, she really started to worry. And while the GP had assured her that Connor was fine, that some children just took longer to hit some milestones than others, Bernie couldn't help but wonder if perhaps their cramped bedsit was somehow to blame. Maybe if they had more room, some outdoor space, and half decent neighbours who didn't play loud music at all hours of the day and night Connor might flourish.

The following morning Bernie went down to the local housing office so early that she was there before most of the staff had arrived. She wanted to be first in the queue to see somebody. She wanted to make sure that she and Connor got the help they needed so that her boy could have the start in life he deserved.

'Good morning, how can I help you?' said the young girl behind the desk as Bernie wheeled Connor's pram into place.

'Two things,' said Bernie, who had made up her mind to be firm but polite. 'I booked to view a maisonette yesterday but when I got there it was on the first floor not the ground like I'd been told, and the man who showed it to me said even though it wasn't my mistake it'll count as one of my offers. Now tell me, is that fair?'

Bernie showed the young woman the listing, and she studied it carefully, and then stood up, opened a filing cabinet behind her, took out a folder and checked the contents.

'Yes, you're right, the listing was incorrect.'

Bernie breathed a sigh of relief. 'So, it doesn't count as one of my offers then?'

The young woman made a sad face. 'That would make sense, wouldn't it? But I'm afraid it's a bit more complicated than that. Had you not viewed the property, you might have been able to appeal but, as it is, you've just got the one offer left now.'

'But the man more or less said that I had to go in and see it!'

'I'm sorry but it's out of my hands. Now, is there anything else I can help you with?'

Bernie wanted to tell the young girl that she hadn't been much help to begin with but for the sake of keeping her onside decided it best not to.

'Okay, just tell me then, has anything new come on today?' She looked down at Connor finally asleep in his buggy after being awake virtually all of the night, and then back at the woman, tears pricking at the corners of her eyes. 'Please, I'm desperate.'

The young woman hesitated for a moment, and briefly checked either side of her to see what each of her colleagues was doing before leaning closer to the glass partition separating them. 'Well, strictly speaking, I'm not supposed to release details of this yet as it's not been officially added to the list, but seeing as I'll be the one typing it up this afternoon, I don't see what harm it'll do. It's a two-bed terrace, over Cossington Park way, which has just had a new kitchen and bathroom.'

Bernie didn't know the Cossington Park area at all, but an actual house sounded too amazing to turn down. 'Does it have a garden?'

The young woman checked her file. 'It says there's a yard.' She looked up at Bernie. 'So, shall I book you in to see it? I should add that if you turn this one down, that'll be it – you'll automatically go to the bottom of the waiting list.'

Bernie's mouth went dry. It really was a gamble. What use was a new kitchen, bathroom, and yard space, if the area was as bad, or indeed worse than the one she'd visited yesterday? What chance would Connor have then? But to stay where they were, and have to wait who knows how long before they got another opportunity to move, would that be even worse?

'I'll see it,' she said trying her best to sound confident. 'As soon as I can please, I'll see it. What's the address?'

Two days later Bernie sat on the number sixty-eight bus, with Connor on her lap heading to a part of Derby she had never been to before. As the bus left the confines of the town centre out onto a long and busy dual carriageway, she couldn't help wondering if she hadn't made a terrible mistake. Everything seemed too busy over this way, too built up, and there were too many buildings that looked like factories and warehouses. But then, the bus turned off the dual carriageway past a Comet, a petrol station and a huge pub on the corner into a road that felt different somehow. Here there was a small parade of shops, a greengrocer's, a newsagent's, a shoe repairer, even a cake shop. She felt herself relax a little and all the more so when the bus passed a primary school, its playground teeming with children letting off steam after a morning cooped up inside classrooms.

Even though Bernie knew there was still a stop to go, she got off the bus and crossed over the road to see more of the neighbourhood first hand. With Connor strapped back in his buggy she walked past a fish and chip shop, the smell from which was so lovely her stomach rumbled, past a hairdresser and a dentist, after which she finally drew parallel to the bus stop where she should've got off.

Turning off the main road she headed along Woodland Street, under a railway bridge, and then turned the corner into Hope Street.

Her first impression was a good one. All the houses looked neat and well maintained, and as she walked along the road she smiled as she saw the chalked outlines for a game of hopscotch, along with some attempts at cartoon characters scribbled on the pavement. Finally, she reached one-two-one, but there was no sign of the housing officer. She was about to check her watch when she heard a front door open behind her, and she turned to see a woman she immediately recognised standing in the doorway.

'Beverley Campbell!' cried Bernie. 'Is that you?'

The woman looked across the road and the moment she laid eyes on Bernie a huge grin exploded across her face.

'Bernie McLaughlin!' she cried rushing towards her, and the two women embraced. 'How long has it been?'

'Too long,' replied Bernie, and she immediately felt bad for not doing more to keep in contact with Bev over the years. 'How have you been?'

'Busy,' said Bev and she looked down at Connor in his push-chair. 'And I'm guessing you have been busy too.'

'Just a little bit,' Bernie replied. 'He's been quite the handful.' She paused and looked at Bev. 'I'm so sorry I haven't been in touch in ages. I know you made a real effort and then I moved, Connor came along and life got busy.'

Bev patted Bernie gently on the arm. 'Don't you worry about it – I understand. It's just the way it goes. It's so good to see you though.' She bent down and tickled Connor under the chin, saying, 'Who's a lovely boy then!' but he was so busy playing with the toy train in his hand that he didn't even look up. 'Anyway,' she continued straightening up. 'What brings you over this way?'

Bernie turned to look at the door of number one-two-one. 'You'll never believe it but I've come to see this place.'

Bev laughed. 'Now what are the chances of that? I've been watching them doing up this house ever since old Mrs Godwin went into hospital and passed away. I think they've put in a new kitchen and I heard one of the workmen saying that they'd moved the bathroom upstairs too.'

Just then, a car pulled up and the very same housing officer that had shown Bernie around the maisonette got out, his face falling the moment he saw her.

'I hope you're not going to give me any more trouble,' he said. 'I had a right earbashing from the boss thanks to you.'

'Well, you won't get one this time,' said Bernie, with a smile. 'Because I've already made up my mind. I'll take it.'

The man raised his eyebrows. 'You haven't even looked around it yet.'

Bernie shrugged. 'I've just got a good feeling about it. This is going to be mine and Connor's new home.'

13

Lila

It's early evening and Niamh and I are sitting in the corner of our favourite bar, conveniently located around the corner from the office. Pulling her most disgusted face, Niamh sniffs, hands my phone back to me and picks up her glass of wine. 'Her roots need doing, that dress isn't doing her any favours and someone needs to tell her that duck-face influencer thing she's trying only really works if you've got decent cheekbones.'

I can't help but laugh at Niamh's caustic assessment of the photo of Gabe's ex-girlfriend, but then all too soon I'm back to feeling maudlin as again I'm forced to face the question of whether she is still his ex or if they've got back together.

'Thanks for that, but it's not actually the question I asked.'

'I know,' says Niamh, 'I was hoping you wouldn't notice.'

'So, you do think Gabe was seeing her before we split up?'

Frowning she takes a sip of wine. 'I'm sorry to say it, but yes. You know what men are like – they're the laziest creatures in the world. They don't leave a good thing unless they've got something else already lined up. And judging from the photo, I'd say she's been lined up for quite a while.'

Niamh's words feel like a punch in the gut but as much as I'd hoped she'd tell me I was overreacting I can't say I'm surprised that she agrees with me. It was the first thought to cross my mind the moment I'd seen the picture of them together. If he'd had nothing to hide she would've been on his Instagram for all to see, with a light-hearted caption, along the lines of: 'Bumped into an old uni mate. Good to catch up, albeit briefly,' but instead she was conspicuously absent. As my granddad always said, 'People with nothing to hide, hide nothing.'

I take a sip of my wine. 'So, what do you think I should do?'

'Definitely have it out with the cheating low-life! You need to know when this started, how much crossover there was, and how he thinks he can justify treating you like this.'

I can't help but laugh. 'Way to go nuclear from the get-go! I was thinking you'd say I should, I don't know, unfollow him on Insta or something – not have a full-on confrontation.'

'And what's wrong with that? Anything less just lets him off the hook and if there's one thing I'm sick of, it's guys being let off the hook. Nope, he's made his bed and put this tart in it, the very least he can do is lie in it. Call him, call him now and have it out with him!'

I shake my head. 'I can tell you now, that won't be happening. I'd sooner parade around Derby city centre naked than call him.'

Niamh refuses to let it go. 'But why? Why should men get to treat us like this and get away with it? At the very least you've got to admit it'll be fun listening to him squirm.'

I drain the rest of my drink and I'm about to ask Niamh if she wants another when my friend snatches up my phone from the middle of the table.

I look at her confused. 'What are you doing?'

'Striking a blow for wronged women everywhere,' she declares and to my horror she unlocks the phone, yells, 'Siri call Gabe!' at the top of her voice and the next thing I know my favourite photo of Gabe fills the screen, as the sound of my phone ringing him fills the air.

I make a grab for the handset but it's too late, the call connects while it's still in Niamh's hand and even over the sound of the music in the bar I can hear a tinny-sounding Gabe say, 'Hello? Lila? Is that you?'

Finally, with a look of triumph on her face she hands the phone to me and whispers, 'You'll thank me for this, maybe not today, maybe not tomorrow, but one day.'

Feeling like I might be sick I press the phone to my ear and begin making my way outside.

'Gabe,' I say once I've found a quiet spot. 'Yes, sorry, it's me.'

'Everything okay? Or did you bum-dial me?'

'Bum-dial, I'm afraid. I'm out with Niamh and I must have accidentally hit your number while I was rooting around for my purse.'

'Oh, okay. No problem, as long as you're alright. I suppose I'll let you go then.'

Relieved, I'm about to leave it at that but before I can change my mind I add, 'Actually, while I've got you . . . do you mind if I ask you a question?'

'Fire away.'

'I'm just curious . . . when we split . . . there wasn't anyone else was there?'

He falls silent for just a fraction too long and then bounces back with a question of his own. 'What makes you ask that?'

Ignoring his response I put the question to him again. 'You can be honest, just tell me. I can take it.'

'Of course there wasn't anyone else. I was always faithful. Look, where's all this coming from?'

I take a deep breath. 'I saw a photo . . . a photo of you and Orla.'

Another pause, this time longer. I feel like I can almost hear him flicking through an index of excuses before finally landing on the one he thinks will sound most plausible. 'Lila . . . I'm . . . I'm sorry. I never meant for—'

'Don't bother,' I say cutting him off as I feel my heart breaking all over again at the confirmation of his betrayal. 'I can't believe you, Gabe, I really can't. All this time I've been thinking our break-up was my fault and all the while you were sneaking round behind my back with her. Well, I'm done grieving for what we had. She can have you – I don't care!'

With that, I end the call, delete his number and promptly burst into tears.

So there it is, all my worst suspicions confirmed. I feel angry, so angry I could break something, throw it against a wall and watch it smash into pieces but more than that, much more than that, I feel stupid and gullible. How could I not have seen this? How could I have been so blind? All his excuses for not coming up to see me, all his lies, they seem so obvious to me now. How had I ever believed them?

I go back into the bar and tell Niamh everything, and despite her suggestion that we should spend the rest of the evening drowning my sorrows I head straight home, take a couple of paracetamol to stave off the headache that has appeared out of nowhere and go straight to bed.

Thankfully I sleep a deep and dreamless sleep, and when I awake the following morning I tell myself that I'm done thinking about Gabe. Instead, I throw myself into my day at work and then that evening head over to Marcus's mum's house to conduct my first interview.

When I'd asked if he could smooth the way for me to talk to his mum, he'd not only agreed but also offered to meet me there and make the introductions. Admittedly my instinct had been to decline – it's not as if I can't handle myself with an interviewee – but then it occurred to me that perhaps his offer might be his way of trying to make amends for his initial hostility, and so, always keen to take an olive branch when one is offered, I'd accepted.

'Good to see you again,' says Marcus ushering me into the small but neat hallway of his mum's flat.

It's a bit strange seeing him again, all the more so when I think of the trust he and Connor have put in me to find Bernie.

'Good to see you too,' I reply trying to sound businesslike and efficient even though thanks to Gabe I feel anything but. 'How's Connor?'

He frowns. 'Not great. He got beat up at the bus stop a few days ago. He's okay now, but it really shook him up.'

'Oh no, how awful,' I exclaim. 'It wasn't anything to do with all the publicity, was it?'

'No, just kids being nasty. I wanted to drive round and look for them but he wasn't having any of it. It's just the way it goes sometimes. When you're a bit different like Connor, you're vulnerable, and people take advantage of that.'

'Well give him my best won't you,' I say making a mental note to send Connor something nice in the post as Marcus leads me into the living room to meet his mum.

Bev Campbell, though small and slim, carries herself with the air of someone twice her size. She greets me politely but I sense a guardedness about her that makes me glad her son is here to put her at ease.

She asks me if I'd like a drink and I gladly accept, and while she disappears to the kitchen Marcus leads me to the living room where we both take a seat on the sofa. The room is cosy and comfortable and the carpet feels thick and luxurious beneath my feet. On almost every inch of the wall there are framed family photos, of babies and toddlers, Marcus, her grown-up daughters and grandchildren.

'So, you want to know about Bernie, do you?' asks Bev, as she comes into the room carrying a tray of tea and biscuits.

'If you don't mind.' She hands a mug to me and then one to Marcus.

'Well, I'll tell you what I can if you think it will help.' She sighs, takes a seat in the armchair opposite and shakes her head sadly. 'Such a sorry business it was. Such a sorry business indeed.'

I open my notepad to a fresh page. 'I'm trying to build up as complete a picture of Bernie as I possibly can in the hope it will lead to something that will help us find out what happened to her. So, first, a bit of background. How long have you known Bernie?'

'Now there's a question!' Bev thinks for a minute. 'It must be thirty years or so. We used to work at Hudson's SuperSave together, then we lost touch but as luck would have it she moved in across the road.'

'And you were good friends?'

'Very,' says Bev emphatically. 'I lost Marcus's dad just before he was born and so found myself a single parent with three children to raise.' I glance over at Marcus who is looking down at the carpet. I didn't know he'd lost his dad but then again I'd only just met him so why would it even come up?

'Bernie was on her own too,' continues Bev, 'so we always looked out for one another. Although Bernie wasn't always what you'd call an easy person to get along with; in fact at the time she went missing we weren't on speaking terms.'

I look up from my notepad. 'Oh, how come?'

'It was to do with the council plans for Hope Street. We'd fought against them side by side from the beginning, but I could see which way the wind was blowing and I told her I was thinking about accepting a ground-floor flat if they offered it to me. Bernie didn't like that and so stopped talking to me. It's one of my biggest regrets that things were so bad between us when she went missing.'

Bev looks down at her hands sadly and as I write all this down I think how awful she must have felt having fallen out with her friend and never being able to repair the damage.

'Thanks for sharing that, Bev,' I tell her. 'I really appreciate it. I know it can't have been easy for you to talk about.' We all pause for a moment, and the only sound is of the three of us sipping our drinks, until finally I break the silence with another question.

'Was Connor's dad ever on the scene?'

Bev shakes her head. 'He disappeared the moment he found out she was pregnant.'

'And what about her family? Was she in touch with any of them?'

Again, Bev shakes her head. 'She came over from Ireland when she was fifteen. I think there was some sort of big family falling-out. In all the time I knew her she never so much as mentioned her parents or talked about having any brothers or sisters, or said that she ever thought about going back to Ireland.'

'She was a bit of a loner then?'

'No, I wouldn't say that. She had friends here in the street and at work too.'

'And how about relationships?'

Bev laughs. 'Bernie always used to joke that she wasn't interested in any of that kind of nonsense.'

'But didn't she ever get lonely?'

'No, Connor was her world, and any time she wasn't with him she was probably thinking about him. That woman really adored her son.'

I glance down at my notes before lifting my gaze to meet Bev's. 'I really get a sense that she was completely devoted to Connor so her disappearance makes even less sense in that context. I mean, this is totally out of character for Bernie by the sounds of it; she'd never done anything like this before.'

Bev takes a sip of her tea and shakes her head.

'In that case what do you think might have happened to have kept her away from Connor for so long?'

Bev studies the contents of her mug for several moments as if the answer to the question lies in there somewhere. 'I honestly have no idea,' she says finally meeting my gaze.

'None at all?'

'All I know is that she would never have willingly abandoned Connor like that. She more than anyone else knew how vulnerable Connor is . . . so all I can say is that if it was in her power to come back, she would've done it by now.'

Knowing how difficult it will be for her to answer, I hesitate before asking my next question. 'So, are you saying you think Bernie's come to some sort of harm?'

'I hope not,' says Bev, 'I really hope not. But I can't think of any other reason she wouldn't have come back before now.'

'So, you think she's . . .'

'Dead?' Bev finishes off my sentence. 'I know Connor truly believes she's going to come home, that one day she'll walk through the door and everything will go back to the way it was, but I just don't think that's going to happen. Not now, not after all this time. As much as it grieves me to say it, I think she's gone, and I've accepted it. So maybe once you've finished doing what you're doing Connor will realise it too and then we can all work towards helping him move on.'

We chat for a while longer, and Bev shows me the photographs of her and Bernie she's sorted out to show me, most of which are of them laughing together. The two women were obviously very close and I can only imagine how hard these last few years have been for Bev not knowing what happened to her friend.

Finally, I thank her and after we've said goodbye Marcus walks me to the front door.

'Was that any help?' he asks as I bend down to slip my boots back on.

'It'll certainly help me start building up a better picture of Bernie,' I reply, 'and given what your mum and everyone else is saying there's no way she would have deliberately walked out and left Connor, so we're looking at either foul play or misadventure, neither of which is great, and neither of which means that Connor is likely to get his happy ending.'

'Poor Connor,' says Marcus. 'You tell yourself that it's better to have certainty than hope but in his case I'm not so sure.'

'Well, for the time being nothing's certain so let's assume we still have something to hope for.'

We're both silent for a moment and then things turn awkward again when I realise I'm not quite sure how to say goodbye. A handshake seems too formal, a hug far too familiar, so all that's left is a horribly self-conscious exchange of smiles.

'Well, I'd better be off,' I hear myself saying and with that I get into my car and head home.

I spend the rest of the evening writing up my interview notes, and then when I'm done, I make myself a quick pasta dinner and watch some TV. Feeling myself nodding off I'm about to head to bed when my phone rings.

'Hello? Is that Lila?'

'Hi,' I reply recognising the voice on the other end of the line as belonging to Marcus's mum. 'Mrs Campbell?'

'Yes, I'm so sorry to bother you. It's just that something's been playing on my mind since you left and I know I'm not going to rest until I tell you.'

'Oh, okay. What is it?'

'Well, do you remember you asked me whether Bernie had ever gone missing prior to this . . . well, I said no but that wasn't exactly the truth. The thing is . . . well . . . this isn't actually the first time. The truth is she went missing once before.'

14

Connor

Adele and I are busy restocking the shelves in the bird and wildlife section of the store when I hear her say, 'Here, Connor, look, what do you think of my new bikini?'

I look up to see her dancing around like a hula girl and holding two coconut shell bird feeders in front of her chest. To get the joke I have to look at the coconut shells, which means looking at her chest, which makes me feel a bit funny inside and I feel the whole of my face go red.

'Very nice.' I laugh because it is funny after all, and then I grab a pair of coconut shell bird feeders and put them on my chest and then I dance around like a hula girl too. Adele thinks this is very funny and she cracks up laughing and we dance around the aisle until suddenly Adele's face changes, and she quickly moves the coconuts away from her chest. I turn around to see what she's looking at and it's then that I see Ryan standing at the end of the aisle with his arms folded.

'You two finished with your comedy routine, yet?' he snaps. We both nod but say nothing. 'Good, then get back to work and don't let me find you messing about like that again.'

We quickly carry on restocking the shelves, and I'm so embarrassed that it feels like the whole of my skin is on fire. I've never been told off at work before, and I don't like it. I wonder if I should go and find Ryan and apologise but as I turn around to ask Adele if she wants to come with me, I see that she is laughing so hard she can barely stand up straight.

'Did you see his face?' she says once she's stopped laughing. 'He didn't know where to look! What he must have thought to find us like that! Honestly, I wish I'd taken a picture of his face! One hundred per cent it'd go viral!'

When I'd decided to be friends with Adele I'd thought it would mean waving hello to her in the morning or saying goodbye to her at the end of a shift. I did not think it would end up with us being actual proper friends but it has. Even though I was careful around her to begin with she is so different to how she used to be and so much fun to be around that I have stopped worrying, and just started to enjoy myself. Adele isn't mean and spiteful like she used to be; now she is always laughing and joking around and is already one of the most popular people at work. And because I'm getting to spend so much time with her it feels like I am popular too, and it's a nice feeling. I've never been popular before and I've never had many friends my own age. People at work have always been nice to me, but not in the same way they are nice to Adele. Now people want to sit with me and Adele at lunchtime and they ask me my opinions on things like TikTok videos and stuff that's been on TV. And it's not because I've changed. I'm still the same old Connor. It's all because of Adele and even though I didn't like being told off by Ryan, somehow it feels worth it to be her friend.

'I heard about you and that Sharpe girl getting told off by Ryan for mucking about,' says Alan later, when I'm sat in the break room. 'What are you doing spending so much time with that nasty piece of work?'

'She's not a nasty piece of work. She's actually really nice. You might like her too if you gave her a chance.'

'I'd sooner put my hand in a nest of vipers,' says Alan, and then he shakes his head as if he is very disappointed in me. 'Look, I know she helped you out the other day but that doesn't mean she's changed. People like the Sharpes don't change. I know you won't listen to me but just have your wits about you with that one, okay? She could easily take advantage of someone like you.'

I wish I hadn't told Alan how Adele had helped me when I got attacked by those boys. I feel like he's using what I told him against me and that just isn't fair. I'm so angry that my face gets all hot. I've had this my whole life, people treating me like I am a child, and I'm sick of it! I have a job, I cook for myself, I keep the house clean and tidy, and still people treat me like I'm not a grown-up.

I stare at Alan, my lips pressed together hard. 'What do you mean, "someone like me"?'

Alan's face changes and he holds a hand up in the air like he's trying to calm down a barking dog. 'There's no need to snap. I didn't mean anything bad, I just—'

'You just what, Alan? You don't think I can look after myself?'

'Of course you can. I'm just worried that's all. Worried that Adele might be taking advantage of your good nature.'

'She's not.' I stand up, dropping the rest of my sandwich into the bin because suddenly I don't feel hungry anymore. 'She's my friend and I thought you were too. And you should know better than to talk about someone's friends in a nasty, horrible way.'

I don't talk to Alan for the rest of the day, even when we are watering the plants in the garden and outdoor section together. He tries to talk to me, mentioning things he knows I like to talk about, but I pretend I don't hear, and after a while he gives up trying, and we just work together side by side in silence. I will forgive him eventually because that's what friends do but, for now, Alan is in my bad books.

That evening after work Marcus comes round. Before my talk with Alan, I thought I might tell him about Adele but I'm worried he will have the same reaction and so I decide against it.

'Listen,' he says after we've finished eating, 'my mum's been on at me again. She's worried about you being here on your own and thinks you ought to start looking at flats.'

'But I don't want to look at flats – you know that. Lila's going to find Mum and bring her home to Hope Street. Why would I want a flat?'

Marcus holds up his hands. 'I know, I know. But you know what my mum's like. She won't take no for an answer, and I have to say she's got a point. I mean, even if your mum does comes back—'

'When! Not if!'

'Okay, when your mum comes back do you really think she's going to want to carry on living here now that everyone else has moved out? At least see what they're offering. No one's saying you've got to take any of them; all we're saying is have a look. I mean, have the housing sent you anything through recently?'

I shake my head even though I know there is a huge pile of letters in the drawer in the back room. I'll tell Marcus about them one day but now is not the time.

'That council,' says Marcus, 'they're absolutely useless. I'll get the website up and we'll take a look.'

He takes out his phone, and after a while he shows me a few flats he thinks are nice. 'So what do you reckon?' he asks when I hand back his phone. 'They're not bad are they?'

I shake my head. 'Marcus, I really don't want to do this.'

'I know,' he says. 'Me either but neither do I want a clip round the ear from my mum. Listen, just do this one thing for me to get her off my back will you? If you do I'll get you an extra-large chips next time.'

I feel bad. Marcus never asks me for anything and never complains about all the things he has to do for me. 'Okay,' I say, 'I don't want you to get in trouble with Bev, and I don't need you to get me an extra-large chips, but I will look at flats so she won't shout at you. Okay?'

A couple of days later, Marcus calls and tells me that he's booked us in to see a flat and will take me there before my shift starts. I'm still eating my breakfast when I hear his car pulling up outside and straight away my heart feels heavy. I really, really don't want to look at any flats and for a moment I think about telling him that I don't feel very well. But then I remember the last time I lied to my friend about being ill when I'd wanted to get out of going to his sister's fortieth birthday party because I knew there'd be too many people there. Bev had got so worried about me that she'd made me an appointment at the doctor's and got Marcus to take me. In the end the doctor tried to give me some medicine and I got so worried about taking it when there was nothing wrong with me that I'd had to tell her the truth and she gave me a real telling-off for wasting her time.

'Alright,' says Marcus, when I answer the door. 'Are you all ready?'

I take a deep breath and then shake my head. 'I'm sorry, Marcus, but I don't want to go and look at flats.'

Marcus sighs. 'Oh, mate, but we had a whole conversation about it. No one's saying you have to go through with it, it's just to show willing, that's all, and get my mum off my back.'

'I am really, really sorry but it just feels wrong to even look at a new place without Mum. It feels wrong to leave Hope Street, like I'm letting her down.'

'You're not letting her down! You're just looking at a flat. Where's the harm in that?'

'There's lots of harm,' I say. 'Mum's coming back, I know she is, and I don't want her to think that I ever, even for a second, gave up on her.'

'And she won't. Connor, you're being ridiculous now! Your mum's number-one priority has always been keeping you safe, and she'd know that if you were looking to move it would only be because it wasn't safe for you here anymore.'

'But it is safe,' I say feeling myself getting angry. 'Nothing bad has happened to me while I've been here. It's my home, it's Mum's home and if I ever do have to look at a new place to live, I don't want to do it without her.' I look at Marcus and I don't want to annoy him but I have to tell him the truth. 'I've decided that I'll wait until she comes back and we can do it together.'

Even though Marcus says he understands I can see he is annoyed, and after he's called the man from the council he leaves without even saying goodbye. I feel really bad when he's gone, like I've let him down, but what else could I do? Like I said to Marcus if I had gone to look at the flat I'd feel like I was letting Mum down, which is even worse.

I feel so sad that I don't finish my breakfast and I'm still sad when I arrive at work for my shift that afternoon. Reaching the staff entrance I'm about to swipe my card when the door opens and Adele comes out.

'Alright, Connor?' she asks but then she sees my face and she puts an arm around me. 'What's the matter? Has something happened? Those boys haven't been bothering you again, have they?'

With tears in my eyes I tell her about my argument with Marcus, and how I don't want to look at anywhere new to live until Mum comes back.

'Of course you don't.' She gives me a big hug. 'I'd be exactly the same if I was you.'

'Really?' I look up at her. 'Do you mean that?'

'Every word.' She kisses me on the cheek. It's warm and soft, and makes me feel like I have butterflies in my tummy.

'How about you and me go back inside, grab a drink and talk everything over?'

I don't move, not because I don't want to go with her but because I'm still thinking about her kiss.

'Are you coming, Connor?'

I look at Adele and for some reason she seems different, and I feel different too and without saying anything I let her take me by the hand and lead me inside.

15

Lila

As I enter the busy café for my meeting I scan the tables. There are groups of mums wrangling their toddlers, couples enjoying a coffee together, and clutches of older ladies talking ten to the dozen. Not a single one, however, fits the description of DCI Halton – the police officer contact of Angela from the crime desk at *The Echo* – who has agreed to meet with me to discuss Bernie's case.

Spying a free table, I set down my bag, order a flat white at the till and then sit down and wait. No sooner has my drink arrived when a tall, slim, smartly dressed woman with curly brown hair pulled back in a clip approaches my table.

'Lila Metcalfe?'

I get to my feet and hold out my hand. 'DCI Halton? Thanks so much for agreeing to meet with me. Take a seat and I'll get you a drink.'

At the counter I order a filter coffee and a couple of pastries for good measure, then return to the table. I'm eager to get straight into it and not take up too much of her time.

'So, did Angela tell you what this is about?'

The officer nods. 'The misper, from three years ago, Bernie McLaughlin, who's been in the papers recently. Angela says you're trying to help the son.'

'His name's Connor and he genuinely believes his mum is alive and out there somewhere, and understandably without knowing what happened to her he's finding it virtually impossible to get on with his life. So, really, anything you can tell me about the case, any leads I can chase at all, will be very gratefully received.'

DCI Halton reaches into her bag and pulls out a notebook and I do the same. 'Bernie's case, while technically still open, isn't live – meaning that there's no one actively investigating at the moment. I did review the file before I came out and jotted down a few notes, but there's not an awful lot to go on, I'm afraid. From what I gather there's nothing to suggest foul play. She was well liked within the community, adored her son, and as far as we're aware hadn't had anything to do with her ex-partner, Kevin Townsend, since before Connor was born. We did look into him but he passed away nine and a half years ago, so that was that really.'

While I was aware that Connor's dad wasn't and had never really been in the picture, it was still somehow something of a surprise to find out that he was dead.

I look up from my notepad. 'And does Connor know, about his dad I mean?'

'I have no idea. As far as I'm aware he never met the man.'

'Oh right, yes, of course.' I take a moment wondering where I should stand on this ethically. Should I just keep quiet about it or pass this news on to Connor? But what would be the point of giving him more bad news when he already has enough to contend with?

DCI Halton glances down at her notepad again as I continue to make notes. 'As far as CCTV goes, it's a pretty patchy story, as I know you're aware. There's footage of her on the bus into town, and some heading across the city, but I'll be honest, at the time half the cameras in town weren't working, and so that's where the trail goes cold.' She refers to her notepad again, and turns over a new page. 'Other than various standing orders, there's been no activity on her bank account, at least none while the case was being actively investigated.'

I stop writing for a moment and look at DCI Halton. 'And what about in the lead-up to her disappearance, was there anything un-usual in her bank activity then?'

'Nothing that's been flagged up. It seems she liked to deal in cash mainly, visiting the bank and taking money out each week. Sometimes it's a bit more than usual, sometimes a bit less, but there's nothing to suggest that she was in any trouble or planning on disappearing.'

'So, she just vanished into thin air?'

DCI Halton opens her mouth to reply but then the waitress returns carrying her drink and she waits until we're alone before continuing. 'Sadly, it's much more common than you'd think. People disappear every day, and it's very rarely anything sinister – more often than not it's to escape a situation to give themselves some breathing space, and they simply don't want to be found.'

'About that.' I shift uncomfortably in my seat. I'm going to have to come clean about Bev's revelation. 'It's just come to my atten-tion that despite what the police were told at the time Bernie did actually go missing once before.'

Without giving away the source of my information I tell her what I learned from my phone conversation with Bev. That, years ago – when Connor would have been only about six or seven – Bernie had gone missing.

DCI Halton raises an eyebrow. 'That's not in the case file.'

'It's . . . it's . . . information that's just come to light. As you might appreciate, I can't reveal my sources but they are reliable. What I can tell you is that she wasn't missing for very long, and it was a time of incredible emotional distress for her.'

Bev's revelation had thrown me at first and cast the whole of Bernie's disappearance in a different light. It not only raised the possibility that she might have deliberately run away this time but also made me wonder whether she'd been driven by her situation to take some even more drastic action.

DCI Halton begins writing something down and without looking back up she says, 'So, what happened exactly?'

Careful to keep the details vague I tell her how Bernie had taken Connor to a friend's house and asked them to look after him overnight so she could have a bit of a break. The friend, all too aware of the stress Bernie had been under, agreed.

DCI Halton fixes me with a look. 'What sort of stress exactly?'

I recall Bev's words. 'She'd had her hours cut at work, was in arrears with her rent, and at the time Connor was really struggling at school and not sleeping, which obviously meant that Bernie wasn't either.'

DCI Halton scribbled this down. 'Okay, so I'm assuming this break didn't go to plan?'

'Apparently, she didn't come back for him the following morning. Of course her friend tried Bernie's mobile and when the calls went straight to voicemail they went round to her house but she was nowhere to be seen.'

'And still, this "friend" didn't go to the police?'

'Well, I think they might've done but then they got a text from Bernie apologising and saying that she'd be back once she'd got her head straight. The friend didn't want to get Bernie in trouble with social services so, she just sat tight, and sure enough, after a couple of days she came back just like she said she would.'

'And did she say where she'd been?'

'She didn't want to talk about it and the friend didn't want to push her. But the friend did say that wherever it was Bernie went, and whatever it was she did there, it seemed to give her what she needed to carry on. According to my source she never did it again, never seemed to need to, and was more devoted to Connor than ever after that.'

Once she's finished scribbling in her notepad DCI Halton sits back and looks at me. 'It would've been helpful if we'd had this information at the time.'

'But does it really make any material difference? I mean, no one knew where she went, what she did there, or who she went with.'

'But what it could've done is indicate some sort of psychological pattern,' says DCI Halton ruefully. 'That when things get tough for Bernie, her gut instinct is to take herself out of the situation and, judging from the files, three years ago was a tricky time for Bernie. Her home was under threat, Connor was still living there and still dependent on her in many ways and she wasn't getting any younger. Who knows? Perhaps this triggered a bout of anxiety much like the time you've described and she convinced herself the only thing she could do was leave.'

'But she came back last time, and she hasn't this time. I mean that doesn't sound anything like the Bernie people have told me about. I've spoken to at least a dozen people now from old neighbours and friends to former work colleagues and they all say how devoted she was to Connor. And to just up and vanish for three years leaving Connor to fend for himself like that just seems completely out of character.'

'True,' says DCI Halton, 'but you'd be surprised by the number of families who hadn't the slightest suspicion that their loved ones were thinking of leaving. People can be very good at hiding their troubles, even, or perhaps especially from those they love most.'

I can't help but feel disappointed. In spite of Angela's warning I'd been hopeful that a fresh lead would come out of this meeting and yet to all intents and purposes what I'm hearing boils down to this: some people just disappear and you might never know the reason why. Connor will never be satisfied with this answer. How could he?

DCI Halton must have seen the look on my face because after a long sip of her coffee she says, 'Listen, thanks for sharing your info. It's much appreciated and when I get a minute I'll take another look at Bernie's case. Who knows there might be something we've overlooked.'

We talk for a while longer. I ask questions to clarify the timeline and then we go on to discuss some of the missing persons cases she's worked on in the past, a number of which have ended happily, others, less so. She's an engaging conversationalist, so much so that I lose track of time and it's only when her phone buzzes with a text and she pauses to respond to it, that I realise we've both long since finished our drinks and the café is much quieter than it was when she first arrived now the early morning rush has subsided.

'I'm afraid I've got to get going,' she says gathering her things together. 'It's been good talking to you.'

'And you too,' I reply, shaking her hand. 'Thanks again for your time.'

'My pleasure,' she says. 'And I've got your number, so if I find anything of interest I'll be in touch.'

The week that follows is absolutely manic, not only do we have to cover an unexpected royal visit to the area, and a local by-election, but in the middle of it all I receive an email from *The Correspondent* informing me I've made it through to the final round of interviews. I can't quite believe it. I'm simultaneously shocked and thrilled. I've been so busy that I haven't had time to give it much thought and now I'm through to the final round. I call my mum straight away and tell her the good news and she is over the moon for me. 'Of course they've called you in for a second interview,' she says, 'you're brilliant at what you do and they'd be lucky to have you.'

When the day of the interview comes round I spend most of the journey frantically preparing for it, but as we draw closer to

London my nerves start to get the better of me. I feel sick, dizzy and a bit like my head might explode and so I decide instead to distract myself by catching up on some calls I need to make. The first of these is to Marcus, as I want to bring him up to speed about the investigation, and specifically the news about Connor's dad, which I'd been worrying about ever since DCI Halton had informed me.

'Connor's dad's dead? How? When?'

'Liver failure about ten years ago; apparently he was a bit of a drinker.'

There's a pause as he takes this in and all I can hear is the sound of machinery and the radio blaring just as it had when I'd visited his work before. 'I mean, I never met the man but Mum always said he was a right waster, and never had any time at all for Connor.'

'Still, do you think I ought to tell him, Connor, I mean? My head says yes, but my heart says no. I'm really not sure what to do for the best so I'm more than happy to be guided by you.'

'It's a tricky one. On the one hand he is an adult and it drives me mad when people don't treat him like one, but on the other, I think he's probably got enough on his plate right now without feeling like he should be mourning for a bloke he's never met.'

'So, he's definitely never had anything to do with his dad?'

'Not as far as I'm aware. Apparently, Bernie met him through work and when he found out she was pregnant he wasn't interested.'

'Sounds like a real charmer. So, you don't think I should mention it to Connor?'

'No, at least not yet. I've never heard Connor talk about him so I say let sleeping dogs lie and all that.'

'Okay.' I'm secretly relieved to hear him echo the thoughts I'd been having. 'Well, if you could pass on my update to Connor, I'd be grateful. How is he by the way?'

'Do you know what? He seems really good at the minute. I mean, we did have a bit of a falling-out over going to see a flat but I saw him the other day and he seemed like he was over it. In fact, it was like he couldn't stop smiling. I asked him what was making him so cheerful and he just shrugged but I'm guessing it must be down to you and the work you're doing. So, thanks, because of you he's more upbeat than he's been in a long time.'

Hearing this I feel a strange combination of pride and guilt. Much as I'm glad that Connor's happy, I can't imagine he'll still be that way if I get *The Correspondent* job and have to break it to him that I won't be able to continue the investigation into his mum's disappearance.

Over the speaker system the conductor announces that we'll shortly be arriving at St Pancras. I'm about to mumble a quick goodbye, when Marcus asks a question.

'I don't suppose you'd fancy going for a curry next week? You, me and Connor? Connor came up with the idea – he just wants to say a little thank you for all you're doing.'

My initial thought is that I can't afford the time, but then I tell myself a girl's got to eat sometime, and anyway, it's a lovely thought and will be a good opportunity to get to know Connor a bit better.

'That sounds great,' I tell him. 'Text me the details and I'll be there.'

As I get off the train I think about Marcus, and how much he clearly cares for Connor. He's not at all the person I thought he was when I first met him, and as I make my way over to *The Correspondent*'s offices I find myself wondering whether he thinks the same about me.

Reaching my destination, I give my name in at reception and as I take a seat in the waiting area and am about to switch off my phone, it rings.

'Hi, is that Lila Metcalfe?'

Recognising the voice, I stand up and shielding the phone from the building's echoing atrium I continue the call.

'Yes, speaking. DCI Halton?'

'Yes, it's about that case we met to discuss the other day, the Bernadette McLaughlin missing persons case. Well, after our conversation I put a few feelers out and I've just heard back from someone at the MP Unit. And . . . well . . . they do have an as yet unidentified body at a facility in Peterborough. Apparently it's been there for some time and I'm sorry to say it matches Bernie's description.'

16

Connor

'Connor? Connor can you hear me? I was just asking if I could have a quick word.'

The moment I look up I see Alan staring at me and I feel my whole face go red. The reason I go red is because I've been thinking about the other day when Adele kissed me. I've been thinking about it a lot since it happened. I think about how she looked, and how her lips felt against my skin, and the smell of her perfume when she got close to me. I think about how it gave me a funny feeling in my stomach, and about how much I would like her to kiss me again and what that might feel like. But I can't tell Alan about any of this because a) he doesn't like Adele and b) I'm still not talking to him.

'Oh, Alan.' I try my best to sound normal. 'I didn't see you there. What do you want?'

'To talk about the other day.' He pulls up a chair next to me at the break room table. 'I want to apologise for the things I said about Adele. It was wrong of me and I should've respected the fact that she is your friend.'

I think for a moment. It is very hard work being annoyed with Alan because we have been friends for so long, and I really want us to be friends again.

'Are you sure you mean that?'

'Scout's honour. I'll even apologise to her if you really want me to.'

'No, it's fine,' I say, because I think Alan might explode if I say yes. 'The important thing is that you have said sorry to me. Thank you, Alan.'

Alan lets out a long sigh of relief. 'Well, I'm glad that's all sorted. I'm not sure how much more of not talking to my best pal I could've taken.'

I smile. 'Me either.' I reach into the pocket of my jacket, pull out a half-empty bag of crisps and offer him one. 'I've never had this kind before. They're really nice and they're ready-salted too.'

'Your favourite,' he says, helping himself to a crisp. He chews loudly and swallows. 'And you're right – they are tasty.' He takes another one and then looks at me. 'So, where is her ladyship . . . I mean Adele? She in today?'

I can't help myself, just hearing her name is enough to put a smile on my face. 'She is but not until two.'

Alan gives me a funny look. 'Do you know her entire rota?'

Without thinking I reel off Adele's shifts for the rest of the week. 'She is working a two 'til eight today, eight 'til two tomorrow and then it's her day off and she's back in the day after with a six 'til two.'

'You really like her, don't you?'

'She is amazing,' I tell Alan. 'She is pretty and she is funny and she knows everything about everything and the other day she even kissed me.'

Alan's bushy eyebrows shoot up. 'She kissed you?'

I feel myself blush. 'It wasn't like a boyfriend/girlfriend kiss though; it was more of a peck on the cheek because I was sad.'

'And what were you sad about?'

'It doesn't matter. The important thing is that she cheered me up. I think I'm going to ask her out on a date.'

Alan's eyebrows shoot up again and almost disappear into his hair.

'A date?'

'I really like her and want her to be my girlfriend.'

Alan doesn't look very happy. 'Are you sure about that, lad? A girl like Adele . . . well . . . all I mean to say is, are you sure?'

'I'm a hundred per cent sure.'

Alan doesn't say anything for a moment; he just looks worried. 'Well, if you are sure then I suppose I should wish you good luck. Do you think she'll say yes?'

It's a question I've been asking myself over and over again since the kiss happened and the fact is I'm not sure at all. I know that we're friends, and I know that she hasn't got a boyfriend at the moment because I heard her telling Briony, but what I don't know is whether she likes me that way.

'Well, if you want my advice, just tread carefully, okay? She might like you like that, but equally she might just want to be friends. If I were you I wouldn't get my hopes up too much. And if it doesn't work out with Adele don't forget there are plenty of other lovely lasses out there. For instance, there's this cracking young lady who works at The Green Mountain Garden Centre who'd be perfect for you. Me and her always have a bit of a laugh and a joke whenever I go there, and I just know you'd like her. All I'm saying is don't put all your eggs in one basket.'

After talking with Alan, I suddenly don't feel as confident as I did before. And as I head back to the shop floor after my break to help out with a stock move in the hardware section, I can't help but think about all the times I've misunderstood people in the past. There have been times when I thought girls liked me when they didn't really. And there have been times when I thought people were being friendly when actually they were making fun of me behind my back. And without Mum to talk to I'm not sure if what I have with Adele is like those times or something different. Whether we are just friends and nothing more or if she actually wants to be my girlfriend.

Just before I reach the double doors to the shop floor someone from behind suddenly covers my eyes with their hands and a voice I know straight away says, 'Guess who?'

'I know it's you, Adele. I'd know you anywhere.'

She takes her hands away and I turn around and grin. She has done something different with her hair and looks prettier than ever. I want so much to ask her out but I just know that I'm not brave enough.

'Hello, Con. How's your shift been so far?'

'Okay, but it's always better when you're around.'

Adele smiles. 'Awww, Connor, you always say the sweetest things. Anyway, I'm glad I managed to catch you. What are you doing tomorrow night?'

Her question really confuses me. 'I don't know. I'm not at work so nothing I suppose.'

'Well, how would you feel about getting together for something to eat?'

'Are all the people from work going out?'

She laughs and the sound of it is beautiful. 'No, I'm not talking about getting together with everyone from work; I'm talking about just me and you.'

My mouth goes so dry that I can hardly get the words out. 'Just . . . just . . . the two of us?'

'Yes. I thought we could have a Deliveroo round at yours and then maybe watch a film. What do you think?'

I can't believe it! Adele has just asked me out! This is the happiest I have ever been in my entire life. 'Yes,' I say quickly, before she can change her mind. 'Yes, I would like that very much.'

I don't sleep that night. I can't. I am just too excited. Adele is coming to my house and we're going to have a takeaway and watch a movie, and it is going to be perfect. I don't let myself think about if she will kiss me again because I know that if I think about it too much it will make me even more nervous than I already am. Instead, I think about how nice it will be to eat a meal with someone on a Friday night rather than being on my own, and I imagine us sitting on the big sofa, snuggled up together. Maybe, if we watch a scary film she will hold my hand in the really frightening bits, and then I will tell her, 'It's okay, it's nothing to worry about; it's just a film,' and she will look at me and smile and say, 'Thanks, Connor, I'm glad you're here.'

I'm not in work on Friday, but I go in anyway because there are lots of things I need and I want to use my staff discount to get them. I buy a box of large candles, and two silver-effect candlesticks; I buy a big bag of potpourri; I buy a grey fake fur throw to cover the stain on the big sofa from when I accidentally spilt a whole can of Vimto on it, and I also buy two posh plates and some new cutlery because all the stuff I use is okay for every day, but not very nice if you're trying to impress someone.

When I head to the checkout, I make sure to go through the self-service because if anyone I know sees what I am buying they will only ask lots of embarrassing questions that I will hate. Luckily, I manage to get in and out of the store without any of my friends seeing me and so from there I go straight to the big Asda where I pick up two large bottles of Vimto and a bottle of pink wine because I know Adele likes rosé.

When I get home, I put all the things I've bought away and then I clean the house from top to bottom, which takes a long time because I haven't really been keeping on top of the housework even though I tell Marcus every week that I am. The bathroom especially takes ages to do, but by the time I'm finished everything is gleaming and smells of pine-fresh cleaner.

Even though Adele had said she would be at my house by seven o'clock there is still no sign of her at seven thirty. I start to worry that maybe she isn't coming, so I send her a text asking if she is okay but get no reply. By seven fifty-six she still hasn't arrived and I am almost certain that she has changed her mind and isn't coming, and that somehow it is all my fault. I send her another message asking if I've done something wrong and I'm still waiting for a reply at ten past eight when there's a knock at the door.

At last, she's here and all my worry disappears and I'm back to being excited again. On the way to the front door I check my reflection in the mirror over the fireplace and can't help but smile. I am wearing my favourite bright yellow 72 Seasons World Tour Metallica T-shirt – the one I only wear for special occasions – and a brand-new pair of jeans. I look good and I think Adele will think so too.

When I open the door she is busy messaging on her phone.

'Hello, Adele,' I say, 'I was getting worried about you.'

She looks up from the screen. 'Yeah, sorry about that – I had a few things I needed to do.'

'Come in,' I say, stepping to one side, and as she does so I notice that she is carrying a large black backpack. Normally when I see her coming into or going home from work she is carrying a small bright pink fluffy handbag, so this looks strange on her.

'Can I take your coat?' I ask closing the front door.

Adele shakes her head. 'Actually, I can't stay long.'

'Oh, but I thought we were going to eat and watch a film?'

Adele shoves her phone back into her pocket. 'You're right, Connor, and I'm sorry. Maybe another time. The thing is, something's come up. It's a long story . . . but part of it is that it's my brother's birthday next week and I had to do some shopping before I came here; that's why I'm late. Anyway, is there any chance you could do me a massive favour?'

'What is it?'

'Well, he's staying at my mum and dad's at the minute and I don't want him to know what I've bought for him. Can I leave this bag with his present in it here, and pick it up in a few days?'

'Okay,' I say thinking maybe we'll have our date when she comes back to get it.

Adele smiles. 'Connor, you're a lifesaver! The only thing is it's a really expensive present and I'm worried about anything happening to it while you're out at work. Do you mind if I put it upstairs out of the way?'

'What is it?' I ask trying to guess what it might be. It looks quite big, and Adele said it was expensive. 'Is it a PlayStation? I bet it is.'

'Yes,' says Adele sounding like she's thinking about something else. 'It's a PlayStation; now let's hide it out of the way.'

I take Adele upstairs, and at first, I think it might be best to put the bag in my room but there are so many things in there that I think it would be the first place a burglar would look, and so instead I take her into Mum's room.

'Just put it under the bed. It will be safe there.'

As we go back downstairs my stomach rumbles.

'Are you sure you don't have time for something to eat?'

'I'd love to but I can't. I've got to go and help my mum with something, but we'll definitely do it another time, okay?'

'Okay, I'll see you Sunday at work.'

'I'm not in Sunday,' she says. 'I swapped shifts this morning. But I'm sure I'll catch up with you soon.'

I walk her to the door and as I open it she says, 'Thanks so much for this, Connor, you're a real friend,' then she kisses my cheek again, and I feel like my heart might explode.

'It's okay,' I say, once I can speak. 'I'm glad I could help out.'

'And oh,' she says as if she's just remembered something, 'about the bag . . . it's just between you and me, okay? No one else can know, not another soul. The last thing we want is for my brother to find out what I've bought for him and have his birthday ruined.'

'I understand.' I am very pleased that she is trusting me with her secret. 'I won't say anything to anyone, I promise.'

17

Lila

'Going home already, are we? You've only just come back from lunch!'

Niamh scowls in Lewis's direction and he immediately looks apologetic. 'Sorry, Lils, I'd completely forgotten about today. That was bang out of order.'

'It's fine.' I slip on my coat and I'm just about to button it when my phone buzzes with the message from Marcus I've been expecting: *I'm here, whenever you're ready.*

Niamh gives me a hug. 'Are you going to be alright, mate?'

I nod, even though I've never done anything like this before and I'm dreading it. 'I'm sure it's going to be awful, but it's got to be done and maybe it will give Connor some answers one way or another.'

As I head down in the lift I think back to that moment, the moment I got the call from DCI Halton. Even though I'd always known the chances of finding Bernie alive and well were slim, Connor's optimism, his belief that his mum was okay and would come home was so powerful that it was impossible not to buy into it. So, the news that this story might have an unhappy ending after all came as something of a blow, and as I'd received it just as I was about to go into my interview for the job at *The Correspondent*, I'd had to use all my strength to compose myself in double quick time.

While I think the interview had gone okay, my head had been so full of Bernie and Connor that it's impossible to be sure I didn't come off a little distracted. Still, I did my best, and once it was all over I pushed it to the back of my mind, headed out of the building and called Marcus to break the bad news.

'She's dead?' His tone was utterly suffused with disbelief and I realised in that moment I wasn't the only one to have been swept up by the tide of Connor's optimism. 'Of course I knew it was possible, but it just feels . . . I don't know . . . different knowing for sure.'

'But that's just it, we don't know for sure and we won't know until she's been identified. All that's certain is that this woman fits Bernie's description, had no ID of any sort on her, and no one else has come forward to claim her yet.'

Marcus fell quiet. 'We can't tell Connor this, at least not until we're sure. Will they let someone who's not a relative ID her?'

'I don't know. I can check if you like.'

'And if they agree to it, then it's something I'd like to do for Connor. There's no point in putting him through an ordeal like that if it turns out not to be her.'

Once I'd finished speaking with Marcus, I'd called DCI Halton back. I explained the situation and thankfully she'd agreed to arrange for me and Marcus to view the body and do an initial identification, which if positive would obviously have to be confirmed by Connor himself. Once this was agreed I'd called Marcus back and we'd arranged to travel to Peterborough together.

Reaching the ground floor, I tap out at security and head towards the exit and after scanning the car park eventually spot Marcus waiting for me behind the wheel of his car. He gives me a small wave and I wave back, but even from this distance I can tell how tense he is. Who wouldn't be? I know I am.

'Are you sure you're okay to drive?' I say climbing into the passenger seat. 'We could take my car. It wouldn't be anywhere near as comfortable as this one, and there's a good chance we might break down along the way, but I'd be more than happy to take us.'

Marcus smiles. 'I like driving. Anyway, it'll help keep my mind off things.'

He asks for the address of where we're going and so I take out my phone, read it out to him and he punches it into his satnav before starting the engine, and in no time at all we're heading out of the city in the direction of the A52, neither of us really saying much at all.

'I'm so sorry you're having to do this,' I say eventually. 'I know it's not going to be easy.'

'I've never seen a dead body before,' he says. 'Still, better me than Connor.' He pauses and for a moment I think he's finished speaking but then he looks at me briefly. 'I just can't get my head around why Bernie would have been in Peterborough of all places? Like I said when you told me, she didn't have any connection to anyone over that way. I even checked with my mum, and she was none the wiser. Of course, then she wanted to know why I was asking and so I had to tell her.'

'How did she take it?'

'She was distraught. It was awful. They were mates for decades, and no matter how practical my mum's trying to be about it all, I think it really shocked her to be confronted with the possibility that Bernie might really be gone.' He pauses and sighs. 'I just want to know how she ended up in Peterborough.'

'Me too. Nothing in my notes mentions Peterborough, and none of the people I've interviewed about Bernie's disappearance have spoken about it either. My police contact didn't have any idea. Her only suggestion was that perhaps Bernie went there to start over, and deliberately chose somewhere that she had no connection with.'

'So, they think she's just been living her life in Peterborough for the past three years? I mean, how – without any money and nowhere to live?'

'That's what I thought too. But who's to say that she hasn't been living rough, or perhaps in a homeless shelter somewhere? But to be honest I'm just speculating. The only way to even have a hope of finding out the truth is to see if this is really her and work out the rest afterwards.'

The silence that had started our journey descends once again, and we don't speak until we reach our final destination: the hospital in Peterborough.

'This is it.' Marcus brings the car to a halt in the vast multistorey car park. 'No going back now.'

We spend a few moments getting our bearings before following signs for the Bereavement Care Centre at the rear of the main hospital complex. The building is so nondescript that if you weren't looking for it you wouldn't even give it a second glance, never imagining for a moment what might be inside.

With Marcus trailing after me, I make my way through the automatic doors and after checking my phone for the details, give my name at reception.

We're asked to take a seat on the hard plastic chairs in the waiting area and as the minutes tick by Marcus jiggles his foot nervously while I stare at my phone, trying my best not to think about my granddad, and how at some point he must have been in a place like this before the undertakers arrived to transport him to the funeral home. Thankfully however, my train of thought is brought to a stop by the sound of the automatic entrance doors sliding open and I turn to see a uniformed police officer approaching the desk. I just know he's our contact and sure enough after a brief conversation with the receptionist, she hands him a clipboard and points him in our direction.

Mike Gayle

'Lila Metcalfe?'

I stand up, introduce myself and then add: 'And this is Marcus Campbell, a family friend of the missing person. He's the one who is going to identify . . .' My voice trails off, and we all exchange awkward looks, and then the officer checks his papers again and nods.

'Pleased to meet you both. I'm Constable Rowe, and I've been tasked with helping you out this morning. If you'd like to follow me, I'll take you through.'

Marcus and I follow the officer along a corridor, through two sets of double doors, to yet another waiting room. After telling us to take a seat he disappears, leaving us alone.

'Are you okay?' I whisper to Marcus.

He sighs heavily. 'I've been better.'

Once again, I think about my granddad's final moments, with me, Mum, Dad and Robyn all gathered around his bed as he slipped away. I open my mouth to reply, to say what, I'm not sure, but then the officer returns, and the moment has gone.

'Right then, if you're okay,' he says, 'they're ready for us now.'

The room we're taken to isn't quite what I'd been expecting. Having watched countless police procedurals I'm surprised to find that it looks less like a high-tech clinical facility and more like someone's disappointing kitchen extension without the benefit of windows. The body, covered in a white sheet, is lying on a stainless-steel trolley, and there is a gowned and masked mortuary assistant standing next to it.

'Before we do this,' says Marcus, 'can I just ask how . . . how she died?'

The officer consults his notes. 'It was an RTA, a road traffic accident. According to an eyewitness she just came out of nowhere and the driver didn't stand a chance of avoiding her.'

I look at Marcus, wondering if this information is in any way helpful.

The mortuary assistant steps forward. 'I know you must be very anxious.' Her eyes are large and expressive over the mask. 'But I assure you, she looks very peaceful.'

Marcus takes a deep breath, and then gives a small nod in the direction of the mortuary assistant who gently pulls back the sheet to reveal the face of the woman beneath.

Straight away I hear Marcus let out a huge lungful of air. 'It's not her.' The relief in his voice rings clear. 'I can see how they thought it might be but it's definitely not her.'

'Are you sure?' the officer asks. 'Take your time. Don't forget it's been over three years since you last saw her.'

Marcus shakes his head. 'It could be thirty, and I'd still say the same thing. This is definitely not Bernie McLaughlin. She's roughly the same age, and a similar build, but other than that she looks absolutely nothing like her. I don't know who this poor woman is but it's definitely not Bernie.'

I've stared at pictures of Bernie long enough myself to be in complete agreement with Marcus, and while the build and age are right, nothing else about her even remotely resembles Bernie. I feel all the tension drain out of my body and I'm so relieved this isn't Connor's mum that without thinking I grab Marcus's hand and squeeze it tightly, only in the next moment to realise what I've done and let it go.

The mortuary assistant covers the poor woman's face again, and the police officer escorts us back to reception.

'I'm sorry you had to go through that. It's never pleasant but I really do hope you find the closure you're looking for soon.'

After thanking the officer for his time Marcus and I head out of the building, neither of us saying a word until we're back in the car.

Marcus turns to me. 'That's got to be one of the most surreal moments of my life.'

'It just didn't seem real, did it? And it's awful, as whoever that woman was she's still someone's loved one, but I'm so glad it wasn't Bernie.'

Marcus nods. 'Right now, someone out there could be missing her and just like Connor is hoping that one day she'll come home and it's weird to think that we know she never will.'

Perhaps it's down to the fact that we're both wrapped up in our own thoughts, or the relief that the worst, for now at least, seems to be behind us but somehow the return journey to Derby seems to take half the time.

As Marcus pulls into the car park at *The Echo*, I thank him for taking us today. 'It's not an easy thing you've done. Connor's very lucky to have you as a friend.'

'And he's even more lucky to have you on his side,' says Marcus. 'We really do owe you big time.'

We briefly discuss the arrangements for the curry later in the week and then I wave goodbye. As I head into the office I suddenly remember I'd switched off my phone at the hospital and so reaching into my bag I switch it back on. Instantly I hear the ping of a notification telling me there's a voicemail waiting for me.

'Hi Lila, it's James Neate from *The Correspondent*. I've tried you a couple of times but I haven't been able to get hold of you so forgive me for leaving a message instead. I just wanted to say that you were an excellent candidate, and it was a very close-run thing, but unfortunately on this occasion I'm afraid to say you weren't successful in securing the position at *The Correspondent*. I really do wish you the best of luck with your career, and should another position with us become available please don't hesitate to apply.'

18

Connor

I haven't been at work today as it's my day off but I've spent most of it wishing that I was. If I was at work then at least I'd be busy doing stuff and not thinking about Adele's brother's PlayStation in the bag upstairs underneath Mum's bed. But because I am not at work and not busy, it has been all I can think about all day.

The bag has been on my mind ever since Adele left it with me yesterday. I had stared at it for a whole hour after she'd gone, thinking about the PlayStation inside, and wondering if it was bundled with a game, or if she'd got the version with the DualSense Controllers, or if she'd spent loads of money and got a version with both. I went to sleep last night thinking about these questions and, when I woke up this morning, they were all still buzzing around in my head.

I really have tried not to think about it today. To keep myself busy I went and did my weekly shop at the Lidl on Moss Lane but it was still on my mind on the bus back home. Later, I tried to take my mind off Adele's brother's PlayStation by watching my favourite film, *Avengers: Endgame*, but I couldn't concentrate and had to switch it off. I put on my headphones and tried to listen to a playlist with all my favourite Metallica songs on it, and I did really enjoy the music but I still kept thinking about the PlayStation. In the end, I even tried turning on my own Play-Station and playing *Red Dead Redemption 2*, but I think that just made things worse. Instead of enjoying the game I kept thinking about how much better playing it would be on the brand-new PlayStation upstairs.

I really like my console but it is quite old now and lots of the new games people talk about online don't work with it. Even though I do have the money to upgrade I know I have to be sensible. Mum always told me that being an adult means learning that you can't just buy everything you want when you want it. You have to think about the future too, things like how you are going to pay the rent and your bills.

Turning off my console I decide to make myself a ham sandwich, and before I know it I have taken it upstairs to Mum's room. After a couple of bites, I lie down on the floor next to the bed and stare at the bag with Adele's brother's PlayStation inside.

Adele's instructions had been very clear.

She said I wasn't to tell anyone about the bag.

And she said I wasn't to touch it either.

She must love her brother very much and so it is understandable that she doesn't want anything bad to happen to his birthday present. But nothing bad is going to happen to it. And so, if nothing bad is going to happen to it then it makes no difference if I take a closer look at it, just to see if it really is as good as everyone says.

Without moving my body, I reach out my hand so that it is very close to one of the bag's handles, and I wait.

Nothing bad happens.

So far, so good.

Next, I stretch my fingers until they are touching the nylon fabric of the bag.

Still nothing bad happens.

So far, even better.

Next, I close my hand around the strap and pull it gently towards me, sliding it across the carpet until it is right in front of my face, so close that I can't even focus on it properly.

Then, I sit up, grab hold of the zip, and taking a deep breath slowly pull it back until the bag is fully open.

The first thing I feel as I stare inside is disappointment. There is definitely no PlayStation in this bag, or anything like one.

The next thing I feel is shock as I slowly realise what I am looking at.

It makes no sense.

Has Adele made a mistake? Has she picked up the wrong bag and given it to me by accident? But why would Adele have something like this in the first place? Is it hers? And if not, where has she got it from?

I reach into my pocket and pull out my phone ready to call and ask her but then stop. If I am going to ask her about the things in the bag I am going to have to tell her that I looked inside it. And if I tell her I looked inside it she will probably be upset with me. After all she'd trusted me and I've done exactly what she'd said not to.

But I think if she is going to be upset with me for looking inside the bag then I can be upset with her for not telling the truth about what was in it. And so really, we are both as bad as each other.

I call her number, but it goes straight to voicemail. And so I end the call and try again but the same thing happens. I think about leaving a message, something like, 'Hi, Adele, hope you're okay. Can you call me when you've got a minute, please?' I try to imagine myself saying the words, but I can't. I think I will be too nervous. And so, I carefully zip the bag shut, put it back under Mum's bed, and tell myself that first thing in the morning I will find Adele at work and talk to her face to face.

I hardly sleep that night. Every little noise the house makes has me turning on the light and checking for burglars. It is only when it begins to get light that I finally drop off to sleep but almost straight away I am woken up by the alarm on my phone telling me it's time to get ready for work.

Even though I am back to my usual shift today, I catch an earlier bus than normal so that I can have some time alone with Adele before work starts. Reaching the break room, I double-check the rota on the wall but things must have changed again. Instead of starting at ten like me it turns out that Adele isn't coming in until two.

'Alright, lad?' says Alan, making me jump. 'Didn't know you were in today. The rotas have been all over the place since Ryan took over doing the staffing. Did you have a good day off yesterday?'

'Yes,' I say quickly. 'But it didn't end very well.'

The words have slipped from my mouth before I've had chance to stop them.

'Oh, that's not good, is it? What happened?'

I think hard about how to answer the question. I don't want to tell Alan about Adele and the bag because I know he won't like it. But then again, I don't want to lie to my friend either. Instead, I try something Mum always used to say whenever she didn't want to go into details, 'It was just one of those days.'

Alan raises an eyebrow. 'I think we all get those from time to time. In fact, I had one here at work only yesterday. We had two late deliveries, not enough staff on again, and that flaming Ryan must've had Weetabix for breakfast or something because he was strutting about the place barking orders like a bargain-basement Musso-bloody-lini.'

I nod and smile while Alan moans but really all I am thinking about is Adele, the bag, and how I am going to get through the morning until I can sort everything out with her.

The next few hours go by so slowly that I keep thinking my watch has stopped but, eventually, the hands creep around until it is nearly the end of my shift. Adele will be in the break room right now getting ready for her shift I am sure, and so even though I'm not supposed to leave the shop floor without permission, I go anyway, two minutes early, and race round to try and catch her.

'Adele!' I call out when I spot her chatting to Briony from the office. 'I need to talk to you. It's important!'

'Easy there, Connor!' she says giving Briony a funny look. 'Whatever it is, I'm sure it's not that urgent.' She leans forward and whispers something into Briony's ear that makes them both laugh, and then she stands up and comes over to me.

'Alright then, Usain, what's the rush?'

I look over at Briony, and then lower my voice. 'Can we go somewhere private to talk please?'

Adele doesn't look happy about this. 'I haven't got time now, I'm just about to start my shift.'

I take a step closer to her and lower my voice even more than before. 'It's about the bag.'

Straight away her face changes, and without looking back at Briony, she takes my elbow and almost pushes me out of the break room and into the hallway.

'What about the bag?' Her voice suddenly sounds cold and mean.

For a minute I'm so worried that I can't find the words to tell her what I've done. 'It's . . . it's . . . not a PlayStation.'

Adele looks confused. 'What's not a PlayStation?'

'In the bag,' I say. 'You said it was a PlayStation for your brother's birthday, but it's not.'

Adele screws up her face angrily and takes a step towards me. 'And how would you know that? Did you look in there?'

'I didn't mean to. I just wanted to see what the box looked like – that's all.'

'You'd better not have touched anything in there or you'll be in big trouble.'

'I didn't,' I say. 'I promise, I didn't! When I saw what was in there, I zipped it shut and put it back where it was.'

'Are you sure you didn't touch it?'

'Yes, I'm sure Adele, really I didn't.'

'Good,' she says. 'Well make sure you—' She stops speaking as the door to the break room opens and Briony comes out.

'No rest for the wicked,' says Briony. 'Got to get back to work, but I'm sure I'll see you both later.'

'Yeah, see you, Briony,' calls Adele cheerily, and we both watch her walk away down the corridor. 'Speak to you soon, hon.'

Adele doesn't talk again until the fire doors at the end of the corridor swing shut and we are alone.

'Not here,' she says firmly. 'I'll come round tonight and we'll talk about it then, okay?'

I nod but don't say anything. I am so confused. First Adele was being lovely to me and now she is being mean and I don't really understand why.

'Good, now, if you don't mind, I've got to go and do my shift,' she says and without even saying goodbye she turns and walks down the corridor to the shop floor, leaving me standing alone outside the break room.

I find it difficult to relax when I get home that afternoon. I feel like the bag upstairs is glowing like it is a radioactive bomb, and all

I want is to get as far away from it as I can. But then later, I check my watch, and see that it is eight o'clock, the end of Adele's shift, and start to get really worried. If she leaves work at five past eight, and then gets on the bus at 8.25, it means I've only got forty-five minutes before she's here and I'm not sure what sort of mood she is going to be in. Is she going to be angry with me? Or might she be nice like she used to be?

Just then there is a sharp knock on the front door. I look at my watch, it is only twenty past eight, far too early for Adele to be here. It must be Marcus, maybe he was passing by and has decided to surprise me. I have to get rid of him before Adele gets here.

Without checking through the spyhole I open the front door but it isn't Marcus standing there, it is Adele. But she is not alone. Standing on either side of her are two young men. They are dressed in black from head to toe and they have their hoods pulled up and the lower half of their faces are covered by scarves. They are both carrying rucksacks like the one under Mum's bed.

I don't like this. I don't like this at all.

'Is it upstairs?' one of the men asks Adele, as he pushes past me.

'Under the bed in the front bedroom,' she says, and she and the other man follow him inside.

'What's going on?' I shout. 'Who are these people, Adele?'

'My friends. They've come to take the bag, and they're going to leave some of their stuff here.'

'But they can't do that. I don't want them to. I just want you to take the bag and go.'

The man standing next to Adele looks at me. 'We don't care what you want. From now on you do what we say when we say it.' Reaching into his jacket he pulls something out just far enough for me to see that he's carrying a knife, and then he tells me to give him my spare set of keys.

I don't want to but I'm scared of getting hurt. Then Adele shouts at me, 'Just do it, you retard! One way or the other we'll get them so you might as well hand them over!'

'I don't understand,' I say to Adele. 'I thought we were friends. Why are you being like this?'

The men laugh, but Adele says nothing. She just stands and holds her hand out for the keys. I give them to her. I don't have a choice. But as soon as they've gone, with my heart racing and my hands shaking, I bolt the door and put the security chain on. And as I sit sobbing on the sofa I realise that for the first time ever I don't feel safe in Hope Street.

Bernie: June 2000

'Mind, out the way, love!'

Bernie turned to look at the man who had just barged into her on the crowded platform at Derby station but no matter how hard she tried she felt as if she couldn't really see him. He was just a blur, a shape, an indistinct object in her field of vision, as was everyone else around her, such was her current state of mind.

Two women stood up from one of the benches overlooking the platform and Bernie sank down onto the empty seat. She closed her eyes, squeezing them tightly shut, hoping beyond hope that sleep would take her but she knew it never would. She had never in her life been so tired, so bone-achingly, brain-scramblingly tired. So tired that she couldn't remember what day it was let alone the hour.

It wasn't Connor's fault that he couldn't sleep. It was just the way his little six-year-old brain was wired. To him, midnight was just like midday, and whenever she tried to put him to bed he would simply get up and come into her room demanding that she play with him. She'd hoped it would get better once he started school and was tired out by the day's activities, but if anything it got worse. Being around all those other children, being asked to follow rules he didn't understand, seemed to have sent him into a tailspin, so much so that if either of them got an hour a night, they were lucky. It wouldn't have been so bad had Bernie been at least able to sleep when he was out at school, but between her job at the minimarket, shifts at the launderette and keeping on top of the housework there wasn't a spare minute in the day.

Still, even if by some miracle Connor began to sleep through, Bernie knew that there were more than enough problems rolling around her head to keep her awake for years, the biggest of which was the loan she had taken from Del who occasionally came into the launderette. Everybody had told her that he was a gangster, everybody had told her not to have anything to do with him, and yet when money had been so tight that some evenings she would sit in the darkness unable to afford to put coins in the meter, she felt she'd had nowhere else to turn. Del had given her the money, and had made it seem like a friendly enough arrangement, and so when Christmas had come around she'd borrowed a bit more to buy Connor's presents.

But then in the new year a man she hadn't recognised had come to their door and told her that he had bought her debt from Del, and she now owed the money she'd borrowed to him plus interest. Much as she'd tried her best to keep pace with the repayments collected every Friday night, the interest was ballooning at such a rate that she couldn't hope to ever get it down. The other week, in lieu of payments, he'd taken the TV even though it was rented, and she wasn't sure what else there was left to give him. She'd shuddered to think what the consequences might be, and it had been then that she'd made her decision.

Calling on Bev, she'd asked her friend if she would have Connor overnight, and much to her relief Bev had agreed without even asking where she was going. As a single mum too, she understood the pressures of trying to hold everything together on your own, and for this Bernie was grateful. The following afternoon having packed Connor's bag with pyjamas, his favourite train, *The A–Z of Derby* he was obsessed with, his toothbrush, night-time pull-ups, spare pants and a fresh change of clothes for the morning, she had taken him across the road.

'You'll be alright with us, won't you, little man?' Bev had said but Connor, as was his manner, hadn't responded; instead he'd continued swinging on his mother as though she were a climbing frame.

It was only after Bev had summoned her son, Marcus, that Connor had stopped what he was doing, looked up and smiled at the gangly young boy who appeared in the hallway holding a huge battered bright yellow Tonka truck. Connor's eyes had widened in delight and releasing Bernie's legs he had moved to take the truck, but before he could escape Bernie grabbed his hand, bent down and gave him a huge hug, kissing him fiercely on the cheek until he squirmed out of her grasp.

'Love you, baby!' she'd called after him as he gratefully received the truck from Marcus. 'Be a good boy for Aunty Bev please and don't give her any trouble, okay?'

Connor hadn't replied; instead, with Marcus following after him, he'd pushed the truck down the hallway making loud 'Vroooom! Vroooom!' noises at the top of his lungs and then disappeared into the kitchen.

For a moment Bernie had stood not saying anything at all, watching the empty space where her son had been, until Bev reached out a hand and touched her gently on the arm.

'He'll be fine,' she'd promised and Bernie hadn't doubted it. She had to, if she was going to go through with what she intended to do. Yes, Connor would be safe here, she'd told herself, Bev and her kids were always so lovely and patient with him. He could be happy with them. Happier than he ever would be with her.

Bev looked at her friend thoughtfully. 'Is everything okay?'

'Yes, fine,' she replied, 'nothing a little sleep won't solve. Anyway, I'd better be getting off.'

Bev smiled. 'You go home and go straight to bed. Don't worry about Connor and I'll see you when you're ready tomorrow.'

Bernie said nothing; instead, she'd hugged her friend tightly, as if this was their last goodbye, and then without looking back had left and caught the bus to Derby station before climbing the stairs to platform two where she now found herself.

An announcement came over the Tannoy: 'The fast train now approaching platform two does not stop here: please stand well back from the edge of the platform.'

This was it. The moment she had been waiting for. As her pulse quickened, she pressed her hand onto her jacket pocket, feeling not only her own heartbeat but also the outline of the envelope within. She got to her feet, weaving her way through the throng until she was close to the very edge of the platform.

She looked down the line to the oncoming train hurtling towards the station, the scraping sound of the wheels getting louder and louder with each passing moment. She drew a deep breath, shut her eyes, quietly summoning the mental and physical strength that would be required to do what needed to be done, and then took a half step forward only to feel someone suddenly grab at her arm. She turned to see a white-haired elderly lady, wearing a navy-blue headscarf and pale green rain mac standing next to her.

'Oh, I'm so sorry, my dear,' she said. 'I think I must have come over a bit funny there. Do you mind if I hold on to your arm? I think I need to sit down.'

Before Bernie could reply, the old lady had steered them both away from the platform edge, through the crowd, past an empty bench and into the station café. Removing a crisp ten-pound note from a purse in her handbag she handed it to Bernie. 'Get us two teas and a couple of packets of biscuits please, dear. Custard creams ideally for me, but if not anything but those horrible Bourbon things. They don't agree with me.'

Puzzled by her own inability to refuse this stranger's requests, Bernie went and joined the short queue at the counter, wondering what on earth had just happened. She looked down at her own hand holding the woman's money and saw that it was shaking. Maybe a cup of tea, a biscuit and a sit-down was just what she needed.

'Oh, I do like a good brew,' said the old lady, as Bernie returned to the table and set down her tray laden with two cups of tea, two packets of custard creams and the woman's change. 'Come on then, love,' she commanded, as Bernie remained standing, 'sit down. You're making me nervous!'

As Bernie took a seat, the woman placed a cup of tea in front of her, and tucked a packet of the biscuits on the saucer, did the same for herself, then after moving the tray aside she held out her hand.

'The name's Jean, Jean Walker. Pleased to meet you . . . ?'

Bernie cleared her throat. 'I'm . . . I'm . . . Bernie, Bernie McLaughlin.'

The woman smiled. 'Oh, what a lovely accent and what a lovely name! And both so musical! So much better than plain old Jean Walker! I never liked it myself, too stern-sounding. Jean Walker is the name of your least favourite teacher at school, the one who's a real dragon. Still, I've always done my best not to live up to it!' She laughed, and then gestured to Bernie's untouched tea. 'Come on then, girl, drink up – don't let it go cold.'

As Bernie sipped on her tea the woman chatted away as though the two were old friends. She told her how she'd lived in Derby all her life, and before she retired, she had worked as a clerk at Derby Magistrates' Court. She'd revealed that while she'd been proposed to twice she'd never been married and had instead dedicated much of her life to looking after a long line of dogs rescued from her local animal shelter. 'You can't go far wrong with a dog,' she said between mouthfuls of custard cream. 'They're loyal, dependable and always pleased to see you when you come home. They've kept me going through some difficult times, I can tell you.' At this the woman looked at Bernie pointedly and said, 'Life's hard. We all need some help sometimes, don't we, dear?'

Bernie said nothing, she just stared down at her cup as tear after tear rolled down her face and onto the table. Jean reached out a hand, and placed it over one of Bernie's saying, 'It's okay, you let it out, let it all out.'

And there, in that half-empty station café Bernie told this stranger everything, about Connor, her exhaustion, her debts and how she'd come to the conclusion that she just couldn't carry on anymore.

'I've made such a mess of everything,' she said finally. 'And I just can't see a way out.'

'There's always a way out,' said Jean firmly. 'Always. You just have to find it, that's all, but I promise you it's there.'

When Jean had suggested that Bernie should come and have a spot of lunch with her back at her house, Bernie couldn't think of a reason to say no. And so, once they had finished their tea, they'd left the café and at Jean's insistence climbed into the back of a black cab and made their way over to her tiny cottage on the edge of the village of Duffield. After a meal of bread and soup, Jean had suggested that Bernie go for a lie-down in the spare bedroom, and she had been so tired, so utterly exhausted that she didn't put up a shred of resistance.

When she woke, Jean revealed that Bernie had been asleep for twenty-hours straight. She could hardly believe it, and she was so apologetic that she immediately began to gather her things to leave, but her new friend would hear none of it. 'A good bath, and another night's sleep, and you might be ready. But go now, and I won't sleep for worrying about you.'

Bernie's thoughts flashed to Connor and Bev. What would they be thinking? How would she ever make it up to them?

'They'll be fine,' said Jean, as if reading Bernie's thoughts. 'And if you give yourself one more day, you will be too.'

And though it felt selfish, though it felt wrong, Bernie did exactly as Jean suggested but after breakfast the following morning, she knew she was ready to go back home.

'I don't know how I'll ever thank you,' said Bernie, as they waited on the doorstep for the arrival of the taxi to take her home.

'There's no need,' Jean replied. 'The only thanks I want, the only thanks I need is knowing that you'll never sink that low again without asking for help. And you will, won't you?'

Bernie nodded. 'I promise,' she replied and as she gave Jean a hug, she heard the sound of a diesel engine followed by the beep of a car horn heralding the arrival of the taxi.

It wasn't until she was halfway across the city that Bernie recalled the envelope in her inside jacket pocket, but when she patted it as she had done before it felt so different that she was compelled to reach inside and take it out. The envelope, which had been sealed, was now open, and the letter to Bev and Connor that she had penned was gone. In its place was a bundle of twenty-pound notes, more money than Bernie had ever seen in her life, along with a note that read, *Money you can replace, people you can't. With love, Jean.*

19

Lila

As I sit in a long line of traffic on my way over to meet Connor and Marcus for our curry, I really begin to wish I'd made my excuses earlier and cancelled. The fact of the matter is I'm just not in the right mood and haven't been since I got knocked back for the job at *The Correspondent*. 'It's their loss,' Mum had comforted when I'd called last night to tell her the news. 'You're great at what you do – you know that. Something even better will turn up when it's the right time. I just know it.'

Even though I could've scripted her response right down to her homespun platitude about fate, it was one hundred and ten per cent exactly what I needed to hear, having had my ego shattered once again. It's one thing to have been rejected unceremoniously by my long-standing boyfriend, but another altogether to be reject-ed professionally, especially when until now I'd actually believed that I'd had a good shot at this job.

Like Mum, Niamh had tried to console me but in her own unique way assuring me I was a brilliant journalist and that 'the job would've been handed to some Oxbridge type whose dad was friends with the editor'. Even though I hadn't got that vibe from the people I'd met at *The Correspondent*, it did however provide a modicum of comfort. I'd even contemplated pitching a piece to one of the other broadsheets about my experience and how the old school tie network was still very much alive and kicking but to be honest my heart just wasn't in it. While admittedly I'd been in two minds about going for the interview in the first place, as I've been rejected the one thing I'm certain of is how much I wanted that job. And while I know there will be other jobs, other opportunities, on top of everything else going on in my life this just feels like the ultimate slap in the face.

Eventually, the traffic starts moving and a short while later I arrive at my destination, The Mazaydar Dynasty, a tiny balti house tucked away on a side street on the outskirts of the city centre. Though thanks to the traffic I'm ten minutes late, there's no sign of Connor and Marcus. A friendly waiter shows me to our table anyway and while I'm waiting I order a Coke. It arrives just as I'm about to give in to temptation and check Gabe and Barnaby's Instagram when I look up to see Marcus striding towards me. To my surprise he's alone.

'Sorry I'm late,' he says as I stand up to greet him. 'I was on my way to pick up Connor when he called to say he wasn't feeling well. It was too late to cancel so I came anyway. Hope that's okay?'

'Of course,' I say, even though I can't help thinking that now it's just the two of us, it'll be a bit weird, like we're on a date or something. 'I just hope he's alright. Is it a bug or something?'

'I've no idea. I asked him if he needed anything but he said he was just going to get an early night. I think I'll swing by after work tomorrow and see how he is.'

'Well, tell him I said hi and get well soon, won't you?'

While Marcus orders a lager, I scan the menu, suddenly ravenous. I'd worked through my lunch break interviewing one of Bernie's old colleagues from the minimart and had only survived the afternoon thanks to a packet of crisps I found in my drawer and a slice of Patrick's birthday cake.

'I've never been here before,' I say as the waiter leaves our table. 'It's a bit off the beaten track. How did you ever stumble across it?'

'I used to do the original owner's car,' Marcus explains, 'and then he offered me and the boys from the garage a discount if we ever fancied a meal and so we had the works Christmas do here and it's been a firm favourite ever since. The old man's retired now and it's his son in charge but the food is still easily the best in the city.' He stops and laughs. 'And it's Connor's favourite restaurant because he reckons they do the best egg and chips.'

I give Marcus a funny look. 'All this amazing food and he just orders egg and chips?'

'Say what you like about Connor,' he replies with a smile, 'but he definitely knows what he likes and he's not afraid to stick with it.'

Marcus's drink arrives and after getting the lowdown from him on the best dishes on the menu we order, and as the waiter leaves our table it strikes me again that this feels a lot like a date, all the more so when I glance around the now busy restaurant packed with couples enjoying a romantic evening out.

I turn back to Marcus and see that he's grinning. 'I know, I know,' he says as if reading my mind, 'I had to check for a minute that it wasn't February 14th. I swear on my life it's not normally like this; it's usually just groups of mates coming for a quick bite after work.'

I can't help but laugh. 'Don't worry about it,' I say wanting to reassure him. 'Maybe they've taken out some advertising on Tinder: Fifty per cent off every meal for any match you take on a date!'

Marcus laughs again. 'Yeah, I can see that or even free poppadoms if you come back on your second date. Whatever they're doing it's certainly working. I've never seen it this busy on a weeknight.'

Just then our waiter brings over a platter of poppadoms and chutneys, and because of Marcus's joke we both laugh, and just like that whatever awkwardness there might have been disappears instantly. As we tuck in to the food Marcus asks about my day and I fill him in about the protest in Allestree over the proposed closure of the swimming baths there and how I'd had to follow up on a rumour that Tom Cruise had been spotted viewing a stately home up for sale in Ashbourne.

'Wow, Tom Cruise in Derby?' says Marcus loading a spoonful of aubergine chutney onto a poppadom. 'Does he need his car servicing, do you know?'

'I hate to shatter your dreams,' I reply, 'but it turns out it was a case of mistaken identity or more likely wishful thinking. In the end it was just some boring tech millionaire, wanting to keep his identity a secret while he looked for a weekend place in the country.'

In return Marcus makes me laugh with an anecdote of his own about a woman who'd stormed into his garage that morning threatening to sue him over her car breaking down after he claimed to have fixed it. 'Honestly, she was absolutely rabid, banging on about how I was a rip-off merchant and how she was going to take me to court and ruin me.'

'And so, what did you do?'

'Well, I had my suspicions but I thought under the circumstances I ought to double-check, so I looked her up on the system and sure enough the last time she'd brought her car in was two years ago. Turns out she'd actually had the work done at a rival company two miles down the road.' He stops and laughs. 'You should've seen her face. She went fifteen different shades of purple when she realised what she'd done and I think if the earth had opened up and swallowed her whole she would've been grateful.'

By the time our main courses arrive we've covered subjects as diverse as prizes we'd been awarded at primary school (Marcus a fake gold medal for a project about climate change, me a small plastic trophy for coming second in the long jump) and the chances of Derby County ever making a return to the Premiership.

'So,' begins Marcus once we've shared out some of the food, 'where do you usually go, when you're looking for a big night out in Derby?'

I reel off the names of a couple of places I've been with Niamh, but then to my surprise I conclude with the words: 'But to be honest I used to spend a lot of my weekends going down to London.'

'What's in London?'

'My boyfriend . . . well ex-boyfriend now.'

This, I realise is the first time I've mentioned Gabe to him, not that I've been keeping it a secret but rather it just hasn't come up. Now it has I feel incredibly self-conscious.

He nods thoughtfully. 'So, you've been in the wars have you?

I smile awkwardly. 'Just a bit.'

'Nice to meet a fellow survivor,' he says putting his fork down and holding out his hand for me to shake.

'You too? What happened?'

'In a nutshell, we were together five years, then a year ago she did the dirty on me with one of her exes, and to rub salt into the wound once she'd packed her bags and left, I discovered she'd taken a bunch of loans out in my name leaving me in thousands of pounds' worth of debt.'

'What a cow!'

Marcus laughs. 'You're not wrong there. But what are you going to do? It'll all be paid off soon enough.'

'What a nightmare! I bet it's really put you off getting back out there.'

'I was on the apps for a while,' he admits, 'but to be honest they're not my thing.'

'Too many nutters?'

'I don't know, I find it all just a bit . . . you know . . . clinical . . . a bit soulless.'

I take a sip of my drink. 'My friend talked me into signing up to one the other day while we were out and a little bit the worse for wear.'

'And?'

'Well, put it this way, I deleted it as soon as I got home. I think I must be like you. I like to get to know people . . . organically.'

Marcus laughs. 'Like vegetables?'

'If only I could afford organic veg! Those bags of bargain wonky carrots and dodgy potatoes are more my thing. I suppose what I'm saying is I just want to meet someone the old-fashioned way.'

'You mean after downing half a dozen vodkas and getting off with some bloke in a dodgy nightclub?'

'Exactly that. I don't want to have to flirt with someone over text. I spend all day every day writing; the last thing I want is to have to write again in order to pull some guy too.'

'Maybe you don't have to,' says Marcus and for a moment I'm confused by his response, but then the owner comes over to check everything is okay with our meals and by the time he's gone, I convince myself that I must have imagined it.

For the rest of the evening we chat like old friends, about anything and everything until finally, I look up to see that the once full restaurant is now empty and the staff all clearly want to go home.

'We should ask for the bill,' I say, and when it arrives – despite my protests – Marcus insists on paying.

'Like I said, this is a thank you from me and Connor for everything you've been doing. You really are amazing agreeing to help him like this. I can't imagine it's easy fitting it in with everything else you've got to do.'

'It's fine,' I say, 'really it is. I like Connor, and I feel like he's been let down a lot in his life, and so if I can do something to help then I'll gladly do it.'

On the way out we thank the staff, and standing outside the restaurant prepare to part ways.

'Well, thanks for a lovely evening.'

'My pleasure. I've had a really good time.' He pauses and then gives me a look that I can't quite decipher.

'What?' I put my hand to my mouth. 'Have I got something in my teeth?'

Marcus shakes his head and then adds mysteriously, 'I meant it you know.'

I look at him confused. 'Meant what?'

He gives me that look again and leans in towards me, head tilted, eyes closed and gently kisses me.

Slightly taken aback, I don't return the kiss, instead I stand perfectly still for a moment, my head teeming with questions, chief of which is how exactly I feel about this latest turn of events.

'Sorry,' says Marcus stepping back and looking suddenly mortified. 'I shouldn't have done that. I've made things weird, haven't I?'

'No, you haven't at all. It's just . . . I don't know, that . . . it's just a little bit strange.'

He pulls a face. 'Was it a bad kiss then? I'm sorry, it's been a while.'

I grin. 'No, the kiss was great, ten out of ten, no notes whatsoever. It's just that . . . I haven't kissed anyone but my ex in five years.'

'When you put it that way,' says Marcus, 'I can see how you might feel a bit weird.'

'But that's just the thing,' I tell him. 'It was weird, but not in like a bad way, it's just different that's all. It's just taken me a bit by surprise.'

'Maybe it's too soon,' he says taking a step back. 'Maybe you need a bit more time to get your head around things.'

'Oh, it's definitely not that,' I say reaching out a hand and pulling him towards me until his face is mere millimetres from my own. 'I think what I probably need, is just a bit more practice.'

20

Connor

There is someone at the door.

But I do not answer it.

Yes, they've got keys now but they cannot get in.

The door is latched and the security chain is on.

They cannot get me.

And if I just stay where I am upstairs in the bathroom with the door locked, maybe they will go away and leave me alone.

I think back to the night Adele and her friends took my keys. I didn't sleep that night; I couldn't. Every time I thought about closing my eyes I kept seeing the knife, the men, and Adele's mean face. Instead, I stayed awake, so angry with myself for trusting Adele that I hit myself with my fists and banged my head against my bedroom wall. How could I have been so stupid? Alan had warned me not to have anything to do with Adele but I didn't listen. Marcus had told me that people didn't change but I thought I knew better.

When morning came I called in sick at work. And when Marcus called to remind me about our night out with Lila I lied and told him I wasn't feeling well and spent the whole evening hiding in my bedroom, with a chair up against the door, scared that Adele and her friends might come back.

They didn't come then but they're here now and I'm so frightened I don't know what to do.

Suddenly, my phone rings, and I jump at the sound of it. I look at the screen and see that it's Marcus.

I answer the call.

'Connor, are you okay mate? Me and Lila have come to see how you're doing but the front door's locked. I've been knocking for ages. Couldn't you hear me?'

I let out a sigh. It's not Adele and her friends.

I go downstairs to let them in. But I can't let them stay for long. What if Adele and her friends come back while they're here?

'Alright, mate,' says Marcus. 'How are you feeling today – any better?'

I don't know what to say. It's much harder to lie to a friend face to face than it is over text.

'I'm not too bad thanks,' I say.

'Are you sure?' asks Lila. 'You look a bit pale.' She puts a hand on my forehead like Mum used to do to check if I've got a temperature. 'Well, you're not too warm so that's a good sign. Have you got any pain?'

I shake my head. 'I'm fine, really, I'm fine. You don't need to worry. You can go now.'

Marcus laughs. 'We've only just got here, mate. How about I go out and get us some fish and chips and keep you company for a while?'

I shake my head. 'You can't stay here. Please, you both need to go.'

Marcus and Lila both look at each other and then at me.

'Connor, what's going on?' asks Marcus. 'Has something happened? Is it those boys again, the ones from the bus?'

'No, I'm fine,' I say.

'No, you're not,' says Lila. 'Please, tell us what's wrong, Connor.'

'There's nothing wrong.' I can't help myself, I look up at the ceiling, thinking about the bags and what a mess I'm in.

Marcus looks at me funny. 'Connor, is there someone here, someone upstairs?' Before I can reply he moves towards the door and I feel sick with nerves.

'Please don't go up there, Marcus! Please don't! I don't want them to hurt you!'

He rushes out of the room and I chase after him but Lila catches up with me in the back room and stops me. 'Connor, who's upstairs? Who said they'd hurt us?'

'I can't . . . I can't tell you . . . he . . . he had a knife.'

Lila's eyes widen in shock and she calls up the stairs. 'Marcus! Are you okay? Is everything alright? Connor's just said something about someone with a knife!'

There is a horrible long moment of silence and then Marcus calls out, 'I'm fine, I'm coming down,' and then he comes downstairs and into the room carrying the two black rucksacks that had been under Mum's bed.

'What's going on?' asks Lila. 'What's in those?'

Marcus doesn't say anything; instead he just drops one of the bags onto the floor at my feet then opens the zip of the second one and shows it to Lila. Inside are rolled-up banknotes, and lots of little clear plastic bags, some with tablets inside and others white powder.

'It's not mine! It's not mine,' I try to explain. 'They're not my bags.'

Marcus looks at me. 'Connor, what's going on?'

I feel like I have no choice. I've never seen Marcus this serious before. 'They belong to . . . to . . . my friend Adele.'

'Your friend? What friend? Where from?'

I feel like my head is all of a jumble. There is so much to say but I'm not sure how to say it. I take lots of deep breaths, then tell them everything about Adele, about how she used to be mean to me at school, about believing that she'd changed, that she was my friend, and how I've found out just how wrong I'd been.

Marcus explodes in anger. 'They threatened you with a knife? Tell me where this bitch lives! I mean it, Connor, tell me where she lives right now!'

I start to cry. This is all too much. I don't want Marcus to get hurt or to hurt anyone. I just want it all to go away, for life to go back to how it was before this all started.

'Marcus!' snaps Lila, putting her arm around me. 'Can't you see you're scaring him? I know you're angry, I'm angry too, but we need to stay calm and think about what's best for Connor.'

'You're right,' he says letting out a big sigh. 'I'm sorry, mate, I didn't mean to shout. How about I get us all a cup of tea?'

As soon as Marcus leaves the room, I feel a lot calmer, as if he's taken all the worry of the past few minutes with him into the kitchen. Lila takes me back into the front room and we sit down on the sofa, her arm around me, my head resting on her shoulder. I close my eyes, and imagine that it isn't Lila next to me but Mum, and it makes me feel much calmer.

'Here we go,' says Marcus a bit later when he comes back into the room carrying a tray of tea and biscuits. He hands out the drinks and then sits down in the armchair. 'Listen, Connor, I'm sorry about before.'

'It's okay,' I tell him. 'I know it was just because you were worried about me.'

'I want you to know none of this is your fault, okay, none of it,' says Marcus. 'And you don't have to worry about anything. We'll get this sorted, I promise you.'

'What we need is a plan,' says Lila, 'and the only one I can think of is to call the police and let them deal with it all.'

I shake my head. I don't want the police to know. I don't want Adele and her friends to be angry with me. I just want it to all be over and I am about to say this when Marcus sits forward in his chair.

'Okay, say we do that, say we call the police and they arrest the three of them, what then?'

'How do you mean?' asks Lila. 'They'll be in custody, won't they?'

'Maybe,' says Marcus, 'then again maybe not. I mean, what if they get bail and are back on the streets in a few days? Or what if their mates catch wind that it's because of Connor their stash and money is in police hands? What then? The thing is I grew up around here, and I know how people like this lot operate. If we go to the police they'll come after Connor, and in a place like Hope Street who's going to stop them?'

Lila sighs. 'So, what do we do?'

'Give them their stuff back,' says Marcus. 'And hope once we've done that, they'll leave Connor alone.'

I sleep better that night because Marcus and Lila stay at my house, taking it in turns to keep watch from Mum's bedroom in case Adele and the boys came back. But they don't and when I wake up the following morning I come downstairs to find them talking in the living room.

'Morning, Connor,' says Lila. 'Did you sleep well?'

'Yes, thank you,' I reply, and then because it is very much on my mind I ask, 'Are we still going through with the plan?'

Marcus and Lila look at each other and then me, and then they nod.

'You don't have to come if you don't want to, mate,' says Marcus. 'But yes, it has to be done.'

I head back upstairs and get ready, and then Marcus, Lila and I drive to the retail park and wait for Adele to arrive to start her shift.

'But what if I got it wrong and she's not working today?' I ask after we've been waiting for nearly twenty minutes. 'Sometimes people swap shifts at the last minute or she could call in sick.'

'Then we'll just have to keep coming back until she is in,' says Marcus checking the clock on his dashboard.

My stomach feels like it's scrunching up and I want to be sick. 'But what if the boys with the knives are with her?'

'Then we'll deal with it,' says Marcus, and he glances down at the baseball bat leaning up against his armrest and the sight of this makes me feel even more sick. 'Don't worry, let's just sit tight for now and see what happens.'

Just then I look up at Marcus's rear-view mirror and see Adele coming slowly down the path towards the staff entrance, not hurrying even though she's already five minutes late.

'It's her,' I say, my heart racing as both Marcus and Lila look over their shoulders to see her better.

'She doesn't look like much of a drug dealer,' says Lila. 'Just shows how deceiving looks can be.'

'She could be wearing a ball gown and a tiara for all I care,' says Marcus grabbing one of the bags and reaching for the car door handle. 'I just want her to leave Connor alone.'

As Marcus and Lila get out of the car, I'm not sure what to do. Part of me is scared of seeing Adele again and wants to stay in the car, but part of me doesn't want my friends to deal with this on their own. I know I have to get out. In the end, I take one deep breath and then another and then get out of the car too.

At first Adele is too busy looking at something on her phone to notice us but then Marcus throws one of the bags down on the ground in front of her and she stops suddenly.

'Don't bother running,' he says quietly. 'There's no way we won't catch you.'

She looks at Marcus, then at me, and then at Lila and then takes out her earbuds and shoves them deep into her jacket pocket.

'Whatever he says he's lying,' she says staring at me. 'He's not right in the head. He's always making up stories.'

'Let me tell you how this is going to go,' says Marcus ignoring her. 'You're going to take these bags back to whichever hole you crawled out from right now, and you're not going to go near Connor again, got it?'

'You think I'm scared of you?' says Adele nastily. 'I make one call, and you're a dead man.'

'Possibly,' says Marcus. 'But I can make a call too, a call that you and all your scummy mates could well end up regretting. So, what's it going to be? The choice is yours.'

'And just to help you make your decision,' says Lila, taking a step towards Adele, 'I think you ought to know that I'm a journalist on *The Echo*. And if anything, I mean anything at all happens to either of my friends here, I swear I'll slap your face, and the faces of all your . . . colleagues, all over the front cover of the paper. And by the time I'm finished with you, everyone will know who you are, where you live and every last filthy thing you've been up to. And that's a promise.'

Adele gives us all a really horrible look as if she wants to scratch our eyes out with those long red nails of hers but I can also see that she is scared, really scared, perhaps even more scared than me.

'Well?' shouts Marcus.

Adele steps forward and picks up the bags. 'You're going to pay for this.'

'I'm not sure we are,' says Lila and she takes out her phone and snaps a picture of Adele holding the bags. 'Just so you know, not only have we photographed the contents of the bags – including the handy list of names and numbers you left in there – but we've also got footage from the hidden CCTV camera installed at Connor's house of everything you said and did. Like I said, this doesn't have to be a police matter, but it can be, if that's the way you want to play it.'

Adele doesn't speak; instead she turns around and starts to walk away until Marcus calls after her.

'Connor's keys!'

She stops and turns around. 'I haven't got them. They're at home.'

Marcus pulls out his phone. 'Then I'm guessing I'll just have to call the police and see if they can get them for me.'

Adele scowls, but putting down the bags she jams her hand into her jacket pocket, takes out my spare keys and throws them on the ground in front of Marcus.

'You need to pick those up,' says Marcus. 'And you need to hand them to me.'

For a minute I get worried because I don't think she'll do it but then she bends down, picks them up and gives them to him.

'Thank you,' he says, closing his hand around them. 'Now off you go, make sure to quit DIY-Depot today—Connor never wants to see your face again—and remember everything we've told you, because I promise you, we won't be repeating ourselves.'

That night, I stay at Marcus's flat. I can't even think about going back to Hope Street yet, I'm just too scared. What if Adele and the boys come back to get me and Marcus and Lila aren't around to stop them? What if they come in the middle of the night while I'm sleeping and threaten me with knives? It's all just so horrible. It's like my home isn't my home anymore and I really don't know what I'm going to do.

21

Lila

'Look at you, threatening drug dealers like some sort of knock-off Liam Neeson!' says Niamh, the following day at work as we sit at our desks. She'd been out on a job when I'd returned to the office yesterday and so hadn't heard about my role in confronting that awful woman who had terrorised Connor.

'I know,' I reply. 'I couldn't believe it when I heard myself talking about plastering her and her mates' mugs across the front page of *The Echo*. As if Peter would ever have gone for that.'

Niamh laughs. 'I don't know, I could actually imagine Peter going for a bit of good old-fashioned naming and shaming. Do you remember the time those kids were causing havoc in his mum's road? It was all we could do to stop him from getting us to do a six-page colour pull-out on the little wasters and their hopeless parents. Still, your threat worked, didn't it? And it sounds like they won't be bothering Connor again in a hurry. Poor lad, how is he now?'

'Not great,' I reply. 'He was really shaken by it all, so much so that he stayed at Marcus's last night, and as it stands, I really can't imagine him wanting to go back home anytime soon.'

Niamh gives me a searching look. 'You really care about him, don't you? This isn't just about the story anymore, is it?'

Part of me wants to deny this, to project some sort of air of professionalism, but the truth is she's right. Connor isn't just part of a story I'm writing anymore, he's someone I care about a great deal. And as for Marcus . . . well, that's a whole other story.

Niamh looks at me quizzically. 'What's that look on your face about? There's something else isn't there? Something you're not telling me.'

I know from experience that once Niamh has caught a whiff of a story she won't let go until she knows everything.

'Come on,' she encourages, 'you know I'm going to get it out of you sooner or later, so you might as well get it over with.'

'It's about Marcus,' I say, and even though Lewis is out on a job for the morning, instinctively I lower my voice.

Niamh raises an eyebrow. 'Yeah, the dishy mechanic – what about him?'

My silence speaks volumes, so much so that Niamh's mouth falls open in shock. 'You and Marcus?'

'We kissed.'

Niamh looks properly scandalised. 'No! When?'

'The other night when the three of us were supposed to be going out for a meal. Marcus came alone because Connor said he was ill – which, now of course I know wasn't true – and so the two of us spent the evening together and ended up having a really nice time—'

'I bet you did!'

I roll my eyes. 'No, not like that. Well, it sort of was like that but not really. It was just a lovely evening, which ended with a very nice kiss. And we were on our way to a second date or really, I suppose a proper first date when we dropped in to see how Connor was and you know the rest.'

'And so how have you left things?'

I shrug. 'How could we leave things? Connor needed help; I needed to get back here. There just wasn't time to talk about anything else.'

'But there's time now isn't there? What's stopping you from messaging him and booking in another date?'

'Well, he's got a lot on his plate with Connor and everything, maybe now's not the right time.'

Niamh pulls a face. 'The right time? What are you on about? You're single . . . I take it he's single too. What are you waiting for? Don't tell me this is about Gabe.'

Again, my silence does the talking for me.

'Urgh, I can't tell you how much I can't stand that man!' she says. 'He cheated on you. Why are you even giving him a second thought? You're not still hoping you'll get back together, are you?'

'No, of course not,' I say. 'It's just that . . . I don't know. You know how when something new starts you just want things to go well and when they do, it's great, you take it as a sign that it's meant to be. But when things don't go right, like last night—'

'—it leaves you wondering if it's a sign that it's doomed from the start,' interrupts Niamh finishing off my thought.

'I just wanted things to go smoothly, that's all, and as it hasn't it's given me way too much time to get all up in my head. You know, all the usual thoughts: am I rushing into this? Am I really ready for something new? Do I like him more than he likes me? Is this all going to end disastrously and put me off relationships for life? You know the kind of thing.'

'Of course, I do,' says Niamh. 'No one can conjure up more reasons not to go on a second date than me! How about that time I talked myself out of seeing that really great bloke who had that gorgeous Labrador? No second date because I was worried about how sad I'd be when the dog eventually passed away. It's all madness! So, don't listen to any of it.'

I sigh heavily. 'I suppose you're right, but the fact is, he hasn't messaged me so maybe he's thinking the same crazy doom-laden thoughts as—'

Just then, my phone pings. I pick it up and check the screen and laughing show it to Niamh.

'Talk about signs!' she says with a grin. 'Go on then, open it.'

I read the message and can't help but smile. 'He's wants to know if I'm free tonight for "a second go at our second date or a first go at a first date".'

Niamh laughs. 'Top messaging banter. I like it, and I like him. Tell him you'll book a table at The Alvaston for tonight. A Bumble date took me there the other week and it's dead cool and really romantic too.'

'I don't remember you telling me you had a Bumble date recently. How did it go?'

Niamh sighs. 'Not great – that's why I didn't tell you about it. You know, you meet those people now and again who have absolutely no sense of humour? Well he could've been their king. Still, the food and the décor at The Alvaston were amazing, and even a night with Humourless Hugh wasn't enough to stop me having a starter and ordering pudding too. Anyway, stop playing for time, I'll go and make us a coffee while you message Marcus straight back.'

And so that's what I do. I tell him about Niamh's restaurant recommendation, and he messages back to say that sounds great and so I book a table for eight, and spend the rest of the day trying my best not to throw up from nerves.

After work I head straight home and spend the next hour scrubbing and preening myself in preparation for my date before trying to pick an outfit. I try on virtually everything in my wardrobe before settling on a hot pink tailored trouser suit I'd last worn to the wedding of one of Gabe's work friends teamed with a new pair of silver heels I'd ordered months ago but haven't had the opportunity to wear yet. Though I say so myself, as I check myself out in the mirror, I have to say that with the exception of my hair – which of course is one hundred per cent refusing to do anything I want it to – I look amazing.

Determined that Marcus should set eyes on me sitting at the bar looking sophisticated while sipping on a French Martini I order an Uber to get me into town well before our meeting time. For some reason, however, no driver on earth wants to accept a trip from my flat to the restaurant and so in the end, like some sort of Luddite, I have to call my local cab firm and they of course take the best part of half an hour to arrive. By the time I get to the restaurant I'm more sweaty and flustered than sexy and sophisticated.

'You look amazing,' says Marcus, waving aside all my apologies for being late.

'Thank you,' I reply, wondering how long I can leave it before I can make my excuses and escape to the ladies' to repair some of the damage the rush over here had wreaked. For the first time I look properly at Marcus, and almost gasp at how handsome he looks in a fitted pale blue suit.

'And you look great too,' I say trying my best to temper the en-thusiasm in my observation before quickly picking up the drinks menu to give myself something else to focus on.

Once I've ordered a drink and the initial awkwardness has worn off, we have the absolute best evening together. We of course talk about Connor and how worried we are about him, but then we're shown to our table and the conversation naturally moves on to lighter topics and we find ourselves gabbing non-stop, so much so that the waiter has to come back three times to get our food order because we keep forgetting to look at the menu.

Niamh was right about this place – it's a perfect first-date lo-cation. The lighting is low, which makes it feel cosy and intimate, and though nearly every table is occupied, the music, some sort of ambient electronic thing, makes me feel like I might be in Ibiza not downtown Derby. To top it all the food is so spectacular I have to resist the urge to take photos of every dish.

Though we order a bottle of wine, and even share a dessert, the evening is over all too soon. As the waiter arrives with the bill Marcus insists on paying again but I refuse his kind offer and put down my card instead, telling myself that nights like these are exactly what overdrafts were made for.

Thankfully, given the heels I'm wearing, we both agree it's probably a bit late to be going on somewhere else and so we decide to share a ride home.

Again, our conversation flows so naturally, so effortlessly, that neither of us pays any attention at all to where we are as we cross the city and so it's something of a surprise mixed with a heavy dose of disappointment when the car comes to a halt and I look out of the window to see we've arrived at my flat.

'Wow, that was quick,' says Marcus, his voice betraying his own regret that the night is coming to a close. 'I had a really, really good time.'

'Me too,' I reply, and I fall silent. With all my focus on getting through this evening I hadn't even allowed myself to think about what I might want to happen if things went well.

I glance at the driver's rear-view mirror to see him looking impatiently back at me. If I carry on like this my perfect five-star Uber rating is going to suffer.

Finally, I turn to Marcus. 'Look, I know it's a school night and everything. But I don't suppose you fancy coming up for a drink? I'm almost certain I've got a bottle of wine and some local craft beers that a PR company sent to the office the other day.'

'Sounds perfect,' says Marcus, and getting out of the car we head up to the entrance to my block, him asking me questions about the area and how long I've lived here and me secretly panicking at the state I'd left the place in my hurry to get ready for the date. As I open the door to the lobby and we head up the stairs I mentally picture each room of my flat and quickly realise that not a single one is fit for visitors.

'Listen,' I say when we reach my front door, 'I know this is going to sound nuts but would you mind just giving me five minutes to sort out the mess in my flat before you come in?'

Marcus laughs. 'I can't imagine it's anywhere near as bad as you think.'

'No,' I reply, 'it's probably a lot worse. Just five minutes, please, or I'll never be able to look you in the eye again.'

He laughs again. 'Honestly, you don't need to do anything on my account. You should see my place right now. With Connor staying it's a right bloke pit, but if it makes you happy, take as long as you need.'

Thanking him I quickly dash inside the flat, and do a frantic run around every room scooping up clothes, shoes, plates and mugs, and dumping everything in the kitchen, the one room I'm almost certain he won't need to go into. Opening the fridge I grab the beers, then go to the cupboard and take out the bottle of wine and two glasses and then carefully manoeuvre myself along the hallway to the living room where I set everything down on the coffee table. Switching on the two lamps at either end of the sofa I close the curtains then scan the room for any rogue elements before checking my reflection in the hallway mirror and making a few minor adjustments. Finally, I return to the front door and open it to see Marcus, a look of extreme amusement on his face.

'All good?' he asks, his eyes twinkling mischievously.

While I know he's referring to my mad tidying session, in that moment I can't helping thinking of his question more philosophically. Is everything good? Is everything the way I want it to be? Is everything perfect? And what's more, does it even need to be? The only answer I have to these questions is the one that instinctively comes to me. Putting my arms around Marcus, I lift my head as he turns towards me, and we kiss, a long, slow kiss, and then taking him by the hand, I lead him past the carefully curated living room all the way to my bedroom, where I close the door behind us.

22

Connor

'I think the one we're looking at this morning is on the sixth floor,' says Marcus over the sound of the air conditioning on full blast as we sit in his car looking up at a very tall block of flats. I don't really like it. It looks too big and too scary and, even worse, as we're looking a man comes out of the main doors with two very vicious dogs who bark nastily at everyone who walks past. But this was my idea and so I take a deep breath and get out of the car.

When I told Marcus after two weeks of staying with him that I didn't want to go back to Hope Street he was really good about it. 'No problem, mate,' he said. 'There's no rush to leave mine but if you're feeling this way then why don't we look online at some council properties and maybe sort out going to see one?' And so that's what we did. We looked through everything on the council website, which didn't take very long as there wasn't much there, and this flat that we're here to see was the best one.

The man from the housing is quite chatty. His name in Luiz and he is short and fat and has very smiley eyes. We talk about the weather and how hot it is and then head inside. The lifts aren't working so we have to use the stairs instead. Going up to the first and then the second floor is okay, but the next two make me really out of breath. By the fifth floor I'm feeling very dizzy and my legs are wobbly and I have to sit down for five minutes, which I think Marcus and Luiz are quite glad about because they sit down too. I have to do the last set of stairs in two parts, having a rest in the middle until finally we reach the sixth floor. Luiz makes a joke that it will be a lot easier on the way down but I don't laugh and neither does Marcus.

As we walk along past the front doors of the other flats I start to wonder about the people who live here. From one flat I can smell fried food, from another I can hear a TV playing loudly, and from another I can smell something like curry and hear a tiny dog barking. Halfway down the corridor Luiz stops outside one of the doors, then reaching into his bag he takes out a big set of keys that have a bright yellow label on them and opens the door.

The first thing I notice is the funny smell, sort of damp, like when I don't dry my jumpers properly before putting them away. The second thing I notice is that a little boy or girl has scribbled on the walls in the hallway with felt-tip pens. There are lines of colour running all the way along it like a very thin rainbow and I think how angry Mum would have been if I'd ever done something naughty like that.

'As you can see it's nice and bright in here thanks to these big windows,' Luiz says taking us into the living room. I walk over to the windows and look outside. The main view is of another block of flats but when I look to the side of it, I can see the pointy bit of Derby Cathedral in the distance. When I look down to see if I can see Marcus's car from here, I notice that all the people on the street outside look really small, and I think it might be quite good fun to watch them from up here.

Next Luiz shows us the bedrooms. There's a big one that could be Mum's, but the second one is tiny, much smaller than my room at home, and I would never be able to fit all of my things in it. After this he shows us the kitchen, which is so small that only one of us can be in it at a time, and it smells funny too. Last of all, he shows us to the bathroom, which is okay, but doesn't have a shower like we have at home, just a bath, which looks really dirty.

'So, that's everything,' says Luiz. 'Why don't I leave you to chat with your friend and when you're done just come and find me?'

We go back to the living room and when we hear the front door close Marcus turns to me.

'So, what do you think? I mean, I know it needs a bit of work, but overall it's not too bad is it?'

'I don't like it,' I say. 'It smells funny, and the lift is broken, and the kitchen is too small and my bedroom isn't big enough.'

Marcus nods. 'You're not wrong, but still, it's only the first place you've seen.'

I shake my head. I can't imagine me or Mum living here. It just doesn't feel right. 'I really don't want to see any more places. I think I want to go back to Hope Street. I know I want to go back to Hope Street.'

Marcus sighs heavily. 'Come on, Connor, tell me you're joking. You must understand you can't go back there. It's not safe.'

'I am not joking,' I tell Marcus. 'I am very serious. Hope Street is my home, it's Mum's home, and it's not fair that I should have to leave it just because of nasty people like Adele and her friends. You even said yourself when you went to check on it, that everything was fine. It's been ages now, Adele has left DIY-Depot and no one has tried to break into my house or smash anything up. I think it might be safe to go back now. I think Adele and her friends have forgotten about me.'

'I get it, Connor, I really do, and you're right, scumbags like Adele shouldn't be allowed to chase you out of your own home but you know how mad my mum got when she found out what had happened to you. How do you think she's going to be if I tell her you're moving back to Hope Street after all that?'

'Maybe you could help me make it safe,' I say. 'We could change the locks and get one of those video doorbell things. We sell them at work – I could use my discount.'

Marcus smiles sadly. 'You've thought of everything haven't you?'

'I just want to go home,' I say, looking around the room that feels cold and empty. 'I just want to go back to Hope Street.'

That afternoon Marcus very kindly calls one of his friends who does odd jobs and arranges for him to fit a brand-new lock, a new security chain and a video doorbell in Hope Street. I managed to get it for a really good price because it was on special offer. The day after it's all done, I move back in, and even though Marcus offers to sleep on my sofa that night to make sure I'm okay I tell him I'll be fine. And even though it is a little bit scary being back here at first, and every time the wind blows and the windows rattle I do jump a bit, after a while I forget all about the horrible things that have happened here because it just feels so good to be home.

'It's a disgrace the way them in charge let those places fall apart,' says Alan the next day at work when I tell him about going to see the flat as we're restocking in plumbing supplies. 'I can remember some of them being built, smart and modern they were at the time, but it's like anything else, without proper maintenance and care they go to wrack and ruin. If it were up to me that lot in Sudbury prison would be fixing places like that up instead of sitting on their backsides all day watching daytime bloody TV.' He tuts again, and shakes his head. 'Still, I'm glad you're back at home if that's what you want. I'll tell you what, I was planning to go to The Green Mountain Garden Centre over in Mackworth after work – their bedding plant selection is miles better than this place – and they've got a cracking café too. Since we're both finishing at two today why don't you come with me and I'll treat you to a couple of new plants for your garden and a nice cream tea to celebrate you being back home?'

In the time we've been friends Alan has taken me to visit quite a few garden centres and we always have a really good time. And so even though I was quite looking forward to going home and playing a new video game I'd bought to cheer myself up, I tell him I'd love to go.

It's nearly half past two by the time we pull into the huge car park of The Green Mountain Garden Centre. It was quite a funny journey because almost everything seemed to be making Alan cross. He was cross about the roadworks near work, he was cross about the young man who beeped him at some traffic lights because he took too long to pull away and he was cross at a tiny old lady in a huge car because she could barely see over the steering wheel and he thought it was dangerous.

The car park is really busy, and at first I'm surprised at how many people aren't at work in the afternoon but when I look at everyone going in through the entrance I see that I am the youngest person here by a very long way and they are all probably retired.

'Right then,' says Alan, grabbing a trolley, 'I say we get the plants first then after that we'll get some grub. How does that sound?'

As we go in through the main entrance I can see right away why Alan likes it so much here. It's massive, and they sell lots of interesting things that you didn't know you needed but when you see them you're not sure you can live without them.

Before we've even got through to the bedding plant section outside I manage to pick up a pot of jam, an ice cube tray that makes ice cubes in funny shapes and a large torch, which said it was as bright as one million candles.

'I told you this place was amazing,' says Alan, as I spot a foldaway fan and put that in the trolley too. 'The things they think of, amazing! I bought a keyring here the other week and if you can't find your keys you only have to whistle and suddenly it starts beeping so you can find them! Genius!'

Reaching the automatic doors we head outside to the bedding plants and Alan starts telling me all about his plans for his front garden and how it needs more colour in there when he looks up, stops what he's saying and waves at someone. I look across and see that he is waving to a girl about my age. She is shorter than me, has bright red hair that is tied up in a swishy ponytail and has a nice smile. She is wearing a Green Mountain staff uniform, and is watering some plants with a hose just like me and Alan sometimes do at work.

'Hi, Katie,' says Alan. 'So lovely to see you. Glad to see you're giving those plants a good drink in this weather. They'll definitely need it.'

Katie smiles a big beaming smile and turns off her hose as me and Alan walk over to her.

'Hi, Alan, lovely to see you too. Are you back for that rose bush you were thinking about getting last time?'

'Afraid not,' says Alan. 'I did a bit of research and roses are a bit too high maintenance for me. All that messing about with manure, special feed and spray to keep all the bugs off. Who can be bothered? I'll stick to what I know I think until I've got a bit more time on my hands.' He turns and looks at me. 'Connor, this is my friend Katie. She always looks after me when I come here.' He then looks back at the girl. 'Katie, this is my friend Connor from work. We've both finished for the day so we thought we'd spend some of our hard-earned money here.'

Still smiling she looks into the trolley and points. 'I've got that exact same torch. It's really good. We had a power cut at home last month and when I turned it on it practically lit up the street.' She laughs at her own joke and then points her finger at me. 'And I've got that too.' For a minute I'm confused and then she laughs and adds, 'I mean, your T-shirt. I've got the same one.'

'You like Metallica?'

She grins. 'My favourite album of theirs is *Ride the Lightning* even though everyone says that *Master of Puppets* is the best. Which is yours?'

Even though *Master of Puppets* is my favourite for some reason I find myself saying, 'I love *Ride The Lightning*, and "For Whom the Bell Tolls" is my favourite track on it.'

Katie gasps. 'That's my favourite too!'

'I don't know what either of you pair are on about,' says Alan. 'You might as well be talking in Chinese for all the sense this is making.'

'We're just talking about music and our favourite band: Metallica,' says Katie, and she looks at me and smiles. 'I don't really meet many people who like them as much as I do.'

'You two should get together and start a fan club,' says Alan, but even though I know he's only joking I suddenly feel embarrassed, so embarrassed that without looking at Katie or saying goodbye I tell Alan I'm going to look at the fruit trees over by the shed display and then I walk away.

23

Lila

As I park my car outside a well-to-do detached house on the edge of the Derbyshire village of Melbourne my phone pings with a message. *Hi, Lila, so sorry, but I'm running late. Should be with you in 10, Toni.* Sitting back in my seat I tap out a quick reply and allow myself to relax a little. Having left the office later than I'd planned I'd had no choice but to race over here at top speed but now I have a moment to myself I can catch up with some of the other items on my burgeoning to-do list, chief of which is calling Marcus.

It's been just over two weeks now since he'd first stayed over at mine and it's funny to remember just how nervous I'd been waking up the morning after. Worried that things might be awkward between us my mind had immediately gone into overthinking mode and I'd fretted about everything from whether he might regret our night together to my insane behaviour in making him wait outside the flat while I tidied up. As it was, however, I needn't have worried. The first thing he did on waking was to turn and kiss me despite my protestations about my morning breath and the very next thing he did after that was ask if I wanted to make plans for later on before we both headed off to work.

The ease of that first morning seems to have set the tone for how things have progressed between us ever since. Instead of feeling constantly on edge, as you do at the start of a new relationship, worried that you're going to put the other person off if you relax even just a little bit, I feel like I can just be myself around him. And even better I'm pretty sure he feels the same.

We chat easily for a couple of minutes, catching up on each other's mornings and dissecting again the dreadful film we'd watched at the cinema the night before then, aware that time is ticking on, I get to the point of my call.

'Anyway,' I say, checking my watch, 'I was just wondering what you're up to at the weekend.'

Marcus laughs. 'Spending it with you hopefully. Why? What have you got in mind?'

'Well, my editor has come up with an idea for a weekly series of articles in *The Echo* called, "Why go abroad when you can have fun in the East Midlands (or thereabouts!)?"'

'Catchy title,' says Marcus stifling a laugh. 'Love it.'

'Well, my friend Niamh has to write: "Why visit Disney World when you can go to Matlock's Gulliver's Kingdom?" And Lewis got lumbered with: "Why visit the Catacombs of Paris when you can go to Nottingham – The City of Caves?" And I was wondering if you'd fancy coming on an all-expenses-paid trip to the seaside while I research, my opus: "Why visit the Costa Del Sol when you can go to Skegness?"'

This time Marcus doesn't even try to hide his amusement. His big, deep laugh fills my ears and puts a huge smile on my face.

'Skeggy?' he splutters. 'You want us to go there for the weekend?'

'Yeah, I know. It's not the most exciting destination for a romantic getaway and you really don't have to, if you don't—'

'I'd love to,' he says cutting me off. 'It sounds like a right laugh, and I haven't been to Skeggy in donkey's years – no pun intended. Besides, I'd go anywhere with you. You know that, or at least I hope you do.'

I feel myself melt and I'm about to reply when in my rear-view mirror I see a car pull up behind me.

'I'm sorry,' I say quickly, 'but my interviewee's just arrived. I'll have to call you back, okay?'

Five minutes later I find myself sitting in the perfectly present-
ed front lounge of Antonia 'Toni' Hardacre. Everything about the
woman who has just entered the room carrying two steaming mugs
of tea – one of which she sets down on a coaster on the coffee table
in front of me – screams posh older lady. From her sensibly stylish
Marks and Spencer clothing to her speaking voice that doesn't reveal even the slightest hint of a Derbyshire accent from the outside
at least she's very much a blue blood. But even so there's something quite solid and straightforward about this slim, white-haired
woman, something that makes me feel she'd be able to converse
as easily with a dustman as she would a minor member of royalty.

'Thank you so much for getting in touch with me,' I say after
we've made polite conversation for a while. 'You said in your email
that you had some information about Bernie McLaughlin.'

'Yes, I did,' she begins. 'Although now you're here I'm afraid
I feel a little foolish taking up your time as I'm not entirely sure
how this will help.' Putting down her tea she crosses the room and
picks up a pale grey manilla folder from on top of a bureau in the
corner. 'I happened across one of your articles about Bernadette
McLaughlin in *The Echo* a few weeks ago while at a friend's house
and the name rang a distinct bell.'

'It did? How so?'

'She was, I suppose, a friend of my late aunt, Jean Walker.'

I lean forward a little in my chair. How on earth had Bernie
McLaughlin become friends with the relative of a woman like this?

'Interesting,' I say. 'I haven't come across that name in my research so far. How did Bernie and your aunt know one another?'

'Well, that's the interesting thing, I never met Bernie and my
aunt never mentioned her to me at all; in fact the first I heard
about her existence was five years ago after my aunt passed away.
I came across her will, and discovered that while she'd left the ma-

jority of her estate to me and my sister, she'd made a number of small bequests, mostly to charities, but one of them was to a Miss Bernadette McLaughlin.'

I'm now leaning so far forward in my seat that I'm in danger of falling off it altogether. Why had this woman's aunt left Bernie money in her will? What was their connection?

'My aunt was of completely sound mind when she passed so I had no reason to question it, but I have to admit I was intrigued and a little puzzled as to why she had effectively left ten thousand pounds to a complete stranger. It was only when it came time to clear her house and I came across these ...' she pauses and hands me the folder '... that things became a little clearer.'

I peek inside the folder to see a collection of letters all addressed to Jean Walker in Bernie's unmistakable handwriting and then look back at Toni for explanation.

'Feel free to take the letters – I've no use for them, but in short, having read them I discovered that my aunt and Bernie seemed to have become friends in the late year Two Thousand after a chance conversation at a railway station and they remained in contact, mostly via letter for the rest of my aunt's life. Apparently, she was very fond of Bernie and I discovered that the feeling was mutual when I received a letter of condolence from Bernie herself via my aunt's solicitor. It was a very sweet and lovely thing to do but in truth I didn't think about her again until I saw her name in your paper. Knowing how much she meant to my aunt I just thought that if I could help in any way, I should, and so I thought I'd offer you these.'

Thanking Toni for her help I take the letters away with me and over the week that follows read every single one. Just as she'd said they document a lovely friendship spanning roughly fifteen years with, from what I can gather, only the occasional meet-up for lunch or a coffee. For the most part it's just two friends exchanging news about their lives and while there's nothing that speaks to Bernie's current disappearance it's only when I'm sharing the story with Marcus at the weekend when we're on the way over to Skegness that something clicks.

'I can't believe I didn't see it until now,' I say suddenly to Marcus as we head along the A158 towards our destination.

'See what?' asks Marcus briefly taking his eyes off the road to look at me.

'That Bernie must've first met Jean Walker around the same time she went missing back in 2000. I'm almost certain the dates tally, and what's more in those early letters Jean seems to be very concerned about Bernie's state of mind, which makes me think . . . I don't know maybe she had a breakdown of some sort and Jean helped her get through it.'

'But I thought this woman died five years ago, and that Bernie knew about it. I don't understand, what's that got to do with Bernie going missing this time?'

'Chances are nothing, really, but if I'm right about this, and Jean really did help Bernie in some way, then I'm almost certain Bernie didn't disappear of her own free will this time like the police are suggesting. She did it once back in 2000, but reading those letters, hearing her express her love for Connor, there's absolutely no way she went missing of her own accord this time round, no way at all.'

'But aren't the alternatives still pretty terrifying?' observes Marcus.

'That's one way of looking at it, I suppose,' I say, 'but on the other hand I think it means there's still hope.'

It's a little after midday as we pull up in the hotel car park. We check in before heading straight out to meet the photographer at a beachfront café as arranged.

The photographer, a freelancer called Jono, is a plump man, with greying hair and a jovial demeanour. He's as old-school as they come, which is perfect for a job like this where no pose is deemed too cheesy or cartoonish. He takes numerous shots of me poking my head through various comical seaside photo stand-ins. In one I'm a burly lifeguard carrying a curvaceous blonde Marcus and in another I'm a sealion balancing a ball on my nose while Marcus, dressed in the bright yellow oilskins and sou'wester of a fisherman, attempts to feed me a fish.

Next, we move on to a row of shops where I'm snapped standing next to a comically enormous stick of rock before moving next door where I pose with a ball of candy floss that's bigger than my head before finishing off in one of the arcades where Jono makes me put on a cheap plastic kiss-me-quick hat, and pretend to look anxious as I manoeuvre the controls on one of those claw-grab machines in an attempt to win a distinctly unofficial-looking furry Minion.

'And that's the last shot,' says Jono, as much to my surprise, the claw grabber picks up the fake Minion and slowly drops it into the prize chute. 'Actually, maybe we should get another one for good luck with your new friend.'

And so, much to my shame, as everyone in the arcade looks on, I stand hugging the cheap yellow toy to my chest with all the delight of someone who has just won an Oscar.

Leaving Jono to pack his kit away, Marcus and I walk hand in hand back along the seafront past the countless penny arcades, fish and chip shops, and bed and breakfasts of Skegness in the direction of the hotel.

'Your job is insane,' says Marcus over the cawing of the hungry seagulls above us. 'But it certainly beats the usual nine to five.'

'It has its ups and downs,' I reply.

'Talking of which,' says Marcus grinning as he points at the waltzers. 'We'll have to have a go on those later. I haven't been on a fairground ride in years.'

'Probably with good reason,' I reply, 'but yes, definitely – let's do it.' I give his hand a squeeze and I'm about to carry on towards the hotel when suddenly, surprisingly, a compulsion overtakes me and I turn to face him.

'Everything okay?'

I find myself grinning like an idiot. I don't know whether it's the sea air, the sunshine or simply the fact that I've got so carried away with my assignment that I really am starting to feel like I'm on holiday, but I realise I want to cast caution aside. In every single relationship I've ever been in I've always tried to play it cool, to keep my feelings in check, to never be the first one to show their cards. But right here, right now, I don't want to do any of that. I just want to tell Marcus exactly how I feel.

'Everything's better than okay,' I begin. 'I know this is going to sound strange but I just want you to know I really like you.'

Marcus smiles, a look of amusement playing in his eyes. 'Okay . . . that's good, isn't it?'

I shake my head in frustration not quite sure he understands what it is I'm trying to express. 'No, what I'm trying to say is . . . I mean it, I really like you.'

Marcus's eyes seem to smile and his grin grows even wider, and suddenly there, slap bang in the middle of the pavement, holiday-makers bustling past us on every side, he takes me in his arms and kisses me.

24

Connor

'So, this lady, Jean, she and Mum were friends for a very long time?' I say to Lila as I break a bit off a poppadom and dip it in the blob of mango chutney on my side plate.

'About fifteen years,' she says. 'Did your mum never mention her?'

I shake my head. Mum had lots of friends from old jobs and things, and she would meet up with them all the time. I didn't know there was a special friend that she wrote to but it doesn't really surprise me because it sounds like something Mum would do.

'Well, I'm really glad Mum was friends with her,' I say. 'She sounds like she was a nice lady. And anyway, if it wasn't for her money I don't think I'd have been able to keep up with all my bills, so I really like her. Here's to the nice lady Jean,' I say lifting my pint of shandy in the air, 'for being such a good friend to me and Mum.'

I clink glasses with Lila and Marcus who are sitting on the opposite side of the table and we all manage to take a sip of our drinks before the waiters bring over our food.

It was my idea for us to come to The Mazaydar Dynasty tonight. Partly it was because I missed out last time but mostly it was because I wanted to say thank you to Marcus and Lila for being such good friends to me. They have helped me so much and I don't know what I would have done without them. Plus, I really like the food here and the waiters are always really friendly.

Marcus has a chicken methi, rice and a naan, Lila has a king prawn karahi and rice, and as usual I have fried egg and chips.

We're all eating and saying how nice the food is when Marcus turns to Lila and gives her a funny look. She then gives him a funny look back and then he turns and looks at me.

'Connor,' he says, his voice sounding serious as he puts down his fork. 'Me and Lila have got something we want to tell you. It's nothing bad, hopefully you'll think it's good, but we didn't want to be keeping it from you or for things to be—'

'I think what Marcus is trying to say,' interrupts Lila, smiling, 'is that he and I are seeing each other.'

I think for a minute. 'What? Do you mean, like you're boyfriend and girlfriend?'

'Exactly that,' says Marcus smiling as he looks at Lila.

'Why would you think that I would think that was bad?'

Marcus shrugs. 'I don't know really – I just didn't want you to feel weird or anything.'

I do not understand this at all. 'Why would I feel weird about one of my best friends going out with another one of my best friends? That would be strange.'

'That's what I said,' says Lila and she pretends to punch Marcus on the arm. 'Anyway, we're just glad that you're glad.'

I let out a big sigh and put down my fork. 'Actually, I wanted to ask you both something about boyfriends and girlfriends. Is that okay?'

Marcus pulls a face, a bit like he's in pain, but Lila nods, gives me a smile and says, 'Fire away! Ask anything you want.'

'Okay, well it's like this: I went to The Green Mountain Garden Centre over in Mackworth the other day with Alan and there was this girl, Katie, who works there.'

'Okay,' says Lila nodding. 'What about her?'

'It turns out that she likes Metallica like I do and she said that she even has the same T-shirt as me at home. Anyway, Alan joked that we should start up a Metallica fan club together and I felt a bit embarrassed so I walked off without saying goodbye to Katie.'

'Oh, don't worry,' says Lila. 'I'm sure she wouldn't have taken offence.'

'Well, that's just it, she didn't. Yesterday, Alan came in to work and said he'd had to go back to Green Mountain to get some more bedding plants and while he was there he saw Katie again. He said that she asked about me and then wrote out her phone number and told him to get me to give her a ring. I wasn't sure what he meant and so I said to him, "Why does she want me to give her a ring?" and Alan wasn't very helpful because he just said, "What do you think she wants, you daft lump? She wants you."'

When I say this Marcus pulls another face, and Lila looks like she is trying her best not to laugh, which I don't mind because it is sort of funny.

'Okay,' says Marcus. 'So, this girl likes you and wants you to call her, and it certainly sounds like you've got things in common so what's the problem?'

'You're worried because of what happened before? With Adele?'

I feel my face go red when I hear her name. Every time I think about back then I feel stupid and angry not just with her but with myself too. How could I have let myself believe that she liked me? I should've known better than to believe that someone could actually like me that way.

'Yes,' I say so quietly that I'm almost not sure I said it out loud until Lila reaches across and gently puts her hand on mine.

'Not everyone is horrible like Adele,' she says. 'Some people are nice and this friend of Alan's sounds like she's one of them. Getting together with someone is always a bit scary at first, because you don't really know them and they don't really know you, and the getting together part is where you learn about each other. And sometimes, I'm sad to say, it doesn't work out, and that's okay, that's life. But then sometimes it does work out.' Lila stops, looks at Marcus and smiles, then looks at me again. 'I suppose what I'm trying to say is that everything's a gamble, but sometimes those gambles pay off. You should call this girl. She sounds really nice, and if it doesn't work, that's okay, because at least you had a go. And if it does, well ...' she stops again, looks at Marcus and smiles '... that is even better.'

I take Lila and Marcus's advice and call Katie the next day, and we have a really lovely long chat and talk about lots of interesting things like video games (her favourite is *Horizon Zero Dawn*) and music (as well as Metallica she likes Nirvana, Bob Marley and Harry Styles) and much, much more. When we've been talking for nearly an hour I take a deep breath and even though I am really, really nervous about it, I ask her if she'd like to meet up. For a minute I think she's going to say no but then she laughs and says, 'I thought you were never going to ask,' and I feel a million times better. The only problem is that neither of us can think where to go. She doesn't really like pubs or bars and I don't like really going to the cinema and so the only thing I can think to do is eat food, and so I'm about to ask if she'd like to go to The Mazaydar Dynasty with me when she has an idea. 'I know exactly what we should do,' she says excitedly, 'but I want it to be a surprise.'

I think about telling her I don't really like surprises even though that isn't always true but I don't want to upset her, and so I ask her for a clue to what we're doing and all she says is, 'wear something comfortable.'

'Maybe she's going to take you ice skating,' says Alan, when I tell him the news about my date with Katie. 'All that flinging yourself about and falling over, you need loose clothes for that, don't you?'

When I tell Marcus about the date, he's got a different idea about where we might be going. 'I think she's going to take you to something like Laser Quest or maybe an escape room,' he tells me. 'She knows you both like gaming, so something like that would be up both your streets.'

To be honest I'm not sure if Alan or Marcus are right or wrong, but I don't have any better ideas and so when the date comes round I put on a Metallica sweatshirt and a pair of jogging bottoms and then catch the bus into town.

'Hi, Connor,' she says when she meets me outside McDonald's. 'Have you guessed where we're going yet?'

I shake my head. 'My friends think it might be ice skating or an escape room. Are they right?'

She smiles mysteriously and for the first time I notice that she is carrying a large sports bag with her. ''Fraid not but it's even better. Anyway, you'll see for yourself in a minute. It's not too far away.'

As we walk through the centre of town Katie asks me about my day at work and I tell her about some excitement we had when a man tried to steal a pair of long ladders. Just as he was leaving the store Ryan and Georgia saw him and it was really funny watching him running across the car park with them chasing after him.

'And did they catch him?'

I have to laugh when I think about it. 'No, he couldn't run very fast carrying the ladders so in the end he just chucked them on the ground and ran off towards the back of Nando's.'

I'm about to ask Katie about her day at work when she suddenly stops and says, 'We're here.' I'm a bit confused to start with because we're standing outside a shop called, 'Glam Nails – UK's Best Professional American Nail Care,' and even though I don't know what that is, I'm pretty sure I don't want it done to me.

But then Katie must see the look on my face because she laughs, and says, 'Not there, silly,' and then she points to a door at the side of the nail shop that says, 'Dave's Dojo – Kick-boxing, Karate, Taekwondo and more!'

Now, I really am confused. 'I don't understand. What are we doing here?'

'Remember when we first talked on the phone and you told me how you used to get bullied at school?'

I nod, but still can't think what we're doing here.

'Well, I got bullied at school too. People used to call me names and beat me up just because I was a bit different. So, my dad brought me here to do taekwondo and I loved it so much that I've done it ever since, and I thought you might like it too. And don't worry, it's a beginner's class today, so you won't get hurt.'

I follow Katie up the stairs to a big, wide room with wooden floors and padded mats spread out everywhere. There are about a dozen people already there and everyone is wearing what looks like a kung fu suit but Katie tells me it's called a dobok. She unzips her bag and takes out a dobok and gives it to me. 'This used to be my dad's from when he used to come with me but he doesn't use it anymore so you can borrow it tonight.' She shows me where to get changed and by the time I get back she has changed into her dobok too, and is waiting for me.

The lesson is so much fun, and feels a bit like playing a live action version of *Mortal Kombat*. Dave teaches us how to block and defend and with Katie's help even shows us how to do a few throws. It all goes so quickly that I'm surprised when Dave tells us that the class is over, and it's only when I look at the clock that I see I've been here for over an hour. At the end we all bow to Dave because he's our sabom, which Katie tells me is a bit like being a sensei like in *The Karate Kid* but is Korean instead of Japanese.

All the way back to my bus stop the only thing I can talk about is how much I've enjoyed tonight. I tell Katie how I wish I'd done taekwondo when I was getting bullied at school, and then maybe things would've been different.

'Dave always says that we shouldn't look back; we should look ahead,' she says. 'And I think he's right. We can't change what's already happened, all we can do is deal with what's in front of us.'

I think about this all the way home on the bus and how maybe what Dave says is right. It was really horrible what Adele did, but I can't change what happened. All I can do is deal with what's in front of me and right now, that's Katie. And so while I'm still on the bus, I take my phone out of my pocket and send a message: *Will you be my girlfriend?* and straight away I get a reply: *Yes, please.*

Bernie: December 2003

'Here's their twenty P's,' said Bernie to the nice lady on the door at the church youth club handing her the subs for Connor, Marcus, and two other kids from the road. 'What's the activity tonight?'

The woman thought for a moment. 'I'm pretty sure it's painting.'

Bernie groaned inwardly, her mind already jumping ahead to picking Connor and the rest of them up only to find her son covered head to toe in poster paint again. Still, he enjoyed coming and always said that painting was his favourite activity, and she was glad of the time it would afford her to do what she needed.

Waving the kids goodbye Bernie checked her watch and then practically ran the short distance home, keen as she was to get started on wrapping Connor's Christmas presents. With him being the way he was, even sneaking presents into the house was a trial, let alone keeping them hidden and getting them wrapped, and so she was grateful for this time alone.

Reaching Hope Street, she let herself into the house, went upstairs and after grabbing the chair from her room, she took it out into the hallway. Standing on it she reached up, opened the loft hatch and took out the bin liner that contained the presents and wrapping paper and then carried everything to her bedroom. Emptying it all out onto her bed she felt a sudden rush of happiness imagining Connor's face on Christmas morning, even though to those less acquainted with her son it might have seemed like a strange assortment of gifts for a ten-year-old boy. There was a boxed Mr Blobby soft toy more suited to a five-year-old, a book about repairing clocks, which was his latest obsession, a pair of red wellington boots, a pair of blue wellington boots, a Matchbox car racing set, a Lego space shuttle and six Cadbury Chocolate selection boxes. It was everything he'd told her he wanted, and when she'd questioned some of the less suitable items at the time he had been insistent to the point of hysteria that he hadn't made a mistake.

Grabbing the car racing set, she reached for the paper she wanted to wrap it in only to realise that she'd neglected to bring up the Sellotape and scissors from the drawer in the back room. Tutting, she headed back downstairs but no sooner had she crossed the room than there was a knock at the door.

Bernie groaned and, reasoning that it might be some of the kids from the street doing some early carol singing, she resolved to ignore it. But then there was another knock, and she wondered if perhaps she was wrong and it was Bev needing help of some kind.

Telling herself that whoever it was she would deal with it quickly, Bernie hurried to the front room and opened the door. To her surprise it wasn't kids carol singing, Bev or even Father Christmas. It was Kevin, from Hudson's SuperSave – Connor's dad.

Bernie stared at him in disbelief. The last time she'd spoken to him had been that evening at her flat when she'd told him she was pregnant, and the last time she had seen him was on his final day at work before he transferred to a store down south. Time hadn't been kind to him. He was losing his hair but had styled it in such a way as if to prove that he wasn't, and he'd put on weight too, which made his face look puffy and bloated. What on earth was he doing on her doorstep?

'Hello, stranger, aren't you going to invite me in?'

Bernie was riled. 'And why on earth would I do that? I don't know how you found me, and to be honest I don't care either. I just want you out of here now!' She reached for the latch ready to push the door shut in his face, but he was quicker than she was and managed to put out his hand and his foot to block the door.

'Now, don't be like that. I haven't come to cause trouble, I just want to talk.'

'And what exactly do you think we'd have to talk about?'

He sniffed, and met Bernie's gaze. 'Well, for starters, my son.'

Bernie could've laughed, it was so ludicrous. 'Oh, you mean the baby you didn't want me to have? He's your son now, is he? Aren't you a bit late for that by about, oh, I don't know, a decade?'

At this he at least had the decency to look shamefaced. 'About that . . . I know . . . well . . . I didn't exactly behave very well back then. But people can change. I'm proof of that and I don't know . . . I just want the chance to explain myself. Please, Bernie, I'm begging you, just hear me out . . . that's all I'm asking.'

Leaving the door open, Bernie turned around and walked back into the room and Kevin followed after her. She sat down on the two-seater sofa while he sat in the armchair opposite. She told herself that she would give him five minutes, and not a second longer and then she would call the police.

'So come on then, out with it!' said Bernie firmly. 'Because believe me if you're hoping I'll make a cup of tea for you, you're in for a long wait.'

Kevin shifted uncomfortably in the chair. 'Look, I get it. I deserve that. I was really horrible to you back then, and I'm sorry.'

'Is that it? Is that what you've come to say? That you're sorry? Well thanks for that. It's made my Christmas. Now don't let me keep you. I'm sure you've got a long list of people you need to apologise to.'

He laughed mirthlessly. 'You're certainly not wrong there.'

Bernie suddenly put two and two together. 'So, your wife finally kicked you out did she?'

Kevin sighed. 'The marriage had been dead for a long time. We'd just been going through the motions.'

'And I'm guessing you having affairs left, right and centre were nothing to do with it? What happened? Did you start up with someone at your new store only she found out this time?'

Kevin looked down at his feet sheepishly. 'Something like that.'

Bernie smiled bitterly. 'Something like that, or exactly that?' His silence said it all. 'And so, what? She's kicked you out, won't let you see your kids, your bit on the side doesn't want you, and now you want to play happy families with me and my son. Is that it?'

'You're getting me all wrong,' he replied. 'It's not like that . . . okay? Well, some of it's right but . . . I have thought a lot about you and the baby over the years, I really have. I just didn't know what to do about it, that's all. I didn't know whether you'd be married, have moved on, had other kids, or whatever, so I just thought it best to stay away. But then, last year after me and the wife split, I moved back here to Derby, and got a new job. Anyway, I was out in town with some mates when I bumped into Maria, with the tattoos, you know; she used to work on the meat counter. We got talking and I asked after you and she told me you'd had a little boy, and as far as she knew you were still living in Derby. Next thing I knew I was looking you up in the phone book, and when I saw you still had the same surname I thought . . . I don't know, that it was some sort of sign, that it might not be too late to be part of my son's life.'

Bernie was furious. How dare this toad of a man think he could just waltz into Connor's life like this! Like the last ten years hadn't happened, like he was owed something simply because of a biological function he'd performed over a decade ago. Like the fact that she'd been the only parent Connor had ever known counted for nothing.

'No,' she said standing up. 'This is not happening, not on my watch! Go on, I want you out of here or I'm going to scream and then call the police, just see if I won't.'

'And what are you going to say when they get here?' snapped Kevin, getting to his feet too. 'That you're refusing to let a father see his only son? I'm sure that'll go down well.' He held up a placating hand. 'Look, I didn't come to fight; I didn't come to cause any trouble. All I want is to see my son. Is that so wrong?'

Bernie looked at Kevin, unsure of what it was she felt. Mostly it was anger at the idea that he genuinely thought he could parachute into Connor's life like this, but there was also something else: an underlying feeling of pity. This man who had once seemingly had everything now had nothing, and though she knew he didn't deserve it and he only had himself to blame, she couldn't help but feel a little sorry for him.

'You really want to see Connor?'

Kevin blinked several times. 'Is that his name – Connor? You won't believe this, Bernie, but that was my dad's name. That's got to be a good omen, hasn't it?'

Bernie wanted to say, no, it was no omen at all, just a stupid coincidence. But she knew it wasn't worth her breath. Instead, she thought about Connor and what he would make of Kevin. She had no idea. He could hate him, he could love him – there was no predicting how it might go. But she couldn't help wondering if at some point in the future he'd start asking questions about his dad, and when he did, did she really want to have to tell him that Kevin had wanted to meet him but she'd sent his father away? Was it even her decision to make?

'Fine,' she said, 'you can meet him but on two conditions: one, you're to come here and I'll be in the house at all times.'

'Yeah, I can do that,' said Kevin quickly. 'I can do that, no problem. What's the other thing?'

'I don't want you to tell him who you are. I'll say you're a friend and no more.'

'But—'

Bernie cut him off, leaving him in no doubt about how serious she was. 'But nothing. Those are my conditions. Take them, or leave them, it's up to you.'

From the moment they agreed a time and date for the meeting to take place, Bernie vacillated between wanting to call it off and being certain that she had done the right thing for Connor. Bev had told her she was crazy to even entertain the idea, exclaiming, 'You don't owe that man a damn thing!' while Carla, her next-door neighbour had declared that she had made the right decision. 'A boy needs his dad, and even if he isn't the best in the world, he's got to be better than nothing.'

An hour before Kevin was due to come round Bernie walked into the living room and much to Connor's annoyance switched off the TV and explained that an old family friend was coming over for a visit especially to meet him. Connor didn't react; instead, clutching his toy train in his fist, he looked forlornly at the TV, and so with a shrug she had switched it back on, and returned upstairs to finish her morning chores.

She was just coming down the stairs with a basketful of washing when there was a knock at the door. Setting down the basket on the dining room table she checked her watch and sure enough it was eleven o'clock on the dot. Kevin had never been punctual for anything other than work when she'd known him and so she hoped this signalled just how seriously he was taking this initial meeting with their son.

She opened the door to see Kevin smartly dressed, clean-shaven and holding an orange football under one arm and proffering a large bunch of flowers.

'For you,' he said, handing Bernie the bouquet. As she stepped aside to let him into the living room she noticed a bright red Ford Escort parked outside, and guessed that such a flashy car could only belong to him.

Connor was lying on the floor about a foot away from the TV and even when Kevin went and stood right next to him he kept his eyes glued to the screen where the presenters of a Saturday morning kids' programme were interviewing a pop group.

'Connor!' At the sound of his mum's voice her son finally shifted his gaze and looked at her blankly. 'Remember, I said we had a friend coming to visit today? Well this is Kevin, and he's come to see you.'

Kneeling down next to Connor, Kevin smiled and said, 'Hello, mate, lovely to meet you.' He held out his hand to shake but Connor ignored it and looked at his mum. Finally, Kevin held out the football. 'I don't know how big your yard is but I thought we could have a kick-about if you fancy?'

Bernie had never seen Connor pay the slightest bit of interest in football, or indeed any kind of sport, but she supposed there was a first time for everything.

'Maybe just sit and watch TV with him for a while,' she suggested, 'while I go and put these flowers in water and make us a cup of tea.'

In the kitchen Bernie put the kettle on and while it boiled she put the flowers in water and opened a brand-new packet of chocolate digestives and decanted them onto a plate. Wanting to give them both time to get acquainted she took a load of washing from the machine and hung it out on the line in the yard before returning to the kitchen and putting on another load. After reboiling the kettle, she made two mugs of tea, poured a glass of Vimto from a bottle in the fridge for Connor, and then finally put everything on a tray.

There was no sign of Kevin when she entered the living room, though the football he had given Connor was sitting on the floor next to him. Confused, Bernie set down the tray and asked Connor if the man who had come to visit had gone upstairs to the loo.

Connor shook his head and with his gaze fixed to the TV now showing the news he pointed a chubby finger in the direction of the door. 'He said he had to go.'

Bernie couldn't believe what she was hearing, and marched over to the door and flung it open, hoping that Connor had misunderstood, but sure enough there was an empty space where the red Ford Escort had been.

Barely able to contain her rage, Bernie slammed the front door and when she turned to look at Connor he was already looking at her.

'Did that man say anything else to you?'

Connor nodded.

'What was it?'

'He said, you should have told him, but I don't know what he meant.'

'Did he now?' she said and as she knelt down she hugged her son tightly. That vile man didn't know Connor like she knew him. That hopeless man didn't know her lovely, kind, sweet and funny boy at all. The only people who knew Connor were those who made the effort to spend time with him, to look beyond his difficulties and see the goodness within. Still, at least they were safe here in Hope Street, amongst their friends and neighbours, people who accepted and loved Connor for who he was.

25

Lila

I hate what I'm wearing. I mean really hate it. I was going for smart casual when I'd picked out a newish pair of jeans, teamed with a white top, oversized navy blazer and heels but as I stand in front of the wardrobe mirror I can't help thinking that I look a bit mad, like someone who started getting ready for work and then couldn't be bothered to finish. Resigning myself to yet another trawl through my wardrobe I'm about to slip off the jacket when my phone buzzes. It's a message from Marcus telling me he's arrived and is waiting for me in the car downstairs. Straight away I go into panic mode, torn between getting changed again and making us late or hating what I'm wearing but being on time. Grabbing my bag, I pick up Bev's present, and the flowers I'd bought for Marcus's elder sister, Claudia, who is hosting, and decide to go with the lesser of two evils. As awful as spending the day feeling like you're wearing the wrong clothes might be, arriving late to your new boyfriend's mother's birthday party would be a million times worse.

When Marcus had invited me to join him, his sisters, uncles and aunts and various cousins at the weekend to celebrate his mum's seventieth birthday I'd been flattered. Though I'd introduced Gabe to my sister within the first few weeks of us getting together, and my parents a few months later, by contrast it had taken a whole year before Gabe had seen fit to introduce me to any of his siblings and it was a whole year after that before I met his parents. So, yes, it was lovely that Marcus felt ready for me to meet his family but as the date grew ever nearer I'd found myself becoming insanely nervous about the prospect.

'What if they don't like me?' I'd asked Niamh and Lewis as the day approached. 'What if I make a fool of myself dropping food down my top or inadvertently insult an uncle or aunt and cause a massive family split?'

Lewis had laughed. 'Has that actually happened to you? I mean, if it was Niamh, sure, one hundred per cent stay away, but this is you we're talking about. They'll love you.'

'He's right,' Niamh had said throwing a small bottle of hand sanitiser at Lewis's head. 'They will love you – you've just got to relax.'

And that's what I've been trying to do, hence the smart casual outfit decision, which as I lock my front door and head down to meet Marcus I hate more and more with each step.

'You look amazing,' says Marcus, greeting me with a kiss as I get into the car, and it takes all the strength I have not to correct him and tell him that I look a mess. Instead I ask about Connor.

'He seems good, actually,' says Marcus. 'Really good, in fact. Bright and bubbly like his old self. So, I think something's gone on because while he didn't outright admit he'd taken our advice about calling that girl, something must have happened to put him in such a good mood. Plus, every time I've tried to arrange to pop round and see him this week, he always says he's busy, busy I assume with this girl.'

'Aww, I really hope you're right,' I say. 'He deserves a bit of happiness and it would be lovely if he's finally found someone.'

It's a little after midday when we arrive at Claudia's house in Nottingham for his mum's party and there are already several cars parked outside, as well as a number of guests making their way up the front path carrying presents.

As I flick down the sun visor above me and check my reflection in the mirror, I feel my mouth go dry and then I feel Marcus looking at me. 'Are you alright?'

'Yeah, of course.'

He doesn't seem convinced.

'You're not . . . worried about meeting my family, are you?'

I nod reluctantly and turn to look at him. 'A bit.'

Marcus laughs and squeezes my hand. 'Honestly, you have nothing to worry about. Mum's the only one who can be a problem and you've already won her over, and as for the rest, believe me, you'll have them eating out of the palm of your hand in no time at all.'

Much to my relief, Marcus's family are lovely and welcome me with open arms. Bev loves her present: a silk scarf full of lilacs and greens that I'd picked out after recalling seeing a lilac jacket hanging in her hallway at home. 'Now, that is lovely,' she'd said giving me a kiss on the cheek before holding it up to the light and calling a couple of family members over to admire it. 'And even better I've got just the perfect outfit to wear it with too.'

Bev and I chat for a good while before she's whisked off to greet a batch of new arrivals. I'm just about to head over to Marcus to ask him to point me in the direction of his sister when I feel someone standing next to me and I turn to see a woman who judging by her resemblance to Bev, must be one of Marcus's sisters. She's tall and elegant-looking, with jet-black, shoulder-length hair and deep brown eyes. She's holding a glass of champagne in one hand and a bottle in the other, which she uses to top up my glass.

'I've been waiting for my ignorant brother to introduce us,' she says playfully, as she sets down the bottle on the coffee table next to us, 'but it looks like I'll be waiting a long time so I thought I'd do it myself. I'm Claudia and I'm guessing you're the famous Lila.'

'Famous? Me?' I shake my head. 'Definitely not.'

I hand her the flowers I bought and she thanks me before continuing in the same vein.

'Well, my mum has been talking about you a *lot*, so much so that I just assumed you must be mates with Beyoncé or something! But seriously, we're all really glad you've taken pity on my brother. He was such a misery when that nightmare of a woman dumped him and left him in all that financial mess. Honestly, you couldn't get a smile out of him for love nor money and now look at him.' We both turn and look at Marcus, who is laughing at something his uncle has said. 'See, I told you, that's your doing that is – he's like a different person.'

'I'm sure it's nothing to do with me. Chances are he would've come round eventually. It's like they say, isn't it? Time heals all wounds.'

Claudia laughs so hard she almost spills her drink. 'Not with my brother it doesn't. When Marcus was small we used to call him Grumpy Gus because of how he was when he lost his favourite teddy bear on the bus.'

I can't help but smile at this image of a toddler version of Marcus, bereft because of the loss of a favourite toy.

'Honestly, you should've seen it. It was an old, crusty, worn-out thing, with half its stuffing missing that he got from a jumble sale for twenty pence. And do you know how long he went on about that bear, even though Mum bought him a brand-spanking-new one? Years, and I'm not even joking. He banged on about that thing for years! But that's my brother for you – when he falls for something, he falls hard. So, when I tell you you've worked a miracle bringing him out of his misery, I'm not exaggerating. It's true, you've worked an absolute genuine miracle. Now, let me introduce you to my kid sister, Lorraine, she'll never forgive me if I keep you all to myself!'

At work the following Monday I barely get to say more than a quick hello to Niamh before I have to turn around and head out to help cover a story about a suspected drug-related shooting. By the time I get back to the office she's been sent to cover a breaking story on the resignation of a local MP following allegations of expenses fraud. When she finally gets back to the office at the end of the day her first words aren't, 'Hi,' or 'How are you?' but a rather more plaintive 'I need a drink.' Normally, we'd invite Lewis to tag along but he's still not back from interviewing the new city crime commissioner, and so we head out to our favourite bar without him.

'How did meeting Marcus's family go?' asks Niamh, as I return to our table carrying two large glasses of house red. 'Was it as bad as you thought it was going to be?'

'You were right,' I tell her. 'I was worrying needlessly. They were all really lovely and made me feel so welcome.'

Niamh grins. 'See, I told you they'd love you. So, did they tell you lots of embarrassing stories about Marcus when he was younger? That's all my family ever do whenever I bring a boyfriend home.'

'A bit,' I admit, remembering Claudia's story about the teddy bear, 'but for the most part they were pretty restrained and I ended up having a really good time.'

'But?'

I have to smile. Niamh's always so brilliant at picking up on my worries. 'It's nothing to do with Marcus, or his family, it's actually more about Gabe.'

Niamh scowls. 'What's Prince Charming done now?'

225

'Gabe? Nothing. I don't know, it's just that things with Marcus are so much easier than they ever were with Gabe, and I don't know why I put up with it for so long.'

Niamh takes a long sip from her glass before speaking. 'Because you wanted things to work, you wanted your happy ending, and when you get like that you always put in more energy than you should trying to keep things together when maybe it would've been better to cut your losses and run.'

I stare at my glass for a moment, thinking about what Niamh's just said. She's definitely got a point. I think because Gabe and I had been together for so long I refused to see all the warning signs along the way, his reluctance to travel up to Derby to spend the weekends with me being the biggest one of all.

'You're probably right,' I tell her, and then I suddenly feel blue thinking about all the time I wasted with Gabe when I could've been with someone like Marcus. In a bid to change the subject and hopefully lighten the mood I ask Niamh how things are going with her on the apps.

She sighs heavily and takes another hearty gulp of her wine before replying. 'Actually, I've deleted them off my phone.'

'Really,' I say somewhat taken aback. Niamh had seemed completely committed to them. 'How come?'

She sighs again and drains her glass. 'Because . . . well . . . because . . . I've sort of been seeing someone.'

Despite my attempts not to react I can't help but let the surprise show on my face. 'You're seeing someone? You kept that quiet. Who is he? Where did you meet? What does he do? Tell me everything.'

'Actually,' she says her expression downcast, 'do you mind if we don't? It's just . . . I don't know . . . it's complicated that's all.'

Now I'm really taken aback. This is not like Niamh at all.

'Oh, of course,' I say, as a million questions run through my head as to why she's being so uncharacteristically cagey. 'Sorry, didn't mean to pry.'

'You're not,' she says. 'I'm still working stuff out that's all but when I've got everything straight in my mind, I'll tell you everything, I promise.'

Though we stay in the bar chatting for another hour things feel a little strained between us and as we wait for our respective Ubers to arrive at just after eight I find myself worrying about my usually so happy-go-lucky friend. My gut is telling me she's involved with a married man. It's the only thing that makes sense of her reluctance to share.

'You are alright, aren't you?' I ask as my ride home looms into view at the top of the road. 'You'd tell me if something was wrong, wouldn't you?'

'Yeah, of course,' she says giving me a hug. 'I'm just being a bit of a drama queen, that's all. I promise it's no big deal.'

In the car on the way home I call Marcus to see how his day has been, and end up telling him about Niamh.

'So, you think she's seeing some married bloke?'

'I can't think what else it would be,' I reply. 'It's just so unlike her. Normally I'm the one screaming "TMI" when she regales me with tales of her love life – not asking for more detail. I'm just worried she's going to get hurt.'

'Well, if she won't talk about it, I don't suppose there's much you can do for the time being other than be there when she's ready to open up.'

Reaching home I kick off my shoes and as my stomach gurgles I head straight to the fridge, open up a packet of pre-sliced Gouda, eat one slice straight away, take another as a backup, and then put on some pasta to boil.

I'm just watching one of a series of funny dog videos on Instagram while I wait for it to cook when my phone rings. I don't recognise the number and my first thought is that it's Virgin Media yet again calling me in a bid to get me to upgrade my package but when I answer it the person at the end of the phone is someone else entirely.

'Hi, is that Lila?' asks a well-spoken voice that sounds familiar. 'It's James Neate here from *The Correspondent*. I'm so sorry to call so late but I've been in meetings all day and this is the first chance I've had. Anyway, long story short I've got some good news, or at least I hope you'll think it is. For reasons too long and complicated to go into now, I find myself in the position to be able to offer you the post you interviewed for at *The Correspondent*, so if you still want it, it's yours.'

26

Connor

'Are you sure you're okay?' asks Katie her face looking worried on my phone screen. 'You just don't seem like yourself.'

'I'm fine,' I tell her. 'I'm probably just a bit tired that's all. I was up quite late playing games so maybe that's it.'

'You should watch out for that. My mum always says that getting enough sleep is as important as getting enough food.'

'I'll try to get an early night tonight then,' I reply. 'Hope your shift goes well this afternoon and I'll speak to you later.'

Just like that Katie's smiling face disappears and I'm left looking at the screenshot on her contact details. I took it when we were FaceTiming yesterday and even though she is pulling a silly face in the photo she looks really lovely.

It's been four days since Katie agreed to be my girlfriend and I can't believe how well I feel I know her already. We talk every day, sometimes just chatting on FaceTime, like today, and then other times we'll play video games online together and we'll talk to each other there too. She really knows how to make me laugh. The other day she was doing silly voices as we played Minecraft and I almost choked on my Vimto.

I like that we can talk about serious things too. She told me a bit more about when she was bullied at school and how unhappy it made her. I really hated how sad she sounded when she was talking about those days. I wanted to be able to go back in time so I could save her from the bullies and I even told her this. She said it was really lovely of me and then said if she could go back in time, she would use her taekwondo on my bullies, especially Adele who she really, really doesn't like.

Katie was right about me not being myself today because I'm not. Even though I've told her about Mum going missing and about how Lila was helping me to find her, for some reason I haven't told her that tomorrow is Mum's birthday and that always makes me sad. I think maybe the reason I didn't tell her is because I know that she will want to try to do something to cheer me up and make me happy but the thing is after spending two of Mum's birthdays without her already, I know that nothing can help. It's just something I've got to get through.

As today's my day off, once I've got dressed, I catch the bus into town to buy a present for Mum. Before she went missing Mum would always drop little hints about things she would like for her birthday and she would be really obvious about it. Like once, when we were shopping in town we went into Marks and Spencer and she picked up a top and said, 'Oh, this is nice, and they've got it in my size too,' and then she looked at me and gave me a wink, put the top back on the rack and then wandered off looking at something else to give me the chance to buy it without her seeing. Then, when I'd wrapped it up and given it to her on her birthday she still acted surprised.

But without Mum being around to give me clues, I really don't know what to get her. On the first birthday after she went missing it was still lockdown so I ordered her a Peter Kay DVD online because I remember she used to really like watching him on the telly and I could hear her laughing even when I had my headphones on. On her second birthday after she went missing I thought about buying her another Peter Kay DVD but then I was cleaning her room one day when I noticed her perfume bottles on top of the chest of drawers and saw that one of them was almost empty.

I took the bottle into town with me and asked a lady in Boots if they had any in but she told me they'd stopped making it. She was really nice though and let me sniff some other perfumes that she said were similar. They all smelt the same to me, but I chose one with a nice pink and gold bottle and the lady wrapped it up in tissue paper and told me that Mum was very lucky to have such a thoughtful son. This time around though, I really, really don't know what to get her. I haven't got any ideas at all.

Reaching town I get off the bus and walk straight over to Derbion, the biggest shopping centre in town. It's quite busy, and there are so many shops that I don't know where to start. After wandering around and getting a bit distracted after I go into Game and look through their second-hand stuff, I go to Marks and Spencer's and head to the section where I bought Mum's top from. This time round though, it's full of ladies' jackets, and though some, like a denim one I pick up, are quite nice I can't really imagine Mum wearing it so I put it back.

After this I visit the following shops: Matalan (nothing there I like), Next (everything in there is too glittery), Frasers (everything there looks a bit too young) and Ann Summers (I only went in there by accident and there was definitely nothing there for Mum).

I feel a little bit dizzy after visiting so many shops and I decide to go and get something to eat from the Food Terrace but on the way I pass a jewellery shop and a gold necklace in the window catches my eye. The label says that it is made out of 9ct yellow gold. The pendant is heart-shaped and the thing in the middle of it that looks like a diamond is called cubic zirconia.

I go into the shop and ask the lady behind the counter if I can take a closer look and she takes it out of the window and shows me. As soon as I see it up close I know that Mum would love it and so even though it is £138, and more money than I would normally spend I buy it. After stopping off for a sausage roll at Greggs, I buy some wrapping paper and a card and then catch the bus back home. I wrap the present straight away, and then write Mum's card, telling her how much I love her and how I hope she'll be back soon and then I take both upstairs to her room. Opening up her top drawer I tuck them carefully inside with all of the other birthday and Christmas presents she hasn't been here to open.

The next day as I'm getting ready for work I get texts from Bev and Marcus telling me they're thinking of me and Mum on her birthday, which is really kind of them. No one at work knows what today is, and I'm really glad, because at least here things can be normal.

I hardly have time to take my coat off before Alan walks into the locker room, and after catching up with how things are between me and Katie he asks me if I've been to see any more flats yet and when I tell him that I haven't he carries on the rant he started last time.

'I saw some of those council places on the news the other night,' he says. 'They're all riddled with mould and whatnot. It's criminal.' He tuts, shakes his head and looks like he's about to say something else when suddenly the door bangs open, and Rob from the warehouse rushes in looking panicked. 'Emergency meeting in the break room now!'

Alan pulls a face. 'Emergency meeting? About what? Don't tell me they're changing the uniform again. I've only just got used to this one.'

'It's nothing like that,' says Rob. 'It's about the store. Word is something big's going on. I don't know what it is, but I'm going to find out.'

Following Rob, we walk along the corridor to the break room to find it is already full of people.

'Blimey,' says Alan, 'if all you lot are in here, who's minding the store?'

'Forget minding the store,' says Briony from the office, 'we all just want to know what's going on.'

Just then the door opens and Ryan walks in, his face really serious. 'I need you all to go back to work right now!' he shouts.

'Where's the gaffer?' calls out a voice from the back of the room. 'We asked to see the organ grinder not the monkey!'

Everyone bursts out laughing and Ryan goes red in the face. 'Andrew's in an important meeting at the minute and can't be disturbed.'

'He bloody can if we all go marching in there!' someone else shouts and lots of people start grumbling.

'Just tell us if it's true what they're saying,' says Briony. 'I've just got off the phone with a mate at head office and she's told me there's rumours flying around that DIY-Depot are in big trouble and might have to close at least half their stores. Is ours one of them?'

Ryan shuffles the papers in his hands and looks really uncomfortable. 'All I've been authorised to say is that nothing's set in stone yet but there will likely be some store closures and ours is a candidate like any of the other 122 stores nationwide.'

I don't understand what's going on. Are they really saying that they might close our store? I feel sick. I can't imagine working anywhere else. This is the only job I've ever had, and I love it here. I love the people, even the annoying ones like Ryan. I love the customers, even the ones who ask silly questions about paint colours, but more than anything I love being part of a team and doing a good job. Once I start my shift I'm not Connor the weirdo, the person other people call names or feel sorry for. I am Connor the customer service adviser, someone who people come to for help, someone who other people rely on to do any task that is given to me. Without my job, I am just plain old Connor, and I'm not at all sure that is enough.

'What sort of bloody use is that to us?' says Alan, angrily. 'This is people's livelihoods you're talking about. You can't just drop a bomb like this and expect us all to carry on as normal! People have got mouths to feed and bills to pay.'

'Alan's right,' says Briony. 'We need to know one way or the other. We need to know if we're safe here or if we should be looking for new jobs.'

Ryan sighs. 'Look, I'm in the same boat as all you lot. I've just put in an offer on a flat with my girlfriend. If this place closes, I'll be right up the creek.'

'But you must know something,' says Rob, 'more than the rest of us anyway.'

'All I can say,' replies Ryan, 'is what I've said. Stores are definitely going to close, but as for which ones and when, I swear on my life, I have no—'

Just then his phone beeps with a text, and as soon as he looks at it his face goes really pale. 'Guys, I'm really sorry, but it's bad news. Head office have just confirmed ours is definitely one of the stores closing.'

27

Lila

'I'm sorry,' I say, looking at Marcus panicked, suddenly aware that he's asked me a question. In that instant I realise I haven't actually taken in a word he's said the entire time we've been walking down the path from my flat to our cars. 'I missed that. What did you say?'

'I asked if you'd had a look at the menu for that new dim sum place we're going to tonight?'

'Oh, right, no not yet. It should be good though. I've heard nothing but great things about it.'

He gives me a questioning look. 'Are you alright?'

'Yeah, of course. Why?'

'It's just that you seem a bit distracted, in fact you haven't been right since you went out with Niamh on Monday. Has she said any more about this married bloke she's seeing?'

'No,' I say, feeling slightly guilty for using Niamh as a smoke-screen. 'Like you said, she'll tell me when she's ready.'

'Okay, well, don't let it play on your mind too much. You're a good friend and I'm sure she knows that. Right, then.' He takes out his keys then wraps me in his arms and kisses me. 'Have a great day and I'll see you at the restaurant at eight.'

As I watch him drive away I feel another sharp pang of guilt. I hadn't meant to keep such a huge thing from him. It hadn't been my intention at all. All I'd wanted, all I'd needed was a bit of space to get my head around the single biggest decision of my career so far, without the added complication of having to think about someone else. All I'd wanted was the time to try and work out what it was I really wanted, to decide whether or not to accept *The Correspondent* job and move my entire life one hundred and twenty-eight point two miles down to the capital.

As I drive to work I think about the call from *The Correspondent* and how it had completely blown my mind when they'd offered me the job they'd initially turned me down for. My gut instinct had been to say yes, straight away. After all this was my dream job I was being offered. How could I possibly have said no? But instead, I'd found myself asking exactly how long I had to make my decision.

'I'm actually off for a couple of days for a family event but I'll be back straight after that so how about we say by the end of the day on Wednesday,' James had responded.

'That's amazing,' Niamh had said when I'd told her at work yesterday. 'Although how I'm going to survive at *The Echo* with just Lewis for company is anyone's guess. But seriously, I couldn't be happier for you. When do you start?'

That's when I'd had to tell her that I hadn't actually accepted the job yet. She'd responded just as I'd expected, just as I would've done had the tables been turned.

'Have you lost your mind?' she'd retorted. 'You've been offered the job of your dreams and you're dithering about whether or not to take it? What's going on? Is it Marcus? Has he said something?'

'I haven't told him yet,' I confessed. 'And the weird thing is I'm not sure I want to until I've made my mind up. Is that terrible of me?'

'Of course not – you need to work out what you feel first. Nothing wrong with that. So come on, tell me everything you're thinking and let's see if we can sort it all out.'

And so that's what I did. I told her about how when I'd first applied for the job, life had been completely different. I was with Gabe, hoping that a job in London would finally fix things between us. And now that had all changed did I really want to uproot myself and start again? Then there was the commitment I'd made to helping Connor find his mum. If I left for London that would be it, no one else would be looking for Bernie, and just like the police I'd be letting him down all over again. Then there were my deeper fears that sprung from my own insecurity. What if I'm no good? What if I fall flat on my face and don't even make it to the end of the probationary period? What would I do then? Then finally, there's Marcus. Yes, we'd only been together a short while but I really like him. What if he doesn't want to do the long-distance thing? And even if he does is it really fair to put such a fledgling relationship under that kind of pressure?

'Mate,' Niamh had replied, 'you're spiralling big time. Who's to say that you won't find Bernie before you leave? And if you don't there's no one in the world can say you didn't give it your all. And as for the "what-if game", it's one we've all played and believe me there are never any winners. I could just as easily say: "What if you love it there? What if you meet loads of amazing people and get to work on tonnes of groundbreaking news stories that genuinely excite you? What if you're so brilliant they promote you after six months? And as for Marcus, if you really are that into him, who's to say that the two of you can't find a way to make it work?"'

Reaching work I head straight up to *The Echo* but no sooner have I sat down at my desk than an eager Lewis pokes his head round his computer screen and whispers, 'So, come on then, put me out of my misery. Have you made your mind up yet?'

I shake my head and immediately regret having shared the news with him yesterday over coffee.

'Honestly, Lils, only you could overthink something like this. I'm telling you, it's a total no-brainer. I mean, this place versus . . .' he looks around theatrically before whispering, '*The Correspondent*. I mean, there's no contest. Just make the call and have done.'

'Leave her alone, you,' growls Niamh suddenly appearing next to me. She sets down her bag and takes off her coat before continuing her reprimand. 'The last thing she needs right now is you piling on the pressure. She's said a thousand times it's not that easy so back off.'

'Alright! Alright!' says Lewis sulkily. 'No need to bite my head off. I was just trying to help.'

'Well, you're not,' says Niamh. 'But you can start by getting us both a coffee, and not the crappy office stuff either. I mean the real deal from that ultra-expensive new café on the corner.'

Much to my surprise, instead of hurling abuse back at Niamh, Lewis just sighs dramatically before dutifully taking orders for a flat white and a caramel macchiato and heading out of the office.

'He's right though, isn't he?' I say the moment Lewis is out of earshot. 'I am making a bigger deal out of this than I need to.'

'No, you're not,' says Niamh calmly. 'And I'm really going to have to question your sanity if you're taking Lewis's life advice seriously. You're you, not him, and you've got to make your decisions your way. It's the only thing you really can do. One thing I will say though, and it's not my wisdom, it's my mum's, imagine yourself six months down the line and ask yourself how you think you'll feel if you turn it down.'

I consider this for a minute. Though every last single one of the reasons I've put forward for not taking the job are all perfectly valid, perhaps they're out-weighed by the fact that I know in my heart that if I don't give it a go I'll always be wondering what might have been. I'll always be wondering if I could've made it work.

'I think I'll regret it,' I say looking at Niamh.

'In that case,' she replies, 'I think you have your answer.'

And just like that I make the call, accept the job and begin the process of changing my life beyond all recognition.

An hour later, having finally recovered from making such a momentous decision it dawns on me that having already done one difficult thing today another now awaits me: telling Peter I'm leaving.

Taking a deep breath, I'm about to head over to his office to break the news when his door opens and he calls out my name.

'Metcalfe, my office, when you've got a minute.'

It's hard to judge his tone. Though he sounds ill-tempered this is pretty much the case for ninety per cent of the time, so it's impossible to tell if I'm in trouble or about to be given a pay raise.

'Everything okay, Boss?'

He gestures for me to take a seat. 'You like it here, don't you?'

'I love it,' I reply, as my stomach lurches, suddenly wondering how I'm going to broach the subject of me leaving. 'Why do you ask?'

'Because I've had a request for a reference, you big dope,' he says, grinning. 'Congratulations on the new job!'

I feel my cheeks flush with embarrassment. Though Peter is smiling I can tell he's hurt. He's always been good to me and I'm sorry to have upset him.

'Honestly, Peter, I'm mortified. I literally only just accepted the position and I was trying to pluck up the courage to come and tell you. I'm sorry you didn't find out from me first.'

'Well, it's done now,' he says waving a hand dismissively. 'And anyway, I always knew someone would snap you up, sooner or later. You're young, talented and ambitious and it's a national. Of course, London seems like where it's all happening but if you change your mind or ever want to come back just know that there will always be room for you here at *The Echo*.'

I can't help myself, even though I've never done anything like it in my life, I walk round to the other side of the desk and throw my arms around Peter.

'That means a lot,' I say trying my best not to cry. 'And I meant what I said, I really do love it here. It's just time for me to try something new, that's all.'

After work I head into town to meet Marcus for dinner as we'd arranged, hoping beyond hope he'll take the news about my new job as well as Peter had. There's certainly no reason he shouldn't, I tell myself as I wait in line to be shown to our table. I still want to be with him, I'll just be living in a different city, and as for the rest we'll have to work it out.

'Hey, you,' he says standing up to greet me as I near the table. We kiss, and then hanging my coat on the back of my chair I sit down opposite him, wondering when exactly the right time will be to tell him my news. Should I do it now, and potentially spoil a nice evening, or put it off until later and risk not doing it all?

'How's your day been?' I ask desperately trying to buy myself some time. 'Good I hope?'

He sighs heavily. 'Mine's been alright but Connor's not so much. He called me this afternoon in tears: his branch of DIY-Depot is closing.'

My heart sinks. I'd heard the rumours about the chain being in trouble earlier in the week but to be honest I'd been so distracted with my own concerns that I hadn't thought for a moment to look into it more deeply.

'Poor Connor,' I say. 'He's already been through so much as it is. Is he okay?'

Marcus shakes his head. 'You know how much he loves that job. It's the only one he's ever had. I'm not sure how he'll cope anywhere else. I asked if he needed me to drop by, but he said Katie was taking him out for pizza tonight to try and cheer him up.'

A waiter arrives at our table and asks if we'd like to order any drinks. Neither of us have even so much as glanced at the menu so we just each ask for a Japanese beer, and then he disappears leaving us alone again.

'Anyway,' says Marcus. 'How was your day?'

I swallow hard, and fiddle with my napkin, desperately wishing our drinks would arrive, to give me something to focus on and hide behind. I don't feel like I can answer this most innocent of questions without telling him about the job, but at the same time I don't know where to start.

'It was good,' I begin, and then my conscience gets the better of me. 'Actually . . . it was good but also weird. Listen, there's something I need to tell you.'

Marcus raises an eyebrow. 'Sounds ominous.'

'It's not – really, it's not. It's just that . . . well . . . do you remember me telling you about that job I applied for at *The Correspondent*?'

He nods. 'I remember you telling me you were really gutted when you didn't get it, but at the same time you were kind of glad because you've been so much happier at *The Echo* lately.'

My stomach tightens hearing my own words recited back to me. I had indeed said that, and I think at the time I'd meant it too.

'That's right, well the thing is they called me late on Monday night after I'd been out with Niamh and whoever they offered the job to has pulled out for personal reasons, and as I was next in line they've offered it to me and I accepted.'

Marcus looks at me confused. 'So, you've been offered a job?'

I nod.

'In London?'

'I know it's a lot to take in. It is for me too, but I don't see why it should impact us. I've done the long-distance thing before, and while it's not ideal, I think we can make it work.'

Marcus holds up a hand. 'Hang on, so they offered you the job on Monday and you're only telling me now, two days later, even though we spent last night together?'

I wince. He's right, this is so much worse than I thought it would be. 'I know it sounds bad when you put it like that, awful even, but I promise, I kept going to tell you but, well, I suppose, I just needed to work out how I felt first.'

'Oh, well, that's okay then. I'm glad you're all sorted.'

I reach for his hand across the table but he pulls it away. 'Please, Marcus, don't be like this.'

'Like what exactly? You know how important honesty is to me. You know everything I went through with my ex. How did you think I'd feel when you've kept something this big from me? And while we're at it, did you actually expect me to be happy that I matter so little to you that you didn't think to mention something this important? Because that's what this boils down to: either you thought I didn't matter or you thought I'd try and talk you out of it. And to be honest neither of those is a good look.'

He stands and I do too, hating the fact that I've hurt him like this. 'Marcus, please, you don't understand. Please sit down and let me explain.'

'I think I've heard enough thanks,' he says. 'I'm pretty sure I understand everything just fine.' He turns as if to leave but then stops and looks back at me. 'And what about Connor? Where is he in all this? I mean, you did tell him you'd help him find Bernie.'

It hurts that he's bringing this up when he knows how fond I am of Connor, but under the circumstances it's a fair question.

'I've tried everything I can,' I say. 'You know that. And if there was anything else I could do, I'd do it, but I've exhausted every avenue I can think of, so yeah, I suppose when I go, that will be it.'

Marcus shakes his head in disgust. 'So you leave this mess behind you and I'm left to pick up the pieces. Is that it?'

'Of course not. I'll talk to Connor. I'll explain everything. You're right – you shouldn't have to be picking up after me.'

'Finally, something we agree on,' says Marcus, and then turning towards the exit he walks away.

28

Connor

I'm just about to leave the shop floor and head home after one of the most tiring shifts ever when a muscly man with loads of tattoos on his arms pushing a trolley full of garden tools, light bulbs, storage containers and rolls of fake grass calls over to me.

'Here, mate,' he says. 'I managed to get myself some bargains but what else you got out the back? You know, the good stuff?'

I don't know what he means. 'I'm sorry, I don't understand. What good stuff?'

'Come on, mate,' he says as if we are good friends, 'we all know when places like this close they put the crap out first for the suckers. Well, I'm after the real bargains and we both know they're out the back, so why don't you tell me what you got, and if you let me have it, I'll throw in a tenner for your troubles.'

'I'm sorry we're just putting everything out as soon as we can,' I explain. 'I don't think there are any special things out the back.'

'Oh, I see how it is!' he says nastily. 'Saving the best stuff for yourself, are you? Typical! No wonder you lot are closing down with customer service like this. I'm surprised it didn't happen sooner.'

It's been like this ever since our store started its closing-down sale: people wanting to snap up all the best bargains before we close forever. The shop has never been busier. It's just a shame these people never came in before when we really needed them.

Since the news came out work hasn't been very nice at all. Everyone seems sad or in a bad mood and some people have said they are already looking for new jobs even though we're not closing for another couple of weeks yet. Alan told me he doesn't think he'll bother getting another job. 'I can't be doing with all that faffing about at my time of life,' he said. 'I think when we're done I'll just hang up my apron and call it a day, spend a bit more time in the garden, maybe even go on one of those cruises people my age rave about, although who knows what I'd do with myself stuck in a tin can in the middle of the ocean for four weeks.'

I can't imagine getting a new job or going on cruises. I can't imagine what I'll do when this job ends. It still doesn't feel real. It still feels like I'm dreaming. This is the only job I've ever had. I don't even know if I'll be able to get another one. After all this time working at DIY-Depot I can't imagine I'd be very good at doing anything else.

Last night everyone got an email from head office telling us that from tomorrow someone will be coming in to the store to do something called 'exit interviews'. When I asked Ryan about it this morning, he said that every DIY-Depot colleague would get one and it would be a chance to talk about what would be happening next and how they could help us. 'They might even help you get another job,' he said, 'although I wouldn't hold your breath.'

Clocking out, I head home on the one-two-five, which for the first time in months is nearly on time. On the way home I think about calling Katie and telling her about how awful my day was but then I remember she's working a late shift and so instead I listen to Metallica's *Garage Inc* album. It's my least favourite. It's really just a lot of covers of other people's songs and some not very good B sides, but sometimes I feel bad that I almost never listen to it, and so every now and again I play it just so it doesn't feel left out.

Reaching home, the first thing I do is make myself some lunch. I get a pizza out of the freezer and because today has been so horrible some chips too, but before I can put them in the oven the doorbell rings. I check the app on my phone that's connected to the doorbell and I'm surprised to see Lila's face looking back at me. She hadn't said she'd be coming round and I start thinking it might be to do with Mum. And it is, sort of, but not in the way I'd been hoping.

'So . . . so . . . you're going to stop looking for Mum?'

Lila bites her lip and looks like she might cry. 'Well, I'm not starting my new job for another month, so I'll do all I can while I'm still at *The Echo*. But yeah, if nothing changes between now and when I go, that will be it, I'm afraid – the end of the investigation.'

I look at Lila sitting next to me on the sofa and she seems so sad that I don't want to say anything that might upset her, but at the same time I don't want her to stop searching for Mum.

'So, there might still be a chance that you could find Mum before you leave?'

She sighs. 'I suppose anything's possible but I have to be honest with you, Connor, I'm not holding out much hope. I've tried everything I can think of and I'm running out of ideas.'

I think for a moment. 'But couldn't me and Marcus help you? He's really clever, and even though I'm not I could still help. Mum always used to say, "Many hands make light work."'

'You are clever, Connor, about lots of different things, so don't do yourself down okay? But I think Marcus is quite busy at the moment and even with your help I don't think it would make any difference.'

'But couldn't you carry on looking for Mum even at your new job?'

'I don't think I'm going to have the time. I'm really sorry, but it's going to be a very demanding job and I just won't be able to fit it in.'

'Oh,' I say, 'I understand. Well, I'm just going to have to cross my fingers and hope that you find Mum really soon.'

Lila smiles but her eyes look sad. 'Okay, Connor, well, I'd better go.'

'Are you sure you won't stay for a cup of tea?'

'Thanks, but no, I've got to get back to work.'

I think for a minute. 'Will I see you before you go? And will I still see you when you come and see Marcus?'

Lila doesn't answer straight away. 'Actually, he and I aren't seeing each other anymore.'

'Oh,' I say. 'I didn't know. Marcus didn't tell me.'

'I don't think he's very happy with me at the moment,' she explains. 'I'm hoping once some time has gone by we'll be friends again. But when I'm next back in Derby I'll be sure to drop in and see how you're getting on, okay? I was really sorry to hear about your job. You must be so upset about it.'

'I am,' I say, thinking about how much worse I feel now that I know Lila is leaving too. 'Very sad.'

'Well,' she says, 'I hope you find an even better one really soon.'

I walk Lila to the door and she gives me a hug but it does not feel like an ordinary everyday hug, it feels like a hug that people give you when they are saying goodbye for a very long time. I watch her get into her car and then wave her off but when I come back inside all I feel is sad. I wish Lila wasn't moving to London. I wish she and Marcus were still friends. But I am sure she will find Mum before she leaves. I just know it. She will find Mum and bring her home, and Mum will give me a kiss and tell me that everything is going to be okay and everything will go back to how it should be.

The next day I get up at seven because I'm working a nine–three. I text Katie to say good morning and then she sends me one back that's full of smiley faces. After a shower I iron my uniform and while I wait for the iron to heat up I wonder how many more times I'll get to wear it. I remember my first DIY-Depot uniform really well. Back in those days you had to wear green trousers and a black short-sleeved shirt. I didn't really like the shirt because it was tight around my neck but Mum said I looked very handsome and she took loads of photos of me in it. Since then, we've had lots of different uniforms. There was one with a green sweatshirt, then one with a blue sweatshirt, and then another where they said we could wear our own clothes but had to wear a light blue DIY-Depot apron over the top. But my favourite is the one we have now: a black polo shirt, smart black trousers and a green apron with big pockets on the front.

Later at work I'm in the middle of helping an old lady with a lawn mower that's on sale for less than half price when I hear my name called over the PA system: 'Could DIY-Depot colleague Connor McLaughlin report to the office please? That's DIY-Depot colleague Connor McLaughlin, to the office.'

'Looks like it's your turn for the exit interview,' says Alan as he takes over helping the old lady. 'Good luck, son. I'm sure it'll all be fine.'

'But I don't want to go,' I say, even though the old lady is listening. 'Can't you go instead? Tell them you can't find me.'

'They might look it, but they're not daft. You clocked in this morning, of course they know you're here.' He brushes some fluff off my apron. 'Don't worry, lad. Just listen to what they've got to say, but don't agree to anything you don't feel comfortable with. And don't go signing anything until we've at least had a chance for the union rep to take a look at it, okay?'

Trying my best to be brave I leave the shop floor and head past the warehouse and the break room through to the office. I stop for a minute to straighten my apron then knock on the door and wait until I hear Ryan's voice telling me to go in.

'Connor,' says Ryan, standing up. 'Come in and take a seat.' He nods to the lady sitting next to him who I don't recognise. She is wearing a smart blue suit and looks very serious. 'This is, Anne, she's from head office HR, and she's here to help us today.'

I sit down and smile at Anne but she doesn't smile back.

'Okay,' she says, shuffling through some papers in front of her. 'Let's begin. I think I should start by saying that we realise this is a very unsettling time for all employees. It's my job to talk you through the various options available, the first of which is potential redeployment to one of our other outlets. Would you be interested in pursuing this?'

I look at Ryan. I have no idea what the lady has just said. 'I think what Anne means to say, Connor, is would you like to work at one of the other DIY-Depot branches if there's a job available?'

I think about the question for a moment. I know there are other DIY-Depot branches of course, but I've never been to one and I can't imagine working at one in a different place with different people.

'I don't know,' I say. 'Which branch would it be?' I think about being at another branch. It would be really strange. The same, but different.

'Well,' says Anne, taking out a piece of paper. 'The nearest branch to Derby would be DIY-Depot, Netherfield.'

'I don't know where that is,' I say. 'How would I get there?'

Anne and Ryan look at each other.

'It's the other side of Nottingham, Connor,' Ryan explains.

This sounds like too far to get the bus to but I don't want to sound ungrateful.

'I'm not sure,' I say.

'Okay,' says Anne, 'in that case we'd be looking at a redundancy package, which will be worked out using the company redundancy calculator, which takes into account age, length of service and weekly pay. The calculation will be made at head office and you'll receive your redundancy offer by email in the next five working days. Does that sound okay, Connor?'

I think about the question. It isn't okay. None of this is. 'Can't you just not close the store? Can't you just leave things the way they are?'

Anne looks at Ryan again.

'I'm afraid not, mate,' he says. 'The decision has already been made. We've just got to try and make the best of things now.'

Anne looks at me over her glasses. 'So, are you okay with the redundancy?'

Remembering Alan's warning, I ask her if I can think about it.

Anne squeezes her lips together and she looks a little bit annoyed. 'I'm sorry but that's not an option, Connor.'

I don't know what to say but when they both just stare at me I feel like I have to say something. 'Oh, then yes, I'm okay with it, thank you.'

'Good,' says Anne, smiling for the first time, 'well, we're nearly done.' She takes out another piece of paper and looks at it over her glasses. 'DIY-Depot takes the welfare of its colleagues very seriously and to this end we've partnered with a recruitment agency to help colleagues with their ongoing career pathways. Is this something you'd like to be part of?'

Again, I look at Ryan to see if he can explain what she is saying.

'I'd say yes if I were you, mate,' he tells me. 'It's just a fancy way of saying, "Do you want help finding another job?"'

Another job. I can't even imagine it. I've got some savings and Mum and I have a joint account that's got some money in too but this won't last forever. Without a job how will I pay my rent and bills? How will I feed myself? How will I survive?

'Okay,' I say.

'Excellent,' says Anne, and then she hands me a clipboard with a sheet of paper attached. 'Just tick the top two boxes and sign at the bottom to say you've had your exit interview and we're all done.'

I look at Anne and then at Ryan, and try my best not to cry. I tick the boxes Anne shows me and then sign my name.

That afternoon I head home, listening to Metallica's *Reload* from beginning to end and trying not to think about how horrible everything is that's going on at work. When I left today, Briony was crying, Ranjit was in a really bad mood and he's almost never in a bad mood, and even Ryan was quiet. It was all so sad, so very, very sad.

As I come up to the house I look up and straight away I notice there's something stuck to the front door. I panic, thinking that maybe it's to do with Adele and her friends and I wonder if I should call Marcus and ask him to come over but then I get closer and see that someone has taped a plastic wallet to the door and inside it is a piece of paper with typed writing on it. I pull it off the door, open up the wallet, take out the piece of paper and read it. At the top in big black letters it says, '**COMPULSORY POS-SESSION ORDER issued on behalf of Derby City Council: By order of the court you have 14 days from the date of this notice to vacate the premises.**'

29

Lila

'How much!' exclaims Lewis looking over my shoulder at the property listings page I have open on my computer. 'Is that to buy or rent?'

'Tell me about it,' I say despondently. 'I always knew it was going to be expensive but this is ridiculous. I mean, look at that one,' I say pointing at the listing for a tiny studio flat in Tooting. 'It's barely bigger than the inside of a wardrobe and it's nearly twice the amount I'm paying for my current place.'

Lewis pulls a face. 'And it's pretty grim too. Still, on the plus side it's so tiny you'll be able to shower, watch TV and cook a meal all at the same time!'

'Thanks, mate,' I say, 'I can always count on you to look on the bright side. Anyway, haven't you got work to do?'

As he heads back to his desk I close the page, kidding myself that if I leave it for a bit and look later then perhaps miraculously something better and cheaper will have popped up. I have to get back to work anyway. I've got a couple of pieces on the go, two news stories and a feature on a local hospice charity celebrating its fiftieth anniversary. The woman I've been dealing with at the hospice had promised to send me some photos but when I check my email there's nothing from her. There is, however, an email from the photographer who took the pictures for my Skegness article. 'Sorry for the delay in getting these over to you,' he writes. 'I got knocked off my bike and broke my arm and so I'm really behind. Apologies!'

I click on the link, and download the photos, and as soon as the zip file has opened I scan through the images, looking for one in particular. It's an extra photo he'd taken once we had all the ones for the piece in the bag, and the moment I spot it I smile even though it makes my heart ache at the same time. Biting my lip, I stare at the jokey picture of me and Marcus, arm in arm, as we both attempt to take a bite out of a huge ball of candy floss. We look so happy, so perfectly carefree that right now, all I want is to be back in that moment and never leave it.

I feel absolutely terrible about the way things ended, and looking back I can see that it was all my fault. I should've told Marcus about the job offer when I'd had it, because I can only imagine how hurt and angry I would've been had the situation been reversed. By keeping it from him I'd denied him any opportunity to be supportive, to show me how much he cared about both me and my future. Instead, I'd removed him from the equation completely, treating him as an afterthought only fit for consultation once I'd already made the decision. It's no wonder he'd felt so slighted, no wonder he felt as if I'd let him down.

Not for the first time, I think about calling him to apologise, to ask if he'd be willing to meet up and talk things through, but like every other time before this, I convince myself that he won't want to know, perhaps even that he's already moved on with someone else. In an attempt to push that dark thought to the very back of my mind I close the picture of the two of us, and open a new document, ready to get back to work, but as I reach for my notebook my phone rings, and though when I check the screen I'm hoping that it's Marcus, to my surprise it turns out to be Connor.

'Lila,' he says in a voice that sounds like he's been crying, 'Lila, please can you come and help me? It's the council. They've put a letter on my door saying that I have to get out of Hope Street.'

As soon as I get off the phone, I grab my jacket and car keys, and telling Lewis to let anyone who asks know that I've had to go and deal with an emergency, I head out of the office. It occurs to me as I make my way over to Cossington Park, that I should've anticipated something like this happening. Even with all the bad press that my initial article about Connor had sparked, the council were never going to put their plans for the development on ice forever. Clearly, they'd been keeping this move up their sleeve hoping that Connor might be tempted out by other means before they had to come down hard. With time ticking on, and building costs skyrocketing by the day, they must have felt as though they had no choice but to bring out the big guns and use the law to get Connor out for good.

The moment I pull into Hope Street, I spot Marcus's car already parked outside Connor's house, and immediately feel nervous. Hearing Connor's distress I'd been in such a rush to get over here that it hadn't occurred to me that of course he would've called Marcus too. Still, I reason as I pull up behind Marcus's car, we're both here to help Connor, and I'm sure we'll be able to put what happened between us aside for a while for his sake.

It's Marcus who answers the door, greeting me in a formal, distant manner, which is somehow worse than if he hadn't acknowledged me at all.

'Connor's still really upset,' he says. 'I was just making us a cup of tea. Come in and I'll make you one as well.'

As Marcus disappears to the kitchen, I sit down on the sofa next to Connor who is hunched over, looking down at a wodge of tissues in his hand, which he's twisted into a knot.

'I'm so sorry this has happened,' I say after giving him a hug. 'Where's the letter you told me about?'

Connor reaches down to the floor by his feet, picks up a plastic wallet and hands it to me. 'They can't do this, can they? They can't force me to leave my home?'

'I don't know,' I say taking the letter from him. 'I really don't know. But try not to worry. Let me find out everything I can and we'll take it from there.'

I read the letter through, and while I've never seen a CPO before it certainly looks official. As Marcus returns to the room with the drinks I take a photo of the document, and then make a call to Jo Fletcher, an old school friend of mine who now works as a solicitor in Birmingham. Although she warns me this isn't her area of expertise, she agrees to look it over and call me straight back.

While we wait I try my best to fill the awkward silence that descends on the room with small talk but with Connor still upset and Marcus barely saying a word it goes almost nowhere and so the three of us sit in silence until Connor suddenly speaks.

'Do you think they've done this because I didn't like the flat I saw?'

'I doubt it, mate,' says Marcus. 'I think this is what they were always going to do eventually unless you agreed to move. But I thought they would've at least had the decency to give you some sort of notice instead of going straight for the nuclear option.'

Connor shifts uncomfortably in his seat and then finally stands up, leaves the room and returns holding a small pile of letters, which he hands to Marcus.

'Oh, mate,' he says, and for the first time he glances in my direction before quickly looking away. 'Are these what I think they are?'

Connor shrugs and starts to get upset again. 'I didn't know. I thought they were just more letters about the flats so I didn't even open them.'

Marcus starts opening the envelopes and I try my best to comfort Connor. 'It's okay, really it's okay. It's done now – no point in beating yourself up over things you can't change.'

Marcus looks up. 'Yup, these are all warning notices advising Connor that unless he accepts alternative accommodation, they'll have no choice but to proceed with legal action.' He hands the letters to me, and I look through them all one by one, and it's exactly as Marcus says.

'If they kick me out, do you think Mum will still be able to find me?' asks Connor after a moment. 'We have to do something. Could we leave a note on the door telling her where I am?'

'That's one idea certainly,' says Marcus gently, 'but it's like Lila said, we need to take this one step at a time. Let's see what her friend says first before we worry about anything else.'

Jo rings back a few minutes later having spoken to one of her colleagues who has a bit more experience in this area and after chatting to her I relay everything back to Connor and Marcus.

'It's not great news, I'm afraid. The CPO is a legally enforceable document and if nothing happens to stop it then, Connor, you will have to leave Hope Street.'

'Okay,' says Marcus, 'that's the bad news, what's the good?'

'To be honest,' I reply, 'my friend didn't seem to think there was any.' I turn to Connor wondering what the right thing is to do. I wouldn't live in Hope Street alone if you paid me, but then again this isn't my childhood home, and I'm not the one holding on to the hope that one day my mum will come walking through the door. 'Look, Connor, I know I haven't found your mum yet, and for that I'm truly sorry. But if it's what you want I give you my word I'm going to do everything in my power to help you stop this from happening. I mean, we've still got thirteen days to do everything we can to fight it and while I can't make any guarantees, what I can do is promise that I'll give it my all.'

After calling Peter and filling him in on the change in Connor's situation the three of us get to work. I task Marcus and Connor with setting up an online petition opposing the order and getting as many people as possible to sign it. Meanwhile I borrow Connor's laptop and start pulling together as damning an article as I can muster for tonight's front page in the hope of garnering enough public support to force the council to retract the CPO. Finally, I call every last single contact I've made in my three years in Derby, everyone from friends at BBC East Midlands through to local councillors who owe me a favour or two, asking for their help in fighting Connor's cause.

By the time we call it a day at just after nine, I'm absolutely exhausted, all the more so because my phone's been ringing constantly, thanks to the waves my front cover has caused. The leader of the council has called me and Peter in for a meeting, Connor has had to book the following day off work because I've filled it with press interviews, and the online petition – boosted by a link on *The Echo*'s website – is already at over ten thousand signatures.

'Right,' I say standing up, 'Connor I'll be back first thing in the morning to take you down to the mid-morning show at Radio Derby, and Marcus, if you could keep tomorrow free that would be great as I'll need you to take over from me as point person for Connor while I have my meeting with the council and if anything else comes up. Is that okay?'

'Of course. Count me in. Whatever I can do to help.'

'Great,' I reply. 'Let's all just get some rest, and try to stay positive. I'm sure everything will be okay. We've just got to try and stay calm.'

After giving Connor a hug, I head out to my car but as I reach it, I hear the front door open again and when I look up, I see Marcus looking back at me.

'Everything, okay? Did I forget something?'

'No, no, no,' he says awkwardly. 'I just . . . I don't know . . . I suppose I just wanted to say thank you, that's all. Oh . . . and to apologise for being such an idiot. I should never have accused you of abandoning Connor when you've only ever had his best interests at heart.'

I give Marcus a small smile. 'It's fine, you had every right to be angry and anyway, I know you didn't mean it about Connor.'

'It's a bit of a bad habit I've got, isn't it? Flying off the handle at you only to have to eat my words later. You'd think I'd have learned my lesson by now.'

'We all make mistakes,' I reply sadly. 'It's just the way it goes.'

'Well,' says Marcus after a very long moment, 'I promise to try my best not to make any more.'

'Me too,' I say, and for a moment we stand there, just looking at each other. I want so much to take a step towards him, tell him how sorry I am and ask if we can try again but then Connor's front door opens and he calls out, 'Marcus, you've forgotten your car keys.'

As Marcus turns to thank Connor, I call out, 'See you both to-morrow,' and with that, I get into my car and head home.

30

Connor

'Just under an hour to go now, lad,' says Alan looking at his watch as he finishes taking down another set of shelves. 'Fifty-eight minutes exactly before we're all thrown on the scrap heap, and the fat cats wash their hands of us for good.'

Ever since I found the letter from the council stuck to my door, and Marcus and Lila said they'd help me stop it, it's been all that I can think about. I've been so busy between shifts, doing interviews for radio and TV and going around town with Katie, getting people to sign the petition that I haven't really had much time to think about DIY-Depot closing. But now that the last day is here, now that there is less than an hour to go before it shuts for good, it is all I can think about. I can't believe that after today I won't be working here anymore. I can't believe any of this is real. I've had so many good times here, made so many friends, and after today all that will be gone forever.

'Oh, I'm sorry, lad,' says Alan putting one hand on my shoulder and giving me a tissue with the other. 'I didn't mean to upset you – I'm just angry, that's all. Angry about the way they've treated us all. Angry that no one seems to care about the ordinary man and woman anymore.'

I dry my eyes, and give Alan a pat on the shoulder too. Even though he says he is angry I can tell that he is sad like me. Even though he moaned about it a lot, he loves DIY-Depot as much as me, and I know he'll miss it just like I will.

'Excuse me,' says a voice from behind us, 'how much for this?'

We both turn around to see a woman holding up a two-litre can of DIY-Depot-brand brilliant white paint.

'Everything's fifty per cent off,' says Alan pointing at the big banner above the woman's head that says, *Everything fifty per cent off!*

'But there's a dent in the side of the tin,' says the woman rudely. 'Can't you take some more off?'

Alan turns a bit purple and so I step in before he says something he'll regret. 'I'm sorry, no other discounts are allowed.'

'Well in that case you can shove your paint!' the woman says nastily, and she throws the tin into a bargain bin of car washing sponges and walks off.

'I'll tell you what, lad,' says Alan, 'if there's one thing I won't miss, it'll be the bloody general public. Bunch of whinging, tight-fisted idiots the lot of them! There's people here who've lost their livelihoods and then there's the likes of her trying to save herself a couple of quid!' He walks over to the bargain bin, takes out the tin of paint and checks it over. 'It's got a dent in it, she says! There's no bloody dent in it. She's lucky I didn't put a dent in her!'

We carry on working, taking apart shelving units and packing up displays but then at twenty minutes past five, when there should've been another forty minutes of shopping left, Ryan's voice comes over the PA: 'Will all customers please make your way to the checkouts as this store will be closing permanently in ten minutes' time. Please note this is earlier than the advertised closing time but this is to enable all remaining DIY-Depot staff to go to the Beekeeper's Arms to drown their sorrows.'

At first Alan and I think that Ryan's announcement must be a joke but then he comes onto the shop floor and starts pointing customers towards the tills, and tells us to do the same. 'I've given seven bloody years of my life to this place,' he says, 'the least it can do is give me half an hour of paid leave so I can get smashed!'

When it's nearly half past five, we all gather round the customer exit as Briony from the office does a countdown over the PA system. When she gets to zero, Ryan gives me a nod, and I put the key into the control panel, and press the big red button that locks the doors. For a moment everyone stands quietly watching the shutters come down, then Ryan comes over to me, puts a hand on my shoulder and says, 'Good work, Connor,' and then taking out the key shouts to everyone gathered, 'First round at the pub is on me!'

Once we've collected our things from the break room we all head to the Beekeeper's Arms round the corner from the retail park. It's where we went for a Christmas party once, but this time it is very different. There is a huge cheer as we approach the bar, and I see that it's not just everyone who has been at work today but all the others who finished earlier in the week are here too.

'That was a great photo of you in *The Echo* the other day, Connor,' says Pam from kitchen designs. 'You looked proper peeved! I don't know what the council made of it but I know I wouldn't mess with you!'

'My friend Marcus said if he saw me coming down the street with that look on my face he'd cross over!' I tell Pam, and she laughs.

'They're having a meeting about you at the council, aren't they?' says Maryam from home furnishings, handing me a pint of Vimto.

'Yes, they are,' I tell her. 'My friend Lila, who is a journalist, has written lots of articles and the council are so scared of her that they have promised to have a meeting about my case next Thursday and if it all goes well I'm going to get to stay in Hope Street.'

'Some of us are going down to support him,' says Alan. 'You should come. We're meeting outside the council office at ten to cheer him on.'

'Count me in,' says Maryam. 'I'm sick and tired of people like us being pushed around; it'll be nice to fight back a bit.' Suddenly, she gives Alan her bag to hold and me her drink, and then she climbs onto the table, puts her fingers in her mouth and lets out a really loud whistle, so loud that everybody in the pub turns to look at her.

'Today's a really sad day for lots of us in here,' she begins. 'DIY-Depot, Derwent, wasn't just a place to work, it was a family too.'

'Hear, hear!' a couple of people shout from near the bar.

'Anyway,' Maryam carries on, 'we might not be working together anymore but that doesn't mean we have to stop being a family. As most of you know, one of our own, Connor McLaughlin, is in trouble and the council are threatening to kick him out of his home. Well, enough! I'm not having it and neither should you! Come out and support him at ten o'clock next Thursday outside the council house and let's show them that when they mess with one of us, they mess with us all! Three cheers for DIY-Depot, Derwent!'

We stay at the pub for the rest of the evening, and even though it's a really sad day we do end up having quite a good time. I chat to people I haven't had a chance to talk to in ages and the main thing on everyone's mind is where they're going next. A couple of people are going to the Netherfield branch. Others have got new jobs at places like Sports Direct and Marks and Spencer, but most people, like me and Alan, haven't got anything sorted out yet. Alan tells people he's not sure he wants another job at his 'time of life' but I know I will have to get one to pay my bills because although I am getting some redundancy money, like Marcus said, I know it won't last forever.

When I wake up the next day it feels weird knowing that I don't have to go to work but I don't have much time to think about it because there is so much to get ready for the council meeting. Alan and Katie come round at ten and we spend the day making placards for us all to carry and, in the evening, Marcus comes round and Lila pops over to give us updates about how everything is going.

'I don't want to jinx anything,' she says, 'but I've got a good feeling about Thursday. Everything I'm hearing points to the council wanting this to go away as quietly as possible, which to me implies they're not going to do anything to make this a bigger story. I really think we're in with a good chance.'

On the day of the council meeting, I get up early to go on BBC Radio Derby again and Derby Community Radio, then afterwards me and Lila walk through town to meet Marcus. As the three of us get to the end of Market Place I look in the direction of the council building and can't believe my eyes. There is a huge crowd of people, more than just Katie and my friends from DIY-Depot outside. They are all holding up banners which say things like, *Justice for Connor*, and *Hands off our Hope (Street)*. The closer we get the more faces I recognise, like Lee, the landlord from the Crown, the Varelas from the chip shop, and even my old teacher, the one who used to come to my house, Mrs Barnett. And if that isn't enough, I see some of my old neighbours from Hope Street too: the Osbournes from number ninety-five, the Shahs from number eighty-one, the Wyatts from next door but one, the Pinocks from the house opposite, along with Bev and Marcus's sisters.

'Wow,' I say, as Marcus stops to take photos of me with the crowd. 'I knew people said they were coming to support you but I never thought this many would be here.'

Mike Gayle

When the leader of the council arrives everyone boos her and starts shouting, 'Hands off Hope Street!' and they carry on doing this as everyone else from the council turns up.

'I really think they're going to listen to us,' I say to Lila, as the last of the council people go into the building. 'There's so many people here that they've got to change their minds now.'

Lila smiles, but doesn't say anything and for the next hour we all stand waiting for the council meeting to be over. At twelve o'clock there is still no sign of anyone coming out and then out of nowhere Alan shouts, 'What do want?' and everyone around us yells, 'Justice for Connor!' and then Alan shouts, 'When do we want it?' and then everyone shouts, 'Now!' They keep on going like this for ages, then the doors to the council building open and three security guards come out. They make everybody stand back and then Jane Mallory, the leader of the council, comes out too and stands at the top of the steps in front of a TV camera and some photographers.

'Don't worry,' says Katie squeezing my hand. 'There's so many people here, they've got to listen.'

When everyone in the crowd is quiet Jane Mallory starts reading from a piece of paper that she has in her hand: 'After much passionate debate and deliberation, I can confirm that Derby City Council will be proceeding with the planned Cossington Park development. This development will not only bring valuable investment and countless employment opportunities to the region but will also provide much-needed essential community resources. This will of course mean that the demolition of Hope Street and its surrounding areas will proceed as planned and while we appreciate that this will be sad news for some gathered here, we feel that the vast majority of Derby residents will understand that we, your councillors, are as always, striving to act in the best interests of our great city.'

264

31

Lila

Having dropped her bombshell, Councillor Mallory quickly retreats to the relative safety of the council building, leaving scenes of anger and sadness in her wake. I can't believe it. I knew it was a long shot but I had hoped at the very least they'd give him a little more time. Instead, it's all over. All our hard work, all our campaigning, has come to nothing. Despite the strength of public feeling the council have just done exactly what they wanted regardless.

I turn to Connor, wondering how much of what had been said he understands, but it's clear from the look of shock and disbelief on his face and the tears that quickly follow that he's taken in everything he needs to know.

'But what about Mum?' he cries over and over as Katie tries her best to comfort him. 'She didn't say anything about Mum!'

'I know,' I say, hugging him tightly, as everyone around us shouts and boos their disapproval in the direction of the council building and I try my best not to cry. 'I know, I know. They've got it all wrong, Connor, so, so, wrong.'

Before I know what's happening, Connor is surrounded by a sea of people desperate to commiserate with him, and I feel terrible, like I've let him down twice over, once in failing to find his mum and now in failing to save his home from destruction. It had been wrong of me on both counts to give Connor false hope. To let him believe that I could do what no one else could. How egotistical I'd been to think that against all the odds I could find his mother when not even the police with all their expertise and resources had been able to do so. How naïve I'd been to think that I could get a legal possession order overturned solely through the influence of local media and people power.

Perhaps it would've been better if Peter had never sent me to Hope Street, if I'd never met Connor, and stuck my nose in where it didn't belong. Perhaps then Connor would've come to accept his fate and instead of being utterly heartbroken like he is now, he'd be settled in a new part of town, in a new home, able to begin the process of mourning a mother who was never coming home. Because that's the stark reality of this situation I've now come to accept: whatever happened to Bernie, wherever she ended up, the one thing about which I'm absolutely certain is that she is never coming back.

Extricating myself from the mass, feeling like I have no place among Connor's comforters, I turn away about to head back to the office, to do the one thing within my power to do, my piece about the morning already forming in my mind. Once again money and commerce have won, and people like Connor are just collateral damage for the 'greater good'. Yes, the Cossington Park development might bring jobs and money to a deprived area but only at the cost of ripping apart a long-established community, and I strongly doubt whether Connor or any of the other former Hope Street residents will ever see the benefit of this latest spate of regeneration. Once again, the real winners in all this will be the developers and owners of the new slick executive homes the people of Hope Street will never be able to afford.

I'm just about to cross the road when a familiar voice calls out my name and I turn around to see Marcus, his face full of concern. Ours has to be one of the oddest break-ups on record, a painful parting of the ways only to be flung back together again to help our friend. To our credit we've worked well as a team, putting aside our feelings towards one another in order to give everything to supporting Connor. But now it's all over, and I feel so wretched about letting Connor down, I can't help but feel Marcus must hate me even more than he did before all this started.

'Hey, Lila, are you okay?'

'Not really,' I say trying my best to fight back tears. 'This is all my fault. I've really let Connor down.'

'That's not even close to being true,' says Marcus firmly.

'But I said I'd find his mum and I didn't, and I said I'd help him keep his home and now they're going to knock it down. If that's not letting him down, I don't know what is.'

'You gave him hope,' says Marcus. 'When everyone around him, even me, said there was none, you gave him something to believe in.'

'And what good was that?' I say bitterly. 'I feel like I've just been stringing him along when all of this was inevitable.'

'That's one way of looking at it; another is that you cared enough about a total stranger to give them the help they asked for. You never lied to Connor. You were always straight with him, and he knows that. I don't know whether you've heard but I was just talking to someone who knows someone on the council and apparently it was a really close-run thing. There was just one vote in it in the end.'

'Oh, wow,' I say. 'I didn't know that.'

'You fought a good fight, Lila. The odds were stacked against us but you fought it all the same and you should be proud of that.'

'Thanks,' I say touched by the kindness of his words even though I've really hurt him and he has every right to be angry, 'that really means a lot.'

An awkward silence follows, as if there's a lot more we still have to say to one another and yet neither of us feels ready or able to say it. Finally, he asks, 'When are you off to London?'

'The week after next,' I reply. 'Peter's very kindly said I can take the last two weeks of my notice as holiday even though they're short-staffed at the minute. I could really do with the time because I haven't even started packing yet, let alone sorted out anywhere to live.'

'Well,' he says, 'I really do hope everything works out.'

'Thanks.' We hug all too briefly. 'Please tell Connor I'm sorry, and that I really do hope he comes out of this okay.'

'I will,' he says, and then digging his hands deep into his pockets he turns back and disappears into the crowd.

The story I write on my return to work later that afternoon pulls no punches. I not only pour all my own anger into the piece, but also that of Connor and his friends and supporters, even using one of their quotes to send a message to the council: 'They've declared war on the working people of this great city and the only way to make them hurt is at the ballot box in the next local elections.' Peter loves the article so much that he once again gives me the front page with the headline: 'No Hope Street: Council declares controversial development will go ahead,' and I would have felt proud of it had I imagined for a moment that it might make any difference to Connor's situation.

I check my email in the hope of finding messages from some of the London letting agents I've been in contact with. While there are a couple, more pressing is the office-wide email I open with the header: 'Reminder!!! Lila Metcalfe's Leaving Do Tonight!!!'

The irony that I of all people had completely forgotten about this, isn't lost on me. When Niamh had insisted I wasn't leaving without a party and asked me for dates, today had been the one I had given her and amongst everything else going on it had completely slipped my mind. And though the last thing I want to do, today of all days, is party, the fact of the matter is that without insulting my friends and everyone else in the office, I don't have much of a choice.

So, that evening, along with the entire office, I head to Beauforts, a cheap and cheerful wine bar five minutes down the road, and try my best to look like I'm enjoying being the centre of attention.

'It's a good turnout,' says Peter halfway through the evening as he hands me a brightly coloured cocktail that I have no intention of drinking. 'Half these lot wouldn't turn up for their own mother's funeral so it just goes to show how popular you are.'

'Thanks, I think,' I say laughing. 'I am going to miss you all, and *The Echo*.'

'Goes without saying,' says Peter. 'It's a special place.' He takes a sip of his beer then grins and shakes his head. 'I didn't half catch some flak for that piece you wrote today. I've had Councillor Mallory's people threatening all sorts including withdrawing all their advertising for the upcoming quarter but I don't care, they had it coming.'

'The paper's going to be okay though, isn't it?'

Peter waves a hand dismissively. 'Us? We'll be fine. We've survived worse than this and anyway, getting a few backs up means we're doing our job, holding them in power to account, letting them know we're watching. Anyway, the reason I came over is to say I'm not going to forget about poor Connor McLaughlin and his mum. I can't promise I'll be as dedicated as you, but I will keep an eye out for any developments, and of course I'll let you know if I hear anything.'

I don't know whether it's exhaustion from the day, his kindness or the fact that Peter reminds me so much of my granddad, but his words move me so much that I burst into tears and gently, very gently, he pats me on the back and tells me everything is going to be okay.

Leaving Peter, I dry my eyes and make my way over to the ladies' loos to repair my make-up but as I pass through the quieter bar to get there to my surprise I spot Niamh and Lewis in what tabloid journalists euphemistically call, a 'clinch'. Niamh catches sight of me first over Lewis's shoulder and lets out a small yelp of shock, causing Lewis to turn around. But before I can process this bizarre turn of events my phone rings. Grateful for the interruption, I take the call only to immediately regret it the moment I hear Gabe's voice.

'Hope I'm not disturbing you.'

'Er . . . no . . . you're not,' I say, looking from Niamh, to Lewis. 'Just give me a minute,' and turning around, I head back through the main bar, through the exit and out to the street, all the time wondering what on earth Gabe could possibly have left to say to me.

'Okay,' I say, having taken several steadying breaths before returning my phone to my ear. 'I can talk now. What's up?'

'Where are you? Out with Niamh?' I shake my head trying to free myself of the image of Niamh and Lewis locked in an embrace.

'Actually, tonight's my leaving do, so Niamh is here but so are the rest of the office.'

'Wow, so you're leaving *The Echo*? Where are you off to?'

'*The Correspondent.*'

There's a long pause then finally he says, 'You're coming to London?'

'That's the plan.'

'When?'

'I leave next week. Anyway, I'm sure you didn't call to get a career update. What's up?'

'I just can't believe it. You're really coming to London?'

He's avoiding the question again. Maybe he's calling to tell me he's engaged, or worse still that he's got his new girlfriend pregnant and thinks he's doing me a favour and doing the honourable thing letting me know. Whatever the reason I'm not sure I care one way or the other.

'Don't worry,' I tell him feeling strangely confident. 'London's a big place; I'm sure we won't be bumping into one another.'

'No,' he says quickly. 'That's not what I meant, it's just . . . I don't know . . . it's just caught me by surprise that's all. In all honesty, I never thought you'd make the move. I thought you'd be at *The Echo* for good.'

'Why? Because I'm not good enough to be on a national?'

'That's not what I'm saying, Lils. You're an amazing journalist, you always have been, and any paper, anywhere would be lucky to have you. I'm just surprised that's all. I didn't think anything would ever drag you away from there.'

'Well, I suppose it's nice to hear you admit that you were wrong,' I say, running out of patience. 'Now I need to get back to my leaving do so for the third time: what is it that you want?'

'You,' he says. 'I want you back.'

I press the phone closer to my ear unsure I've heard him right and he tells me that he made a mistake ending our relationship. 'I thought I was ready to let you go; in fact I was sure of it, but it turns out I was wrong.'

I'm so shocked I almost drop my phone.

'And . . . and . . . what about Orla?'

'It's all over. I ended things. And if you don't believe me, feel free to check with whoever you want. The thing is, Lils, I made a massive mistake letting you go. Orla wasn't you, and it's you I want. I think we should give us another go and I hope you do too. But don't give me an answer now – just tell me you'll think about it. That's all I'm asking – just think about it.'

32

Connor

'It'll all be alright you know,' says Marcus picking up the mugs from the table. 'We'll find you a really nice place tomorrow, I promise. I know it's not what you want; it's not what any of us want, is it? But we'll make it work won't we, mate? Just wait and see.'

As Marcus takes the empty mugs into the kitchen I sink back into the sofa. I really can't believe what a horrible, horrible day it's been. It had started so well, and I had felt so happy, because I really did think that the council people would listen. So many people had signed the petition and so many of my friends had come out to support me. But as soon as I saw the lady from the council come out of the building, I just knew there was something wrong. She didn't look smiley like you might look if you'd just saved someone's home. She looked serious like people do when they've got to give someone else some very bad news.

Even though she had used lots of words I didn't quite under-stand when she gave her speech, I knew it was all over. I couldn't believe it. These people I didn't know had decided it would be okay to knock down my home. The thought of this happening made me feel so sad, that I just couldn't stop crying. Not when Katie put her arms around me, not when Lila and Marcus gave me a hug, or when Alan and all my friends from work came to talk to me. It was horrible, but nothing could make me stop.

I was so upset that Marcus drove me home and stayed with me for the rest of the day. He even bought us fish and chips for lunch even though we'd already had them earlier in the week. He ate all of his but I left most of mine because I was too sad to be hungry.

After we'd cleared away the plates and cups, I knew I didn't want to think about anything bad and so after having a long chat with Katie on the phone I spent the rest of the afternoon playing video games with my headphones on while Marcus made lots of phone calls and looked things up online. It wasn't until he was getting ready to leave half an hour ago that I realised what he'd been doing was trying to arrange a new home for me.

'I've told the council you're prepared to leave without making a fuss,' he said, 'and in return I've got them to agree to not only give you five grand for the inconvenience but also got you a fifty per cent discount on your rent for the next six months. To get it all you've got to do is agree to take one of the flats they're offering and be out of here by the end of the week.'

'But I don't want to see any flats,' I said quietly. 'I want to stay here.'

'I know you do, mate,' Marcus replied. 'But we've tried everything, and it just hasn't worked. The only thing we can do now is find you somewhere nice to live, somewhere you'll be safe and happy.'

After washing up the mugs, Marcus comes back into the living room. 'Right then,' he says, drying his hands on his jeans, 'I'd better be getting off but I'll see you bright and early tomorrow and we'll do our best to find you a new home.'

I don't say anything. I can't. I'm just too sad. And so, I stand on the step and wave to him and then go back inside. I look around the room. It feels really strange to think that this isn't going to be my home for very much longer, that this is the last week I will be here. I reach out a hand and touch the wall. It feels cool and solid, and I just can't imagine that one day soon this place I've lived in my whole life will be a heap of rubble, a load of broken bricks, wood and glass.

With my hand still on the wall I look across the room at the big picture of Mum on the shelf above the fireplace. Then I look at my DIY-Depot uniform neatly folded up on the edge of the sofa. And then I look down at my house keys on the shelf next to me and suddenly I don't just feel sad anymore, I feel angry too.

Why is life so unfair?

Why am I not allowed to be happy?

First, I lose my mum, then Adele was cruel to me, then I lost my job, and now after all this, they want to take my home! It's just not fair. It's not fair at all. Well, I've had enough!

Picking up the picture of Mum I sit down on the sofa and stare at her face for a long time. The longer I stare, the more upset I get, and the more upset I get, the more I wish she was sitting here next to me, telling me what to do for the best. 'Mum, Mum, they want to take our home from us,' I say to her picture with tears rolling down my face. 'They want to knock it down, and I don't know how to stop them. You always said you'd never let them throw us out. You always said you'd fight them to the end but, Mum, I don't know how to do that. I don't know how to fight them like you would. Please, Mum, please, show me what to do.'

Mum doesn't say anything of course, because she can't. She's not really here no matter how much I wish she was, and even though I know that wherever she is, she is thinking about me, it's not enough to help me now. Right now, I'm on my own; right now the only person I can really count on is me. Marcus wants me to look at flats, Lila is leaving, and even though Katie and all my friends from work have been so kind, I know they think I should leave Hope Street too. So, I've got to work out what to do on my own, I've got to find a way to stop them taking what belongs to me and Mum by myself.

Just then I have an idea, an idea from one of the video games I've been playing all afternoon and evening. In the game there's a part where zombies are after you and you have to barricade yourself in a room to stop them from getting you and I think to myself that maybe I can do the same thing. If I can build lots of barricades, if I can stop anyone from getting in, then just like the zombies in the game the people from the council won't be able to get me. And if they can't get me then they can't get the house and I can stay here until Mum comes back and makes everything okay.

Standing up, I grab my keys from the shelf and go to the front door. I double-lock it and put the chain across like I do at night-time but that doesn't feel like it's enough. I look around the room thinking about the game and how you have to use anything you can find to block the doors and so because it's the biggest and heaviest thing I drag and push the sofa across the carpet until it's in front of the door.

For a moment I stand there wondering if it will be enough to keep the people from the council out. In the game, if you don't do a good job of blocking the door the zombies can break through because there are so many of them. So, I start piling up even more furniture on top of the sofa to make it really, really heavy. I start with the armchair, which I have to put on upside down to stop it from falling off and next I put on my gaming chair, and after carefully clearing all of Mum's pictures and ornaments off it, I put the top half of the shelving unit on the pile too.

When I've finished I stand back and look at what I've done. I don't think anyone could get through the front door now, not even an army of the undead. Next, I go into the back room, and as I take everything off the dining table, I notice that Marcus has accidentally left his wallet there. I put it carefully to one side and then pull the table into the kitchen and wedge it against the back door. In the game there is more than one door and the zombies can get into those doors too and so I decide to make the back door safe as well. There isn't much furniture in the back room, so after I've stacked up all the dining chairs on the table and pushed them in front of the door I put the ironing board and two bedside tables from upstairs on top too.

My phone buzzes with a message. It's Katie asking if I'm free to talk. I don't reply to her though; I haven't got time. I have to finish what I've started. I have to make sure no one can get in.

Putting away my phone, I go round the whole house closing all the curtains, and the bathroom blind. Because there aren't any blinds in the kitchen, I grab a blanket from the airing cupboard and nail it to the window frame so that nobody can see in. After this, I go to the kitchen drawer, take out a box of matches and put them into my back pocket, and then go around the house lots of times checking all the doors and windows, making sure no one can get in. This is my house. My home. And I'm not going to let anyone take it from me.

I am tired after moving all the furniture around and so I go and lie down on my bed, but then just as I'm beginning to fall asleep I hear the sound of a car pulling up outside. Hope Street is really quiet at night so I hear every little sound. Leaving my room I walk along the hallway to Mum's room at the front of the house and pull back the curtains a bit and when I look out of the window I see that it is Marcus. I suddenly remember his wallet downstairs. He must have realised he'd forgotten it and come back to get it.

When I look on my doorbell app I see him take out his keys, try the door a few times, and then look confused. He rings the doorbell and then tries knocking on the door instead but still I don't answer. Then on the app I see him take out his phone and then my phone rings but I don't answer it.

As I watch him on my phone Marcus looks up at the house but then he moves away from the camera and doesn't come back. I don't hear his car start up, so I know he must still be outside. I hear a noise at the back of the house and rush to my bedroom. I carefully pull back the curtain a bit and look through the window and see that Marcus is in the yard trying his key in the back door. He tries lots of times and then he disappears and the next thing I know my phone is ringing again. He must have gone back round to the front of the house because I hear him calling my name through the letterbox.

'Connor! Connor! Are you in there?'

He sounds worried. He sounds scared. I don't want to upset my friend and so the next time my phone rings I answer it.

'Connor, are you alright? I'm outside your house and I can't get in the front door or the back. What's going on?'

My throat feels tight and my hands are shaking. This is it. This is the moment Marcus finds out what I've done. I have to be strong, for me, for Mum.

'I'm . . . I'm . . . sorry Marcus, but I can't let you in. I've decided that I'm not going to leave. I can't. I don't want to live anywhere else. I want to stay here and wait for Mum to come home. She's coming soon; I just know it. But she won't find me if I'm not here.'

'Mate, listen to me. You have to let me in. It's too late for all this. We tried everything we could, but the decision's been made. You have to let me in. I need to see that you're okay. Why don't you come and stay with me again tonight?'

'I can't. If I'm not here they'll knock down Hope Street. But if I stay they can't. It's illegal. The police will arrest them.'

'Connor, mate, please, please, please, please let me in. It's not safe for you in there. Just let me in.'

'I can't, Marcus, I'm really sorry but I can't.' I reach into my back pocket, take out the box of matches I got from the kitchen drawer and stare at them. 'And if anyone tries to get in, I'll burn the house down with me in it.'

Bernie: August 2019

Sitting down at the dining room table, her early morning mug of tea having long since gone cold, Bernie read the letter again still unable to quite believe that it was real: they wanted to knock down Hope Street. In fact, not just Hope Street but the two roads behind it too. And this was going to be all in the name of progress, all to make way for a new 'Cossington Park' urban regeneration development. A development that would allegedly revitalise the area, providing thousands of new jobs and new homes, and replace the long since derelict fifty-acre Cooper-Parkin Engineering Works.

Bernie was stunned. They wanted to knock down her home, the home that she and Connor had now lived in for almost twenty-five years. The home Connor had grown up in, the only home he had ever really known. The one place Bernie had felt safe all these years, the one she'd worked so hard to maintain and keep nice. It was the home that had seen her raise her son single-handedly, creating a haven from an often cruel and unfeeling world.

Slipping off her reading glasses, Bernie put the letter down and looked around the little room. The sliver of morning sun through the back window casting patterns on the wall. The photos of her and Connor on the mantelpiece. Her son's framed certificates from work for passing the various courses he'd been on, some even with a merit. The expensive green and blue bird wallpaper that Connor had managed to get for a bargain when it had been discontinued. Finally, she looked down at the very table she was sitting at where she and Connor had enjoyed so many Christmas dinners and birthday celebrations. They couldn't just sweep all of this away like it meant nothing. She wouldn't let them. Not while there was still breath in her body. She got to her feet, snatched up the letter and, after jamming on her shoes, left the house, crossed the road to Bev's and knocked on her door.

'Have you seen this?' she asked holding the envelope aloft.

'Snap,' said Bev, holding up an identical letter of her own. 'I was just on my way over to see you. This can't be right, can it?'

'Whether, it is or it isn't, it doesn't matter,' Bernie said as Bev ushered her inside the house. 'I'm telling you now, it's not happening.'

Following her friend down the hallway into the kitchen she leaned against the counter while Bev put on the kettle.

'I bet this is the last thing you need,' said Bernie, thinking about her friend's recent spell of ill health. 'That bloody council dropping a bomb like this, when you should be concentrating on getting better. It's a disgrace.'

Bev sighed as she took two mugs from the drainer and popped a teabag in each. 'You're not wrong there. The kids have been good though. They're always checking in on me, and making sure that I'm alright, but yeah, this is not the best timing.'

The kettle came to the boil, and Bev made the tea, passed one to Bernie and then the two friends went to sit in her bright, cosy living room.

'So, what do you think we should do?' asked Bev. 'We can't just stand by and let them break up the community like it's nothing. There are people in the road that have been here over fifty years!'

'And the rest,' said Bernie. 'You know old Mrs Collins on the end? Well, her grandparents were one of the first families in the street. Her granddad worked at Cooper, as did her dad, and her husband too. She's never lived anywhere else but Hope Street.'

Bev blew on her tea and shook her head sadly. 'We can't let this happen. I mean, what are we supposed to do, just up and leave? And where will they send us? I don't want to live on one of those new estates with all the ruffians, and I certainly don't want to live in no high-rise either. I don't want to be anywhere else. I just want to stay here.'

Bernie put down her mug. 'Then we'll have to fight.' She reached into her pocket, removed the letter, slipped on her reading glasses and scanned it. 'According to what it says here there's going to be a consultation process so that's got to mean that nothing's set in stone yet. And there's also a meeting next week at the old Methodist Church on South Street. I say we get everyone together, and we go down there and we tell them that we're not going anywhere and maybe once they see that we're not going to be pushed around they'll change their minds and leave us all alone.'

Over the days that followed, despite their various ailments, Bernie and Bev knocked on every door, on every house, of every street affected, making sure that everyone was aware of what was at stake and how important it was that they turned up to the meeting as a show of force. 'Once they see that we mean business,' Bernie said to a young couple who had only lived in the road nine months, 'they'll have no choice but to back down.'

When the day of the meeting finally arrived, Bernie and Connor made their way to South Street arm in arm.

'Do you think they'll let us stay in Hope Street?'

She looked at her son, who had been fretting about the future of their home ever since she'd told him about the council's plans. 'I'm sure they will. They'll have to; it's our home.'

Connor fell silent for a moment. 'But what if they don't? Where will we go? I don't want to move.'

She reached out and patted his arm gently. 'I know you don't, sweetheart, and neither do I, so we just have to make sure that they know that, don't we?'

Her response seemed to bring her son a degree of comfort. He was twenty-six now, at least a decade past the age she herself had been when she'd left not just home, but also the little that constituted her family, and her country to move to England from a tiny village in southern Ireland. Before he was born she'd never have imagined that he might be still living with her at his age. If anything she'd have pictured him settled down with some nice girl somewhere and maybe a couple of kids of his own. As it was, she doubted that he would ever move out to live on his own, not that she now wanted him to, of course. He was too naïve about the world, too vulnerable, and anyway she loved having him around too much for him to go now. But above all else, Bernie was a practical woman, well aware that she wasn't going to be around forever, which is what made this meeting all the more important. If Connor did ever have to live alone then she wanted him to be able to stay in Hope Street in the home that he loved with people around who knew and cared for him.

As they turned into South Street, Bernie was pleased to see that her and Bev's door knocking had paid off, and the normally quiet road was a hive of activity: cars looking for parking spaces, people streaming into the church and a number lingering outside as though waiting for friends or family members.

Entering the Victorian building, once a vibrant church but now a so-called community hub, Bernie scanned the packed room and spotted Bev waving to her from the front row.

'It's a good turnout, isn't it?'

'Not bad at all.' She cast a glance in the direction of the tables set up with various microphones at the front. 'Now, let's just hope all our hard work has been worth it.'

The meeting opened with a very dry and boring address from the leader of the council in which he attempted to highlight all the positives of the proposed development. Halfway through it, however, people's patience started to wear thin, and when someone called out, 'And what about our houses!' the interruption was met with such a tumultuous round of applause that the council leader's face turned almost purple with embarrassment, and when he continued Bernie got the sense that what followed was a much-truncated version of the speech he had wanted to make.

Once he'd sat down, one of the council's planners put up some slides showing what the new development would look like, and after this someone from the council's housing department explained the options open to those who would have to be rehoused and assured the audience that no one would be sent to a home or an area they weren't happy with.

'Don't trust them!' called out a voice from the back. 'They'll say what they think we want to hear now, just to shut us up. But when it comes to it they'll do whatever they want: Say no to Cossington Park!

At this the room erupted into shouts and jeers, and then almost as one everyone began stamping their feet and shouting, 'Say no to Cossington Park!' and refused to stop even when the councillors practically begged them to. Instead, the chants went on right up to the moment when the meeting was abandoned, and the people from the council made a hasty exit, which was greeted by resounding cheers.

Bernie had no idea who had started the chanting, but she was glad they had because as a show of force it had been faultless. If the council had come to this meeting thinking that the residents of Hope Street were going to be a pushover, they had certainly been disabused of that notion. The community had come together, united, and had sent the council a message loud and clear: Hope Street wasn't for sale and never would be.

The following day's front page of *The Derby Echo* carried the headline: 'Hands off Our Homes!' followed by an in-depth article about the proposed Cossington Park development and locals' anger. There was even a quote from Bernie herself, who they described as a sixty-four-year-old long-term resident of one of the streets earmarked for demolition. 'Hopefully the council will see sense now they know how strongly local people feel. People don't need new developments; they need community!'

In the weeks that followed, the council went quiet and Bernie felt sure that it was because they had been cowed into submission, and were just waiting for the right time to release the news that the project had been abandoned. But then, one afternoon, she'd been in the newsagent's on Linton Road when she bumped into Mrs Nowak, one of her neighbours.

'Did you hear the news?' she asked, as soon as she saw Bernie. 'A couple at the other end of the road, number forty-five I think, and another at eighty-one, have apparently accepted offers from the council.'

'Offers? Offers for what?'

'To move of course. And get this, they've been given fancy three-bed semis over in Mickleover of all places!'

Bernie couldn't believe it. The council hadn't given up at all. They were playing dirty. Of course, families in cramped two-bed terraces would leap at the chance of a three-bed semi in a nice area like Mickleover. Who wouldn't? The council knew that, and it wouldn't matter that there wouldn't be enough of these properties for everyone to get one. All that mattered was to get the exodus started because once one house was boarded up, it would send a clear signal: the council had won, the fight was over and the end was inevitable.

Leaving her shopping on the counter unpaid for Bernie rushed out of the shop and back to Hope Street as fast as she could. She had to change these people's minds. She had to make them see that the battle could only be won if they all stuck together.

Passing her own front door, she marched to number eighty-one and rang their doorbell, but while she heard the barking of a small dog from inside no one answered. Undeterred, she moved on to number forty-five and this time she was in luck; a young woman came to the door holding a baby.

'Sorry, to disturb you, love, really I am. I'm Bernie and I live at the other end of the road, number, one-two-one. I've just heard that you've accepted the council's offer to move. Is that right?'

The young woman looked uncomfortable. 'As it happens, we have, not that it's any of your business.'

Bernie held up a hand. 'Don't get angry, love. I'm not having a go, I promise. It's just that . . . well . . . the council, they're using you to break us. That's what they want. For us all to do our own thing. But if we stick together, if we tell them where they can stuff their offers then they can't force us out.'

The young woman remained unmoved. 'So, you want me and my family to turn down the lovely new home they've offered us in a nice area with good schools just to stay in this dump?'

Bernie gritted her teeth. How dare this girl insult this road, this community. But she didn't dare to give vent to her anger.

'I know it's asking a lot. But please think about it before you accept.'

The young woman shook her head. 'No, I'm sorry, love, but you're having a laugh. The central heating here's been on the blink for months, the backyard's barely big enough to swing a cat, and I'm pretty sure the bloke who lives in the house across the road is dealing drugs! So no, we're not staying, we're out of here, and I don't care what you or anyone else thinks! Now clear off!' And with that she slammed the door shut in Bernie's face.

33

Lila

It's only nine-thirty but I'm more than ready to make my excuses, leave the party and go home. While I'd always expected my leaving do to be an emotional night given how many friends I'm saying goodbye to, the bizarre turn the evening has taken has got my head in something of a spin. First seeing Niamh and Lewis getting off with each other, then Gabe calling out of the blue to tell me he wants me back. All I need now is for Peter to reveal that he's been having an affair with Angela from the crime desk and I'll be fully weirded out.

Putting aside Niamh and Lewis, who have both been deftly avoiding me all evening since I saw them kissing, the main thing on my mind is Gabe's call. Though he had made it clear that he wasn't asking for an immediate answer from me, even if he had I wouldn't have been able to provide one. His call was just so unexpected and I was so taken aback by what he'd said that I was completely lost for words. In the end, somewhat stunned, eventually I'd managed to mumble something non-committal along the lines of having to get back to the party only to then end the call, and spend the next half hour standing in the cold trying to work out exactly how I felt.

Before this moment the only thing on my mind had been concerns about Marcus and the mess I'd made of things. But now, thanks to Gabe's call, I was thinking about him too. I can't help wondering if there isn't something about this situation that was meant to be. After all, one of the big reasons Gabe and I had split up had been because we were living so far apart, but now thanks to *The Correspondent* I'm on my way to London, and for the first time since our uni days we'll finally be living in the same city. On the one hand it feels a lot like kismet, like my destiny is calling, as though after all these years the pieces of a very intricate jigsaw puzzle are finally falling into place. But on the other hand, maybe his call was nothing more than a desperate guy panicking after realising that in checking out whether the grass was greener he'd made the biggest mistake of his life.

Back inside the bar I'd searched high and low for Niamh, desperate for someone to talk this through with, but I couldn't find her anywhere. She must have already left the party with Lewis and now all I want is to go home myself.

As I start to order an Uber my phone rings. My first thought is that it's Gabe calling back, but then I catch sight of my screen and see that it's Marcus.

'Lila,' he says breathlessly, 'I need you to get over here now. It's Connor – he's completely lost it. He's barricaded himself in at Hope Street and is talking about burning down the house with him in it rather than letting the council knock it down.'

There's no mistaking the very real panic in Marcus's voice. This is horrible, so horrible, and I can't help but feel like it's all my fault.

'I'm on my way,' I say trying my best to keep a lid on my emotions, trying my best not to think of how badly this could all end. Changing my destination in the app to Hope Street I head straight outside to wait for the car, growing more anxious with each passing minute.

As we drive across the city, past all the busy bars and restaurants, I go over and over everything I've said and done since meeting Connor and wonder what if anything I could've done that might have prevented this outcome but I draw a blank. I didn't set out to get pulled into Connor's story; it came and found me. And, of course, I never set out to make him my friend; it just sort of happened. But I'd never meant to let him down so badly. I'd never meant for this thing to end this way.

As we reach Hope Street, the driver meets my gaze in his rear-view mirror, assessing me carefully and then finally he says, 'Are you sure this is the place you want, love? There's nothing good down here, I can tell you. They're knocking it down. No one lives here anymore. Maybe you've made a mistake?'

'No, this is definitely the place,' I say as I spot Marcus's car. 'This is exactly where I need to be.'

Getting out of the car, I head straight towards Connor's house where Marcus is standing outside frantically calling up to the upstairs window even though it's closed and the curtains are drawn.

He brings me up to speed, explaining how when he'd left Connor earlier that evening he'd obviously seemed down but there was nothing to indicate that anything like this was coming. Later, having realised he'd left his wallet behind, he'd come back to find both the front and back door not only locked and bolted but blockaded with furniture too.

'I don't know what to do,' he says. 'The last thing I want is to spook him into doing something stupid, but I just don't think he's safe in there on his own.'

'And do you really think he meant what he said, you know about . . .' I don't finish my sentence, but I don't have to.

Marcus runs a hand over his head anxiously. 'The state he's in, I really don't know. You saw him in the pub that time when I said his mum wasn't coming back. When he gets like that he's not thinking straight and there's no telling what that will lead to.'

Determined to do whatever I can to stop something bad happening I scan the pavement and seeing a few pebbles on the road, I pick up a handful and throw them at the front bedroom window until finally the curtains part a little and Connor's face appears in the gap. I signal to him to open the window, and after a few moments of hesitation he does.

'Connor, please!' I shout up. 'We're your friends! Let us in! Let's talk about this.'

'I can't,' he calls down. 'If I do, they'll get in, they'll make me leave, and I won't be here when Mum comes back. I have to stay; I just have to.'

'I know how you feel, really I do, but, Connor, we're worried about you. We're worried you might hurt yourself, so please let us in so we can talk about this.'

'I don't want to talk about it. There's nothing to talk about. This is my home! Mine and Mum's, and I'm not going to let anyone take it from me!'

With that he closes the window, but even so – as we stand helplessly by on the pavement – we can hear him sobbing and screaming inside. It's so horrible, so heartbreaking and as the tears I've been holding back begin to fall Marcus wraps me in his arms.

'There's nothing for it,' I say, as we part. 'I'm out of my depth. We both are. We're going to have to call the police.'

'But what if doing that pushes him over the edge? What if he really does follow through with his threat?'

'He might do that even if we don't call them – just listen to him. It's like you said, he's not thinking straight. We've tried everything we can. We need help.'

I pick up some more stones and throw them at the window again until Connor reappears and opens it. I take a deep breath thinking over what I'm about to say. It's a gamble I know, but maybe it will be enough to make him see reason.

'Connor, listen to me very carefully. Marcus and I are worried, really worried. It's not safe for you in there and as your friends we wouldn't be doing the right thing by leaving you alone. So, you've got a choice: either you let us in so we can help you, or we're going to have to call the police.'

Connor doesn't say anything to begin with, he just lets out a loud and painful cry and then screams, 'No, no, no!' at the top of his voice.

I look at Marcus and he looks back at me, his face grim.

'Maybe we shouldn't do this. Look at the state he's in. I've never known him this bad before.'

'We've got no choice.' I try my best to sound certain even though I'm not. 'It's gone too far for us to sort out now. We have to get help.' I turn back to the house, look up at Connor and hold my phone in the air. 'Connor, I'm going to give you one minute exactly to let us in or I'm going to have to call the police.'

Yelling at the top of his voice, Connor moves away from the window and I tap 999 into my phone, my thumb hovering over the call button.

Fifty seconds.

He appears briefly at the window again, his face pale and twisted in anguish then disappears out of view.

Forty seconds.

My stomach lurches as I hear something smash inside the house but I try my best to stay calm.

Thirty seconds.

To my relief Connor reappears at the window and shouts down at me, 'Please, Lila, no,' and for a moment I think maybe he's wavering but then he slams the window shut and closes the curtains.

Twenty seconds.

His screams, though muffled now, are still painfully audible.

Ten seconds.

I feel all hope of a peaceful resolution draining away and I look at Marcus, his face full of sorrow and fear and then finally, he nods and I make the call.

We don't talk as we wait outside the house on that cold, desolate street. I'm too wrapped up in my own thoughts about how all this will end and I'm guessing Marcus is too. I go over and over everything in my head, wondering if I've made things worse or better, but before I can come to any sort of meaningful conclusion my attention is diverted by the sound of far-off sirens getting nearer by the second. Finally, they are so close that their noise is all I can hear, and the blue flashing lights of the police cars and ambulance hurtling towards us are all I can see.

As the vehicles come to a halt in Hope Street, an officer gets out of one of the cars and approaches us and we explain the situation as best we can.

'Is there any risk that your friend might hurt himself?'

Marcus and I exchange glances.

'He's threatened to set fire to the house,' says Marcus, 'and he's so overwrought that he just might do it.'

The officer nods thoughtfully.

'And is the back door blockaded too?'

'From what I could see through the kitchen window,' says Marcus, 'he's piled a load of furniture up behind it.'

'And is there any other access to the property?'

'Other than through the windows, which are all shut, no.'

'And whereabouts in the house do you think he might be?'

'Up there.' I point to the upstairs window. 'It's his mum's bedroom.'

The officer says something into his radio but I can't make out anything apart from the word 'enforcer', which I don't like the sound of at all.

'You're not going to hurt him, are you?'

The officer gives me a reassuring look. 'No, don't worry, he'll be fine. We'll have him out in no time.'

He walks towards the house and looks up at the front bedroom window. 'Connor?' he calls up in a loud, authoritative voice. 'Can you hear me, son? My name's Officer Dave Farrell, but you can call me Dave. I've been told that you've had quite a rough week and aren't feeling your best, so I'm here to help.'

He turns his head as if listening keenly but there is no sound coming from inside the house.

'Okay, Connor,' says the officer keeping his tone light but firm. 'So, you don't want to talk right now – that's fine by me, I'm not much of a talker either if I'm honest. But, Connor, I was wondering if there's any chance you could do me a massive favour and pop downstairs and open the door.'

He gives Connor a few moments to respond before he speaks again.

'Okay,' he continues. 'So you don't want to come to the door. That's okay. But could you please come to the window and give us a wave so that we know you're safe? You don't have to talk, just a wave will be fine.'

We all look up at the window anxiously but there is no sign of Connor, no sound or movement whatsoever.

Lowering his voice, the officer speaks into his radio again before turning his attention back to the bedroom window.

'Connor, we're very concerned for your safety at this point and so we have no choice but to forcibly gain access to the property. All I ask is that you stay well away from the front door while we do this. Is that understood, Connor? Stay well away from the front door.'

With that the officer signals to two others standing by wearing helmets with face visors. One disappears to the rear of the police van and returns carrying a large red battering ram-type contraption, the kind that until this moment I've only ever seen on TV when the police are raiding the home of a criminal.

I turn to Marcus feeling like I might be sick. I can't imagine how terrified Connor must be right now. I can't believe I've made this happen.

34

Connor

Bang!

The whole house shakes like a car has smashed into the front of it at full speed, and everything inside the room looks blue because of the flashing police lights outside. I crouch down in the corner of Mum's bedroom and scrunch myself into a tiny, tiny ball, squeeze my eyes shut and put my hands over my ears. I feel sick. I feel scared. I want all of this to stop now.

Bang!

The whole house shudders again and there is a crashing sound near my head. I open my eyes and see that Mum's picture of a poppy field has fallen off the wall and smashed. My heart is racing and I can hardly breathe and there is plaster dust from the ceiling all over me.

Bang!

It's not just the house shaking now, but me too. Through the floorboards I can hear men's voices inside the house all calling out my name. They have broken through the front door. They will be up here soon. I don't know what to do. I don't know how to stop them. I look over at the barricade I made in front of Mum's door and just know it's not strong enough. It's only the bed pushed against the door with her chest of drawers on top of it.

I get up and try and move the wardrobe but it is too heavy. Then I hear the sound of footsteps running up the stairs and men calling my name. My hands are shaking as I hear them try Mum's door and then one of them shouts, 'He's in here!'

I lean against the wall and slide down onto the floor. They will be in here any minute. I just know it. My hands are really shaking now and I reach into my pocket and take out the matches. Did I really mean what I said to Marcus? Would I really set fire to the house with me in it? I don't really want to do it, but I do want people to listen and nobody is. All I want is to stay in my home. All I want is to be left alone while I wait for Mum.

'Connor!' a voice shouts through the door. 'It's officer Dave Farrell here. I don't know whether you heard me but I was the one talking to you through the window. Please, Connor, will you open the door so we can see you're okay?'

I say nothing. I open the matchbox and take one out.

I don't want to die. But I don't want to leave here.

I don't want to die. But I don't want to leave here.

I don't want to die. But I don't want to leave here.

'Connor!' says the voice through the door. 'Connor, we're going to have to break down the door, and if you can hear me you need to stay well back so that you don't get hurt.'

I look down at the match in my hand again.

I don't want to die. But I don't want to leave here.

I don't want to die. But I don't want to leave here.

I don't want to die. But I don't want to leave here.

I strike the match. There's a huge bang.

The house shakes again and I drop the match but it goes out. Mum's door cracks and splinters, the bed is pushed across the room and the chest of drawers crashes to the floor. There is dust everywhere. The blue lights are still flashing outside and all over the walls and ceiling.

I close my eyes.

I can't breathe. I feel like I am dying.

I can't breathe. I feel like I am dying.

I can't breathe. I feel like I am dying.

Everything is a blur.

There are people. There are sounds. There are voices.

Everything is a blur and my heart feels like it's going to explode.

And then it all goes black.

When I wake up, I am in hospital. It is not the day I think it is, but a different day. I know this because Marcus, who is sitting by my bed, tells me I've been here for two days. 'You've not been well, mate,' he says. 'Apparently, as well as treating you for shock, you also had some sort of kidney infection too.'

'Oh,' I say feeling weak and tired. 'How did I get that?'

'Well, they don't know but my guess is that with everything going on, you probably haven't been taking good care of yourself.'

'And the house?' I ask. 'Is it okay, will I still be able to go back there?'

Marcus looks down at his hands. 'One thing at a time, mate. Let's concentrate on getting you better first.'

Over the next few days lots of people come to visit me. Katie comes and brings me a bottle of Vimto and a teddy bear wearing a blue T-shirt that says, 'Get well soon.' I think Alan must have told her what happened because she doesn't ask me about it. Instead, she chats to me about work, and taekwondo, and tells me about a new level she's got to in a video game she's playing. Lila also visits me, and so do Alan and Bev. And one afternoon Briony and Maryam come and bring me a big bunch of flowers with a card that says, 'Get well soon, Connor, from all your friends at DIY-Depot, Derwent.' It is lovely to see everybody, and they are all so kind, but whenever I ask anyone about Hope Street they all say the same as Marcus. That I should just concentrate on getting better.

I am lying in bed thinking about Hope Street when the doctor comes round to see me. He looks at my notes and the nurse takes my temperature and checks my blood pressure.

'I think we're all done here,' the doctor says. 'I'm happy for you to go home now, Connor. Sorry it's taken longer than you'd hoped but we wanted to make absolutely sure you were in tip-top condition before we released you back into the wild!'

The doctor starts laughing, and so does the nurse standing next to him but I don't even smile.

'Not a fan of my jokes, eh?' he says when he sees I am not laughing. 'Can't say I blame him, eh, Nurse Phillips?'

The nurse rolls her eyes and smiles at me. 'Come along, Dr Aksoy, patients come here to get better not to be made worse by your jokes! Connor, I'll let your friend know you're ready to leave and hopefully it won't be too long before you're out of here and back home where you want to be.'

When I am dressed and sitting next to the bed Marcus arrives to take me home. But it's not until we are in the car that he tells me he isn't actually taking me to Hope Street.

'Why not?' I ask feeling panicked. 'What's happened? They haven't knocked it down, have they? What about all my things? All Mum's things?'

He taps on the steering wheel and turns down the radio. 'All your stuff is safe. You know I wouldn't let anything bad happen to it.'

'Then why can't I go home?'

'Because . . . well . . . because it's not safe for you anymore.'

'But it's my house!'

'I know it is . . . was . . . but remember, it's the council's now and there's nothing anyone can do to change that.'

'But it's not fair!'

'I know, I know, mate, but it's just the way it's got to be. Me and a few of the lads from work moved most of your stuff into storage and the rest is at mine. I thought you could stay with me until we get you sorted.'

This is all too much. My home, the place I have lived in ever since I can remember is not my home anymore. And all my things and Mum's things are everywhere except where they should be. I always said that the minute I left Hope Street it would be taken away from me and I was right. I've only been out of the house for a few days and already it has been emptied without my permission.

I want to cry, to shout at the top of my voice about how unfair this is. All I want is to be left alone, to go home and wait for Mum to come back. I know that everyone secretly thinks she will never come back, that I am stupid for believing anything else, but I know, in my head, my heart, in every part of me that they are wrong. Mum would never leave me, not if she could help it, and she would never give up trying to get back to me, just as I will never – not now, not ever – give up on seeing her again.

We drive along in silence for a bit before I feel Marcus looking at me.

'So, what do you think?' he asks as we slow down at a set of traffic lights. 'Are you happy to stay with me for a few days?'

I turn to look at my friend. He really has been so kind, helping me, looking out for me, always trying to do his best to keep me safe, but this just has to be done.

I nod at Marcus, and as soon as he looks back at the road I reach down, unfasten my seatbelt and before he can stop me I open the passenger door and get out of the car as the traffic lights change colour. I race across the road, dodging cars beeping their horns at me, until I make it to the other side. Scrambling over the metal barriers I start running faster than I have ever run in my whole entire life.

I don't know where I'm going; all I know is that I have to get as far away from Marcus as I can. I run through a council estate, into a park and out the other side before reaching a small row of shops. I'm really out of breath and thirsty, so, so thirsty. I would give anything for a cold can of Vimto but when I check my jacket and trouser pockets I realise I don't have any money and my phone is still in the bag I'd left in Marcus's car.

After getting my breath back I start walking down the road trying to work out where I am but it isn't until I see a road sign with the names of places I recognise that I realise I'm quite far away from Hope Street and to get there I'll need to catch a bus into town and another back out again. If the buses are on time I could be there in less than forty minutes, but walking will take much longer and after all that running, I don't think I have the energy.

Reaching the bus stop I let a few buses go by, waiting for my moment. When there are enough people at the stop who are all trying to get on a bus into town, I wait for someone to ask the driver a question and then sneak on. Even though I think some people see me do this no one does anything about it.

With my heart beating really fast I take a seat on the top deck, pulling up the hood of my sweatshirt to try to make myself invisible. A short time later the bus reaches the centre of town where after waiting until the driver is busy talking to someone, I join the crowd of people getting off.

I'm too scared to get on another bus without paying so I decide I will walk back to Hope Street from here. I make my way across town through the busy Corn Market, past the shops and hair salons on St James Street then out of town along the dual carriageway until I start to see a few places I know like the petrol station, the Crown pub and the old Comet building. Finally, I am on Linton Road, walking past St Mary's – my old junior school – and the open door of The Fresh Fryer Chip Shop.

Soon after I reach Margaret Road, and it is then I realise I have another problem. I haven't got my keys with me, and I don't even know where they are. I think I might have left them in the house, which would mean Marcus probably has them or has given them to the council. I make up my mind that I am not going to let a little thing like this stop me. This is my home I am trying to get back into, and so even if I have to take a brick and smash a window, I will do it.

As I turn into Hope Street the first thing I notice is Marcus's car parked outside my house. Of course, he has guessed where I was running to; he isn't stupid. Where else would I go? I think about running again but then realise that I barely have the energy to stand up anymore. I tell myself that perhaps I will be able to talk to Marcus and convince him that letting me go back to Hope Street is the right thing to do.

As I walk further down the street the car door opens and Marcus gets out, and even from a distance I can see that he is in a bad mood. Then I look at my house, and I can't believe it. The front door and windows are covered in the same metal grilles that have been used on all the other houses on the street. One-two-one Hope Street now looks more like a prison than a home.

'Marcus . . . what have they done?' I cry, as tears begin rolling down my cheeks. 'I'll never be able to get in there now, and no one will be there to meet Mum when she comes back.'

35

Lila

'Right then,' says my new editor, Beth Warwick, as she stands up and starts to gather her things, 'everyone knows what they're doing so let's get back to work.'

Immediately the meeting room buzzes with noise and chatter as the rest of the team start making their way back to the newsroom, and I'm about to do the same when Beth calls me back.

'Just wanted to say how impressed I was by your piece on the schoolkids and their climate change protest yesterday,' she says. 'It was really good work.'

'Thanks,' I say feeling myself blush. 'That really means a lot.'

'Well, I remember what it's like being the new kid on the block,' says Beth, 'and how easy it is to doubt yourself in a place like this. So, I just wanted you to know that you're doing a great job and I look forward to reading a lot more of your work in the future.'

As I walk back to my desk feeling about ten feet tall, I find it almost impossible to believe that it's only been a month since I left *The Echo*. So much has happened that it feels like much longer.

It had been hard leaving my life in Derby behind, all the more so because of the way things ended for Connor. That night back in Hope Street is one I'll never forget. The horror of seeing him being physically removed from the home he had loved so much, and fought so hard to stay in, had nearly broken me. Though I'd visited him while he was in hospital he'd looked so defeated and I'd felt so guilty for letting him down that I never went back. Instead, I'd concentrated on getting ready for the move to London: finishing up things at *The Echo*, packing up my flat and most challenging of all finding somewhere to live.

Despite several days spent searching solidly for accommodation in the capital I came up with nothing, but just as I was about to give up hope I had a call from an old uni friend who had heard about my move to London and the difficulties I was having. She told me about a friend of hers who was moving out of a flat-share in Stratford, meaning there was a room available. I didn't even bother going down to look at it; all that mattered was that it was empty and I could afford it. I called up straight away and told them I'd take the room, reasoning that anything had to be better than a daily commute on unreliable public transport that would undoubtedly cost an arm and a leg, not to mention driving me slowly insane.

As it turned out, however, the room was not only the second biggest in the flat and more than enough for my needs, but my new flatmates all seemed like lovely people too. That weekend I hired a van, loaded all my things into the back and headed down to start my new life in London.

My first day at *The Correspondent* was both terrifying and utterly thrilling, dropped as I was right in at the deep end. Within my first hour I was charged with helping cover a state visit and by the time I'd finished the day I'd not only done that but also interviewed the Mayor of London for a piece another journalist was working on, and attended a press conference for the launch of a new eight-part drama series on BBC One. From that hectic first day I've gone on to write pieces on everything from all-female running groups to a recent rise in dognapping, from the state of the UK rental market through to a financial scandal at a prominent private hospital.

All of it, every last single minute, has been everything I'd hoped working at a paper like *The Correspondent* would be. It's been tough certainly, but there hasn't been a day when I haven't felt alive with the excitement of it all. And yet, I can't say I haven't missed *The Echo*, for all its faults and shortcomings. And, of course all the people I left behind in Derby too, not least Marcus.

While we've exchanged a few texts since I came down here, for the most part they've been updates about Connor, each of us careful to avoid talking about anything else for fear, I suspect, of saying the wrong thing. None of it is the way I would've left things in a perfect world, but things are the way they are and I keep telling myself that I'll just have to learn to accept that.

I work solidly until just after one-thirty when I stop for lunch. Normally I'd eat at my desk or sit and have a catch-up with some of the other newbies, but as I've arranged to have a virtual lunch break with Niamh I stick in my AirPods, and grabbing my coat I head out of the office and walk the short distance to Battersea Park. Though it's a cool October day it's dry and bright, the perfect sort of day for sitting on a bench overlooking the boating lake when you're wrapped up warm.

'Hello, hot shot,' says Niamh, when she picks up. 'How are you?'

'Not too bad at all, thanks,' I reply shooing away a pigeon that's a little bit too interested in my tuna salad. 'How's your week been so far?'

'Well, you know, all the usual glitz and glamour of *The Echo*. First thing this morning I interviewed a family over in New Normanton who have got raw sewage coming up through the manhole cover in their back garden. After that I wrote a quick piece about a kid banned from school for having a Nike logo shaved into the back of his head and this afternoon I'm covering a Governance, Ethics and Standards Committee meeting at the council. So, you know, yay me.'

'Oh, mate, I feel your pain,' I say and, not wanting to make her feel worse telling her about my day, I change the subject. 'And how are things going with Lewis?'

Much to my surprise, I'd learned that Niamh and Lewis had been an item long before their entanglement at my leaving do. There had been no married man causing Niamh to wrestle with her conscience but rather a reluctance on her part to get involved with Lewis. The two had been sparring partners for so long that I think she'd found it difficult to take their fledgling relationship seriously at first, but now, much to everyone's surprise, they were solid.

'Really, really good,' she says. 'He cooked for me last weekend and it was actually edible.'

This doesn't sound right at all. 'Lewis cooks? From scratch you mean? Not just zapping stuff in the microwave?'

'Oh, he cooks alright: crispy mustard chicken with breadcrumbs and a lemon garlic kale salad followed by fresh ginger cake and vanilla custard. I'm not kidding, Lils, it was gorgeous.'

'Wow,' I say. 'He certainly managed to keep that side of himself very well hidden. The most cooking I ever saw him do was peeling back the foil on a pot noodle and pouring in hot water.'

'Well, clearly he's trying to impress me and he's going the right way about it. Anyway, enough about all that. What about you and Gabe? Have you decided what you're doing about him yet?'

Gabe.

Since he dropped his bombshell about wanting us to get back together I've been all over the place when it comes to Gabe. While he's messaged several times since that night my replies have at best been vague and at worst downright rude. I've told him I'm busy, I've told him I've got too much on my mind with the new job, and I've even told him that if he wants an answer now then it's no. But each time his response has only ever been calm and considered, telling me that he understands that all this is his fault and that he'll wait as long as I need him to. Last night, he'd messaged again under the guise of asking me how my new job was going and feeling that this state of limbo had to be brought to an end one way or another, I'd suggested that we meet for drinks after work this evening.

'So, you've made up your mind then?'

It's a good question but I'm not sure I know what the answer is.

'Not even close.' A huge swan comes in to land on the water right in front of me in an action that is as graceful as it is noisy. 'I haven't a clue what I'm going to say to him.'

'Well, how do you feel about him?'

I stab my fork into my salad and think for a moment. 'I know I used to love him but now I'm not sure. I mean, you can't just switch off feelings, can you? But do I really want him or is it a case of the comfort of the familiar?'

'Do you think things would be a bit clearer if you and Marcus hadn't happened?'

I feel a little pang at the mention of his name. 'I think Marcus showed me there could be life after Gabe, that I don't have to settle, that I can be happy with someone else.'

'But nothing's changed though, between you and Marcus. Has it?'

'Nope, still the same.'

'And you don't think there's any chance it will?'

'Not really – too much has happened for us to make it work now.'

Niamh sighs heavily. 'So, the choice is get back together with Gabe or live the single life in London?'

'Pretty much. So, what do you think I should do?'

Niamh laughs. 'You're asking the wrong woman. This time last year I wouldn't have touched Lewis with a bargepole and now look at me! Clearly, I'm not to be trusted! But you've always had a good instinct so like Peter's always telling us, trust your gut, and I'm sure that whatever you decide it'll be the right thing.'

That night, having turned down an offer from a group of my co-workers to join them for drinks, I head over to the Shard to meet Gabe. The location was his choosing. If it had been left to me we'd have met in a nice down-to-earth pub in Soho, some-where we could tuck ourselves away in a corner and talk properly. But he'd suggested this and while I'd expected it to be swanky, it's only as I get out of the lift on the 31st floor that I realise quite how upmarket it is. All the men are wearing expensive-looking suits and all the women are sophisticated in designer evening wear. Meanwhile I'm still dressed in my work outfit of jeans, a smartish top and blazer, and although I'm sure I look out of place, I'm so caught up in my thoughts about our meeting that I'm not sure how much I actually care.

I spot Gabe almost immediately, sitting at a table overlooking the river, London Bridge and the lights of the city. He looks almost exactly as I remember: tall, handsome, immaculately dressed as always, though his straight black hair inherited from his Chinese mother had been cut a little shorter than normal.

'Lila,' he says, and as I approach the table he stands up and greets me a little awkwardly with a kiss on the cheek. 'It's so good to see you. Let me get you a drink. What do you fancy? A gin and tonic or a cocktail?'

'Gin and tonic would be great,' I reply, even though I'm not sure I can afford orange juice in a place like this.

As I sit down, he calls over a waiter, orders my drink and then at last, it's just the two of us.

'So how are you finding living in London?' he asks, glancing in the direction of the view. 'I'm guessing it feels like a million miles away from life in Derby.'

'You're not wrong there,' I reply. 'Still, I'm sure this place will catch up with the Midlands one day soon.'

Gabe smiles.

'How are you?' I ask, after a moment.

'Good thanks,' he replies, and he goes on to tell me how busy he's been at work and how he might be in line for a promotion.

'Congratulations.' The waiter arrives with my undoubtedly very expensive drink and it dawns on me that not only is getting back together with Gabe not what I want, but I'm not sure if he was ever what I'd wanted. Not really. It strikes me that most of the five years we were together were spent thinking about what we might be in the future as opposed to what we were in the moment. Perhaps it was the distance between us that had kept us together all that time. He and I were such different people, with such different ways of looking at the world, and I can't help thinking that had I moved to London instead of Derby, our relationship would've naturally run its course a long time ago.

I look up and meet his gaze. 'I don't think this is going to work.'

He's silent for a moment and then says, 'Are you sure?'

Taking his hand in mine, I meet his gaze once more, 'I'm sorry, but yes, I am.'

He looks at me and I look back, and I can see that he wants to put up more of a fight, but knows me too well to try because my mind's made up.

He nods, as if to himself, and then sighs. 'It was good while it lasted, wasn't it?'

'Yes,' I say, not wanting things to end on a sour note. 'Yes, it was.'

With that we embrace, and then, turning around, I leave without once looking back.

Out on the street I make my way to the Tube, my head full of thoughts about what's just happened. I feel liberated. Lost. And more than a little sad and yet at the same time strangely at peace with my decision.

As I cross the road my phone rings, and to say that I'm surprised to see who's calling is an understatement but that's nothing compared to the shock I feel at what they have to say. The moment the call is over I break into a run.

36

Connor

'So, what do you think?'

Marcus is looking at me for an answer but I don't really know what to say. The flat we are standing in is nice. It is a ground-floor flat just two streets away from where Bev lives. It is modern, tidy and clean, and on the way in we had a chat with a nice old lady who has lived in the block since it was built. She told us it is the best place she has ever lived because it is quiet and all the neighbours are friendly. And she even said that she would never live anywhere else. But I don't really think it matters where I live anymore because any place that isn't Hope Street and doesn't have Mum in it will never feel like home.

'It's nice,' I say, not wanting to upset Marcus.

'I mean, I know it's only got one bedroom and you wanted two, but it does have a lot going for it. It's not a high-rise, it's in great condition, and it's dead quiet too. I really think this is the one. How about you?'

I shrug. 'It's okay. If you think it's the best one then so do I.'

Marcus looks a bit disappointed that I'm not more excited.

'We could look at some of the others if you like,' he says. 'One came on this morning not far from Rykneld Park, which seems okay. We could book a viewing before we make a decision on this one.'

'No thanks,' I say, feeling like I haven't got the energy to look at any more. 'This one will do fine, thank you.'

'Are you sure?'

'Yes,' I say. 'I'm sure.'

Marcus sighs. 'Okay, mate, in that case I'll go and have a word with the bloke from the council and tell him you've made a decision.'

As he goes out into the hallway, I walk back to the living room and stand and stare out of the front window at the small lawn and the house opposite. It is a much nicer view than the one I had of boarded up houses on Hope Street but I still wish I was back there.

It has been over a month since the council boarded up Hope Street, since the only home I can remember was taken from me. At first, I was angry – really, really, angry. With the council, with the police, with Lila, with Marcus. Because if it hadn't been for them, I'd still be in my house waiting for Mum to come home. But now, I don't feel angry anymore. I just feel sad – really, really sad – and nothing anyone, even Katie, does to try and cheer me up works because I can't stop thinking about how if Mum goes to Hope Street to find me, I won't be there. That she'll think I've given up on her, that I gave up fighting for our home.

After a bit Marcus comes back. 'Nearly sorted,' he says, holding a clipboard that I'd seen the man from the council carrying. 'You've just got to sign the paperwork and the keys will be yours.'

I sign my name on the place Marcus shows me and then give the clipboard back to him, and he takes it to the man from the council and comes back with a set of keys.

'These are yours, mate,' he says handing the keys to me and smiling. 'Congratulations, you've just got yourself a new home.'

The next day Marcus and I get up early and drive to a storage unit near the Rams' ground. There is a white van parked outside and two of Marcus's apprentices are standing next to it waiting for us and after saying hello, we all start taking some of my things from the unit and loading them into the back of the van. Because I have only got a flat, I can't take everything so we have to leave most of the big furniture from Mum's bedroom and some of the things from the back room in the storage place too. It makes me feel sad thinking of Mum's things being left behind but Marcus promises me that it will all be safe until we think what we want to do with it.

When the van is packed, the apprentices drive over to the new flat while Marcus and I follow behind. When we get there, Marcus tells his apprentices where to put everything because I don't really know where I want things to go. It feels weird seeing all my things in this strange new place and I don't really like it but I don't say anything because there's no point.

'Still feels a bit a strange, doesn't it?' says Marcus, that night, as we stand in the kitchen putting away the shopping we have just bought from the supermarket up the road.

'A bit,' I say reaching for a can of beans and putting it on the shelf in the cupboard next to me.

Marcus gives me a small smile. 'I remember when I first moved out of Mum's and into my own place, it took a while for it to feel like home and I think it'll be the same for you. But trust me, once you've been here a couple of weeks and arranged all your things just the way you want them it'll get better.'

Once we're done Marcus stays for a bit and watches TV but then about nine o'clock he stands up and says, 'Right, then, I'd better be off.'

I walk him to the door, and then he gives me a big hug. 'You look after yourself, okay? Remember if you need anything at all, just give me a bell, and don't forget Mum's invited us both over for dinner tomorrow night.'

After Marcus leaves, I FaceTime Katie.

'So, how's the new place?' she asks.

'It's okay,' I say and I take my phone around the flat and show her.

'I really like it,' she says, 'and it'll look even better when you've put up all of your pictures and posters. I'll help you do it.'

'Maybe,' I say, still feeling weird about being here, and after we talk a bit more I tell her I'm feeling tired and will call her tomorrow.

I don't really feel tired. I just don't feel very much like talking. Instead, I stay up late playing video games with my headphones on so that I don't disturb any of my new neighbours. Around two in the morning I am really tired so I switch off my console. I brush my teeth and then get into bed, but I just can't settle. Everything looks strange, everything smells strange and all the noises around me are just too different.

In the end I take my duvet and lie down on the sofa in the living room with the TV on but with the sound down low, and as I close my eyes, I pretend to myself that Mum is sitting on the sofa next to me, rubbing my back, and telling me everything will be okay.

The next morning, I wake up to the sound of my phone ringing and I think it's Katie checking to see if I'm okay but when I answer it, it's a lady's voice but one I don't recognise.

'Hi there,' she says, 'am I speaking to Mr Connor McLaughlin?'

'Yes,' I say, wondering if it is someone from the council checking about the new flat.

'Great,' she says, 'I'm Greta Hughes from HGN recruitment. I was given your details by your former employer, DIY-Depot. I'm calling with some good news!'

'Oh,' I say feeling confused. 'Have they changed their minds about closing the store?'

'Well, er, no, but I am pleased to tell you that you've been selected to interview for a position as a customer fulfilment associate at the Wyvern Square branch of SuperBargains. Can I book you in for this afternoon?'

I have to get a bus into town then another one out and then walk for ages to get over to Wyvern Square and I nearly get lost on the way. The retail park where I am having the interview is really big, much bigger than where DIY-Depot was and it has a lot more shops too. As I walk to the big SuperBargains I go past a Sports Direct, a Homesense, a TK Maxx and a Deichmann's as well as two different department stores and a massive food court that is already full of people even though it is only eleven o'clock in the morning.

I take off my headphones and suddenly feel dizzy. Everything is so busy and noisy and all I want to do is turn around and get back on the bus. I don't really know how I feel about the idea of getting a new job. Of course, I know I'll have to get one eventually, because like Marcus said my savings won't last forever, but I don't feel ready. I've not even had time to get used to my new flat or living in a new area, and now this. I've never worked in a su-permarket before, and SuperBargains is a really big one that sells food and clothes and even has its own opticians. I'm not sure I'm going to like it.

I'm just about to turn around and leave when I remember how I'd promised Greta from the recruitment agency that I would come for the interview and I don't like to break my promises if I can help it. And then I remember too that when I had my interview at DIY-Depot I was nervous then, and that turned out really well, so who knows? Maybe this will be the same.

When I reach the store, at the far end of what is called the east wing of the Upper Mall, I look around for signs to help me work out what to do next, but there aren't any. In front of me is a big line of checkouts and everyone in uniform seems far too busy to help me. After wandering around up and down the aisles for a while I end up in the underwear section of the clothing department, where I see a woman in uniform who looks a bit less busy than everyone else.

'Excuse me,' I say, trying not to look at the tiny coat hanger with the lacy black knickers on it the woman is holding, 'I'm here for an interview and I don't know where to go.'

'Interview?' The woman pulls a face. 'I wouldn't bother if I were you – this place is a nightmare to work for.'

I swallow hard but don't say anything and thankfully the woman speaks again, 'Over there in the corner where it says "Customer Services",' she says using the pants to point with, 'they'll call up to the office and someone will come down and collect you.'

I do what she says and eventually a young man comes out of a door behind the desk marked 'Staff Only' and after checking my name off a list he takes me upstairs to a room where there are two women in SuperBargains uniforms. One is younger and wearing lots of make-up and the other is older with very black hair scraped up into a bun on top of her head.

'Connor McLaughlin for you, Danielle,' says the man who brought me upstairs, as he turns and leaves the room.

'I suppose I'd better be off too,' says the older woman, who looks me up and down then gives her friend a funny look before getting up and going.

'Yeah, see you later, Jas,' the younger woman calls after her. 'I shouldn't be too long. This guy is the last one for a while.'

I look at the chair in front of me and wonder if I should sit down even though I haven't been asked to. I feel sick, and nervous, and wish more than ever that I'd had time to talk to Alan or Marcus about the interview. I've never even heard of a customer fulfilment associate before and I have no idea what the job is, and so I am very much, as Alan would say, whistling in the dark with this one.

'Take a seat,' the woman behind the desk says eventually, in what I do not think is a very friendly or professional way.

'So, do you drive?'

I look at her confused. I didn't know this job was about driving. 'No, I don't. I don't even have a licence.'

The woman pulls a horrible face. 'Then how are you going to get to work for the four a.m. shift?'

I'm not sure what to say. Greta hadn't said anything about starting that early.

'I don't understand,' I say. 'I'd never be able to get here for four o'clock in the morning. The buses by me don't even start until after five.'

The young woman swears under her breath. 'Right, so another time-waster then. Thanks very much. You can go now.'

'But I haven't had my interview,' I tell her.

'There's no point if you can't get here on time, is there?'

'But Greta, the woman from the agency, didn't say anything about starting that early. Aren't there other shifts?'

'Not for a CFA there aren't. And that's what we're recruiting for so if you don't mind . . .'

I want to say that I do mind. I want to say that I had spent the whole journey over here worrying about this interview and what they might ask me. I want to say that I've had to take two buses to get here, haven't had time for lunch and now have a really bad headache. I want to say that I've just been forced to move house after living in the same place for nearly all of my life. I want to say that I feel lonely and afraid in my new flat, in an area that I don't really know very well. I want to tell her that I miss my old job, and the friends I used to work with. And then as well as all of that I want to tell her just how much I miss Mum, how much it hurts that no one seems to care about her apart from me, and how I'd give anything, absolutely anything to see her again. I want to tell her that the last thing I need right now is to waste my time talking to rude people like her about jobs that hadn't been explained very well. But there is no point in saying any of this to Danielle or anyone else here because it is obvious that they do not care, and so without saying anything, I stand up and leave.

As I wait at the bus stop, I try my best not to cry but it is very hard because I feel so sad. I don't feel like going back to my new strange flat, but I don't know where else to go. Katie is at work so I think about going to visit Alan, and I take out my phone to try and work out which bus I need to catch to get over to his house but as I'm looking at the journey planner website my phone rings.

'Hello, Lila,' I say, pleased to hear a friendly voice, 'how are you? Are you still in London or are you back in Derby?'

'Actually,' she says, and her voice sounds funny, 'I'm in Manchester. Connor, I've got some absolutely amazing news: I think . . . I think . . . I might've just found your mum.'

Bernie McLaughlin:
Wednesday 11 March 2020

– The afternoon of the day she goes missing

'Good afternoon, ladies and gentlemen,' came the voice crackling over the coach PA system, 'this is your driver Vernon speaking, just letting you know we'll shortly be arriving at Manchester Central Coach station where this service will terminate. Please remember to take all your belongings with you and wait until the bus has come to a complete stop before taking off your seatbelts. Thank you for travelling with BudgetBus, enjoy the rest of your day and we look forward to taking you on your next adventure very soon.'

There was a small flurry of activity as Bernie, along with the handful of other passengers on the 9.15 Derby to Manchester coach, began preparing for arrival. Checking that she had her bag and phone, she reached into her coat pocket and removed the piece of paper on which she'd written down the address and directions to her destination and carefully looked it over. The next leg of her journey involved getting from the coach station to Piccadilly Gardens, something she wasn't completely confident about. She'd never been to Manchester before and though she'd been told it was only a short walk from the coach station with it being so much bigger than Derby she was only too aware of the possibility of losing her way.

Thanking the driver as she got off the coach, Bernie then stood for a moment trying to get her bearings before making her way towards one of the exits. Spotting a sign for the city centre she walked along Chorlton Street until she met something that looked like a main road and checking her directions, she was relieved to find herself on Portland Street, which at least meant she was going the right way. Reaching a posh-looking restaurant/bar place called The Slug and Lettuce, Bernie crossed the road as per her instructions but then felt a little unsure about where to go next. Spotting a young couple coming the other way she asked them for directions to the bus station and they happily obliged and told her she wasn't far. 'See Primark over there,' said the young woman in a broad Mancunian accent, 'just aim yourself towards that and when you're about halfway you'll see it on the other side of the road. You can't miss it.'

Sure enough, the bus station was only a short walk away and after checking an information panel Bernie made her way over to the stand for the number eighty-six and after a brief wait it arrived.

'I need to go here,' she said showing the driver the address on her piece of paper. 'Can you give me a shout when we get to the right stop, please?'

'It'll be announced,' the driver replied. 'Just listen out for the Dane Road stop in about half an hour.'

Glad of the chance to catch her breath Bernie took a seat near the front of the bus and after checking her watch looked out of the window. She couldn't help but smile thinking about Connor and how he'd be at work right now without a single clue where she was and what she was doing. She'd been so careful to cover her tracks, making sure not to leave a single clue as to where she might be going. He really was going to be surprised when he found out what she'd been up to, and she couldn't wait to see the look on his face when she told him all about the adventures she'd had.

Sure enough, about thirty minutes into the journey a recorded voice announced that the next stop would be Dane Road, and gathering her things Bernie got up and waited by the driver for the bus to come to a halt. Thanking her profusely she got off and then consulted her piece of paper again for the next step in her directions.

Lifting her head she spotted Majestic Wines on the corner of the road, which was the landmark she'd been told to look out for. Heading towards it she then turned into Dane Road, and walked down it for a short while until she came to the third road on her right, Harrisons Avenue. Halfway along it she stopped outside number sixty-four, and after one final check of her paper to make sure that it did indeed have a yellow front door and a ramp up to it for disabled access, she rang the doorbell.

'Hello, Ross? I'm Bernie McLaughlin,' she said when a man in a wheelchair opened the door. He was young, about Connor's age, and had a short brown beard, kind smiley eyes and was wearing black jeans and a black T-shirt that said, 'Red Dwarf', in red writing on it just like one Connor had at home.

'Pleased to meet you, Bernie,' he said wheeling himself away from the door and holding it open for her. 'Come in and I'll make you a cup of tea. I bet you'll need one after your journey here today.'

'You're not wrong there,' she said. 'Milk, two sugars please if you have them.'

Bernie followed the young man into a kitchen, which had clearly been adapted for him. She'd never been in a house like this before and thought it was amazing what they could do these days. All the counters were low and everything was in his reach so he didn't have to rely on anyone else to help him do everyday things.

'So how was your journey?' he asked as they waited for the kettle to boil.

'Oh, not too bad at all,' she replied. 'There's a cheapo coach from where I live and it only cost a few quid to get here. Your directions were grand, thanks, so I haven't had any problems.'

'Sorry again, that I couldn't meet you halfway like you suggested but I don't drive and even though according to my watch it's the twenty-first century public transport can still be a nightmare for people like me.'

'It's no problem,' said Bernie with a smile. 'It's been a bit of an adventure to be honest. It's nice to do something different now and again.'

The kettle came to the boil and Ross made two mugs of tea, handed one to Bernie and then led her through an open set of double doors to his living room at the back of the house.

'Is that it?' she said setting her mug down on the coffee table next to her and nodding towards a slim rectangular box propped up on the sofa.

'It is indeed,' he replied. Putting down his mug, he picked up the box, removed the object inside and handed it to Bernie. 'A signed, framed gold disc of Metallica's *Master of Puppets* album. I guarantee your son is going to love it.'

The idea to get this for Connor's birthday had come to Bernie a few months earlier when she'd been watching *Antiques Roadshow*. These days it seemed, anything from toys from the Seventies to clothes from the Eighties could be considered collectible. If there were enough people out there with an interest then you could be sure there would be a queue of other people willing to sell them whatever it was they were into.

One chap on the show had brought along a lot of signed Beatles memorabilia worth a small fortune and this had given Bernie an idea. What if she got something for Connor's upcoming birthday that might be worth some money in the future? Unlike when he was little, these days she had no clue what to buy him for Christmas and birthdays. If she asked for ideas it was always this gory-sounding video game or that horrible-looking DVD, and while Connor would always be grateful when he got them, because of the way the world is there would always be a new one out in a couple of months, which he absolutely had to have.

No, this time, she decided, she was going to buy him a special present, something he'd always cherish and that's when the idea came to her: she would get him a gift to do with his favourite band. Something rare and special that he could treasure and might even go up in value as the years went on.

It hadn't been easy. She'd had to do all manner of things she'd never dreamed of doing like setting up an eBay account and talking to strangers online but she'd done it because she adored her son, and wanted nothing more than to make him happy. With her budget, her choices were limited. There were rare T-shirts, jackets and Japan-only releases, but nothing that looked quite special enough. And then one day she saw it, a shiny gold disc, framed beautifully and signed by the band members themselves, and straight away she knew how much Connor would love it.

She'd made an offer, a hundred pounds under the asking price and it was rejected, and even though it was beyond the limit she'd set herself she'd upped it by fifty pounds and thankfully it was hers. It was only then, however, that she realised the gold disc had been advertised as collection only. She tried to cancel the order but she couldn't work out how to do it and so reasoning she'd come too far to turn back she'd looked into it, found the cheapest way of getting to Manchester and now here she was.

'Oh, it's grand.' She stopped and admired her purchase. 'My Connor will love it. Why ever are you selling it?'

'I had a few unexpected bills,' Ross replied, 'and anyway, my girlfriend's been nagging at me to get rid of some stuff for a while now so it had to go.'

'Well,' said Bernie, handing it back, 'it'll certainly be going to a good home – you can be sure of that.'

As he carefully wrapped it up for her, Ross told her a little about his life. How he'd been in a car accident as a teenager, losing the use of both legs as a result. 'It took me ages to get my head around it,' he said as he taped up the box, 'that I'd never walk again, and I was really down for a long time, but then I got some help and it really seemed to do the trick. Now I work part-time for a disability rights charity and I'm getting married in the summer.'

'Oh, congratulations,' said Bernie. 'Well, here's hoping all that stuff in the paper is over by then.'

He raised an eyebrow. 'You and me both, my girlfriend will do her nut if the wedding gets cancelled. Now,' he said holding up the securely packaged gold disc. 'Have you got a bag for this?'

Though she could now see it wouldn't be remotely big enough Bernie reached into her handbag, removed the Aldi bag for life she'd brought along with her and held it up.

'Don't worry,' he said. 'I think I've got one of those big blue IKEA bags somewhere. I'm sure that'll sort you out.'

He left the room and returned a short while later carrying the bag and, refusing Bernie's offer to pay him extra, he put the package inside and handed it to her.

'Will you be okay, finding your way back?' he asked at the door, after she'd paid him.

'I think so,' she replied. 'It's just up the road, turn left, get back to the main road and then cross over to catch the bus into the city centre.'

'That's it,' he replied. 'Well, good to meet you, Bernie. Have a safe journey home, and wish your son a very happy birthday from me.'

Bernie was fine getting back to the bus stop, feeling braver and more excited now she'd completed her mission, and when the number eighty-six arrived she was surprised to see that it was the same driver who had driven her from town.

'Hello again.' She gave the driver a smile.

'So, you got to where you wanted to go then?'

'All done. Now all I need to do is get home.'

Once again, she sat down near the front of the bus, but as she settled into her seat, she started to feel a bit funny, and suddenly her head was pounding. Reaching into her bag she searched around for the headache pills she'd bought the day before, but it was only as she did so that she had a sudden image of them on her bedside table, where she had left them after taking some last night.

Looking up, she saw a parade of shops. She rang the bell for the next stop, telling herself she would find a chemist, buy some more tablets and maybe find somewhere to have a drink and something to eat. She'd made good time and it was pointless dashing around for no reason. It was ages before the coach left for Derby, so a little detour wouldn't make that much difference.

'You know this isn't town don't you, love?'

Bernie tried to explain what she was doing to the bus driver but couldn't make her mouth say the things that were in her head, and so she just waved at her and got off the bus, clutching Connor's present.

Looking around she couldn't see a chemist but spotting a passing family, a mother walking with her two young children she asked for directions. The woman didn't seem to understand and the harder Bernie tried the more concerned the woman looked until finally she walked away, a protective hand on each of her children. Confused she tried to ask someone else, a young man in a baseball cap, but when she spoke he too acted as if she was talking another language. As she carried on down the road, somehow, Connor's present slipped from her grasp, and when she tried to bend down to pick it up, her head suddenly felt like it was spinning, and she crashed to the ground.

For a moment, as she lay there, blood oozing from a cut on her forehead, strange faces, a man, a woman and a child loomed into view. She tried to speak, to say she wasn't feeling well, but no words came. She had the oddest sensation like she was sinking into the cold, hard pavement beneath her, and then finally, as if a switch had been flipped, everything went black.

37

Connor

'Are we nearly there yet?'

Marcus looks at his satnav and shakes his head. 'Afraid not, mate. We're just coming up to Stoke, so we've got another hour to go.'

'An hour? But that's too long.' I feel like I've got so much energy and nervousness in me that if I got out of the car and started running, I could get there in five minutes. 'Can't you go any faster?'

'I'm going as fast as I can. If we get pulled over for speeding that's going to take even more time. Trust me, I know how desperate you are to get there, and I promise I'm doing my best. Why don't you stick the radio on, sit back, try and relax and we'll be in Manchester before you know it.'

I do what Marcus says, and turn the radio on but even though I go up and down all the stations twice nothing feels right. The fast music feels too happy, the slow music feels too sad, and all the stations where it's just talking are all too boring. Instead, I switch it off, and try looking out of the window at the other cars, at the sheep in the fields, at the lorries in the slow lane, but none of it takes my mind off thinking about how long this is taking. I just want to be there now. I just want to be with Mum telling her how much I have missed her.

I'd been on my way home from the horrible, horrible interview at SuperBargains when Lila called and told me she thought she'd found Mum.

I couldn't believe what she was saying. I'd thought my ears were playing tricks on me, that I was wishing too hard, that I'd been missing her so much I was imagining things.

'You've . . . you've found her? You've found Mum?'

'Well, I think so . . . I'm almost certain I have . . . but I need you to be here so we can be sure. I didn't want to break it to you like this, but I've already tried calling Marcus a few times and for some reason he's not picking up. You need to stay calm, get hold of Marcus and get him to bring you up to Manchester as soon as you can. I'm already up here so I'll text you both the address and postcode and I'll be waiting for you, okay?'

I had so many questions racing around in my head. 'But I don't understand? What's Mum doing in Manchester? Is she okay? Can I talk to her? Where has she been all this time?'

'Listen, Connor, I'll explain everything I can when I see you. But for now, concentrate on finding Marcus and getting up to Manchester. Just find him and get here as soon as you can.'

The moment Lila ended the call I tried calling Marcus but it just kept going to his voicemail. So I called the garage and spoke to Carmel on reception and she told me that Marcus was out on a test drive and must have left his phone behind by accident. 'He shouldn't be too long though, Connor. Do you want me to tell him you called?'

'Yes,' I said quickly, 'yes, please tell him to call me as soon as he gets in! Tell him it's very, very important. Tell him we've got to go to Manchester straight away. Tell him that Lila has found Mum.'

For a moment after ending the call, I wasn't quite sure what to do. I thought about getting the bus over to Marcus's garage but I just knew it would take ages. Then I thought about getting a taxi, but I didn't have anything like Uber or Bolt on my phone and I didn't know the number for any taxis. I was about to look up mini-cabs online when I remembered that there was a special phone in SuperBargains where people could call taxis for free, and so turning around I ran back to the store.

I must have been really lucky because it only took a few minutes for a taxi to come. I gave the driver the address of the garage and as we pulled away, I tried Marcus's phone again and again but he still didn't pick up. I told myself to stay calm, and reminded myself that Carmel had promised she would give him my message as soon as he got back but I was so desperate to get up to Manchester that even one minute felt like an hour. I was about to try Marcus again when suddenly my phone rang.

'Connor? Everything alright? Carmel said it was urgent.'

'Yes, Lila called me. We have to go to Manchester – she's found Mum.'

Marcus went quiet. 'She's . . . really? How? I mean . . . where?'

'I know you have lots of questions, Marcus, and so do I, but we haven't got time for that right now. We have to get to Manchester and we have to get there now.'

Together we worked out a plan. I would carry on to the garage in the taxi while Marcus sorted out things at work so that he could drive me to Manchester and if he had time he would try and talk to Lila too. It felt like all the traffic in the world was in the way of my taxi, and even worse there were roadworks too so my driver had to take a longer route. Even though he had a satnav, I looked up the journey on my phone and tried to give him directions so we could get there quicker, but he got a bit annoyed and said that he would work it out. The drive to the garage had taken forty-five minutes, double what it should have, but I was so glad to finally get there, I didn't care. I just gave the driver a twenty-pound note and then got out of the taxi and ran over to Marcus's car where he was already waiting for me.

'Are you, okay?' he asked as I got into the passenger seat sweating and shaking.

'I'm fine,' I said. 'I just want us to go.'

'And we will, I promise. Lila texted me the details and it's in the satnav, but you need to calm down and catch your breath. The last thing we need right now is me having to take you to the hospital because you've passed out.'

I took a deep breath, and then another. 'I'm okay, see? I really am. Can we go now, please?'

He started up the engine, and though I'd told myself not to ask any questions they seemed to come out anyway.

'Did Lila say anything about Mum? Did she say how she found her? Or how come she's in Manchester?'

'I only know what you know, mate,' said Marcus, as we pulled off the forecourt past the taxi. 'She said she's pretty sure this is your mum but can't be certain until you see her. And look, while I know she wouldn't have called unless she was at least ninety-five per cent sure, there's still that five per cent chance that it isn't. I need you to prepare yourself for that, okay?'

'But it is her – I know it is.'

'And I hope it is too,' said Marcus, 'but while I know it's difficult, I think you should try not to get your hopes up until we know for sure, okay? It won't be long now, so just try to stay calm and sit tight.'

I told him I would try but the truth was it was too late; my hopes were already up, up and away. The thing is I just knew the woman Lila had found was Mum. I just knew it and nothing Marcus said could change that. Mum and I were going to be back together. She would come and live with me at my flat and we would be happy again.

An hour and a bit later, at just after half past four, Marcus finally pulls over, switches off his engine and we both sit looking at the sign outside the address the satnav has brought us to.

'Berkley Court Care Home,' I say reading the sign out loud. 'Are you sure you put the address in right?'

Marcus takes out his phone and checks it. 'This is the one Lila sent me. Is it the same as the one you've got?'

I take out my phone and check it too. 'Yes, it's the same. But I don't understand. What is Mum doing in a care home? Do you think she works here?'

Marcus shrugs. 'Possibly, but there's no point us speculating now we're here. Let's go and find out.'

Out of the car we stare at the building in front of us. It is a large, old building that looks like it might have been a big house or a school a long time ago. It has lots of windows and there is a huge new-looking extension on the side of it with a sign over the door that says, 'Reception'.

We walk over and ring the bell and after a bit a smiley lady in something that looks like a nurse's uniform opens the door and lets us in.

'We're here to meet Lila Metcalfe,' says Marcus. 'She's a friend of ours.'

'Oh, yes,' says the smiley lady. 'We've been expecting you. She's waiting for you in the day room. Just sign in the visitors' book then follow me and I'll take you through.'

Marcus and I walk behind her down a long corridor past lots of open doors that I look through as I go past. All of the rooms have a bed in them but some of the beds are empty and others have an old man or an old lady in them. One lady waves at me as we pass by. She doesn't look anything like Mum but I wave back anyway. Another lady we walk past is singing a Christmas carol even though it is not Christmas and it sounds quite nice because she has a nice voice.

We follow the nurse into a big room and walk through one half, which is filled with lots of chairs and tables, through to another bit where there are bigger comfier-looking armchairs. There are lots of old people dotted around, some are talking, some are asleep, some are watching TV and some are even playing board games. None of them are Mum.

We see Lila sitting in a chair next to the window looking at her phone and as we get closer, she looks up and, smiling, she rushes over to us.

'It's so good to see you both,' she says and gives me a big hug. 'Look, I didn't mean to be mysterious on the phone but if this is your mum then there's a lot to explain, and I thought it would be better if we did it face to face. Long story short, the lady I'm about to take you to see has been a resident in this care home for coming up to three years now, which of course is about how long your mum has been missing. The thing is, she was found without any ID and hasn't been able to communicate with anyone. She's suffering from something called aphasia, perhaps as the result of a stroke, meaning she's lost the ability to speak so no one's been able to find out who she is or where she came from. The staff call her Daisy because when she arrived there was a pale blue scarf with daisies on it amongst her things.'

I feel a huge lump in my throat. 'Mum has a scarf with daisies on it. She has. She definitely has.'

'And was she wearing it on the day she went missing?' asks Lila.

I think hard, harder than I've ever done but I just can't remember. 'I don't know. I think so, but I can't really be sure.'

'Okay,' says Lila, 'well, don't worry. We'll know one way or another soon enough.'

My heart is racing as we all follow the nurse out of the day room and along another corridor. I feel sick with nerves and my legs are all shaky. What if I'm wrong about the daisy scarf? What if this isn't Mum after all? I don't think I could take it if it's not her. I don't think I could carry on.

About halfway down the corridor the nurse stops outside one of the rooms, and I look at the door to see that it has the name 'Daisy' on it.

'Are you ready?' says Lila putting a hand on my arm.

'We're right here with you, mate,' says Marcus doing the same.

'I think I am ready,' I say, and then taking a deep breath I follow the nurse into the room.

38

Lila

The room is tiny and with four of us in here standing around the bed – Connor and the nurse on one side, me and Marcus on the other – it feels even smaller. And yet besides the gentle snoring of the woman lying between us, there isn't a sound. I can barely breathe for watching Connor so intently, hoping, praying, to see a look of recognition in his eyes, some clue, some hint, some indication that I haven't just dragged a vulnerable man halfway across the country only to torture him in the most painful way possible. But despite all my hopes he just stands there staring at the figure in the bed, nothing in his expression betraying what might be going on inside his head.

I wonder for a moment whether the intensity of the situation has overwhelmed him. After all, if I was in his shoes I know I'd be struggling. For Connor, who has gone through so much these past few months, let alone in the time that has elapsed since Bernie first went missing, it must be almost impossible to deal with.

I silently scold myself for not having taken more time to think this through. Having done what checking I could I'd been so convinced this was Bernie, so excited about the prospect of reuniting Connor with his mum that I'd just barged ahead not thinking about the consequences. Perhaps I should've sent a photo first, or maybe even asked Marcus to confirm Bernie's identity before involving Connor; in fact, in this moment I can't help thinking that anything would've been better than seeing him like this.

I think about trying to reassure Connor again, letting him know that he's not in this alone, that we're all here with him, but before I can do anything the woman in the bed stirs slightly, and this seems to be enough to jolt Connor out of his reverie. He blinks several times, rubs his eyes and then with tears rolling down his cheeks he looks at me. 'It's her,' he says as he gently takes one of the woman's frail-looking hands in his own. 'It's Mum, it definitely is. I'd know her anywhere.'

I turn to Marcus for confirmation and he gives me a barely perceptible nod, his face full of emotion. 'That's Bernie, all right. She's older and thinner than I remember, but yes, I'd stake my life that it's her.'

What I'd hoped would be a sigh of relief comes out as more of a sob, and before I know what's happening I'm crying too. I'm just so happy for Connor, so glad that he and his mum are finally reunited. Throughout everything he's been through, all the terrible lows, all the disappointments he's had to face, unlike the rest of us he's never given up hope, never once doubted he'd see her again. And while it might not be the happy ending he'd envisioned, his mum returning to Hope Street and the two of them living happily ever after there, seeing them together like this it's undeniable that this is a happy ending nonetheless.

As Connor stands, holding her hand, Bernie's eyes open just a fraction, but when she sees us gathered around her bed they widen even more until there's almost a hint of fear behind them. Seeing this, the nurse leans over to reassure her and as she does so Bernie seems to relax a little.

'It's okay, Daisy . . . I mean Bernie . . . these lovely people have come to see you. And look, here's your son. He's been searching for you for a long, long time.'

Without moving her head, Bernie gradually shifts her gaze towards Connor and fixes him with an unyielding stare. But then her expression changes as she looks down from his face, to her hand held in his and then back again until their eyes meet. It's hard to tell but in that moment it feels like there's a connection between them, something unspoken, something intangible, and yet very real.

'Hello, Mum,' says Connor, his voice trembling. 'It's me, Connor. Mum, it's me.'

For the first time, and with what looks like great difficulty, Bernie turns her head as if to get a better look at him, and her face breaks into a broad but lopsided smile. At first, I don't even notice, but as I stand looking on, I see that her lips are moving as if she's trying to say something.

'Well, this is a first,' says the nurse. 'I've worked here since the day she arrived and I've never seen her even try to speak until now. Is there something you want to say, Bernie?'

Bernie doesn't take her eyes off Connor and her breathing quickens as if she's trying to summon all the strength in her tiny frame, but there's something else, the slightest inclination of her head, as if she's desperately trying to communicate her desire.

'Mum,' says Connor, so gently, so tenderly that tears prick at my eyes, 'it's okay, I'm here. We're all listening.'

There's a long silence as Bernie struggles with a body that will no longer do her bidding, but then slowly, surely, her mouth opens, and a sound comes out that though quite faint is unmistakably the word 'Connor.'

None of us can help ourselves. This one utterance is like a spark igniting an explosion of cheers and exclamations from everyone in the room. It's her, it's really her. The woman in the bed is without a doubt Bernadette McLaughlin.

'She said my name!' Connor grins from ear to ear as he wipes away the tears in his eyes. 'Did you hear her? She said my name! She knows who I am.' He turns back to Bernie. 'Yes, Mum, it's me

– Connor. I'm here, I'm right here. And I've missed you, Mum; I've missed you so, so, much. And I'm going to look after you. You're never going to have to be alone. I'm going to look after you, always, just like you looked after me.' Leaning over the bed he gives his mum the gentlest of kisses on the cheek, and as he pulls away, I can see that there are tears of joy in Bernie's now smiling eyes.

Without discussion the nurse, Marcus and I leave the room to give Connor and Bernie some time alone, and we head back to the dayroom, where the nurse offers to get us a drink while we wait.

'That was really something wasn't it?' says Marcus, after we've sat in stunned silence for a while.

'It really was. Like I told you, I was ninety, maybe ninety-five per cent sure it was Bernie. Every detail I was learning just made me more certain, but until Connor identified her there was always that nagging doubt that maybe this was more a case of me desperately wanting it to be true, and seeing connections that weren't really there.'

'So, come on, you've got to tell me. How on earth did you manage to track her down? I thought you'd stopped looking for her when you moved to London.'

'I did. I had. And then a couple of days ago I got a call from Peter, my old editor at *The Echo*. He'd been contacted by a reader whose father-in-law had just been moved into a care home in Manchester. While talking to the staff, she'd heard about the mystery around the identity of a woman who had been brought to the home not long after lockdown. She had apparently suffered a stroke and no one knew her name, where she'd come from, or anything about her and even after appeals in the local press no family had come forward to claim her. The woman's story rang bells with *The Echo* reader as she'd followed Bernie's story quite keenly because they were about the same age and so when she got back home she called

The Echo, and told them what she knew. Not wanting to bother me for nothing, Peter called the care home and when everything seemed to check out he called me.'

'And so, what happened then – you came racing up here?'

'Well, the moment I got home I dug out all my files then called the care home myself, and emailed them a photo of Bernie along with links to all of the coverage from *The Echo.* They seemed pretty sure it was the same woman. Of course, I had my doubts because nothing I'd uncovered suggested any link to Manchester, but it was the best lead I'd had in all my time looking for her and I couldn't just ignore it, so I persuaded my new boss to let me take a couple of days off to follow it up and, well, you know the rest.'

Marcus shakes his head. 'This is blowing my mind. I mean, Manchester of all places. What was she doing here?'

'That was my big question, and to be honest I'm still not one hundred per cent sure I know the answer. But the story I got from the home goes like this: she was found unconscious on the street near some shops in a Manchester suburb then taken to Wythenshawe Hospital by ambulance where they found she'd had a massive stroke. They did the best they could for her but then there was the small matter of a global pandemic.'

'And of course, they discharged all the old people into care homes to free up the beds.'

'Exactly. And to make matters worse, she couldn't speak, and when she was found she had no bag, no purse, no keys, no ID, nothing on her to say who she was. Initially the police thought she might be a local woman who, confused in the early stages of the stroke had left her home and collapsed nearby, or perhaps was someone who had managed to wander out of a local care home unnoticed. But all the local appeals they made drew a blank, and of course with Covid raging, care homes on extra tight lockdown, and the world turned on its head, it was like a perfect storm. Everyone everywhere was struggling so much to get through each day that solving the mystery of this woman just wasn't a priority.'

'But I don't understand,' says Marcus. 'How was she not on any police database? How did no one make the connection between a missing woman in Derby and an unclaimed woman in a care home in Manchester?'

'Your guess is as good as mine but I spoke to my police contact this morning who helped us before, and although she didn't use these words, and wouldn't go on the record, I think it's safe to say there's been a monumental cock-up, and it was a case of the left hand not knowing what the right hand was doing.'

'And is there even a working theory about how she ended up in Manchester?'

'None as yet. But from what I've learned about her, there's no way Bernie would've come all this way without good reason, and there's no way she would've been able to get here without money, bank cards, or at the very least a lift. What that good reason was, I've no idea. Had she come to meet someone? Was it someone she used to work with who I didn't manage to contact? Was it a family member, someone from Ireland who got back in touch with her? But then there's the question of what happened to her phone and keys. She had her bag when she went out in the morning, but according to the police reports she had nothing on her when she was found, which means that either she got rid of them herself, which makes no sense, or someone took them from her.'

'So, you think she was attacked?'

'The police didn't find any evidence of that, but it's possible that someone took her belongings somewhere between her collapse and the arrival of the ambulance. It's not unheard of; in fact I covered a couple of cases like it at *The Echo*. Opportunists, spotting the chance to benefit from someone else's misfortune.'

Marcus shakes his head in disgust. 'I tell you what, if I ever saw anyone doing something like that, I'd make sure it was the last thing they ever did.'

The nurse returns with our drinks but then is immediately called away to deal with something, leaving the two of us alone.

'So, what happens now?' asks Marcus. 'Will we be able to get her transferred to a home in Derby so Connor can see her?'

'I'm sure there'll be a lot of bureaucracy around it but I really can't see why not. The police shouldn't take too long to confirm that Daisy is in fact Bernie and once that's done, hopefully the rest will start to fall into place.'

'And Connor will finally have his mum back. I don't know about you, but it's almost enough to make you believe in happy endings, isn't it?'

'Almost.' I look at Marcus trying to gauge his expression, wondering if he's only referring to Connor's situation or if there's more to his words. 'I've missed you, you know.'

Marcus smiles. 'The feeling's mutual.'

'Mutual enough to give us another shot?'

He leans forward in his chair and takes my hand. 'I think so,' he says, with a twinkle in his eye. 'With all this hope in the air, I'd be crazy not to.'

39

Connor

I've been telling Mum about everything that has happened since she went missing, well, nearly everything. I've left out anything to do with Hope Street, and the house being boarded up because I don't want her to get upset but I have told her about Katie and how nice she is. And, I'm just about to finish off by telling her all about DIY-Depot closing and my horrible job interview at Super-Bargains this morning when there's a knock at the door and a care assistant comes in pushing a trolley with a plate of food on it.

'Hello, my name's Chizzy, and I'm here to feed Daisy . . . I mean Bernie. Is that okay?'

I tell her it is fine, even though I am not really sure what she means. I watch as she presses a button on the side of Mum's bed, which makes her sit more upright, and then she covers Mum's top with a big paper towel sort of thing and after telling Mum that she's got fish pie and carrots for dinner she starts to feed her like a baby.

It is very strange watching Mum like this. Before she went missing she did everything for herself and lots of things for me, but I can see that she can't do that now. She can't even hold her spoon; the lady has to do it for her, and sometimes when she's chewing the food falls out of her mouth.

When I first came into the room, I recognised Mum straight away, even though at the same time, I didn't. Lila had told me that Mum had had a stroke, but I wasn't really sure what that meant. Alan's wife had died from a stroke, so I knew it was bad, but I didn't know it could be like this. So, when I saw this lady who looked like

Mum but didn't act like Mum it felt strange. This lady had Mum's face, her eyes, nose, mouth and hands, but at the same time she wasn't anything like the Mum I remember.

But then she moved in her bed, and there was something about the sound she made that was so like one Mum used to make when she fell asleep watching TV on the sofa at home that made me feel sure it was really her.

Holding her hand had made me feel even more sure. It was warm and soft just like Mum's and even had the same little round scar on it from when she hurt herself on one of the washing machines at the launderette.

Me being sure it was Mum was one thing, but I was scared that Mum might not know who I was, worried that she might not remember me. I would've loved her just the same if she had forgotten who I was, but when she said my name, it was the best feeling ever. It was like a million Christmas days at the same time, like all the hugs she'd ever given me all at once. I knew who Mum was and Mum knew who I was. And that was all that mattered.

'She's a good eater, your mum,' says the care assistant feeding Mum another spoonful of food. She turns to Mum and says, 'Fish pie is your favourite, isn't it?'

Mum smiles, and she doesn't just gobble up her fish pie, but her apple crumble and custard pudding too, and afterwards Chizzy wipes Mum's mouth with a paper towel, and then clears everything away and leaves. We're only alone for a minute or two when there's another knock at the door and Marcus comes in.

'Alright, mate? Lila's just taking a call so I thought I'd come and check on you. How is she? Everything okay?'

'She is fine. She has just had her dinner and pudding . . . but this nice lady, Chizzy, had to feed it to her.'

Mike Gayle

Marcus comes over and puts a hand on my shoulder. 'That'll be because of the stroke. I'm guessing your mum isn't able to feed herself anymore.'

'It doesn't matter,' I say, 'I'll feed her when I take her home.' Marcus doesn't say anything and so I turn to look at him. 'I can take her home, can't I? I will be able to look after her, won't I?'

Marcus sighs. 'Listen, mate, it's early days and there's a lot to sort out but I just don't think it's going to be possible. Your mum is going to need full-time care, twenty-four seven for the rest of her life. Even if you didn't have to work and didn't live in a one-bed flat it would still be impossible.'

I feel sick. I've only just found Mum again. I can't leave her here. 'But I'll take really good care of her, I promise. I'll take the best care ever, just you wait and see.'

'I know you would, mate, but that's not what I'm saying. I'm saying that even with support, it just won't work. Your mum needs to be in a place like this, where they've got the staff and the equipment and the know-how to look after her.'

'But I live in Derby. Will I have to move to Manchester if I want to see her?'

'Of course not,' says Marcus. 'I've already spoken to the social services here in Manchester and explained the situation, and although they say they'll have to talk to social services in Derby first, they can't see it being a problem to find a care home near you. Just think about that, if we got your mum moved to a place like this in Derby, you'd be able to see her every day.'

I lean back in my chair and look at Mum. She's fallen asleep again and is snoring gently. This isn't the way I thought things would be at all. I thought she'd get to come home with me; I thought I'd get to look after her just like she'd always looked after me. But maybe Marcus is right, maybe I wouldn't be able to take care of her in the

342

right way, like they do here. Maybe, having her in a care home near me would be for the best. At least then, like Marcus said, I could see her every day, but still know that she was safe if I have to go out to work or do the shopping.

'Okay, but please can we get her back to Derby quickly? I don't want her to think we're leaving her here forever.'

'Of course, mate.' Marcus gives me a gentle pat on the back. 'There's no way I'm going to let that happen, I promise you that. In the meantime, until it's sorted, we'll figure out a way to get you up here at least once a week, and the nurse was telling me they've got a couple of iPads so you'll be able to chat to your mum on that whenever you like.'

There's a knock at the door and Lila comes in and I'm so grateful for everything she's done, so happy that she found Mum, that the minute I see it's her I get up and give her the biggest hug I can manage.

'Thank you, Lila, for finding Mum. Thank you for bringing us back together.'

I ask her lots of questions and she tells me the story of how she found Mum. It is all very complicated, and I'm sure I'll have to ask her about it again. But the one thing I really am struggling to understand is why Mum didn't tell me the truth about where she was going that day, and why she came all the way to Manchester when I didn't think she knew anyone here.

'Those are definitely two of the big questions we'd all love answers to,' says Lila. 'But there's a good chance we might never find out. Still, the important thing, the only thing that really matters is that the two of you are together again.' She pauses and looks at me as if she has something else to say. 'There is one more thing . . . and say no if you really don't want to do it but Peter – my old editor at *The Echo* – has asked me if I'd write a piece about you getting your mum back. And, if that's not enough, my boss at *The Correspondent* has asked me to do a piece on you and everything that happened as well. Obviously, it's a lot to ask but I think it would be really nice for everyone who's been following your story to see that it has a happy ending. What do you think?'

I look over at Mum who has just woken up and is smiling at me, and then look back at Lila. 'Yes, I think that would be nice. Without you and *The Echo* we would never have found Mum, and anyway, I think she would like to be in the paper too. She always used to like having her photo taken.'

While Marcus sits with Mum, Lila and I go and sit in the care home's garden to do the interview. There are lots of flowers in the beds, and lots of benches to sit on and four bird feeders and a bird table with lots of little birds on them and I watch them as I try my best to answer Lila's questions. It's funny going over the story of me and Mum again like this, especially because this is the first time I'm getting to tell it with a happy ending. If it hadn't been for Lila and *The Echo*, Mum might have stayed here alone without me, and I would've stayed in Derby without Mum, and we both would have been missing each other forever. But now we're back together and it is all thanks to Lila.

A few minutes after we've finished talking a photographer arrives, and she takes pictures of me and Lila in the garden, and pictures of me and Mum back in her room. As she takes the pictures, she asks me to tell her about my story, and even though I have just finished telling Lila I tell her too and when I get to the end she gives me a big hug and says she's never heard a story like mine, and that she'll make sure to buy both papers when they come out.

When the photographer's gone, Marcus tells me it's time for us to go too. 'I'd love to stay,' he says, 'I really would but I've got to get back for work in the morning.'

I tell him I understand, because I know I can't stay with Mum in the care home and I don't know anyone in Manchester, and then after saying goodbye to Mum, he and Lila leave the room while I say my own goodbye.

'I've got to go back to Derby now.' I take hold of Mum's hand and squeeze it gently. 'But me and my friends are making sure you will be back home there soon. I will speak to you every day on the iPad, and Marcus says that he might be able to bring me up to visit you again, maybe at the weekend.'

I look at Mum to see if she understands what I'm saying but it's quite hard to tell. She looks happy though and I'm glad about that.

'Before I go, there's just one thing I need to tell you, but it's quite a big thing.' I bite my lip, trying my best not to cry but I can't stop myself. 'I tried Mum, I tried really hard, but I'm so, so sorry, I couldn't stop them from taking Hope Street from us. I couldn't stop them from taking our home. I'm sorry, Mum, I'm sorry. I've really let you down.'

I close my eyes, as tear after tear falls down my face, but then something strange happens, and when I open my eyes I see that Mum has somehow moved her arm so that her hand is now on mine. She looks at me and smiles, and I feel like a huge weight has been lifted off my chest. Even though she can't speak, I know she's telling me it's okay, that she understands. And when she smiles at me, I know she is telling me not to worry. I know she is telling me that everything will be alright in the end.

Epilogue

Lila: The following spring

Quite how word got around that Hope Street was finally being knocked down, is anyone's guess. Perhaps someone knows someone on the demolition team, or an old resident has a friend at the council planning office. But however it's happened the news has been relayed so successfully that much to the workmen's surprise and amusement there's now – along with me, Connor, Marcus, Niamh and a photographer from *The Echo* – a sizeable crowd gathered behind the temporary fencing erected at the end of the road.

Marcus turns to Connor who is standing holding Katie's hand. 'Are you absolutely sure you want to be here for this, mate? It's not going to be pleasant.'

'Yes, I am very sure,' says Connor. 'I know it won't be very nice but I'm not just here to say goodbye to Hope Street from me, I'm here to say it from Mum too.'

I completely understand Connor's need to see this through to the end. Upsetting as it doubtless will be to watch this street and the home he loved so much reduced to rubble, to bear witness to its destruction and say a proper final farewell is something that has to be done to complete the circle. Anyway, there's an inner strength to Connor, a steely core that's not immediately obvious to the casual observer, but is there nonetheless, and I don't doubt for a second that he'll get through this as he has so much else in his life, and he'll emerge stronger than ever before.

The deep rumble of several diesel engines starting up grabs our attention and Niamh, who has spent her morning interviewing Connor, along with other former residents of Hope Street, quickly directs her photographer towards the action. Climbing a set of stepladders he begins taking a few shots of the excavators as they trundle into place. There's no ceremony, no speeches, just a strangely silent group of people looking on as these huge and powerful machines, staggered at intervals along the road, begin tearing into the fabric of the houses on Hope Street.

Watching these homes being torn apart and the startling ease with which the excavators – like man-made dinosaurs – bite, chew and claw apart sturdy roofs and solid walls, as if they're made of mere tissue paper, is as compelling as it is heartbreaking.

As I turn to look at Connor, there are tears in his eyes and I'm glad of the comfort of Marcus squeezing my hand in solidarity. I rest a hand on Connor's shoulder, telling him we can go if he wants to but, drying his eyes, he shakes his head.

'I'm okay,' he says. 'I want to stay until they're finished.'

And so that's what we do. We stand and watch until the entire row of terraces has been flattened, completely changing a once familiar landscape into something strange and alien.

'That was horrible, wasn't it?' says Niamh. 'It must have been awful for poor Connor. I hope he's okay.'

I look over at my friend now standing with Marcus and Katie, chatting to a few old neighbours. 'He will be. It might take a bit of time. But he'll get there.'

'Still,' says Niamh. 'I'm sure his surprise will cheer him up. Have you told him anything about it?'

'No, he thinks I just came up for this. We're heading over to see his mum now and I'm going to spring it on him there.'

Niamh grins. 'He's going to love it, isn't he?'

'Love it? I think he's going to be over the moon.'

'Right, well, I'd better be going. But I'll see you and Marcus at ours for dinner later. Lewis has been desperate to try out a new cookbook I got him for his birthday so come hungry because the last time I spoke to him there were four courses and he was toying with adding a fifth!'

After giving Niamh a hug goodbye, I head over to join Connor and Marcus.

On the short drive over to Bernie's new care home I take several calls from colleagues at *The Correspondent* about various pieces I'm working on and about which they need my input. Even now, six months on, I sometimes have to pinch myself just to confirm I'm not dreaming, that I do actually work at one of the best national newspapers in the country. In recent weeks alone I've written a piece that was discussed on *Newsnight*, and I've appeared on *Woman's Hour* talking about an article I wrote about inequalities in women's healthcare, and even interviewed a famous Hollywood actress turned spokesperson for a new UN food programme for the cover of the Saturday weekend magazine. It's all a far cry from *The Echo* and yet at the same time I feel as much at home at *The Correspondent* as I once did there. It's funny how quickly we adapt to new realities.

As soon as we arrive at Ashwood Lodge, right on cue Marcus suggests to Connor that he and Katie go in ahead of us and see his mum. 'Lila and I have just got a few things to sort out, but we'll see you in there in a sec.'

Eager to see his mum, Connor thankfully doesn't ask any questions; instead almost dragging Katie behind him, he practically runs up the path towards the entrance, taps in the code and disappears inside.

'The coast is clear,' says Marcus pressing a button on his dashboard to open the boot.

Making my way to the rear of the car I retrieve my carefully wrapped parcel just as someone pulls up next to us. For a moment, I assume it's just another person come to visit a relative but then I hear the driver greet Marcus by name and realise who it is.

'Hello, Alan,' I say closing the boot. 'I'm so glad you could make it.'

Alan gives me a cheeky wink. 'Wouldn't miss it for the world. Can't wait to see the look on Connor's face. Although, I did nearly give the game away when I saw him at work yesterday. Not thinking, I said, "See you tomorrow," and he gave me a funny look and reminded me that neither of us were on the rota for today. I passed it off as a bit of a senior moment and I don't think he thought anything of it.'

'I'm just glad you're here,' I say. 'How are you both getting on at the garden centre? Good I hope.'

Alan smiles. 'I tell you what, love, it's a dream come true. Never thought in a million years I'd get another job at my age, let alone one where I get to work alongside my old mate Connor, and the lovely Katie too but it just goes to show, miracles do happen.'

I politely decline Alan's offer to help me carry my parcel and we all head inside the building that has been Bernie's home since her transfer from the care home in Manchester was finally given the green light at the beginning of the year. All reports from Connor and Marcus so far have been really positive. The home itself is in a beautiful leafy setting, the staff are all lovely, and best of all it's just a single bus ride from Connor's flat, which means he can visit her every day, just like he wanted.

We reach Bernie's room to find that Bev is already there, just as we'd arranged, chatting to Bernie, Connor and Katie. We all say our hellos and then much to his confusion, Connor catches sight of Alan.

'Alan, what are you doing here? Do you know someone who lives here too? What room are they in? Maybe Mum knows them.'

Alan looks at me and so I step in and explain. 'Alan's not here to visit someone else. I asked him to come along, just like I asked Bev to make sure she'd be here too.'

Connor gives me a questioning look. 'What's going on? I don't understand.'

'Don't worry, it's nothing bad. It's really good actually, in fact wonderful. Remember that article I wrote in *The Correspondent*, the one all about you and your mum being reunited?'

Connor nods. 'Yes, it's in my scrapbook at home.'

'Well, a few weeks ago someone got in touch who had read the article and had some new information about your mum they wanted to share.'

'Who was it?' asks Connor. 'What did they say?'

'You know how we've never been able to figure out what your mum was doing in Manchester? Well, I think I know now. She was buying a present for you for your birthday.'

Connor is so stunned that it takes him a moment to react. 'Mum was in Manchester buying me a present?' he says eventually. 'Why did she have to go all the way over there?'

'Because it was very special, something that she knew you'd love, and the person she was buying it from lived in Manchester and going there was the only way she could get it.'

I take the parcel I'm holding and hand it to Connor. 'Open it – it's for you.'

Puzzled, Connor carefully sets about opening the package and, once he's done so, sits staring wordlessly at the object in his hands for several moments.

Mike Gayle

Eventually he turns to me, eyes wide. 'Is this real?'

I nod. 'It's not the one your mum bought, sadly. Judging from what the man who sold it to her said, she had the signed Metallica gold disc when she left him to get the bus back into town. This was confirmed by a bus driver I managed to track down who remembered seeing your mum with a big blue IKEA bag, and also recalled the fact that she got off the bus early, which was probably because she was starting to feel unwell. She must have had her stroke and collapsed shortly afterwards but by the time she was picked up by the ambulance the IKEA bag along with her purse and handbag had disappeared. So, I think we have to assume they were stolen.'

'That's horrible,' says Connor. 'Who would do something like that?'

'Lowlifes, that's who,' says Alan. 'But don't pay no mind to them, lad, listen to the rest of this story. It's going to blow your socks off.'

Connor looks over at me expectantly. 'What? What is it?'

'Well, once I heard this I brought it to the attention of *The Correspondent*'s music editor and asked if he could pull some strings with Metallica's record company, and see if we could get it replaced. Well, their PR went one better: not only did they send over a gold disc, signed by all the band, but also tickets for their next gig in London. And guess what? You've been given backstage passes so you get to meet them too.'

'I can't believe it,' says Katie. 'Connor, you're going to meet Metallica! That's amazing.'

'Well, you're coming with me, aren't you?'

Katie plants a kiss on Connor's cheek. 'Ah, do you mean it? I'd love to.'

After setting down the framed gold disc carefully on the table next to the bed, Connor stands up, wraps his arms around me and gives me the biggest hug.

352

'Thank you, Lila, thank you so much!'

'Don't thank me,' I tell him. 'I barely did anything. Really, this is all thanks to your mum.'

Connor smiles, and turning to Bernie who is gazing at him contentedly he gives her a gentle hug, and kisses her cheek tenderly.

'Thanks, Mum,' he says. 'Thanks for everything.'

As Connor and Katie marvel at the gold disc and summon every passing care assistant in to hear how excited they are about the prospect of meeting their favourite band, I take Marcus by the hand and lead him outside to the benches overlooking the front gardens.

'Well done, you,' says Marcus. 'That is one very happy Connor. You really excelled yourself.'

'Not quite.' I can't help but grin. But only because I know what's coming next. 'I've still got one last surprise, but this one's for you.'

Marcus raises an eyebrow. 'Okay, I'm all ears. Is it tickets to see Beyoncé? Because that would be amazing.'

I punch him on the arm playfully. 'What would be the point when you're totally in love with me?'

Marcus grins and puts an arm around me. 'You've got me there. So is my surprise you singing a medley of Beyoncé tunes while I act as your backing dancer?'

'Not with my singing voice, thank you very much,' I reply. 'Nope, your surprise is something different. You know how we've been doing the long-distance thing?' Marcus nods. 'Well . . . you know how difficult it's been with me missing you, and you missing me?'

He nods again. 'Don't remind me. Anytime we're together it's always over way too soon.'

'Well, what if it wasn't? What if I came back to Derby?'

'And give up everything, you've worked for? No way. I'd sooner sell up the garage and start something up closer to you. We'll be fine. We'll make it work. There's no way I'm going to let you give up that job for us.'

'What if I don't have to?'

Marcus looks at me confused. 'How do you mean?'

'It's not going to be straight away – it could take up to six months to come together – but *The Correspondent* is looking to expand their regional content. I'm in line to be their reporter in the Midlands, which of course means—'

Marcus's eyes widen. '—You're moving back to Derby?'

'That's the plan, at least.'

'That's amazing,' he says, wrapping me in his arms. We kiss and as the sun shines down on us, and the birds sing their joyful chorus, everything, absolutely everything, feels right with the world.

Acknowledgements

Huge thanks to everyone at Hodder especially Jo Dickinson, Al Oliver, Kate Norman, Alainna Hadjigeorgiou, Alice Morley and Helena Fouracre. And huge thanks too to everyone at United Agents especially Ariella Feiner, Jennifer Thomas and Amber Garvey. Additional thanks to Helena Newton and Philippa Willitts. Thanks as ever to The Board, and all the amazing authors who have said nice things about my work, especially Lisa Jewell, Jojo Moyes, Lyndsey Kelk, Jenny Colgan, Ruth Hogan, Alexandra Potter, Beth O'Leary, Sophie Kinsella, Holly Miller and Clare Mackintosh. And as always, huge thanks to Claire for everything.

Meet the residents of
Hope Street

Jessica McGuinness

Beate Herrmann

Angela Owen

Natalie O'Donoghue

Johanna Bell

Cheryl Drury

Shazzie, Reader at Work

Bryony Phelps

Emma Louise Walker

Lotte Don

Charlotte Millar

Jemma Hartley

Laura Drinkwater

Jo Fisher

Imogen Fowles

Andie King

Sarah Collins

Sarah Friday

Kim Kings

Theodora

Shona Holmes-Berry

Lex

Karen Osman

Lisa Harding

Helen Appleby

Ruth Lethem

Ruth Ng

Sarah Goldthorpe

Claire Holder

Angela Lawman

Heidi Minchin

Sophie Berrill

Jane Morley

Joanne Nuttie

Ashley McKee

Jenny McQuillan

Reading Group Questions

1. It was Connor's love for his mum that made him stand his ground. Can you think of a time when you've stood firm by your beliefs when everyone around you is trying to persuade you to do something different?

2. If you were Connor's friend, would you have let him stay on Hope Street or tried to convince him to leave?

3. At the start of the book, Lila feels completely disillusioned with her career choice. Eventually, the flame of passion for her profession is rekindled. Can you think of a time when you've felt like giving up, only to be reminded of why you chose the path you're on to begin with?

4. What do you think *Hope Street* is trying to say about local news? And how important do you think local news reporting is today?

5. Lila initially describes Connor as 'a poor local lad who has clearly fallen between the cracks of a broken system'. How true do you think this is?

6. Bernie was afraid of losing the sense of community on Hope Street, partly because she worried about Connor. Was she right to worry?

7. Would you describe Bernie as stubborn or strong?

8. Bernie says to a woman thinking of leaving Hope Street: 'Don't get angry, love. I'm not having a go, I promise. It's just that . . . well . . . the council, they're using you to break us. That's what they want. For us all to do our own thing.

But if we stick together, if we tell them where they can stuff their offers then they can't force us out.' If you lived on Hope Street, do you think you would have fought to stay or taken up the council's offer of new accommodation?

9. There are lots of examples of friendships in *Hope Street* like Connor and Alan, Bev and Bernie, Lila and Niamh. What do you think *Hope Street* has to say about friendship?

10. Is Adele a complete villain? Or do you think there's more to her story?

11. What do you think went wrong with Lila and Gabe? Was it just down to the pressures of a long-distance relationship, or do you think the problems were more fundamental?

12. When Lila confesses to Marcus about her new job, he's hurt and explains: '. . . either you thought I didn't matter or you thought I'd try and talk you out of it. And to be honest neither of those is a good look.' Do you think his response is justified?

13. In Chapter 31, Lila says: 'I've let him down twice over, once in failing to find his mum and now in failing to save his home from destruction. It had been wrong of me on both counts to give Connor false hope.' Is it ever wrong to be hopeful, or are we always better off trying to be more pragmatic?

14. Do you think Katie will be good for Connor? And if so, why?

15. At one point Bernie says: 'People don't need new developments; they need community!' Is she right? And how important is community to you?

About the Author

Mike Gayle was born and raised in Birmingham and moved to London to pursue a career in journalism, working as a feature editor and agony uncle. He has written for a variety of publications including the *Sunday Times*, the *Guardian* and *Cosmopolitan*.

Mike became a full-time novelist in 1997 following the publication of his *Sunday Times* top ten bestseller *My Legendary Girlfriend*, which was praised by the *Independent* as 'full of belly laughs and painfully acute observations'. Since then, he has written eighteen novels including *The Man I Think I Know*, Richard and Judy Bookclub bestseller *Half a World Away*, and *All The Lonely People*, which the *Guardian* hailed as 'a heartbreaking and ultimately uplifting look at isolation'. His books have been translated into more than thirty languages.

He lives in Birmingham with his wife and daughters. You can find him online at mikegayle.co.uk and on X @mikegayle.

Mike Gayle: emotions you'll never forget, stories you'll want to share

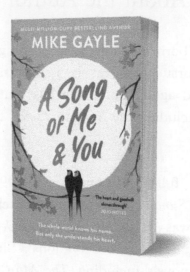

'Mike Gayle creates real, warm characters you will recognise. Amid real human dilemmas, the heart and goodwill always shines through'
Jojo Moyes

'Moving, uplifting, unforgettable. Mike always writes from the heart and creates stories we fall in love with'
Lisa Jewell

'Funny, real and unexpected, a story that will keep you hooked to the very last page'
Alexandra Potter

'This second-chance romance comes from the sure hands of Mike Gayle, known for his ability to pluck the heartstrings'
Daily Mail

Stay up to date
with all the latest news from

Mike
Gayle

Scan the QR code to sign up
to Mike's newsletter:

www.mikegayle.co.uk